Lawrence's England

Companion volumes

D.H. Lawrence: the Early Fiction, Macmillan 1986

D.H. Lawrence: the Early Philosophical Works, Macmillan 1991

D.H. Lawrence: 'Sons and Lovers', Cambridge 1992

Lawrence's England
The Major Fiction, 1913–20

Michael Black

in association with
St Antony's, Oxford

© Michael Black 2001

All rights reserved. No reproduction, copy or transmission of this publication may be made without written permission.

No paragraph of this publication may be reproduced, copied or transmitted save with written permission or in accordance with the provisions of the Copyright, Designs and Patents Act 1988, or under the terms of any licence permitting limited copying issued by the Copyright Licensing Agency, 90 Tottenham Court Road, London W1P 0LP.

Any person who does any unauthorised act in relation to this publication may be liable to criminal prosecution and civil claims for damages.

The author has asserted his right to be identified as the author of this work in accordance with the Copyright, Designs and Patents Act 1988.

First published 2001 by
PALGRAVE
Houndmills, Basingstoke, Hampshire RG21 6XS and
175 Fifth Avenue, New York, N.Y. 10010
Companies and representatives throughout the world

PALGRAVE is the new global academic imprint of
St. Martin's Press LLC Scholarly and Reference Division and
Palgrave Publishers Ltd (formerly Macmillan Press Ltd).

ISBN 0–333–56626–2 hardback

This book is printed on paper suitable for recycling and made from fully managed and sustained forest sources.

A catalogue record for this book is available from the British Library.

Library of Congress Cataloging-in-Publication Data

Black, Michael, 1928–
    Lawrence's England: the major fiction 1913–20 / Michael Black.
    p. cm.
    Includes bibliographical references and index.
    ISBN 0–333–56626–2
    1. Lawrence, D. H. (David Herbert), 1885–1930–Criticism and interpretation. 2. Lawrence, D. H. (David Herbert), 1885–1930–Knowledge–England. 3. National characteristics, English, in literature. 4. England–In literature. I. Title.

PR6023.A93 Z567 2001
823'.912–dc21   2001036992

10 9 8 7 6 5 4 3 2 1
10 09 08 07 06 05 04 03 02 01

Printed and bound in Great Britain by
Antony Rowe Ltd, Chippenham, Wiltshire

Contents

A Note on the Jacket Illustration		vi
Acknowledgements		vii
1	Spontaneity and Revision as Aesthetic in Lawrence	1
2	'Theorising myself out': After *Sons and Lovers*: The 'Burns Novel' and 'Elsa Culverwell'	16
3	*The Rainbow*: Memory, Metaphor, Myth and Projection	39
4	*The Rainbow* as History	55
5	*The Rainbow*: Language and Imagery	69
6	*The Rainbow*: 'The Bitterness of Ecstasy'	89
7	*The Rainbow*: Recurrences, Religion, Dependency	116
8	*The Rainbow*: Scenes by Moonlight	133
9	*England My England*	152
10	*Women in Love*: Introduction	184
11	*Women in Love*: The Chapter as Focus: 'Breadalby'	191
12	*Women in Love*: Birkin and Lawrence: Loerke	208
13	*Women in Love*: The Project	217
14	*Women in Love*: Character	226
15	*Women in Love*: Lawrence's England	233
Index		242

A Note on the Jacket Illustration

Mark Gertler's 'Merry-go-round', in the Tate Gallery, London, was painted in 1916. Lawrence had already written, in *The Rainbow*, that people, good ordinary citizens, seemed to his Anton Skrebensky 'So many performing puppets, all wood and rag for the performance! ... He watched the citizen, a pillar of society ... saw the trousers formed to the puppet-action: man's legs, but man's legs become rigid and deformed, ugly, mechanical.' When he saw Gertler's picture, he must have felt his own insight had been crystallised, and wrote to Gertler: '... It is the best modern picture I have seen ... the great articulate extremity of art.' And in *Women in Love*, the original puppet-figure is altered: the German sculptor Loerke says to Gudrun that there is no point in her going to Paris – 'one had better ride on a carousel all day'. Loerke is a complex and unsympathetic character, who develops ideas on the place of art in the modern industrial world which Gertler might disavow. Hence a letter of December 1916 from Lawrence to Gertler in which he says: 'In my novel there is a man – not you, I reassure you – who does a great granite frieze for the top of a factory, and the frieze is a fair, of which your whirligig, for example, is part. – (We knew a man, a German, who did these big reliefs for great, fine factories in Cologne) –'

Acknowledgements

My principal debt is to the scholars who have produced the volumes of the Cambridge Lawrence which I have made use of here. They have not only established the texts: their introductions and notes are sources of much valuable information.

It is a pleasure to acknowledge years of friendship and collaboration with the other members of the Editorial Board: James Boulton, Lindeth Vasey and John Worthen: I am indebted to them in particular. Our discussions and correspondence have been a continuing resource – and very enjoyable. So too with David Ellis and Mark Kinkead-Weekes as co-authors of the Cambridge Biography and as friendly correspondents.

Some recent books about Lawrence which I have found helpful have also given me the sense that a new approach is being created as if in a kind of implicit collaboration. The authors have become correspondents and friends: Fiona Becket, Michael Bell, Janice Harris, Virginia Hyde. Among the pioneers of an earlier generation I think in particular of Keith Sagar, whose *The Art of D.H. Lawrence* started me thinking along certain lines in 1964, when I worked on it as publisher's editor.

Chapters 1 and 2 appeared in an earlier form as articles in *The Cambridge Quarterly*: I am grateful to the editors for permission to use them in this revised draft.

Quotations from copyright material in the Cambridge Lawrence are used by permission of Cambridge University Press and the Estate of Frieda Lawrence Ravagli, represented by the Literary Executor Laurence Pollinger Ltd – and I take the opportunity to thank Gerald Pollinger for his helpfulness over many years.

Michael Black

1
Spontaneity and Revision as Aesthetic in Lawrence

This is the third in a series of volumes giving a commentary on the principal prose works of D.H. Lawrence in chronological order – so far as that is practicable. The difficulty is that from early in his writing life Lawrence found himself working on a number of works which he had initially composed, often rapidly, in a free improvisatory mode. He wrote fast, and could produce a draft in days or weeks rather than months. He then often laid aside what he had written for a future reworking and embarked on something else. So he had, at any given time, a number of works in progress. He used to bring them towards publication by revising them more than once, sometimes radically, taking them through a number of drafts, and later revising again in proof. The scholar pursuing the writing life in detail would not only have to move from draft to draft of any one work, but from this draft of one to that draft of another, and then perhaps to the inception of a third or fourth before returning to the next draft of the first. My three volumes simplify by keeping to works in published form[1] and published order; but one must be aware of this underlying process of composition and its implications for critical argument.

The Cambridge edition has been in progress since the 1970s and is near completion. The scholars editing the works have not only produced strikingly improved texts, and some entirely new ones: their work is also giving us insights into this writing process and Lawrence's meanings. These need to be developed into new critical perceptions, helping us to abandon the old Lawrence of the 1960s. The starting-point now is that

---

[1] I use the Cambridge text. In my first volume (*D.H. Lawrence: The Early Fiction*, 1986) for *Sons and Lovers*, this was not yet available, but I have in a later study dealt with that important case: see Michael Black: *D.H. Lawrence: 'Sons and Lovers'* in the series 'Landmarks of World Literature' (Cambridge 1992).

Lawrence is a conscious artist, and the art is in everything he wrote. In this chapter I develop some implications of his composition-practice. In the next I examine two texts made available in the Cambridge edition, examples of brilliant improvisation which also show Lawrence reflecting on what he has been given by his genius. I then analyse *The Rainbow* as one of the most extraordinary novels of the twentieth century – itself the product of his characteristic mixture of spontaneity and revision. I give it most space because it has been underestimated. The wartime short stories then lead into a discussion of *Women in Love*.

It may be that the Cambridge Lawrence is demonstrating what might be shown in other classic authors if a comparable wealth of evidence had survived. Most probably, the edition establishes the far end of a continuous range: I believe Lawrence takes things further than other writers. All authors revise as they write, sometimes extensively. But I see a difference between the revisions of a Flaubert or a Joyce, where the authors posit a distinct aesthetic of conscious or deliberate composition, and the case of Lawrence, who has a different one which we need to identify. If there is one spectrum, they are at opposite ends. It has gone on being thought that Lawrence was merely 'a genius but ...' (Aldington's phrase) who didn't have the discipline of lesser men, and that his works are unequal for that reason. My argument is that he was a great and conscious artist, though he had the advantage of a phenomenal natural gift, and his instinctive method is one condition of his success.

The works of an author can be read as representing that author's mind or 'world', its development and deployment (the idea behind this series). Lawrence's works have a unity, a closeness of expression, a personal identification which goes beyond 'style' and which one tries to catch in such terms as 'It is as if it was all there from the start, waiting to be expressed'. That simplifies. To avoid teleology or determinism, the best metaphor would be Lawrence's: the growth and flowering of a perpetual plant, where in successive seasons an internal dynamic is played out in changing circumstances, producing first these flowers, then those. Yet they are all from the same originating organism. The linking factor between the composition of each work and the production of the whole is this continuity, this procession of draft after draft, followed in important cases by revision after revision.

This argument is qualified in a way which confirms it by observing that some things we most admire came out virtually perfect in a single draft, and remained in that form, preserving their miraculous spontaneity. I comment on two of these – the so-called 'Burns' fragment and 'Elsa Culverwell': brief outcomes of a single improvisation, abandoned for reasons worth pondering, and now available in the Cambridge edition. Because they are unfamiliar, readers coming upon them are likely to be taken with their freshness, their originality.

But there are works we know well, also written in a single draft. Lawrence thought his 'Introduction' to Maurice Magnus's *Memoir of the Foreign Legion* one of his best things: it was revised as he went along – every writer does that – but came out in a single draft. 'Honour and Arms' (better known as 'The Prussian Officer') came out in one draft. *The Lost Girl*, which most readers enjoy, was a single draft, though it had a long incubation, which started with 'Elsa Culverwell'. Like *Mr Noon*, *Aaron's Rod* was a single spontaneity, and can be read as starting a later period movement towards freedom and away from afterthoughts. Hence *Kangaroo* reads as dangerously spontaneous, and is a critical issue partly for that reason. Conversely, *The Plumed Serpent* was much revised, but the pondering does not endear it to most readers.

In editing Lawrence, work on each text has had to be based on the evidence available: the documents of composition and publication – manuscripts, typescripts, proofs, early editions – complemented by evidence from the biographical record, especially Lawrence's letters. The editor constructs the story of composition in all its stages, concluding that the edited text must use as its base one document which represents Lawrence's developing intention at a crucial point. This state of the text must be emended to recover authoritative readings from earlier and later states. The base-text is often manuscript; where it is a revised typescript, it has to be emended to incorporate readings from manuscript – especially to recover Lawrence's punctuation, always expressive but often overridden – and readings from proofs or printed editions, where a change was made by Lawrence. The edition aims at an ideal first publication, given that the actual first publication was always in some way defective.

Now that so many volumes have been published, we can characterise the phenomenon: Lawrence as author. The best description is a technical one. Lawrence is a 'constantly revising author'. The phrase begins to account for the fact that for major works we may have several drafts, where the first differs to such a degree from later ones that they seem like different works. Moreover, in later stages of composition Lawrence always took new transcripts by others (typescripts, proofs) not as a chance to check for accuracy but as opportunity for further revision, sometimes drastic. This went on all the way to publication, so that one can see publication as interrupting a process which might have gone on indefinitely. That temptation needs to be restrained: with most of his works Lawrence did think that he had finally got them 'right'. However, there was then external interference from publishers, editors and other censors. If he was the fruitful plant, they were the gardeners or farmers, processing and marketing the crop. He became accustomed to this, assenting to things he could not avoid. He had to live.

To turn back to the beginning – the manuscript drafts of a particular work – these can differ substantially, and Lawrence signified the gap by using different titles. The first two of the four drafts of *The White Peacock* were called 'Laetitia' after the central female character. The third became 'Nethermere', a name from the locale: the place is now seen to represent, to form, the people living in it. The first three drafts of *Sons and Lovers* were called 'Paul Morel'; at a very late stage in the two-year writing process 'Paul Morel IV' was suddenly renamed *Sons and Lovers*, as if something in the book so strenuously rewritten had crystallised in Lawrence's mind. The even longer composition-process which split into *The Rainbow* and *Women in Love* began as a single work called 'The Sisters', then 'The Wedding Ring'. The titles show that he started with the idea of a pair of contrasting siblings, but went on to contemplate a cycle of relationships. By then he had adapted, like other novelists of the time, the idea of 'the saga', to imply what sociologists call a 'longitudinal' study of a family, group or class.

The redrafting process could be so radical that, although where all the drafts survive one can trace the process and infer such changes of conception, the relationship between first draft and final text can become very tenuous. Some drafts stand on either side of a fault-line. The rift is so wide and deep that the editor of a final reading-text often cannot incorporate in the textual apparatus readings from an earlier draft where there is no verbal link between the two texts. So we now have editions of 'Paul Morel' and 'The Sisters' (more properly called 'The First *Women in Love*') to set alongside the First and Second versions of *Lady Chatterley's Lover,* and 'Quetzalcoatl' beside *The Plumed Serpent*. The student of these major works can now follow the progression from first draft to published text.

Contemplating that rift between drafts, one has to go beyond the notion of revision of a gently evolving text, and posit another process: returning to a source. Lawrence at these points began again, dived back into the pool of spontaneity where he always started, and which he always trusted more than second and third thoughts. So we are dealing with two phenomena which shade into each other. For the critic, redrafting – going back to the start – must be more significant than less radical revision. The two processes are aspects of the same thing – the working habit of basic spontaneity followed by continual revision – and both have critical as well as textual interest. But the major changes force a change of emphasis, because this habit is also a method, which needs to be theorised as an aesthetic, even if it started as an unconscious one. For Lawrence became aware of what he was doing, and was, to put it paradoxically, deliberately spontaneous.

The phrase 'constantly revising author' can cover a different case, the classic or Flaubertian case of the author revising to achieve a previously determined intention. The phrase 'final intention' used by textual editors is ambiguous, since it covers both possibilities. The final intention which one calls Flaubertian is that in which the author who conceives each work as a planned closed system finds, as he/she composes, even on reading the proofs, refining touches which perfect the system. So the author, in Henry James's phrase,[2] demonstrates 'a controlling idea and a pointed intention'. These preconceived and long-elaborated schemes govern any late contribution, which must be designed to support the existing whole.

That aesthetic was pressed on Lawrence by Ford Madox Hueffer as Editor of *The English Review* and Edward Garnett as reader for Duckworth. They both thought Lawrence was a genius, but inexperienced and undisciplined. Hueffer urged Lawrence to seek a Flaubertian 'form'. That preoccupation goes with the habit of making a plan and associated notes, in the manner of Henry James or of Flaubert, who took it so far as to revise his synopses. Lawrence rarely made plans, and only, it seems, at the beginning of his career. The equivalent in the visual arts is that the classical painter makes sketches of the whole and studies of detail, finally transferring to a squared-up canvas all that he has separately evolved, in order to produce a highly finished whole. The 'final intention' has been worked out in advance, and is now realised. In Lawrence's case, this notion is a fundamental misconception.

Garnett edited *Sons and Lovers*, reducing it to its published form of 1913 by cutting it by about a tenth. At base, his aim was simply to reduce a 'sprawling' novel – one of James's 'loose and baggy monsters' – partly to make it more readable, partly perhaps to reduce the printing costs. He had made perceptive comments to Lawrence on the previous

---

[2]In the *Times Literary Supplement* article of 1914, where James deplored this lack in, among other recent novels, *Sons and Lovers*.

draft, but now felt disappointed, with a feeling, confirmed by a letter from Walter de la Mare, the reader for Heinemann, that the long Part I was otiose and repetitive. Now that we have the restored text, I have made the opposite case: those 'repetitions' carefully establish the narrative rhythm, and still more the emotional patterns, of the whole book.

By his process of revision Lawrence established his form. It was not planned in advance, for the good reason that until he had rewritten it into final form he did not see how to get it there, still less what the form was. The fundamental limitation in a pre-planned scheme is that unless you transcend it you are at the end no wiser than at the planning stage. You have only realised what you projected: your thought, your ideas, your will have determined the outcome in ways which may be fatally limiting. For Lawrence, or for artists who work like him, the work has to tell you where it wants to go, and it may surprise you. Certainly it will break any mould you try to cast it in.

Well-meaning advisers like Garnett and Hueffer were, with their Flaubertian ideal, pressing Lawrence back towards a classical past, though they thought their Francophile sophistication was 'modern', by the standards of the 1900s.[3] It has gone on seeming modern until recently.

It is essential to distinguish Lawrence's aesthetic from that one. It is also important not to think that if his final intention was not the Flaubertian one of seeing the last exquisitely finished mosaic-piece drop into place, the only alternative was to stumble about in the dark changing things until they seemed right, or time ran out and he had to send the text off to the publisher. Yet that was a consideration, for after 1912 Lawrence had to live by his writing. He did have to complete, rapidly, a succession of works, which had to be accepted by publishers as marketable, to sell well enough to give him an income, and persuade publishers to go on backing him.

This commercial semi-imperative was, equally, a pressure on the publishers. It accounts for their attempts at sexual censorship. The circulating libraries would buy or not buy many copies of a new novel,

---

[3]Both Hueffer and Garnett worked with Conrad. The late Yves Hervouet's study *The French Face of Joseph Conrad* (Cambridge 1990) establishes Conrad's extraordinary, almost superstitious, dependence on Flaubert as model, especially in this matter of 'form'. From this relationship, from the more distanced respect of Henry James's critical writing, and via influential intermediaries like Garnett and Hueffer/Ford, an aesthetic became embodied in critical works on 'The Art of the Novel' and in some degree survives. It has inflected critical attitudes to Lawrence.

and the buying was done by the conventionally-minded guardians of the taste of conventionally-minded readers. In *The White Peacock*, that first innocent novel, Lawrence was begged to tone down some mild physicalities and milder expletives, and agreed. 'Paul Morel' was declined by Heinemann, among other reasons, for its sexual outspokenness. Lawrence later reported Heinemann as saying that it was the 'dirtiest' book he had ever read. Garnett expunged the boldest elements, though to his credit he left a surprising amount, for that time. Later, timid publishers attempted to remove things behind Lawrence's back – and quite often succeeded.

The modern editor has to trace the text through all its stages of development, recorded in its transference – revised by the author and corrupted by transcribers – from document to document. The editor has to eliminate the interferences of scribes, typists, editors and compositors: also to correct errors of transcription, including those of the author. At some points the editor has to adjudicate between two readings which are both authorial. Lawrence hardly ever compared the draft now before his eyes with the previous one. Discovering a copyist's error or ambiguity, he would not bother to resolve it by checking what he wrote, but by producing a third form. The editor has to opt for one form, and to put the others in the apparatus, perhaps with a note.

Moments like that, repeated and combined with the revisions which Lawrence inserted in each draft, cumulatively have a large implication. Having grasped the nature of Lawrence's method, and having seen that it became deliberate, it is natural to convert it into an aesthetic. But that needs careful definition. One aesthetic which I have discounted is the simple notion of endless change, or the indeterminate text as intention, now a much canvassed theoretical concept. It would be possible in the case of Lawrence – it has happened in the case of Joyce – to say that the justification of the editorial role is not the provision of a final, stable reading-text. A mere reading-text is a publisher's requirement; it enables him and the author to make a living, and it enables the ordinary reader to buy and to read, perhaps only once, a commercial product. Rather, one should imagine the whole compositional process unrolling before one's eyes, and it is that *process* which matters. CD-ROM or the latest interactive device would do justice to this: one would see the text forming and re-forming like clouds, or opening up like flowers: a sequence taking place as if in real time.

The idea is interesting and sympathetic, in so far as it places emphasis on the concept of compositional development; but I reject it as manipulated by literary theorists with an a priori position about textual indeterminacy complementing relativist views of the reading-process. Though he had moments when the publication business disgusted him, and the suppression of *The Rainbow* was a lasting trauma, Lawrence at first wanted and later needed to place finished works before the public, even though the process of publication, for him as for Joyce, often looks like an interference, a termination of pregnancy, or at any rate a Caesarean, rather than a natural birth.

There is danger in letting the argument be taken over by analogies and metaphors, but we are in the area of models or formulae, with their inevitable limitations. The edited text is a construction, corresponding entirely to no single actual document, but derived from those which survive and a posited compositional process. Applying it to Lawrence, one has to bracket the fault-lines created by the abandoned drafts. These may be peculiar to Lawrence, at any rate in the degree to which they differ. Their effect is to breach the continuity, whether you conceive it as the process reconstructed in editing the text or, to return to my main argument, as a Flaubertian reaching for an intention already defined. Lawrence's breaking off and starting afresh is not a disclaimer of any intention, but a recognition that the thing so far written is not the thing sought, so he has to start again and try to find it this time, or the next.

This was not something he could state or discuss with an editor or friend, because he had not yet got out the thing he might discuss. Think of Paul Morel in *Sons and Lovers* taking his pictures to Miriam Leivers so that she can make *him* conscious of what he has done; one reason why he needs her is as reflector who helps him to focus his own intentions and discover if this is what he wanted to stand. In actual life, Jessie Chambers, asked to read 'Laetitia', had to tell Lawrence that it was 'story-bookish', a false start, so he began again. Faced with an early draft of 'Paul Morel', Jessie again told him that he had not made it real; again he went back to the beginning. But once he had found the true path with any work, no reader could tell him anything very useful, since no reader could intuit Lawrence's own evolving consciousness of what he was aiming at. He was committed to the process of intense creation and repeated revision in answer to the dictates of something internal and as yet unformulated.

This accounts for some remarkable statements in the Letters, such as this one, often quoted, about 'The Sisters':

I am doing a novel which I have never grasped. Damn its eyes, there I am at page 145, and I've no notion what it's about. I hate it. F[rieda] says it is good. But it's like a novel in a foreign language I don't know very well – I can only just make out what it is about. (*Letters* I, 544; 23 April 1913)

Lawrence's consistent practice was to sit down and write, and see what came. It would not be true to say that he had nothing in his mind. He had his thoughts and experience, and his previous writings, including a fair number of drafts, unpublished and unrevised, there as if in a waiting-room of the mind; at any moment he might feel the need to return to them, revise and take them a stage further. These drafts were, so to speak, hinting at a direction, converging or diverging. But there is also a sense in which, especially at the outset, he pointed himself at the page, at an unknown about to come into being. When it began to appear he could begin to know it – to take it further. He then engaged with it in a prolonged wrestling, like Jacob with the angel.

The transformations which the works underwent are most obvious in the poems, to the extent that versions of one poem are different poems. Lawrence was aware of this, and the reason for it. In the 'Foreword' of May 1928 to his 'Collected Poems' he wrote a retrospective account, looking back, not long before his death, to his youth:

And I remember the slightly self-conscious Sunday afternoon, when I was nineteen [twenty, actually], and I 'composed' my first two 'poems' [....] [M]ost young ladies would have done better: at least I hope so. But I thought the effusions very nice, and so did Miriam.

Then much more vaguely I remember subsequent half-furtive moments when I would absorbedly scribble at verse for an hour or so, and then run away from the act and the production as if it were a secret sin. It seems to me that 'knowing oneself' was a sin and a vice for innumerable centuries, before it became a virtue. It seems to me, it is still a sin and a vice, when it comes to new knowledge. – In those early days [....] I used to feel myself at times haunted by something, and a little guilty about it [....] Then the haunting would get the better of me, and the ghost would suddenly appear, in the shape of a usually rather incoherent poem. Nearly always I shunned the apparition once it had appeared. From the first, I was a little afraid of my real poems – not my 'compositions,' but the poems that had the ghost in them. They seemed to me to come from somewhere, I didn't quite know where, out of a me whom I didn't know and didn't want to know, and to say things I would much rather not have said: for choice. But there they were. I never read them again. Only I gave them to Miriam, and she loved them, or she seemed to. So when I was twenty-one, and went to Nottingham University [....] I began putting them down in a little college notebook, which was the foundation of the poetic me. *Sapientiae Urbs Conditur,* it said on the cover. Never was anything less true. The city is founded on a passionate unreason.

To this day, I still have the uneasy haunted feeling, and would rather not write most of the things I do write – including this note. Only now I know my demon better, and, after bitter years, respect him more than my other, milder and nicer self. Now I no longer like my 'compositions' [....] And I must have burnt many poems that had the demon fuming in them [....] Save for Miriam, I perhaps should have destroyed them all. She encouraged my demon.

[Of 'The Wild Common'] It has taken me twenty years to say what I started to say, incoherently, when I was nineteen, in this poem. [...] To the demon, the past is not past [....] Only now perhaps can I give it more complete expression [....]

It is not for technique these poems are altered: it is to say the real say [....] The demon, when he's really there, makes his own form willy-nilly, and is unchangeable. (Appendix I in *The Complete Poems*, ed. Vivian da Sola Pinto and Warren Roberts, 1964, pp. 849–51)

This is not a process of revision to bring a work closer to a foreseen intention. It is a return, time after time, to the source of a spontaneous outflow. It is a deliberate attempt to avoid the reshaping that might be proposed by the will, the intelligence, the consciousness, because they only offer what is already known in terms of thought, and already written in terms of 'form', and Lawrence wanted to go beyond these things.

This is the root meaning of originality: direct transmission from the sources, the springs, uncontaminated by the channel of the personality. In this sense Lawrence is a late romantic, one of the greatest. As Leavis pointed out, his closest affinity in English literature is with Blake, who said of his paintings, 'Though I call them mine, I know that they are not mine.' He also said, mysteriously, 'Jesus was an artist.' If we are to make sense of that, it may be by reflecting Lawrence's perceptions onto Blake. One thinks of those texts, especially in the Fourth

Gospel, one of Lawrence's favourite books of the Bible, in which Jesus speaks of himself as a channel of the spirit, the voice of the unseen Father, and the source of living water – one sent to testify to that spirit, who had to say what it was laid on him to say. As so often there is an affinity between Lawrence and Rilke.[4] Lawrence's function as artist is that of the fountain-mouth, the marble mask through which the one pure saying passes, on its journey from far back and deep down.

Leavis, in his late writings on Lawrence, pointed in the same direction in using the distinction between what he called Lawrence's 'Ahnung', the internal impulse, and his 'nisus', the long effort of articulation. The technical terms did not naturalise in English, and in his last book Leavis dropped them, expressing the whole process more happily as 'the emergence, as he experienced it, of original thought out of the ungrasped apprehended – the intuitively, the vaguely but insistently apprehended: first the stir of apprehension, and then the prolonged repetitious wrestle to persuade it into words'.[5] This process reveals itself retrospectively as the whole writing life.

There are series of works by Lawrence which can be shown to be rewritings of immediate predecessors – attempts to come closer or to see from another aspect what in the earlier writing had been partial or from a single perspective. In my second volume,[6] I showed this in the early 'philosophical' works. There, the first strange brief utterance – a mere half-dozen pages – the Foreword to *Sons and Lovers* suddenly throws out a bunch of metaphors and metonyms, and sketches a kind of argument which is also a form of Scripture. This was taken up and developed in a rapid series of rewritings. The continuity of the series is attested by the recurrence of the images and a sort of technical terminology. Readers who have the Foreword suddenly thrown at them like a handful of pebbles, but pursue a dogged way through the series find that by 1917 and 'The Reality of Peace' they have learned this branch of language, this way of thought, and can make sense of it. They also see that Lawrence is thinking out, or working out, a set of figurations

---

[4]There is also an affinity with George Sand. In her letters to Flaubert, she is often to be found taking a 'Lawrentian' line, in her gentle but persistent criticism of his radical perfectionism. Consider for instance her letter of 29 November 1866 about her own writing: 'Le vent joue de ma vieille harpe comme il lui plaît d'en jouer ... au fond ça m'est égal pourvu que l'émotion vienne, mais je ne peux rien trouver en moi. C'est l'*autre* qui chante à son gré, mal ou bien ...' Gustave Flaubert–George Sand, *Correspondance,* ed. Alphonse Jacobs (Paris 1981) pp. 102–3.
[5]F.R. Leavis, *Thought, Words and Creativity* (London 1976) p. 124.
[6]Michael Black, *D.H. Lawrence: The Early Philosophical Works* (London 1991).

and attitudes. The involvement produces anguish as well as 'thought'; he is not moving by logical steps to a position where some proposition is satisfactorily established. It is more a piece of internal adventuring.

I have called this romanticism: it also has an affinity with a tradition of modern art. I think in particular of the basic procedure of the Surrealists and other important artists of the 1920s and 1930s who were not formally part of that movement but shared the belief in spontaneity; and especially their successors, the Abstract Expressionists. What in Surrealism has been called 'liberating the unconscious' was a psychoanalytical appropriation of the endeavour, a reduction; and the Freudian and other grids imposed by theorists have proved a parochial limitation and a banalisation. What matters is the initial risk-taking gesture of the painter who leans forward and begins to mark the canvas without having made initial sketches or studies; who lets the process take place; who may at a certain point radically repaint the whole; or who may decide to do that in the next picture. The apparent paradox is that a pondering process can be as much part of the whole as the first inspirational moment: the patron saint of that first moment is Pollock; and of the succeeding ones, Braque.

As for the constantly-to-be-recovered spontaneity, my figure of diving back into a pool is Lawrence's: a key metaphor. It applies to all art. Here is Aaron Sisson at the start of *Aaron's Rod*:

> Then he cocked his eye over the sheet of music spread out on the table before him. He tried his flute. And then at last, with the odd gesture of a diver taking a plunge, he swung his head and began to play. A stream of music, soft and rich and fluid, came out of the flute. (AR 12: 35–9)

And here is Lawrence himself as painter:

> I disappeared into that canvas. It is to me the most exciting moment – when you have a blank canvas and a big brush full of wet colour, and you plunge. It is just like diving into a pond – then you start frantically to swim. So far as I am concerned, it is like swimming in a baffling current and being rather frightened and very thrilled, gasping and striking out for all you're worth. The knowing eye watches sharp as a needle; but the picture comes clean out of instinct, intuition and sheer physical action. Once the instinct and intuition gets into the brush-tip, the picture *happens*, if it is to be a picture at all. ('Making Pictures', in *Phoenix II*, 603)

And finally, what I have described as a working method, and then as an aesthetic, is identified with a religious perception of the creative impulse itself:

> The mystery of creation is the divine urge of creation,
> but it is a great strange urge, it is not a Mind.
> Even an artist knows that his work was never in his mind,
> he could never have *thought* it before it happened.
> A strange ache possessed him, and he entered the struggle,
> and out of the struggle with his material, in the spell of the urge
> his work took place, it came to pass, it stood up and saluted his
>   mind.
>
> God is a great urge, wonderful, mysterious, magnificent
> but he knows nothing before-hand.
> His urge takes shape in flesh, and lo!
> it is creation! God looks himself on it in wonder, for the first time.
> Lo! there is a creature, formed! How strange!
> Let me think about it! Let me form an idea!
>   ('The Work of Creation', in 'Last Poems': *Complete Poems* II, 690)

Lawrence left another record, in the note he supplied to his first bibliographer, Edward McDonald: 'Books to me are incorporate things, voices in the air. [...]' He went on to say that he never re-read any of his published books (we know that he re-read *The White Peacock,* but the claim is plausible, since his relatively brief life was necessarily taken up writing the new ones). No book for him has a date, or even a binding. 'The miserable tome itself' he sees as delivering him over to 'the vulgar mercies of the world.' He goes on: 'The voice inside is mine for ever. But the beastly marketable chunk of published volume is a bone which every dog presumes to pick with me.' So, he says, 'I always hide the fact of publication from myself as far as possible. One writes, even at this moment, to some mysterious presence in the air. If that presence were not there, and one thought of even a single solitary actual reader, the paper would remain for ever white.' 'Since *The Rainbow*, one submits to the process of publication as to a necessary evil: as souls are said to submit to the necessary evil of being born into the flesh.' He moves into another of his favourite metaphors, associating necessary process with a momentary perfection: 'To every man who struggles with his own soul in mystery, a book that is a book flowers once, and seeds, and is gone' (*Phoenix*, I, 232–5).

While last year's flower and seed may be gone, an author is a perennial plant, or a tree. Lawrence seeded and flowered for a score of seasons; while each flower was itself, they are all from the parent-plant, identifiable and comparable, unique and generic.

The critical implications in all this extend beyond the single work. A hostile reader may say of deliberate spontaneity: this is to surrender to the first thing which comes into your head; and there are places in Lawrence where, if you don't see what he is doing, that is an easy thing to say. It goes with the old commonplace that the natural writer has no art, like 'sweetest Shakespeare, fancy's child'. But there are subtler ways of putting this. Not to have a clear sense of an audience, or rather to feel that you are light-years ahead of your audience – and Lawrence was, as one can see by reading the reviews he got from his most intelligent contemporaries – is to feel that you are on your own, except for the 'mysterious presence in the air', so that anything goes. There are places (some passages in *Study of Thomas Hardy*, for instance, or some of the 'riffs' in the second half of *Mr Noon*[7]) where Lawrence may be thinking 'nobody else may ever read this' and where he pursues his bitter jokes or abandons himself to his associational processes. (Strangely enough, these can be followed, since they have their logic.) After *The Rainbow*'s suppression, one can sense a hostility to the audience, which comes out in the later novels. Critics have taken as facile or commercial writing what is both a provocative challenge to the reader and an exhilarated flouting of convention, with Lawrence poking his head through the frame.

Most important, the fact that there has been both spontaneity and revision in important works may lead the sympathetic critic to say approvingly: *this* is spontaneous, and, more critically: *that* comes from the constructive effect of revision; or even this is Lawrentian, and that is Flaubertian. This is an issue in the discussion of *The Rainbow*. But both elements are essential. Often in short intensely expressive works, especially poetic sequences, you can identify the poet's 'inspirations' – the loci where that linguistic gift is being used at its most characteristic, with no fore- or afterthought. But you can also see places, usually

---

[7]Cf. STH 10: 30–11: 36, and the commentary in BEPW 152ff. In *Mr Noon*, see the improvisations on 'spooning' in chapter 2, or the schoolboy humour of the apostrophe to 'uplift' on pp. 156–7. This starts almost as doodling, or as letting go – and then the thought occurs that this may be a way of stinging the conventional reader into a reaction. This is pursued in *Aaron's Rod* and *Kangaroo* as a conscious tactic.

when a larger structure is being articulated, where poets have to get from the place where they are now to the place where they need to be next, or to make clear how this place relates to, chimes with, that one. So the last lines of a poem in a sequence may have to be transitional to the first lines of the next. Thought, reworking, is needed; one has to ponder relationships, find links, make connections: and this is deliberate, may seem cold-blooded.

The Rainbow is a big book, and very highly organised: *Women in Love* even more so. They could not have reached that complexity of structure in a single spontaneous writing: it had to be worked and reworked. The surprising thing is not that some elements seem too neat or too willed. It is by comparison with the rest that one says so; the astounding thing is that the rest is so inspired, while the structural engineering is always characteristic and never banal.

2
'Theorising myself out': After *Sons and Lovers*: The 'Burns Novel' and 'Elsa Culverwell'

In Italy, in November 1912, Lawrence finished the last revision of *Sons and Lovers* and sent it off to Duckworth. It is commonly supposed that with the final rewriting of that book he had drawn a line under the first part of his life. In that mood the question, what next? might be answered by – something different, and not personal. Having been 'unEnglished' by his weeks in Germany, being for the moment settled in Italy and absorbed in the new experience, he could now look back at England and the English. And if one reflects about *The White Peacock*, *Sons and Lovers* and certain early short stories, it is possible to be too interested in the personal aspect. One other strong element is an attempt to say something penetrating about the people, the community, Lawrence grew up among, and the place they lived in. Here, perhaps, was a way forward which was not a total departure.

There are references in the Letters to a novel 'purely of the common people' (*Letters* I, 431, August 1912) and this is named 'Scargill Street' in October (*Letters* I, 466). This may have been an unfulfilled plan. The writings which we actually have from these months are the 'Burns Novel' fragment, written in November, and the slightly longer fragment now called 'Elsa Culverwell', which is just conceivably 'Scargill Street.'[1] The 'Burns Novel' was abandoned and not taken up again, ever. 'Elsa Culverwell' takes up again a theme – the actual Cullen family – eliminated from 'Paul Morel' before it became *Sons and Lovers*, and then used as the germ of 'The Insurrection of Miss Houghton', written in January–March 1913, and abandoned in order to begin 'The

---

[1] On the argument that to move from Nottingham Road, where Elsa was born, by marrying someone in Scargill Street is to move from the shopkeeper class into 'the common people'. Such a marriage would be like that of Miss Louisa in 'Two Marriages', later revised as 'Daughters of the Vicar'.

Sisters'. It was lost sight of during the War because the MS was in Bavaria, and then taken up once more as a novel which, after the disaster of *The Rainbow*, had to be 'popular'. It became *The Lost Girl*, rewritten from the start in a single draft in 1920.

Both fragments – the 'Burns Novel' and 'Elsa Culverwell' – are spontaneous writing of high quality: vivid, fresh and full of interest: works of genius.[2] An ideal 'Portable' or 'Omnibus' Lawrence selection would include both, since they are still unfamiliar, and making them widely available would revive interest. They are vivid pieces written by Lawrence in his great period of hopefulness and overflowing genius. They strike the reader over-familiar with Lawrence's classic work with all the more force. They are unrevised first drafts.

The 'Burns' fragment gives the opening pages of a novel which translates the figure of Burns, making him a native of Lawrence's own Midlands, the country of his heart. Burns was, despite his father's relative prosperity, his own literacy and his command of literary written English, a working man, a countryman, with an instinctive gift, like Lawrence's. His vernacular poetry was popular and came out like song – his great poems *are* songs, of and for his own people, in their language. Emotionally, he was immediately instinctive, responsive to impulse. This made him a natural lover, and got him into trouble. Later, as famous literary figure and national treasure he had to be made respectable by the unco guid. Lawrence read Lockhart's 'Life', and essays by Lang and Henley; when he re-read Lockhart in 1927, he told Donald Carswell it 'Made me spit! Those damned middle-class Lockharts grew lilies of the valley up their arses, to hear them talk' (*Letters* VI, 231). What he valued, and felt as instinctive brotherhood, was that Burns came direct from his place and people, wrote or sang from that unconscious life, in a speech not made genteel by education and an art not sophisticated by academics, teachers, critics, or editors and censors.

But Burns was a Scot, removed in time, place and language. Lawrence must have felt that his equivalent would have to come from his own country and be a speaker of his own dialect – which he, Lawrence, had not as his mother- but as his father-tongue. His Burns-figure is therefore John Haseldine, known as Jack. He lives at the Haggs

---

[2]The first is an appendix on pp. 201–11 of the volume *Love Among the Haystacks* in the Cambridge edition, edited by John Worthen. 'Elsa Culverwell' is an appendix on pp. 343–58 in the Cambridge *The Lost Girl*, also edited by Worthen.

Farm, the home of Jessie Chambers, Miriam Leivers in *Sons and Lovers* and the Saxton family of *The White Peacock*, and the imagined site of a number of early short stories. The time is unspecified, but must be before Lawrence's grandfather's time, for mining in the Eastwood area is still using the old gin-pits, before the days of deep shafts in about 1820. Jack is not a miner, but a farmer's son. He is literate, is teaching himself arithmetic from a book. His personal gift is a fine tenor voice: he is known for it, and sings in the evenings in public houses, where he is welcomed and admired, since his gift is recognised as an art.

I have abstracted these 'facts' as pieces of information, in the way one does from one's reading. The fragment itself is brilliant because it does *not* abstract, but conveys information in the way one naturally receives it, as immediate impression, or as deduction, incidentally, while something is going on. One is just *there*, seeing and overhearing; what one calls, after the event, description, and what one receives as the narrative come out as the purely instinctive art which the tale is about.

He was writing in November, and remembering how it must have been at home. So, in the narrative, it is a fine late November afternoon turning towards night: always one of Lawrence's favourite times, the meeting-point between states or realms. The fragment takes us through the evening: establishes a crucial first contact between a man and woman, then a later confirmation of the new relationship. What happens is beyond or below words – though simple words are used by the characters for communication. Other ways of making contact are more important.

The time of day starts as what we call nightfall; but Lawrence had shown in *The White Peacock* and elsewhere that night does not fall, it rises, as shadow in valleys and dells, like a tide rising, while up in the sky a vivid light changes. So here, Lawrence's painter's eye records the notations. This is how it starts:

> There was the clear sound of a man's whistling, but no one was to be seen on the common. The afternoon of the beautiful November day was drawing to a close. Overhead the sky was of fine, high blue, but in the west it grew mild as turquoise, then glistened green near the dark rim of the hill. Under the blue sky the fawn-coloured leaves standing dry and chavelled upon the young oaks shone sharply as the levelling light caught them. (LATH 201: 3–9)

But he is more than this eye, he is a whole attentiveness, so immediate as not to be conscious of itself. If you look back to that first sentence, you become aware that as in life the sound has made you look, but attention is then caught by the scene, and the sound is forgotten. The paragraph goes on, to look upwards and around, and to feel the changing light on objects. And now it introduces two women into the landscape – a focusing:

> Then two women were seen, with reddish kerchieves over their heads, bending among the oak-scrub. (201: 9–10)

'Were seen' is passive, neutral; there is no observer. The women are just there, not identified. They are, we deduce, collecting brushwood for kindling (locally this is called 'sticking', we learn later), and this is a hint about the period, the way of life, a peasant economy. The next paragraph begins:

> The whistling ceased, there was heard the sharp quick strokes of an axe. (13–14)

The further sound draws attention back to the whistling by stopping it and substituting itself. It must be made by the unseen man who was whistling (it is not womanly to whistle, especially at work). It is part of the same economy that women gather, men use axes. What is hanging in the air here is that the man has made a sound which might have been a soliloquy, but might have been a signal. It has had no response.

The eye then fixes a young holly-tree, and the notations give it a strong presence, not human, but powerfully value-laden, as if wanting to be an analogy:[3]

> It was a perfectly healthy young tree, erect, with all its berries burning among the dark and glittering leaves. Quite alone it stood, and radiant. (18–20)

---

[3]The notation is taken up and amplified in the later short story 'England My England': 'Winifred! She was young and beautiful and strong with life, like a flame in sunshine. She moved with a slow grace of energy like a blossoming, red-flowered bush in motion' (EME 6: 14–17). And cf. the moment in action in France, when the first shell bursts: 'He only noticed a twig of holly with red berries fall like a gift on to the road below' (32: 5–6).

'One of the women' now moves into focus. The colour of her 'crimson and fawn kerchief' and her hair 'red as a squirrel about her pink and white face' link her with the holly-tree. She glances at the 'radiant young' tree, and the adjectives silently transfer to her. 'She walked valiantly with her great armful of twigs': that produces a suggestion of strong personality. Then, by moving, a donkey comes into focus, grazing. It had been 'almost invisible on the common, in its greyness. Moreover it was belted round with sackcloth fawn like the oakleaves.' This does what a good painter might do, suggesting through colour a deeper harmony of belonging together. The donkey is linked tonally with the background, while the girl is linked with the holly-tree. More directly, it tells why we had not seen the donkey until it raised its head and caught the girl's eye, and ours.

Still the notations go on unfolding: how the light changes, how the shadow rises. It is established that the girl 'was a slim, light thing of about eighteen'. She approaches the holly tree, looks for the best bunch of berries. 'Suddenly the whistling stopped' (so it had been going on again, not noticed) and there is a third sound, from the same source: a man's voice, 'strong and cheerful', shouting. It is calling a name, 'Bill'. The girl guesses that it is the donkey's name. As the man goes on calling, and the donkey refuses to move, she calls in reply 'He's here!' The man is guided by her voice to his donkey, and appears.

> 'Was it you as shouted?' he said.
> 'I knowed it was you,' she replied [....] (202: 37–8)

The implications of this reply emerge later. What has happened is not just that the girl has told the man where his donkey is. Having heard the broadcast of his whistling, having heard his axe, having heard his voice (and recognised it), she has now called to him, thus converting his noises into a signal to which she has given an answer. In Lawrence's terms this is momentous: a contact has been made; a claim, even, established. This is one of the ways in which people who do not know each other meet. They now talk a little, rather constrainedly on her part. He admires the holly-bush ('It's a rare red bush') and tries to make contact with her: the remark might be a compliment to her, for she too is rare and red. He asks where she is from, learns her name, Mary Renshaw;[4] startles her by asking if she likes her name, says it is 'pretty-sounding' – another coded

---

[4]The name of the Brinsley family Lawrence's uncle had married into. Emily Saxton in *The White Peacock* marries a Renshaw.

compliment. He learns that her father is a miner; tells her he is from the Haggs. Then,

> 'How did you know it was our donkey?' he said.
> ''Cause I've 'eered you singin', and I could tell your voice.'
> 'An' 'ad you seed me?'
> 'No.' (203: 32–5)

This suddenly tells us a lot; if she could recognise his voice when he simply called the donkey's name, then it was a voice she had listened to very intently on some previous occasion, or more than once. So, one thinks, she was already attracted, but may not have known that, has been predisposed to answer his call, which she instantly recognised as his.

However, they have to be getting on with what they are doing, so have to part. She explains that she must go back by another road, with her companion. When he asks why, she replies 'Because I mun – I on'y 'eered yer singin.' We infer that she must go back with the woman she went out with, or family and neighbours will make deductions which will harm her reputation; the relationship between him and her is so far only this odd chance link that she recognised his voice. But then, it is being established that that is a strange and interesting thing. He points out that there will be a dance on Saturday night (an invitation to be there, and to hear him sing again) but she says that she does not go to dances.

They part without farewell; he loads his cart, harnesses the donkey, and goes off his own way.

> Above the dark, shaggy common, the sky was bright green and purple, but it gave off no light. The earth was a great shadow. One big white star hung between the purple and the darkening green of the west. (204: 32–5)

This is like Hardy's placing of small, lone figures in a huge landscape. Above the two humans the transition continues between day and night, the two states, notating Lawrence's constant sense of the relativity of our alternation of light and dark down here, our clock-time, and the unchanging present time up there, of the planet related to the sun:

> Suddenly he lifted his head and began to sing. He had a fine tenor

voice that rang out in the frosty, clear evening. The girl, climbing the hill in the other direction, bowed beneath her load of wood, heard the wild singing as she tramped.

'That's Jack Haseldine,' said the woman accompanying her. 'He knows more songs than any lad i' th' country.'

'And a good singer,' said the girl. (204: 39–205: 5)

This is the first time we have heard his name: he has been 'a man', 'the youth', 'the lad'. But the two women know him as a voice, a talent, as well as a name.

As for the 'wild singing', it may be what he habitually does as he walks along by himself after work, as the whistling might be what he does while he works by himself, but it now also has, across the widening gap between them, an intended audience – her. It is like the wild singing which, in her dream, March will hear in the later story 'The Fox'. It is also like the singing of Count Dionys in 'The Ladybird', calling Daphne without knowing that he is calling her, so that her appearing in his room at first startles him – 'Darkness answering to darkness and deep answering to deep'. These later reworkings of the theme develop it considerably, at the cost in 'The Ladybird' of becoming over-elaborate, literary, uneasily poised between naturalism and romance, and over-solemn. Here at this early point, the brief and natural statement could pass unnoticed: it is when we read later fictions that we realise that 'singing' is one of Lawrence's ... I don't know what the right term would be: 'theme' is too weak; one needs the old rhetorical term *topos*.

This works both ways: we are now alerted to things less developed in earlier writing. There is the very first fiction, 'A Prelude', the little story entered for a newspaper competition and printed in 1907. This too has its thematic holly and its young lovers in the Haggs trying to make contact across a separation – to declare love – first by performing the centuries-old guyser's play, and then, successfully, by singing. Acting, singing, dancing are ways in which the body expresses itself directly, and we receive messages at a level below and beyond speech, or are able to 'say' what we need to say without using words. One remembers also that Lettie Beardsall in *The White Peacock* leads on her young men by playing and singing to them: her choice of song always has a point. George Saxton, her 'Burns' lover, naturally turns to folk-song.

Jack makes his way home, and Lawrence follows him in his memory across country to the remembered Haggs. When he enters the house, meets his father and brother, has his meal, the scene borrows something from Italian peasant families seen around the Garda. Watching them, Lawrence must have felt in touch with the earlier age of his own region, was being briefed, so to speak, for the first part of *The Rainbow*.

Jack spends a little time with his book and his slate, but some restlessness, some sense of incompletion, takes him back out into the open. His declared purpose is 'to look at my snares', but underneath there is an undeclared lack. There follows a Lawrentian night-scene. Orion duly appears: another *topos*. This was Lawrence's personal tutelary constellation:

> The night was brilliant with stars, the wood was black. He walked down the high, bald fields, along the hedgerow. Orion was just heaving up above the wooded hill opposite. Everywhere the ground was dark, everywhere the heavens glittered. He clenched his hands, wanting to grasp something. (206: 20–4)

The relationship with Hardy is felt again: but Lawrence does not imply that the universe diminishes his humans. The notation of the hands is yet another *topos*. Two pages back, Jack's 'hands and wrists were big, raw-boned as he grasped the purple and grey twigs, but they moved with an intimate intelligence'. His father's hands, as he sits by the fire, were 'folded and asleep'. Hands are instinctive creatures, as if independent, know better, do things without being told, and betray what is going on deep inside.[5]

> He stood and listened. There was scarce a sound anywhere. And yet the night seemed to breathe. He felt his breast burning [....] There was a rush and flurry down in the hedge. It was a rabbit in one of his snares.

'Wee sleekit cow'ring timorous beastie', the reader may remember. Jack perceives it first as just a thing: 'The thing was afraid of him.' Then it is 'a little live thing with his wire round its neck'. Then it 'was a living little rabbit-person with dark eyes, and it was afraid of him'. More, he talks to it as a female.

> He held it in his big hands against his chest, murmuring:
>   'Are ter frit, my little missie. Are ter frit, Tiss, Tissie?'

---

[5]BEF index 'hand, hands'. Also 'Orion'.

But he was more frightened himself. He dared not kill it. Feeling the palpitating thing crouch and warm his breast, he was stifled. The stars glittered, staring like thousands of eyes. Slowly, very carefully, fumbling, he felt for the twine round the rabbit's neck. It gave a convulsed movement. His heart leaped like a ball of fire. Half trembling, he loosed the noose. When it was free of the rabbit, he began to breathe again. He cuddled the thing against his breast.

'Say nowt!' he said. 'Say nowt.'

Then glancing round, he lowered the little beast and set it on the grass. It sat there in a bunch, not moving. He stood quite still. Suddenly, like a shot, it was gone into the darkness. He felt a load off his breathing. The night seemed to expand big and clear again. He stood and looked round. It seemed another world than that he knew by daylight. He was half frightened.

There was something he wanted, out of the glittering night. He stood quite still, fronting it all. He ought to be going back to the house, but he did not want to. He wanted to get away from something – he wanted something. Turning swiftly, he set off across the fields up-hill. (207: 2–22)

'Fronting' was the word used of Mrs Morel, facing the vivid sunset sky in the powerful scene when she decides to call her baby Paul, having held him up to the sun. What has crystallised in Jack, we discover, is the unspoken decision to go to the girl's house and to speak to her: to make verbally the claim that might have been implicit in his singing.

He makes his way to her house, identifies it as the end-house, as Lawrence's had been when the family lived at The Breach. He watches, and she comes out to get some coal. The brief description is arch-Lawrentian: in the light of her candle 'He saw her small serious face ruddy as a moon' (207: 31–2). 'Ruddy' links with the red notations of her hair and the holly at the beginning, is one of Lawrence's most frequently used adjectives,[6] always indicates vitality and is usually an approval-indicator; as for the moon, it is a frequent presence, a kind of challenge, most notably in *The Rainbow*. His action is characteristic: 'Softly, he began to whistle a tune.' He approaches, speaks, asks her to 'come an' ha'e a word wi' me', then to 'come a bit of a walk'. She is reluctant; the children have to be sat with, her father will come home and be angry. Then he grasps her to him just as he had held the rabbit, and they have this exchange, in which he 'explains' why he has come

---

[6]It makes its first appearance in the second line of 'A Prelude'.

– because she called him that afternoon – and she 'explains' why she had called. They are recognising a kind of claim on each other, which they feel but can hardly verbalise:

> He put his arms round her, and folded her to him suddenly.
> '"He's here!"', he suddenly said, curiously and lovingly imitating the voice in which she had called to him on the common. '"He's here!"' – I thought it was a witch of the woods callin'.'
> He had got her tightly clasped to his bosom, and was trembling.
> 'What made thee ca' to me?' he asked.
> 'I niver thought,' she replied.
> '"He's here!"' he repeated softly, 'that's what I heard. An' Bill vanished clean out o' my mind, as if he'd gone off in a wisp. – I wonder if you could shout again like that –?'
> 'Like what?' she asked.
> 'Like that. You called straight to me.'
> 'I'd heered you singin' an' whistlin',' she said.
> 'What did I sing?' he asked.
> 'You sung "Gentle Annie".'
> He held her fast in his arms, very warm.
> 'I catched a rabbit tonight an' I let it go again,' he said.
> 'What for?'
> 'I dunno!' (208: 24–209: 2)

The rabbit is associated with her, so he tells her about it. What the narrative has rapidly noted, the reader may brood over, perhaps make too much of. Was that capture and release symbolic? Did it symbolise tenderness? Or lack of constancy (catch them and let them go)? Is Mary Renshaw the next rabbit? But that is the business of consciousness. What is happening here is unconscious, though the narrative voice is putting extraordinary things into words, and we are suddenly in the universe of *The Rainbow* – or more exactly in Lawrence's own extraordinary mode of writing, where terms like 'narrator' and 'person' are left behind:

> She put up her mouth to him. He found her lips. The end of her small nose, quite cold, brushed his cheek. He was breathless and astonished in all his being. Holding her fast, he moved his lips over her face, her cheeks, her shut eyes, her brows. The discovery was amazing. The whole secret of the night and the stars was in these soft, smooth grooves and mounds and hollows. It was her face! Yet

it seemed to include big distances and wonderful things. The flashing lights overhead were no further off than the strange roughness of her eyebrows under his lips, the arched, dark sky didn't frighten him more than the firm domes of her eyes under the softly closed eyelids. And she was breathing against him, live and warm like the rabbit. And it was the darkness he was kissing, discovering. It was the night he had his mouth upon.

Suddenly she sighed, and raised her face from him.

'Dost love me?' he murmured, not knowing. 'Dost love me?' (209: 8–24)

'Live and warm like the rabbit' makes the connection. But to go on to 'And it was the darkness he was kissing, discovering. It was the night he had his mouth upon' goes right through the connection to the mystery which the rabbit also represented: the amazingness of living otherness, one might say. But that is intellectualisation, putting into concepts what was put in strange words. And who speaks them? Is Jack putting them into words for himself? No: the words represent his wordless intuitions. He is a sort of poet, then. Also his intuitions may mean that the momentary objects of his attention, his desire, are the focus of a larger desire that transcends them: a hard role for the other person to play. And 'darkness' does not just mean the night-time they are in at this moment: *The Rainbow* will make that clear.

She asks him if he loves her.

> He took her close in his arms again. She let her self melt against him quite naturally, as he pressed her to his breast.
> 'I do,' he whispered. 'I do! I do!'
> She sighed again as he kissed her. (28–31)

They are interrupted by the sound of a door opening. She 'withdrew from him', goes back indoors, where he sees 'the dark ruddiness vanish from the interior as she mended the fire'. He leaves, 'Feeling warm, with a warm, rich sensation in his chest and arms'. He comes to an inn, where he is welcome as the singer who brings in customers to hear him, and keeps them drinking while they listen. He is given a place of honour at a strange raised hearth such as Lawrence had recently seen in Italy. As it is Thursday, the men have a five days' growth of beard – another Italian detail. And we are suddenly told what Jack looks like – 'a raw-boned, big youth, with a high domed head on which the black hair hung straight. He was swarthy and ruddy, his dark eyes were full of fire and laughter' (210: 24–6). We realise that for the first time we are seeing him in a full light, then look back a line or two and see he has taken his hat off and is sitting in the firelight: this is why we can now see what he really looks like, after ten pages and a good deal of incident.

The fragment ends: we suppose he is about to sing. He has been characterised as 'something of a king among the men, because he was clever, and a great singer, and something of a fiddler'. We see also that he is on easy terms with the company.

Another four-paragraph fragment records Jack waking, presumably the next morning. It is one of Lawrence's 'break of day and dawn of consciousness' setpieces, very brief. The observed birth of light, the transition towards sunrise, preoccupied him as complementary to the other process at the end of day. The notations here are characteristic: 'a stealthy look about the room that seemed like dawn'; 'He lay quite still, watching the window, seeing nothing, neither conscious nor unconscious, but like the dawn, indefinite, only silting towards realisation.' 'The gold came up behind the hill, and with it, joy for everything.'

Reflecting on this subtle, accomplished and powerful writing, and trying to see why Lawrence abandoned something so good, one finds it shedding a light in both directions, backward and forward. Here we are again in the woods and fields and hills round the Haggs. Is Jack Haseldine going to be a Lawrence-figure? There is an intrinsic likelihood; Lawrence said in a letter that Burns 'seems a good deal like myself – nicer in most ways. I think I can do him almost like an autobiography'. There, perhaps, is the beginning of a disadvantage, in his mind something to be avoided, and gestured towards in a letter to Garnett about an unnamed piece of writing – most probably 'Elsa Culverwell': 'I've stewed my next novel inside me for a week or so and have begun dishing it up. It's going to have a bit of a plot and I don't think it will be unwieldy, because it will be further off from me and won't come down on my head so often.' It may be that he feared the Burns story was *not* sufficiently far off from him and would, if continued, have 'come down on his head'. I doubt if Lawrence wanted to deflect his Burns-figure towards himself; rather he wanted a central character who has a talent, not necessarily his, and certainly not his psychic heritage. For that reason Jack Haseldine is more like George Saxton of *The White Peacock*, who is a farmer's son, lives at the Haggs, sings folksongs, sets snares for rabbits but has no hesitation about killing them, is physically attractive and profoundly at home in his setting – but whose awakening to consciousness is the end of wholeness and the beginning of a disastrous decline.

It is not clear from the fragment whether Jack Haseldine is more conscious than George Saxton; and this is, curiously, a question of period or era. Jack has more talent, indeed an art, but the cliché - understanding of such figures is that they were instinctive or untutored geniuses, the 'native woodnotes' cliché. Lawrence knew better than that: would have recognised from Burns's sophisticated English verse that he was bilingual in the same way as himself: was, like him, well- if largely self-educated, and in many ways self-conscious. Jack Haseldine seems more of a true peasant than Burns.

The instinct to move back into the past may spring from the sense that the present in both *The White Peacock* and *Sons and Lovers* – that is, the present of Lawrence's own lifetime – is felt as modern in dangerous or troubling ways. Walter Morel, the miner-father, is like the survivor of an earlier race of men: he has lived on into a time which is beginning to have no use for his sort: his son finds him primitive, and the author of the book is in two minds about him. George Saxton too has been born out of his own time: towards the end of the novel he exemplifies his own fall into consciousness by reflecting that he is a failure, 'ought to have made something of myself [....] a poet or something, like Burns [....] But I am born a generation too soon' (WP 288: 11–16).

Alternatively, he is several generations too late, and is visibly destroyed by his inability to cope with the life he has fallen into. The fabulous Annable, the intellectual turned gamekeeper, thinks he can revert into a natural life on the fringe of society, but fails and dies – or destroys himself. There is an impulse to say that there was an earlier time when men with these qualities, that natural vigour, could be shown as fully at home in their bodies and their communities and homelands. That might seem nostalgic for a lost Eden – or so a modern sceptic would say, as a way of not listening. But this whole topic of the relationship between present and past, and the kind of being that the two periods fostered is going to be crucial in *The Rainbow*. In principle, Lawrence was committed to the view that people must live onward in time, becoming what they have it in them to be. But there is a possibility that that will not be allowed, or at any rate not approved.

The advantage of choosing an artist as representative is that he can be taken as growing-point. That would make him (Lawrence was moving towards the thought that it might equally be her) a source of scandal to contemporaries who do not want change. The disadvantage of the device is that it produces the cliché-figure of the artist at odds with 'bourgeois' society; separates off the artist as unrepresentative or superior, and his art as what separates him; and casts the community as the object of Flaubertian hatred or irony, or, as in *Buddenbrooks*, nostalgia. Going back in time to a Jack Haseldine is possibly a solution of the problem. There was a time when a popular artist was representative of his community, and comfortable in it. As folk-singer Jack is welcome in the inn, applauded by his hearers, liked as a man. It would, one suspects, be his love-affairs which would get him into trouble – first of all with Mary's father, perhaps.

But from Lawrence's ultimate viewpoint there is a flaw in the scheme: it looks as if it will deal with only one generation; and if it occupies only a few years in the late eighteenth century, it is lost in a single past which can be looked back on as a time-capsule: magical, mythical, at any rate lost. There is just a hint of *Wuthering Heights* in the air: Emily Brontë's novel, which has a long time-span and encompasses two distinct generations, shrinks in the memory to one brief legendary time, long ago: a warning. The important point made in *Sons and Lovers*, a clear advance on the prolonged but clumsily handled time-scheme in *The White Peacock* and the inordinately brief present in *The Trespasser* (one week in 1909), is that change works through successive generations, and the change is of consciousness itself.

I guess that some such thoughts made Lawrence abandon the fragment: Jack Haseldine 'done almost like an autobiography' might come out too much like Paul Morel: if he came out like a successful George Saxton, that was still too much like self-repetition. Above all, being locked into a period so long ago would bring all the unrealities of the historical novel and would never get Lawrence to his main concern, which was being alive in *his* century and having to realise that and cope with it, and especially managing to love.

One successful feature of the fragment is that it is not yet too obviously in any time that one can identify (it might almost be the Italy he was living in then) but, before he had gone much further, period 'authenticity' would have been bound to press its claims. If you take that seriously, you have *Romola*; if you take it lightly you have *Kidnapped*. What he was working towards, without yet knowing it, was *The Rainbow*, with its three generations taking us from someone like Jack Haseldine to someone like Paul Morel and beyond, ending not just 'now' but pointing onward; and recording on the way an evolution into consciousness, and then into self-consciousness – also from a male-led world to the arrival of the female as focus. But he had not got there yet. What the fragment brilliantly does is to make us see in Jack an original confident unconsciousness, a strength and openness of being, an at-homeness in the world, like a starting-point.

In 'Paul Morel', the late draft of *Sons and Lovers*, readers will find the first in the succession of writings which culminated in *The Lost Girl*. The actual Cullen family of Eastwood: George Henry Cullen the shopkeeper with his pretensions and grandiose projects, his invalid wife, the capable and distinguished governess who gave piano lessons, the daughter Florence whom the governess looked after and who became a trained nurse, the dour middle-aged woman supervisor of the working-girls who turned out cheap goods on the top floor of the big house in the Nottingham Road – this group fascinated Lawrence, and he first turned them into the Staynes family in 'Paul Morel'. Paul has piano lessons from the governess, and (surprisingly to readers of *Sons and Lovers*) one of the two daughters is the Miriam whom he loves.

'Elsa Culverwell' is the second handling of this family group. Now the shopkeeper is Frederick Culverwell, eleven years younger than his wife. She married him at 32; had two children, was mortified to find she was living over the shop, was too ladylike to admit shopkeeping into her consciousness, and turned aside into invalidism. We are in Arnold Bennett's territory, derived from Balzac: the observation of provincial life, the lower-middle to middle-middle class, a keen interest in how money is made in small family businesses, and how lives can be made or unmade by it; with an equally keen interest in 'character', especially the distortions produced by the setting. So the huge brick house, the immense and funereal mahogany furniture, the things sold, their price, all these things lead up to the question: who – given your station in life – you can marry if you are Elsa Culverwell; what marriage would be like if it is based on all that, and what is the alternative.

The opening sentences, 'My mother made a failure of her life. I am making a success of mine' (LG 343: 2) convey two things. Here is 'character', in one classic sense: this is a strong-minded person who gets straight to a point, has self-confidence. Is it misplaced? Perhaps we shall see. But the real surprise, for a reader of Lawrence, is that this is a first-person narrative.

'The Insurrection of Miss Houghton', begun in January 1913 and abandoned in March after 200 pages, was the next use of this 'Cullen' material, but since the MS is lost we do not know whether it too was written in the first person. Lawrence incorporated no part of it in the eventual *Lost Girl*, which was completely rewritten. This would have been necessary if he had used the first person in 1913, and, rereading the draft in 1920, was clear about the fatal limitation – for him – of the technique. A reason for thinking that he went on using it for a time is that the first draft of 'The Sisters', begun in April 1913, did use it, though no part of this draft survives which shows it in use. This is the implication of two letters to Garnett:

> I shall make it all right when I rewrite it. I shall put it in the third person. All along I knew what ailed the book. But it did me good to theorise myself out [....] I'll make it into art now. (*Letters* I, 550, 19 May 1913)

> I have nearly finished The Sisters – p. 283. I think the end is good. I am rather keen to re-write it in the third person. (*Letters* II, 20, 1 June 1913)

That suggests that Lawrence had done quite a lot of experimenting with first-person narration, and had 'theorised' himself to the point where he saw that it would not serve all his purposes. The purpose it would serve was to be 'dramatic', to use another voice, to write from inside another personality. Moreover, since his 'I', Elsa, is a woman, he was attempting what was still in 1913 quite a bold thing. One reflects that Dickens had done it in *Bleak House*, but equivocally. 'I know I am not clever', says Esther Summerson in Chapter 3; which raises the question: who, then, has just written two of Dickens's most extraordinary introductory chapters, with their sweep and power? Dickens as narrator can be the only answer; the switching between voices in the progress of the novel is an ingenious device, but the contrast between the voices is unsettling, and making Esther 'not clever' is equivocal. Emily Brontë handled her first-person narrators in *Wuthering Heights* brilliantly: their being 'not clever', or at any rate more ordinary, less demanding than the almost mythical main characters, makes a dramatic point about both kinds of person. But Lawrence must have bumped up against the limitation inherent in the technique, which is not simply that contemporary readers might be disconcerted by strong-minded women. His Elsa *is* clever, or some such word, but that produces a problem of its own.

One difference between the two narrative methods is presented by our current critical terminology – which fails to make an essential distinction. The 'omniscient' narrative voice using the third person can be allowed to know and tell everything; the intermediate narrator or 'I' can only know what he/she knows. In *The White Peacock* the narrator Cyril Beardsall is soon telling us things he could not have known. It is more to the point that he is soon thinking thoughts, indeed just seeing and feeling, in ways that only Lawrence could rise to. Paradoxically, the reader accepts this, since Cyril is so obviously an alter-ego, a young Lawrence-figure. But is he to be thought of as a writer, indeed a genius?

Of Elsa Culverwell as persona, one can say that a dramatising intelligence would give her her first energetic sentences, expressing her will and self-confidence; and would go on to keep her sentences short and her language simple: she is not a writer. The same intelligence would get a little sly pleasure (remembering his own childhood) in the shift of viewpoint which gives this:

> We used to go walks with our mother and Miss Niell. In winter, Lucy and I had fur tippets and muffs and fur hats, and, as we went along the street where the miners' children were running, in their quaint clothes that had been made for somebody else, we felt very grand indeed. (349: 18–22)

That is 'in character', but seems to limit her, both her intelligence and her sympathy. A reader like Garnett would think, 'Yes, she would be a little snobbish: perhaps only as a child, though.' And perhaps it is a trap for the simple reader, for she may be being sardonic about her past childish self, class-bound in an immaturity she is now able to be honest about. Is she in fact very intelligent?

Garnett might have said, as I do, that the person who could write that and mean it without afterthought could not write this, of her father:

> There was a pleasing sensation about his eloquence, like the stroking of silk, like the glisten and change of silk. (348: 37–9)

And of his 'enjoyment' of religion:

> It seemed to me a kind of wallowing, or like a cat when it gets quite frantic in its voluptuous rubbings and slidings. (349: 3–6)

Oh, one begins to think, we have a *writer* here, and one turns back to the first page, where it says, of the mother:

> I can see her in her photograph, wistful, with a touch of langour, waiting to be awakened, fearing almost to sleep all her life [...] (343: 17–19)

'Sleeping beauty', one murmurs: he had used the theme in *Sons and Lovers*, and often later, but it is well hidden here. Then a sentence at the end of the paragraph about Miss Venner, the supervisor of the working-girls, says simply:

> Nothing seemed to leap straight up in her, as it did in Miss Niell. (349: 12–13)

I suppose an unsophisticated person, not a writer, might manage something as brilliantly simple, as if by instinct, as they might manage the aphorism a few sentences earlier: 'She always was more moral than vital.' A lot depends on our accepting the convention, not listening too suspiciously, and accepting that this voice is indeed Elsa Culverwell's. She might have got this out of Dickens, about the young man with the tenor voice that Miss Niell has a soft spot for and she, Elsa, is jealous of: 'He was rather a tall young man, with a very assertive chest.' But when we read

> He was leaning against the piano, his strong, hard chest thrust out [....] (354: 1)

and

> He stood erect; thrust out his chest [....] (354: 18)

the word 'motif' may suggest itself. And the description of the man's singing, so expressive of his nature, is simply brilliant:

> [...] his voice came ringing through the house. It was as if it were produced in some fine steel instrument, so hard and clear [...] It seemed as if the music were hurt in his throat [....] He suddenly tore the recitative out of his throat. (353: 28–354: 19)

Here one sees the strength of the writing. Readers brought up on Esther Summerson, even readers impressed by Forster's Schlegel sisters, are hearing a woman's voice which is strong, indeed sharp and tough, and willing to show its unladylike aspects. There are excitements and shocks ahead for such readers. But still, there is this problem about not being a writer – for here is one of Lawrence's personal *topoi*, for one thing. One can imagine Garnett and Hueffer not being shocked so much at the absence of conventional femininity, but on the verge always of saying 'But that sort of person couldn't say that, couldn't think it' because it implies a writer's gift. It might seem merely snobbish, but it is near a truth or it wouldn't get said. It is linked with conventional notions of 'character' – the thing Lawrence was profoundly undermining.

The ultimate limitation of the technique, and the attendant thought about 'character', is not that it produces this minor argument, but that it absolutely precludes anything like the night-scene in the Burns fragment: not just the beauty of the 'descriptions' but specifically the moment when Jack is holding the rabbit or later holding Mary Renshaw, and Lawrence is free to intuit in him, to put brilliantly into words, the things Jack quite possibly cannot say but which nobody is entitled to say he cannot feel.

Not having the words is not the same as not having the feelings, and is in any case the point. Normally, these things *are* wordless, and it is Lawrence's paradoxical genius to get them into words. And in Jack Haseldine Lawrence has chosen a special nature: it is specifically in him to have these feelings, though his only way of expressing them may be in song. It is in these passages, and similar passages throughout Lawrence's work, that the subterfuge, or the happy unconsciousness of a problem, in Cyril's narration in *The White Peacock* is stripped away, and we are confronted with the absolute genius of the writing.

It is Lawrence's gift to reveal the world of submerged consciousness in which we all move for a large part of the time within the world we also inhabit. If you look back at the passage in the 'Burns' fragment beginning 'She put up her mouth to him' and the question which it raises: namely, who is saying this? the immediate answer can only be 'Lawrence'; but he is feeling himself into a representative situation and saying what we all might if we had the gift – which starts as the power to grasp that wordless feeling, and becomes Lawrence's gift of getting it into words. Does it have anything to do with what used to be called 'character'? No; but it has to do with individuality felt at its deepest level: that of a true unconscious which is not identified by psychoanalysis. The 'Burns' fragment is about the way that unconsciousness worked in an imagined past and the fact that we can receive it now is a bridge with that time: a universal is implied. Our 'minds', to use a dangerous word, still work in that way. Moreover the exposition of this universal in the specially talented Jack links the artist, even the genius, with the rest of us. We are on the way to extraordinary things in *The Rainbow*, which are difficulties for some readers, but which must be grasped as related to the universal ability to 'project' .

There is a limit to what he can let Elsa Culverwell say as narrator without the reader concluding that she is a genius or indeed a Lawrence. (Not many writers have this problem, but *he* did.) He does strain the limit in some places which can be identified. The experienced reader of Lawrence comes on the sentence: 'He was like his father, fair, strongly made, with the straightest stare in his blue eyes that has ever been seen since the Vikings looked over the sea at England' (357: 17–19). Elsa has met a young man below her class, and it seems as if they are going to have a love-relationship – perhaps she may marry him. The sentence is just within Elsa's range, but one feels, trembling behind it and wanting to come out, another *topos*: the whole set of images about Northern fair-haired, blue-eyed men which haunts about Gerald Crich, for instance, and has its post–1913 'theoretical' statements both in *Twilight in Italy* (the notion of the races of North and South, and the mid-point in the Alps where they confront each other) or in *Movements in European History*.[7]

Throughout (except for the passage about Elsa's father) there is no obvious metaphorical virtuosity; the language and syntax remain simple, the tone retains an equable though flexible directness. But one can say flatly that at a certain point even a Lawrence who wanted to remain 'popular', to appeal to the Arnold Bennett- and Galsworthy-reading public, would find that, in order to say what he wanted to say, he had to go through the wall of their set of conventions, about 'character', about the description of locale and event, above all about consciousness.

But the two fragments show Lawrence searching in the way he always did – by writing and seeing what came, dropping some things and returning to others, and then rewriting radically. 'Elsa Culverwell' also shows that – as in the early fictions and even after the War, in the group of three two-part novels *The Lost Girl, Mr Noon, Aaron's Rod* – he is firmly centred on Eastwood and the country round it. So, for that matter, is the 'Burns' fragment, for all the time-gap. One fragment is

---

[7]BEPW index: North, Northern; South, Southern See also SL 11: 11: Paul's brother William has 'a touch of the Dane or Norwegian about him'.

set in the town he knows, and the people; the other is in the country setting, but long ago. He is still concerned, in 'Elsa Culverwell' with his own generation or cohort, but is now saying 'Suppose I take a woman? Suppose she is from the shop-keeper class?' That gets him away from his own case: it widens the perspective.

Lawrence is still asking, if you were born and brought up where he was, what did life offer, why was it like that, and was it enough? In Elsa, he is looking at the life, the society, indeed the tribe, through the experience of a strong-minded person, who is not, for all that she does not conform, an artist. In the 'Burns' fragment the central consciousness is more gifted, but is the kind of artist you do not find now; who was at one time accepted by the tribe as its bard, its singer. The implication is that this integration of the talent into the group has been lost, so that one has to look back several generations to find it. The transformation of Burns's case is turning him into something not known from direct experience, which has to be imagined, though Lawrence can borrow a touch or two from the Italians he is now living among, and who put him in contact with what it must have been like in England before the great change to modern life.

It may have occurred to him during 1913–14 that he needed to combine elements of these two writings. He needed to turn the two-generation scheme of *Sons and Lovers* into a longer process, over at least three generations, so that he could bridge the historical and cultural gap between Jack Haseldine and Elsa Culverwell. A later thought might have been that the brother and sister of *The White Peacock* could become two sisters with contrasting natures and fates, as in *Middlemarch* and *Howards End*.[8]

He had done this already in 'Two Sisters', soon to be revised as 'Daughters of the Vicar', where the choice of a mate by Miss Louisa and Miss Mary brought into focus the social values of particular classes, and the transcendence of the issue when one sister decides she is not going to make a failure of her life in the way her mother had done and her sister was doing. What he now needed was a long family evolution punctuated or illustrated by such crises. Perhaps a later thought was that to make the lover of one sister a Lawrence-figure would give himself a voice, but let him distance it by setting others against it. He could place that figure historically by bringing him in in the final 'now' of the writing – which turned out to be a post-1918

---

[8]The device goes back to Sophocles' Antigone and her sister Ismene. Eliot, Forster and Lawrence were conscious of the tradition, well examined in Masako Hirai's *Sisters in Literature*.

'now'. The War, which overtook him as he was working all this out in the writing of it, was a cataclysm, and he had to show his representative people changed by it – and also how it expressed the tribal consciousness.

So what followed began as 'The Sisters', turned into 'The Wedding Ring', and split into *The Rainbow* – which shows the link between the old world and the modern one – and *Women in Love*, where the continuation of what the sociologist would call the 'vertical' study, over time, becomes the 'horizontal' one, of the larger society.

There is another element which begins to emerge in comparing these writings and seeing them in the evolving totality of the work. For instance, 'song' becomes a *topos*. Both fragments show this. Miss Niell's young man is placed by his singing, as Jack Haseldine is. But Jack is not just a singer, he is an artist. More: one can sense in the possible use of the Burns story, and the probable analogy with George Saxton in *The White Peacock* who cannot manage love and is destroyed by it, that Jack could become an Orpheus, who transformed the world with his singing, went down to hell for his love, came back, lost her and was finally torn to pieces by ecstatic maenads. This set of mythical or allusive harmonics produces structural metaphors and whole incidents: a tissue of effects linking the separate works. There is the rabbit which Jack snares and releases, and which he perceives to be related to Mary Renshaw. This may bear on the inclusion in *Look! We Have Come Through!* of the poem 'Rabbit Snared in the Night' which is not obviously germane to the story of Lawrence and Frieda. There the rabbit is an explosive energy, which evokes a corresponding violence in the hands holding it: so the feeling is the exact opposite of Jack's tenderness. There is a link with the rabbit Bismarck in *Women in Love*, and how its brutal energy and the wound it gives Gudrun seals her and Gerald in a knowledge of the violence of their relationship: a consciousness which is obscene.[9] Then one thinks further forward to the relationship between Henry Grenfell and the fox which he both kills and becomes, or, much later in the canon, the Australian political leader whose name one cannot remember because he so powerfully *is* Kangaroo. It was not long after writing these earlier fragments that

---

[9] The original source, in life, of this rabbit-*topos* is given in the sketch 'Adolf', now included in the *England my England* volume in the Cambridge edition. The affinity between the miner-father and the baby rabbit he brings home as he walks back from the pit culminates when the rabbit in its wildness turns its white tail to the human world as if to say *Merde!* to it. The same rabbit appears in 'Paul Morel', and is shown to the Cullen-Staynes family.

Lawrence read *Totem and Taboo;* as so often in his reading, he must have felt that this was a *topos* which he had come upon himself. It reinforces the essentially figurative or indeed mythopoeic nature of his writing, beneath a surface which most readers took – still take – at face value, as ordinary realism.

3
The Rainbow: Memory, Metaphor, Myth and Projection

Women in Love has been accepted since Leavis's work on it as Lawrence's masterpiece. *The Rainbow*, its prelude, has an equivocal place, since most readers like it more, in places, than they do *Women in Love*, but find it unequal as a whole. *Women in Love* is a study of English life in Lawrence's time, with a wide social scope and a penetrating analysis of individual relationships: it seems to be the real point of the whole endeavour. *The Rainbow* is the diachronic study which precedes that synchronic one: it is an account of how things came to be what they were, taking a single family over three generations as embodying the transition from a traditional way of life to a modern one. In that respect it can be taken as merely introductory.

It is well known that originally the project which split into the two works was meant to be one, and it may have been conceived as Lawrence's answer to attempts by Bennett, Wells and Forster – even Galsworthy – to produce, in a family saga, something wider in scope and deeper in implication than the ordinary single novel. Looking at their work may have helped him to see that what he was doing had to be conveyed in more than one volume, and the division must at first have seemed a neat one. But his revisions to *Women in Love* after the first publication of *The Rainbow* widened the gap between the two, and in their after-life the two books have seemed to drift even further apart, so that it is not possible now to take them as merely sequential.

So much is common ground. On the other hand, despite reservations about parts of it, and the sense that it must be less important than the novel which it was meant to usher in, for many readers *The Rainbow* is their next favourite Lawrence novel after *Sons and Lovers*. The trouble is that some parts are much loved, but others, especially in the second half, seem a falling-off; whole scenes seem baffling. This leads to a familiar procedure with Lawrence: the 'good' parts are read willingly, and we think we know what is going on in them; the rest is skipped, as Lawrence falling below his best, or riding his hobbyhorses, or writing badly. In this way, we fail to get to grips with him.

I attempt to get behind this over-familiarity; to convince the reader that the book is a deeply considered whole: one of the great books of the twentieth century. What makes it that is its language and especially what we single out as 'imagery'. One aspect of this language is the voice which speaks – to what extent it is Lawrence's, or the characters', or some status in between. A related aspect is the strange things said, and our difficulty in understanding. Once one has learned the language and distinguished the voices the difficult places make more sense and fit into the whole. The approach needs some tact: in particular questions like, who is speaking here? Is this statement or projection? That term itself needs definition.

Another problem was identified by Leavis: writing about *Women in Love*, he pointed out that every sentence, every touch, is significant. It would follow that the way to establish the unity and continuity of the book would be to expound it sentence by sentence, explaining how this notation prefigures or echoes or transforms that one, and how the structure building up in this way is then modified, and on and on. The commentary would become longer than the text. But until you go on to the end, you haven't done justice to the astonishing evolution of the whole book.

In the sections which follow, I have avoided that problem by dividing the material into categories which are, so far as they go, usefully analytical, and accepting that in the end they collapse, so that I find myself following paths which cross, and lead to the same central areas from different directions. The categories break down because everything in the book is figurative. Yet important things are said about human behaviour at a time and place which, although imagined, corresponds to our sense of history, humanity and Englishness in the century just passed, our century still.

Like Wells and Bennett and Forster, Lawrence wants to go beyond a family chronicle to touch on issues of national and historical significance. Unlike theirs, his books have what can only be called a religious dimension. In a century which was moving away from religious affiliations, Lawrence wanted to identify a continuing spiritual force which was not traditional Christianity, and not the twentieth-century substitute, politics masquerading as religion, but a spiritual sense surviving as undoctrinal feeling and perception, and willing to go on using the figures and the words of the old religion where they represent a permanent insight. Where he did not remake the old language he had to find a new one – which is part of our problem with the book – and he ran the risk of being misread by two sorts of literalists – the religious and the anti-religious literalists. The first group would have an investment in the literal truth of the inherited creed and the old meanings of the well-known words; the others in their literal incredibility. The risk is that neither could actually read him because Lawrence, in addition to this problem of deciding who at a given moment is speaking, developed subtle forms of speech – a language with a large component of metaphor, which can be misread as literal, or of which it can be said, 'But you are being *merely* metaphorical'. But in these matters one can't be anything else.

A metaphorical structure begins as intuition, spontaneous and personal, accepted as vivid and for the moment powerful. Extended and repeated, it ends as a deliberate structure, which can look contrived because it has been pursued for formal and rhetorical reasons as well as intellectual consistency. This becomes a critical issue in *The Rainbow*. One can say that the central image-chain: the rainbow itself, the archways which are the terrestrial counterpart of the arch in the sky, the related 'doorway' images through which characters pass at crucial stages in their lives, the whole notion of 'the widening circle' of experience – these metaphoric shifts are intelligible, logical, effective, and can be taken as the 'meaning'. But they are willed, and even a bit obvious: they enable Lawrence to get from point to point in the book considered as argument, and so – one can quote him against himself – they can seem too mental, too much an operation of ego, will and idea.

But there is also in his language and imagery another element which he was aware of and wanted to free by standing aside to let it work. This is an unforced kind: less conscious, more personal, more like instinctive memory.

When one has identified the two elements, looking like counters to each other, reflection collapses the opposition by saying, but you need both, and they reinforce each other. Another strange outcome is that the 'instinctive' images can seem no less structured, for they come from the associative process, which issues from the memory-store of a particular individual, and this is in its own way systematic. We have through the text privileged access to this 'mind', to use a term Lawrence distrusted. We find that it works in ways which we come to understand as we learn a language, ways which form a network or structure. It is personal and unique, but also human, and is making itself available. I take a small example which shows the two powers working side by side.

At the end of the opening five pages, that epic prelude, the narrative focus narrows to the Brangwens of the 1840s and after, showing them becoming aware that the world beyond their land is changing. There are two brief paragraphs of pregnant description of what they see, a locus to which I must return because it is a foundation. Then follows the notation which I isolate here, which is that as they farm, 'the sharp clink-clink-clink-clink-clink of empty trucks shunting on the line, vibrated in their hearts' (R 14: 29–30).

Four hundred pages later, Anton Skrebensky and Ursula Brangwen, who earlier had a first young love, have met again and are pursuing a serious affair. They stand looking at the same scene: are about to make love for the first time; they hear 'the tiny clink-clink-clink of the wagons' (417: 36–7).

Other elements of both passages tie them into the structure, and in a complex way link them. But pondering this particular echo, one asks, is this a deliberate touch, part of the conscious working-out? My own guess is that it is not a conscious repetition. The train does become an important motif, and one can feel this beginning to happen in the first locus. There are a good many trains in the book – this was the age of rail travel and industrial rail transport before the car and the truck. At first this seems 'historical', but then it dawns on us that a theme is being developed. The 'clink-clink-clink-clink-clink' is of things chained together, running along fixed lines (we have all had this thought about trains); and it is noted that the Brangwens, hearing the sound, also see 'the blackened colliers trooping from the pit-mouth', and smell 'a faint sulphurous smell of pit-refuse burning'. This is an inferno of lost souls outside the Eden of the Brangwens' valley. One memory, the sound, which I take to be almost automatic, has conjured up and inflected another, which turns out to be a literary one, to contribute to the orchestration of the whole piece.

So the two uses of the sound itself are not, at first, a deliberate repetition, but emerge from Lawrence's unforced childhood memory of the shunting trains in the siding by the pit, heard every night as he lay in bed: so that 'clink-clink-clink-clink-clink' comes both times, to use his own phrase, 'unbidden' from his pen, is like his own private cliché. But these notations come inflected by, or they inflect, the situation in which they recur. So, in the first passage, the association with the colliers brings with it the association with the pit, with blackness, with sulphurous fumes, and that underworld, which is contrasted with the Eden on this side of the arch of the aqueduct.

There is another passage near the end of the book where Ursula watches a passing train, is anguished by the sight and the thought, and when one asks what the source of her emotion is, it is that she unconsciously identifies the train with Skrebensky and all who are like him (most men in the last century). There was a hint of this in that first lovemaking, when the 'clink-clink-clink' recurred. They 'saw the sweeping brand of a train past the end of their darkened field' (418: 11–12). The observation seems charged: the word 'brand' does it. Possibly there is a subliminal connection with the next sentences:

> Then he turned and kissed her, and she waited for him. The pain to her was the pain she wanted. [...] She was caught up, entangled in the powerful vibration of the night.

It is as if 'the sweeping brand' has scorched her, but she wanted it to. When we look back to the first passage of all, we now notice that the 'sharp clink-clink clink-clink-clink *vibrated* in their [the Brangwens'] hearts with the fact of other activity going on beyond them.' 'Vibration' is another recurrent notation. There is an obvious connection with hearing, but it turns the message into something which shakes the hearer. (That still doesn't account for the 'brand', to which I must return.)

To go back to the sound itself, that childhood memory, it arrived unbidden, and yet we have seen it becoming an element of metaphor, something beyond cliché, a personal aspect of that kind of perception which is the reaching-out for a meaning by way of the correspondence between perceptions, or the distinction between them – a kind of physical meaning.

We recognise metaphor as a mode of perception-becoming-cognition. A new experience begins to be apprehended by bringing up alongside it something which one already has, as the only way to grasp it. One is not simply making a comparison, because the two elements are not identical; there is a tension between them. The tension is our consciousness of the newness of the experience, the difference. If the old one completely assimilates the new one, we have a cliché, have not moved on. If the new one maintains itself alongside the old one, indeed modifies it while being itself modified, we have the necessary extension of experience which is also self-extension. New knowledge is coming into being, is identified against old experience and defined by the difference. The mind has moved outwards, and taken in something strange, which is formulated in the comparison-process. Metaphor keeps the new sustenance distinct from the assimilating organism by maintaining its identity, as an initial unknown which is not us, or of us, yet is held against what is known by us.

It is a primary mode of cognition. It can be verbalised, as when writers utter it as metaphor. The verbalisation can be their form of becoming conscious – though Lawrence's writing is constantly showing us that there is a lot which comes before the consciousness is aware of it, and some artists as a matter of aesthetic try not to intervene too much – to let as much as possible come unbidden, because what comes that way has not been interfered with like what is summoned up deliberately. For other people, not artists, this whole process may remain unspoken: a momentary movement of the muscles of the mind, an internal sensory event.

Lawrence was aware of this part of his gift: it is a main element of his 'style'. He was aware of it too as his way of getting behind the modern mentality which splits what is felt from the person feeling it, as well as the technique of the ordinary novelist whose narrative depends on making overt such elements as 'As he said this, he was aware that...' This turns into verbalised concept what was felt as something physical. It is not said of Ursula that 'As she saw the train she felt that there was a certain correspondence between it and...' The first train sweeps through the blackness with its train of bright sparks spreading out on the bends. The later train is a tragic perception. The analogy with her feelings is not pressed, not suppressed either. If you come back to the first passage it is given half its meaning by the later one, when if one had been able to ask her why she was weeping over this train, she might, after thinking, have replied 'Well, I suppose I sense a relationship with Skrebensky. I have suddenly become aware – no, actually I was not aware, instead I wept. When I ask why, my mind supplies this answer. He and the train are alike. Most men are.'

We know we shouldn't try to have conversations with characters in novels. Actually, it can have a good deal of point. This sort of thing is going on for much of the time, especially in the second half of the book. It accounts for a lot of the mystery, what people have felt since 1915 as its difficulty. And yet Lawrence was always being profoundly insightful about human behaviour: so much so that his readers could not recognise it.

The Rainbow: *Memory, Metaphor, Myth and Projection*   45

The imagery of the book is, I have suggested, of two kinds. One is spontaneous, related to personal memory. The other is generated logically, by association, extension or metamorphosis – though the root-figure may be instinctive-memorial, so that the two kinds start off as related.

The overt structural images are a family. The book is called *The Rainbow*; the last chapter has the same title. Two chapters are called 'The Widening Circle'. The point on p. 14 where one first ponders 'clink-clink-clink-clink-clink' follows the crucial paragraph where 'the dark archway of the canal's square aqueduct' is a first notation – this actual arch in a remembered actual aqueduct – and as you look through, the vista it permits of a dangerous changing industrial world beyond the Edenic valley.

It metamorphoses later into other arches in church and cathedral, which are significant for the gazer; and that generates the notion of a dependent person as a broken arch, of secure persons or couples as having both ends of their arch planted firmly in the earth, of children being safe and hopeful beneath the rainbow. It metamorphoses into the rainbow itself, as arch or half-circle in the sky; the Bible reminds us that this is the symbol of God's promise that he will not again destroy his own creation. The Bible also supplies 'doorway' figures, implying that one can go in and out of a house, a secure home, where husband and wife are doorkeepers, or as a place one must leave when childhood is over.

By association the Marsh Farm can be seen as an Ark, and the patriarch Tom Brangwen as a Noah-figure. And indeed, he dies in a flood which is the end of the book's Genesis. The reader grasps that this is a structural principle; it lends itself to rather easy guiding remarks from the narrative voice, especially at the ends of certain chapters. This is the deliberate, Flaubertian aspect of the book, the sort of thing which might have been recognised in the 1920s and 1930s by writers on 'The Art of the Novel' if they had not been so nonplussed by the art of this novel.

It is in the nature of metaphors, as of memories, to elide into each other in this sort of progression, since they are both processes of association. Lawrence's willed, structural devices are related to his spontaneous ones. They have a logic one can follow, and which he needs in order to give the book a narrative structure. Though there are places where it seems heavy, he can't do without it, and the fundamental process is his personal gift.

So this does have something to do with the 'clink-clink-clink' –

Lawrence's memorial processes: his access to the way his mind (to use that word) worked – the way all minds work.

Also, to enter a controversial field, it is related to the way minds worked in other times. The momentary sense of significance, felt as a perception of something out there, is like the moment before the metaphor is realised in words, and it has been predicated as characteristic of the preliterate or pre-modern mentality. That sense of 'the momentary god' was seen as the archaic religious experience, which in later ages conceptualised itself into polytheism or animism, or, over time, was formulated into myth.

The basis is universal experience: a man or woman stepping into a patch of light or shade, feeling a breeze, hearing a sound, or seeing something move, and transforming that inkling into the sense of a divine presence: something which one approaches but does not touch – like a rainbow, which is seen but is only an appearance, a sign. This is so far from being remote or prehistoric that if you move around the southern Irish country landscape today, you see little hillside groves or valleys, where there is a spring or a copse or a grotto in the rocks, and the white plaster Virgin is evidence both of the original feeling and of the meaning given to it: a metaphorisation, some will say, though others observe that the statue is factory-made and like all the others: actually a literalisation. Nevertheless, one is impressed that Irish people from the nearby towns and villages put on their suits and get into their cars and come to stand or kneel before the figure in silence. The factory-image has not for them made things too literal, or turned the metaphor into institutionalised cliché. It remains an index (Wordsworth's word) a recognition of what is beyond – a word which rings like a bell in the early pages of *The Rainbow* – and our capacity to receive it.

Lawrence pondered, and demonstrated, this capacity in himself and others in the chapter 'The Crucifix across the Mountains' in *Twilight in Italy*, written concurrently with *The Rainbow*. As he moves up into the high country he imagines what the crucified male figures mean, and how they are transformed as the journey progresses. In the first peasant-like figure down in the plain the maker has embodied someone like himself, with his relationship to the land. He is a sort of anguished Brangwen. Lawrence moves on, to the last, broken cross up in the mountain pass. He sees the male victims not only as images of the Christian murdered saviour but as expressions of the people who made them – their sense of their own nature and fate, first as they are

The Rainbow: *Memory, Metaphor, Myth and Projection* 47

bound to the life of the plain but can lift up their eyes to the hills, and then as they move up into the high place where life is suspended. This signifying process is all-pervasive and not confined to some time long ago or some department separated off as 'religion' and dismissed by many for that reason. This is a large element of the life of the mind (spirit would be a better word).

To go back to the 'sweeping brand' which Ursula glimpsed as the train went by: literally, she saw the train leaving a trail of sparks and steam. The 'sweeping brand' is her metaphorisation: she sees the train *as* that. And then, by another natural process, a memory stirs. The sense that something complex is going on makes one dwell on the sweeping brand itself. The dictionary says a brand is 'a piece of wood that has been burning on the hearth, or a torch. It is also a mark made by burning with a hot iron, therefore a source of infamy. It is also the blade of a sword', and it adds, imaginatively, 'Perh. from its flashing in the light.' Waiting behind the definitions are the allusions, literature as memory: from the Bible 'a brand plucked out of the fire' (Zechariah 3:2), and from Milton the very last lines of *Paradise Lost*:

> They looking back, all the eastern side beheld
> Of Paradise, so late their happy seat,
> Waved over by that flaming brand; the gate
> With dreadful faces throng'd, and fiery arms.
> Some natural tears they dropped, but wiped them soon;
> The world was all before them, where to choose
> Their place of rest, and Providence their guide.
> They, hand in hand, with wandering steps and slow
> Through Eden took their solitary way.

You could sum up the story of Ursula, the last of the Brangwens, and Skrebensky by saying that they suffer a comparable Fall, and are finally expelled from the Eden which is so powerfully figured at the beginning of the whole book.

That may seem a lot to unpack out of the 'sweeping brand'. The words are Lawrence's supplying Ursula's metaphorisation, which we all do all the time, wordlessly. It has here been put into words. It is an instance where my two factors, the spontaneous and the planned, are indistinguishable. There is no doubt that the notion of a Fall from Eden is thematic, a structural principle of the book, so that the Miltonic reference naturally harmonises with the Biblical theme. Equally, one may think that Ursula's sense of a flaming sword, her perception of being branded, are for her instinctive, unscripted, subliminary. But she has had Lawrence's and his peers' education, has read Milton and the Bible, and like the rest of us may quote unconsciously.

The other term for a related process is 'projection', now a psychologists' technicality, but originally a metaphor, and like most metaphors partly about itself. The word has a history which has included alchemy, geometry, map-making and architecture, and only reached psychology in 1836. It reached religion at the same time, largely through Feuerbach, and, as used by Marx, Nietzsche, Freud and since has become a sort of swearword. The result is that a word which first implied a vigorous or subtle outgoing of the mind, imaginative, creative or dominating, turned into the head-shaking, even sneer, which its use presents today. It needs to be rescued, first of all by recognising that the activity is primary and universal, like metaphor, which is closely related.

Some would say that the postulated original religious feeling is a projection, as if that was a criticism rather than a necessary understanding. The old Pre-Socratic saying, all things are full of gods, encapsulated that experience. To say, as we might now, all things are full of metaphors, or even, all things are full of projections, sounds like a reduction, where things have dwindled into the light of common day; but Lawrence shows that the light is not common in the pejorative sense, but is what we share with our ancestors, the power of figuration.

It is seen quite early in Lawrence's work. In the short story 'Second Best' in the *Prussian Officer* collection there is this moment:

> The two girls sat perfectly still. Frances watched certain objects in her surroundings: they had a peculiar, unfriendly look about them: the weight of greenish elderberries on their purpling stalks; the twinkling of the yellowing crab-apples that clustered high up in the hedge, against the sky; the exhausted, limp leaves of the primroses lying flat in the hedge-bottom: all looked strange to her. Then her eyes caught a movement. A mole was moving silently over the warm red soil [...] Frances started, from habit was about to call on Anne to kill the little pest. But today her lethargy of unhappiness was too much for her.

Anne does kill the mole, producing this transformation in the scene, or how it is felt:

Frances suddenly became calm: in that moment, grown-up.

'I suppose they *have* to be killed,' she said, and a certain rather dreary indifference succeeded to her grief. The twinkling crab-apples, the glitter of brilliant willows now seemed to her trifling, scarcely worth the notice. Something had died in her, so that things lost their poignancy. (PO 115: 6–16; 117: 21–7)

The perception of surrounding objects as first 'unfriendly' and then 'trifling' conveys the mysterious mood-swing caused by the killing, which is turned into an enabling sacrifice: the universe had seemed at first to be admonishing her (Wordsworth's term) and then to be encouraging, except that she now will not acknowledge it.

That is strangely perceptive, but is not much more than a psychological oddity neatly rendered. It is a minor form of projection. In *The Rainbow* the phenomenon is pervasive and profound; and is having its spiritual sense returned to it.

It also has remarkable psychological penetration. One should approach *The Rainbow* as the novel in which projection in all its senses is most powerful and pervasive. Partly for this reason readers of the novel in 1915 and since were baffled by the feeling that the characters do not behave like those in other novels. It is a mistake to think that Lawrence's people do not behave like social and individual human beings. I have suggested that one source of the error is that Lawrence so often omits guidance in formulae such as 'When he said this, she felt that...', or 'when he entered the room she had the sense that...' The trouble with the formulae is that they make conscious, give as a socialised currency, familiar verbalisation, what is really internal wordless feeling: 'feeling' itself, another familiar verbalisation, is no help. What is needed is an equivalent for what goes on in us wordlessly, often as what the psychologist would call projection. The paradox is that Lawrence has to project other people's projections, but that is one of his talents. In the 'Burns novel' fragment, rendering Jack's internal movements, he is seen doing it momentously.

It can be shown in small things as well as large ones. When Will Brangwen first visits his relatives at the Farm, arriving as a stranger kinsman, he is described in ways which seem mutually conflicting. He is seen as a number of animals which share no characteristics: a cat, a hawk, a leopard. An irritated reader might say 'make up your mind. What *is* he like?' The narrative first approaches him in unspecific terms: Anna finds he has a curious head: it reminded her she knew not of what: of some animal, some mysterious animal that lived in the darkness under the leaves and never came out, but which lived vividly, swift and intense. She always thought of him with that black, keen, blind head. (100: 22–6)

A few pages on, he has begun to transmute into specific animals. The inconsistency is soon resolved: an occasional aside in the traditional convention, such as 'Brangwen irritably thought', shows that the resort to animal-imagery represents Will's strangeness, as of another species, felt by the family group; the *choice* of animal represents the projection with which Anna (mostly) or Tom personally characterise a momentary grasp of this strange being. To her he is a hawk or a leopard: not just a strange animal, but threatening to impinge or predate, and needing to be withstood. Meanwhile Lawrence's long-running image for Will is also as an animal, but he crystallises Anna's half-perception and identifies the creature, the mole, which represents his blind subterranean questing, his persistence, and his ability to rise to the surface from time to time in a moment of limited vision.

Anna, on the other hand, has to grasp that he is neither a totally strange animal nor 'just the bright reflex of herself'. That half-acknowledgement is complemented in her contrary perception that at moments 'he seemed to expect her to be part of himself, the extension of his will'. So the small detail of the animal-imagery opens out into the large area of the conflict between the two selves, in which at times the other seems hostile and threatening (or leopard-like), or, conversely, *her* absence threatens *him* with collapse. This is a conflict of projections, which can best end with a perception of what is going on, or simply the truce which Will and Anna finally manage.

There are extensions or intensifications of this method which have from 1915 until today exercised readers, to the point where they find parts of the book incomprehensible. The objection is well expressed by Jacques Berthoud: one must be grateful to him for taking us so far:

> By definition, the unconscious is not directly available to the conscious mind: it cannot therefore be treated mimetically – even when [....] the authorial voice itself becomes the mimetic medium. If we consider, not the cathedral episode, in which Will's dark self irrupts into his response to the nave, but a parallel and more extreme case, Ursula's 'destruction' of Skrebensky, something of the point of this objection will be illustrated. Ursula's dark self, which

turns so savagely against her lover, is translated into a whole complex of material equivalents. For her Skrebensky becomes 'a loadstone', 'a dark impure magnetism'; her own hands are 'metal blades', she is 'bright as a piece of moonlight', she 'seethes like some cruel corrosive salt', her soul 'crystallises with triumph'. I can feel the intensity of this writing, but I do not really understand it: I cannot even imaginatively recognise this experience. The reason, I suspect, is not that we never lose our heads or our humanity, but that we never experience the unconscious as directly as this.[1]

The difficulty is increased by the introduction of the unconscious. Apart from the paradoxes which its name brings with it, the whole realm has been so colonised by psychoanalytical theories that it is best abandoned, for its use can produce logical as well as categorical errors. The projection discussed here has nothing to do with the Freudian unconscious. It is a mode of consciousness, though not of self-consciousness. One can, usually does, perhaps *must*, project without being conscious of doing so, though one may come to realise one is doing it. The words supplied by Lawrence as narrator are not words the persons use, nor are they components of their individual psyches. They are Lawrence's way of representing wordless feelings or states of consciousness which are intense but not reflexive. The metaphors (moonlight, salt, blade, and so on) are parallels Lawrence hits on as the way of projecting in words what is neither self-consciousness nor, for that reason, verbal representation of itself to the person feeling it. In the visual arts, this is Expressionism; we feel happier with visual representation, since it does not force on us the paradox of using words for what was wordless. That is what Lawrence does; but once one has jumped the apparent fence, it works. And actually, it is not more paradoxical to use words than pictorial images, only more obviously so.

Virtually all the last chapter, significantly called 'The Rainbow' is projection. This is the chapter in which Ursula fears she may be pregnant, writes an abject letter to Skrebensky asking him to take her back, then takes that walk through the wood, where for the last time in the book we meet Lawrence's personal central metaphor: the circle of perception taken as secure or threatened:

---

[1] Jacques Berthoud, '*The Rainbow* as Experimental Novel', in *D.H. Lawrence: A Critical Study of the Major Novels*, ed. A.H. Gomme (Sussex and New York 1978) p. 68.

> There, the vast booming overhead vibrated down and encircled her, tree-trunks spanned the circle of tremendous sound, myriads of tree-trunks, enormous and streaked black with water, thrust like stanchions upright beneath the roaring overhead and the sweeping of the circle underfoot. (450: 35–9)

What is elsewhere vision is here nightmare. Emerging from the wood, she comes upon the grazing horses, and feels them too as a threat. They rush past her, frightening her further. She escapes, collapses, falls into a traumatised state in which she feels like a stone at the bottom of the stream (another of Lawrence's personal recurrences). She struggles home, undergoes some kind of breakdown, then gradually recovers. If there was a child, it miscarries; she hears Skrebensky is married. She has her final equivocal vision, of a rainbow which is 'arched' in the blood and spirit of 'the sordid people who crept hard-scaled and separate on the face of the world's corruption'. She saw

> in the rainbow the earth's new architecture, the old, brittle corruption of houses and factories swept away, the world built up in a living fabric of Truth, fitting to the over-arching heaven. (459: 5–8)

If you reread the chapter from the beginning, it becomes clear that everything in it is conveyed as felt by Ursula, as projected by her on the screen of her consciousness. The child, for instance, is not certified by a medical examination: its possibility is felt as a 'kind of swoon', 'the heaviness of her heart'. 'Her flesh thrilled, but her soul was sick. It seemed, this child, like the seal set on her own nullity' (448: 26–7). It may be only a dread, a threat. For Lawrence's narrative purpose, the possibility of a child needs to be imagined, but to imagine it as a dreaded outcome, even a phantom pregnancy, is appropriate. The effect on Ursula of the mere possibility is the point. It should be a joy, and is a fear, the result of a failed relationship. In social-historical terms, this is a realism. In 1900 to be pregnant was to be forced into marriage or to suffer disgrace and exclusion.

The wood is a real wood: one could walk to it today. But the wood as felt by Ursula is the last of Lawrence's roaring circles of wind and rain-darkened light. It is felt as giant menace, the threat of freedom removed. The trees 'might turn and shut her in as she went through their marshalled silence'. They are witnesses or accusers. This is evident projection, though of a powerful and subtle kind.

The Rainbow: *Memory, Metaphor, Myth and Projection* 53

The horses too are real. The question might be: do they really threaten her, or is it she who feels them as threatening? She transfers to them the hostility and accusatory power she has felt in the trees. Horses do race about in a high wind, since they are disturbed by it more than humans. Their rushing past could be felt as another threat, would have an element of danger: but the point is that in her actual state Ursula projects a different kind of threat, a spiritual one. The horses are felt as all that is pressing on her in her life. Lawrence says so: 'She knew the heaviness in her heart. It was the weight of the horses.' The nightmare of getting past them and out of the field is compounded of extreme mental distress and physical collapse, what we call a panic state, conveyed with all Lawrence's power.

Clinically depressed, traumatised, cold, wet, exhausted – and possibly pregnant into the bargain – she struggles home and gets into bed, where she 'was very ill for a fortnight, delirious, shaken and racked'. In that state, she is aware, beneath her delirium, that something binds her still to Skrebensky: the possibility of the child.

Collapsed in the field, she had been like 'a stone at rest on the bottom of the stream, inalterable and passive, sunk to the bottom of all change' (454: 15). (Strikingly, that image links back with the sense of trauma in the homoerotic episode with Winifred Inger: a sense of cold, silence, darkness.) As the illness reaches its height, the inalterable stone metamorphoses, in one of Lawrence's most personal imageshifts, familiar from other contexts:

> And again, to her feverish brain, came the vivid reality of acorns in February lying on the floor of a wood with their shells burst and discarded and the kernel issued naked, to put itself forth. She was the naked, clear kernel thrusting forth the clear, powerful shoot, and the world was a bygone winter [....] (456: 20–4)

Stone becomes kernel, or so one might hope (and we do call the kernels of edible fruit 'stones'). And then, when the illness has passed, we are simply told, 'There would be no child.' So: she has had a miscarriage, perhaps, or perhaps there never was a child. There is no point in speculating: the significance of the pregnancy, real or imagined, was its effect on her spirit, how she receives it or projects it. And that is the meaning of all the events in the chapter. Things happen, certainly, and there is a relationship with how she feels them; but how she feels them and in places projects their meaning onto her world is the deep concern and accounts for the language used.

What is figured in that recurring stone/kernel image is the possibility of resurrection, and that is how we are meant to take her recovery. It leads to the final paragraph: her vision. How do we take that? Is it the near-hysterical euphoria of convalescence after severe illness? I think so. But does it also project a hopefulness about what might follow a return from the depths? That too. Is it, then, really a matter of faith rather than a solidly-based estimate? Yes: but what else *could* it be? It is a projection by the author himself, if you like: he is putting himself behind his character, creating, through her, an Apocalypse to balance the Genesis at the beginning of the book.

All these projections are the continuous part-metaphorical activity of perception-mixed-with-creation which is our normal intercourse with the world. In that sense it is ordinary. In Lawrence it is linked with his own continuous sense of what lies behind, underneath, beyond. He reminds us, that is, how normal or everyday the old sense of the momentary god still is, or could be if most people had not blocked out that possibility of openness or wonder. To bring it back within a twentieth-century consciousness he has therefore to provide his extraordinary-seeming images, and to resort to hints of analogy in the form of familiar myth. Lawrence's allusions are usually so discreet that most readers are not aware of them, but the constant Biblical and classical-mythological analogies that the enquirer comes upon, and is at first startled by, are part of this strategy. He is not being merely allusive or syncretistic. The seriousness of the allusions is meant to take the reader out of the positivist world of modern people, even modern believers, and reanimate a universe which has always been penetrated by a sense of the other, the mysterious, the beyond, which has been sensed in the past and conveyed in certain stories, certain figures. To those who say 'These are only metaphors now' he would reply that they always were, and that was always their point, their force, their purchase on the mind. We have no other way of approaching the unknown – never had.

So far as *The Rainbow* is concerned, readers allow the force of the mythopoeia in the early chapters, and enjoy it. It is suggested, partly for this reason, that the second half is a decline. This is a misjudgement. The story of Will and Anna, and even more that of Ursula and Skrebensky, combines what the modern reader has demanded in terms of realism about our world with a demonic inversion of the opening myth. The whole book has a remarkable continuity and force, and the conclusion is as extraordinary as the opening.

4
The Rainbow as History

Mark Kinkead-Weekes's helpful chronology of *The Rainbow*[1] shows a time-span running from about 1840 to 1905. We have a sense, reading the book, of a kind of memory which starts as folk-memory, but sweeps from remote past to near the present of the writing. Within the novel's time span three generations of Brangwens come to maturity. At the beginning we still hear the echoes of earlier generations; at the end we face a horribly different future – and that future, we realise, is the century which has just ended, our century. So the book is about us, whether we happen to be English, or European, or in any way the inheritors of the world inaugurated here.

Tom Brangwen is born in 1838, to a family which, he tells his prospective wife Lydia in 1867, has been at the Marsh Farm for 'above two hundred years'. Like the Earnshaws in *Wuthering Heights*, equally deep-rooted, they are yeoman farmers, independent landowners living a traditional life, content in their world, cut off from the wider one. When Tom courts Lydia, knowing how foreign she is, he finds that her people too were landowners, but in a very different place and mode: they had aristocratic blood, and a feudal relationship with their peasant dependants in the vastness of central Europe. That other ancient mould has been broken by political insurrection against Russian domination, in 1863: so Lydia's first husband, a doctor, had to leave Poland for exile in England. Tom hears the far-off echo of great events on the mainland: feels the strangeness of that other life.

In his own life there are nearer echoes, sounds from across the canal which serves to separate the Brangwens from what is going on in the

---

[1] Appendix IV of the Cambridge edition. See also his chapter 'The Sense of History in *The Rainbow*' in Peter Preston and Peter Hoare, *D.H. Lawrence in the Modern World* (London 1988), pp. 121–38.

Midlands and North of England. The developing collieries throw up their workings: the headstocks, the tips, the new colliery towns. The railway extends, to serve the pits. All this is glimpsed through that arch in the aqueduct; it is beyond their Eden-valley, their horizon. This is what is going on in England: the revolution is industrial, not political; but it alters things more thoroughly over time: it changes the landscape for ever and produces a new race of people.

In the first cycle of *The Rainbow*, in Tom's lifetime, this is offstage, but audible in the 'clink-clink-clink', and producing that whiff of sulphurous fumes when the wind is in the right direction. But so far as Tom Brangwen is concerned, towns are places where he goes to local markets and has a sociable drink after the day's trading. Yet his ancestors have always had a sense of what was beyond their horizon. Before he meets Lydia, he is impressed by the distinguished foreign man he meets at Matlock one day: it is like a message from the outside world. When he first meets the foreign woman Lydia, and has the instant admonishment that she is to be his wife, his servant Tilly puts things neatly by saying that the unknown woman is 'fra the Pole' (you can't get further North than that). She then corrects herself by saying she *is* a Pole. Remembering *Twilight in Italy*, we think of the strongly thematic meeting of Northern and Southern peoples as a hidden principle in the deeper history of the whole continent of Europe.

Tom's death in 1892 is caused by an accident: the canal bursts in a rainstorm, and he is drowned. This is significant: the canal is what we now call the infrastructure of the new industrial world, and it sweeps away this representative of the old one. Since he is a patriarch, a Noah, who has at the Farm been steering an Ark in which the creatures of the old life have been saved from death in the new one, the Flood which drowns him presages an undoing of the old creation. One might ask, what kind of new creation follows? It is not announced by a rainbow as God's promise not to repeat his destruction. That sign is withheld until the end of the book, where it appears equivocal, and may only be the desperate holding-on to hope of the convalescent Ursula.

Tom's step-daughter Anna Lensky, now Anna Brangwen, marries Will Brangwen, from the side of the family which went to live in town; and with their marriage the second cycle of the book is inaugurated. When Tom has presided over the wedding, his role is over and he is free to go. Will is a transition towards modern man in that while he chooses to live at Yew Tree Cottage by the church in the village, he works in town. That was one of the nineteenth-century transitions:

from working at home, or on the farm, or in the village, to work in a factory. He works in the Nottingham lace-making industry as a draughtsman. That sounds 'creative', but the work is mechanical and his heart is not in it. He does it for the wage, and this too is a characteristic predicament of the new age: but so is his whole lifestyle. There he is, in the 1880s, taking the train into Nottingham every morning, and coming home in the evening: a commuter. His heart is still in the country life; he clings to the old ways, especially as associated with the church, where he is organist. The cycle of the Christian year, for him as for his daughter Ursula, represents something they value, want to hold on to, though they, and Anna, are disappointed by the verbal and intellectual formulations of religious doctrine.

What is first conveyed in the opening paragraphs of the book as the sense of the beyond which the Brangwens have, and which the women make half-conscious as openness to a spiritual world, translates into two forms: the willingness to meet the stranger, even to marry into foreignness, and the apprehension of an ultimate beyond traditionally represented in the church. Will's creative impulses: his carving which dwindles into carpentry and finally into the teaching of craft; his music which dwindles into accompanying hymns, is his modern form – growing in consciousness – of the wordless instinct which led the men working in the fields occasionally to lift their eyes up to the hills, and to rest them on the church steeple which stands there – and which at the end of the book is still seen, now standing up 'in hideous obsoleteness'.

Will's being caught in a form of life which does not satisfy him is transformed, for him and his daughter Ursula, by another twist of modernity. The Education Act of 1870 organised the State schools to which most English children went, and was followed by extensions of the system which in the 1890s and after give Will a new start as advisory teacher of handicraft, so that in 1902 Will and Anna move out of the village to Beldover – that is, Eastwood. Will now rides a motor-bicycle (a strikingly modern move) so he can visit schools throughout the county. The work gives him a new social status: he is now entirely a town-dweller, and in the professional class, if at its lowest level, and also he finds some modest outlet for his creativity.

To return to Tom Brangwen: back in the 1850s he had gone unwillingly to the grammar school in Derby, knowing that it was not really for him. He is stirred when he hears poetry read aloud, but cannot on his own read books. They are alien to him; moreover 'there was nothing palpable, nothing known in himself, that he could apply to learning' (18:

9–10). Lawrence's perception translates into our formula that he belongs to a pre-literate, pre-modern culture. But his nephew Will does read. Though he has no paper qualifications, he has educated himself in matters he cares about, in a time when that was encouraged by the public library system which did so much for Lawrence and his peer-group. So when as a young man he first visits the country cousins at the Marsh, he turns the conversation into talk about English church architecture. He knows the technical terms: not just the main styles, but words like sedilia, rood-screen, hatchet-carving.

His father, Tom's brother, ancestor of the modern townsman, doesn't go to church, is presumably a rationalist – this is 1882, so he would have heard of, or read, Darwin and Huxley. We are told that he reads Herbert Spencer. The mother does go to church, and Will himself has an intense, not altogether coherent religious feeling which centres on the symbolisms of the religious building, stained glass, carvings. It is an aesthetic stance. We infer that he gets his technical terms, his passion for the old vernacular architecture, from writers like Pugin or Morris, most probably Ruskin. So he would have some sense of the debate about the condition of England. His disgust with the mechanical designs of the lace-factory might be fuelled by the same kind of reading and current of feeling, and his attempts at wood-carving, which he abandons in un-self-confidence would spring in part from that influence. Similarly, his modest final flowering as respected teacher of handicraft is a humble analogue of the post-Morris, post-Ruskin Arts and Crafts movement.

What I am collecting here is inference from the details which come along naturally in the course of the narrative; but if one looks around in this way it is remarkable how substantial this sense of the intellectual and spiritual life of the time becomes – how much it is part of Lawrence's enterprise in the book, and how much it anchors what might be dismissed as the poetry. In his way Will is a man of his era, a representative follower, in factory and schoolroom and organ-loft and committee-room of the intellectual movements of the age.

Will's relative smallness serves retrospectively to give Tom his stature. Tom can't read, effectively, and doesn't in the same sense have 'ideas', or not from books. Any idea he has must be inherited or the fruit of his own experience. Yet in his mild way he is remarkably open: for instance to the foreignness of the distinguished monkey-faced man in Matlock. Later he is impressed that his brother has a mistress, and that she is an intelligent strong-minded woman. So he does not resent or oppose the unfamiliar: is not merely tribal. His attitudes to women are uniformly sympathetic. Above all, he is miraculously open to the revelation that the strange foreign woman Lydia must be his mate. In his 'bit of courting-like', in the scene in which from outside the house he contemplates her sitting inside like a Madonna with her equally strange child, it is he who has an Annunciation. Later, when he takes the child into the barn at night while his wife is giving birth, it is given to him to perform the action which takes Anna into another world, his world. In the scene where he sees Will and Anna kissing, and feels the jealousy of the older generation being pushed aside, and the later moments where he expiates the jealousy by generous giving, and by presiding over the wedding ceremony, he is a man moved by natural impulses of a generous kind. It is a real gift.

Given this difference of personality – Tom is strong where Will is not – the other difference between them is one of consciousness. Like Paul and Walter Morel in *Sons and Lovers*, they stand on the same ground but not in the same world. If in the early pages the Brangwens have an eye on the horizon and an ear cocked for the sound of the outside world, by Will's time the messages are coming fast, some as sounds like the 'clink-clink-clink' of the railway, some in printed form, but mostly as new forms of life which demand an increase of consciousness.

In the third generation the process reaches a critical phase. Ursula, born in 1883, Anton Skrebensky born in 1877, come to consciousness at the turn of the century. Anton comes to the Marsh in 1899. Tom had no sense of politics that we can discern; one guesses that Will's 'Arts and Crafts' affinities and his position in the educational world might align him with liberalism or guild socialism, unless his passionate feeling for the medieval and his patriarchal family-feeling led him the other way. That is speculation. But Anton Skrebensky has thoughts, concepts of a kind, and they inaugurate an aspect of the disastrous twentieth century.

His choice of profession is crucial. Young men of some social standing then had a choice – medicine, the church, the law, the armed services, public service – if they declined to enter manufacture and trade, leaving them to the pushing middle class. But the choice could reveal a deep instinct. Anton chooses the army, and it leads to puzzlement and apprehension in Ursula, who wants to love him. Their reported conversations are brief, natural and unforced, but Lawrence packs into them enormous implications without making them seem deliberately planned to open up intellectual issues.

When Anton says he would want to go to war, if there was one – 'I should be doing something. [....] It's a sort of toy-life, as it is' (288:

2–3) – Ursula points out that this is a kind of game, and he replies: 'It's about the most serious business there is, fighting.' A century later, we know the truth of that. Actually, the whole conversation conveys his awful innocence about war, and leads to her devastating summing-up of him and the 'nation' which he offers to die for:

> 'You want to have room to live in: and somebody has to make room.'
> 'But I don't want to live in the desert of Sahara – do you?' she replied, laughing with antagonism.
> '*I* don't – but we've got to back up those who do.'
> 'Why have we?'
> 'Where is the nation, if we don't?'
> 'But we aren't the nation. There are heaps of other people who are the nation.'
> 'But they might say *they* weren't, either.'
> 'Well, if everybody said it, there wouldn't be a nation. But I should still be myself,' she asserted, brilliantly. (288: 20–31)

This was published in 1915, and was not what people wanted to hear during that War, or the second one. In the 1930s, the phrase 'room to live in' would translate as *Lebensraum*. At either point in time, the challenge to nationalism, to collectivism, would have seemed subversive. And a more serious point is being made, since 'being myself' is the positive that the whole book is unfolding. Tom was himself without trying, without consciousness of it; later generations have to discover what it might mean, and work at it. This leads to Ursula's devastating summing-up:

> 'What do you fight for really?'
> 'I would fight for the nation.'
> 'For all that, you aren't the nation. What would you do for yourself?'
> 'I belong to the nation and must do my duty by the nation.'
> 'But when it doesn't need your services in particular – when there *is* no fighting? What would you do then?' [....]
> 'Nothing. I would be in readiness for when I was needed.'
> The answer came in exasperation.
> 'It seems to me,' she answered, 'as if you weren't anybody – as if there weren't anybody there, where you are. Are you anybody, really? You seem like nothing to me.' (289: 5–18)

He is 'nothing' in her perception, but also – and for that reason – is an ancestor of all those who in the twentieth century assumed that they only had meaning as part of a collective. It was a way of turning their unacknowledged sense of nothingness, their not being themselves, into a false positive. It has been a century-long nightmare, and it was prophetic to have written this in 1915. Like the other discussions – quarrels even – between the two, it is done at the level of young people saying what comes into their heads under the pressure of the moment. It is not philosophical or political debate, yet essential things get said. The result is that Skrebensky is ultimately rejected by Ursula for being what he is: modern social man, the willing cog in the machine. If one looks back two generations, to Tom, thinking that he is archaic, tribal, and so ought to be anonymous, without definition, one sees that the old society actually encouraged individuality, even oddity. In the next two generations, where Anton finally gives in, Will had been, however baffled, struggling to get clear. This is the force of the 'mole' image:

> Blindly, like a mole, he pushed his way out of the earth that covered him, working always away from the physical element in which his life was captured. Slowly, blindly, gropingly, with what initiative was left to him, he made his way towards individual expression and individual form.
> At last, after twenty years, he came back to his wood-carving [....] (330: 1–6)

A further huge implication is caught in terms which the modern reader (for reasons which the book is *about*) may not quickly grasp. There are those moments when Tom submits to something – not as a conscious decision, but as a relaxation into the movement of life. Lawrence has to find words for him, since it is a wordless inclination of his whole being. To say 'He submitted to that which was happening to him, letting go of his will, suffering the loss of himself' (38: 32–3) is to conceptualise for a moment, and the narrative voice may do this by standing back and abstracting in this way. To say 'he knew that he did not belong to himself' sounds as if it is doing something similar. However that sentence began 'But during the long February nights with the ewes in labour, looking out from the shelter into the flashing stars [....]' and it continues 'He must admit that he was only fragmentary, something incomplete and subject. There were the stars in the dark heaven travelling, the whole host passing by on some eternal voyage. So he sat small and submissive to the greater ordering' (40: 2–8).

One ponders – is meant to ponder – the relationship with Skrebensky's later sense of nothingness, and his relapse into the nation's supposed demands. There is both a contrast and an undoubted affinity; one might say that Tom's impulse is pre-religious and Will's is pre-political, though neither is conscious. However, there is a relationship, and it is increased by the statement 'without her [Lydia] he [Tom] was nothing.' Tom is aware of his dependence, and later both Will and after him Anton are cripplingly dependent in love: this dependence is also one of the great themes of the book, and I touch on it below. What is so remarkable is that the need of the particular person, the lack or dependency, is so penetratingly related to the whole nature of the individual social being, and to marriage.

The neat formulation about belonging or not belonging to oneself is set between these glances to the heavens, from an actual moment in the farmer's year, when the birth of lambs announces the new season. The quasi-Biblical phrase ('Ye are not your own': 1 Cor. 6:19) – what I have elsewhere called Lawrence's Job-mood – offers to translate into words what is more like a posture or movement of assent, a feeling.

On the other hand, think of Anton in church, listening to one of the Biblical texts summing up that message, about belonging: 'The very hairs of your head are all numbered.'

> He did not believe it. He believed his own things were quite at his own disposal. You could do as you liked with your own things, so long as you left other people's alone. (302: 35–8)

It is so wonderfully simple-minded, and to some, so sympathetically modern, that one has to expand a little on the significance. The text, in Matthew 10, follows the one about the sparrows: 'Are not two sparrows sold for a farthing? and one of them shall not fall on the ground without your father.' It can be taken as comforting: God looks after sparrows. But actually, God doesn't, and it isn't what Christ said. Rather God knows about, therefore accepts, indeed wills the fall of the sparrow. Anton doesn't look for the false comfort: but then he doesn't want, either, the sense of being part of the whole that Tom had, nor does he relate it here to his more modern sense of being part of the nation. He comes out, or Lawrence comes out for him, with this also childish phrase about 'his own things'.

It is the source of the modern attitude that for instance my body is my own and I can do what I like with it as long as I don't visibly harm another person. It offers to be a morality, but is like that of a child wanting its own way. It coexists in Anton with the quite opposite but equally undeveloped morality of the social cog. Intellectually it is a muddle; but as a social phenomenon, a prophecy, it is profoundly grasped.

I have been talking about the three generations of men; they provide the background. Ursula Brangwen is born in 1883. She is of Lawrence's own generation. He was born in 1885, and Ursula's childhood and family life, and her experience as a teacher are like those of several members of his peer-group, notably Louie Burrows, born in 1888, to whom he was engaged in 1910–12. Ursula is the central character in the Brangwen saga, and the important thing about her is that she is not a man, and is born at a moment when women began to move into roles hitherto reserved for men, and could be independent economically. The more important question is: would they slip into male patterns of thinking, or would they be independent in their response to the world?

Ursula is 'about eight' when her grandfather Tom is drowned, and has an important relationship with her grandmother Lydia, who dies when she is 15. She would have the child's clear memory of that generation, is to that degree in touch with people born in the far-off 1840s. At the end, in 1905, she is 22; and we meet her again as the central female character of *Women in Love*, which has the 'feel' of being post-War, say just before 1920, the time of publication. Actually, the time-scheme becomes vague, here: if it were really after the War, the principal male characters, especially Gerald Crich, would be traumatised by their experience as officers in France. Gerald is equivocally presented as having been a soldier, but when one looks into it, that was in the Boer War. *Women in Love* is best taken as mainly of its time of writing, so 1913–14, with some details from its time of revision and publication, 1917–21. It follows that Ursula is by then about 30 or a little more – approximately the age at which Frieda met Lawrence; and indeed the later Ursula is one of the Frieda-figures who succeed the Jessie- or Louie- or Helen-figures in the earlier fictions.

But this is finicking. More important, Ursula, born on the 170th page of a 450-page book, is the developing consciousness which links the first generation, the grandparents of the Marsh Farm, with the second generation, of her parents at Yew Tree Cottage and then Beldover – and then with whatever follows them in an opening-out future. A normal life-span would take her to the 1940s or 1950s. Frieda lived until 1956.

Ursula is Tom's grandchild, Will's child, Anton Skrebensky's sweetheart, lover and annihilator. If the men represent the successive generations, she is the product, the link, the inheritor, and importantly the developing consciousness, the critic and the way into the future. The grandmother Lydia has her undoubted identity, is a power in her own right, but is not the focus of attention in the way that Tom is. Given the time she lives in, she has to find her meaning in life as wife and mother. Anna is rendered much more fully, has a considerable force of nature, but is none the less conceived as a kind of foil to, an opposition to Will, who makes the moves which Anna counters. The social-historical implication is that in Lydia's time, even in Anna's, a woman had to expect to be a wife, and would in that role either confirm or oppose her husband – or if she turned from it could devote herself to her children, as Anna finally does.

By the 1890s women with an education would find the easiest profession to enter was teaching, where the development of the State system needed to recruit a great many young people of both sexes, and gave them a preliminary training: Lawrence himself, his sister, Jessie Chambers, Louie Burrows, Helen Corke – to name only the obvious cases. It was a remarkable phenomenon, since it facilitated a social migration, out of the upper working class onto the lower rungs of the professional class. The wider social implication was that independent women with a salary and status were not faced with the same pressure to marry young, or to marry 'well', or at all.

There is a footnote here. Like the actual Helen Corke, Winifred Inger, with whom Ursula has that passing but damaging homoerotic experience, represents a social as well as a sexual phenomenon. An independent woman professional is also free to be lesbian. Something previously hidden emerges, even defines itself, as part of the social transformation. It was perhaps wilful of Lawrence – it seems deliberate – that he marries off two anomalous people, Winifred Inger and the younger Tom Brangwen. It is as if he is suggesting that their social roles match, especially his as modern technologically-oriented colliery manager, with his cynical acceptance of all the mechanical hollowness of the industrial civilisation he serves. Serve him right if he gets as partner this dangerous Diana-figure. There seems an animus in it. Or is it tragic? They are both people who see through the system, are not of it, but join it and forward it, in a betrayal of their own insight. In any case, the transformation of the role of women must include this component to be complete.

With Ursula the female line becomes the central focus of consciousness, and the line into the future. There is a strong impulse here, which might be taken as feminist. The account is saying that men have hitherto been dominant and are now like Will and Anton Skrebensky dwindling into acquiescence of all sorts: a woman cannot be content either with what men want or what they allow themselves to become. It takes a strong woman to say, 'I won't be like that myself, and I won't marry into it.' This is actually Lesson Two for feminists, since it doesn't come immediately. At the beginning of her adult life Ursula is pressed to enter the man's world and make herself an equal member of it. This was Lesson One: be equal, or compete in that arena. At first she wants this herself.

Entering the world of work and dedication to the task of building it is memorably shown in Chapter XIII, actually called 'The Man's World'. Ursula has to fight her parents to get their permission to work: they won't let her leave home yet, and she has to start as a pupil-teacher in the local school. She has taken advice from her former headmistress, who says what such a person might well have said then and since, though it reads ironically in the light of what happens later:

> 'I cannot tell you how deeply I sympathise with you in your desire to do something. You will learn that mankind is a great body of which you are one useful member, you will take your place at the great task which humanity is trying to fulfil. That will give you a satisfaction and self-respect which nothing else could give.' (332: 36–40)

> 'I shall be proud to see one of my girls win her own economical independence, which means so much more than it seems. I shall be glad indeed to know that one more of my girls has provided for herself the means of freedom to choose for herself.' (333: 12–15)

This is not contemptible, is in a conventional way to be respected; but the rest of the chapter throws a terrible light on it. Teaching in one of the old elementary schools was a searing experience, in which those who, like Ursula, thought they would be very nice and make the little children love them were themselves taught a horrible lesson. Successful teachers worked an inhuman machine. Ursula has to learn how to work it: the crucial experience is the one in which she loses her old self by thrashing a particularly horrible child, as pathetic as he is horrible. It is important that he is seen as both, and Lawrence sees to it. The reality of the trauma is conveyed, and the reader is shocked.

Only one aspect of that school is in the past: having to teach a huge class in a space in which other huge classes are being taught, so that everyone can hear what is going on and indiscipline in one class will infect the others. The teachers impose iron discipline in every little thing, and are judged by their capacity to enforce it, which means their willingness to become cogs in the industrial machine, or officers in the army. Naturally, Ursula on her first day does not know how to march her class into school. It is a military drill, with a known set of commands and movements. The children march in like robots. The whole school day is rule-governed, even for the teachers, from the allotted peg where you hang your hat and coat on coming in to taking them off it when you go. It is like an army, a factory, a prison.

Lawrence is writing about something which he knew from the inside, which he had rejected, and had had time to think about. He makes sure that the reader grasps how much school life is a preparation for adult life in a society of anonymous social units, not people with selves. The horrible and pathetic Williams, who has the instinct to cause trouble and gets himself thrashed, is both product and victim, and so is the Ursula who thrashes him. It would be a mistake to overlook the parallel with contemporary disaffected or outsider-children, who baffle teachers no longer able to meet (one can't say solve) the situation in Ursula's way.

The upshot of Ursula's experience is that she is accepted by her colleagues as having passed a test, having graduated into professionalism. She accepts that that is in some sense true, and can feel some pride in having passed, but it is also a fall from innocence, a degradation, a violation. Hence the remark about Lesson Two for feminists: if that is the men's world, who really wants to be in it, and why can't the men see it?

This is why the relationship with Skrebensky has two phases; first the girlhood first love, and then the serious adult affair. The phases are separated by this teaching experience, and the insights gained at college. It is crucial that Ursula has had this tempering before Anton comes back into her life and offers her his – he thinks – superior branch of the man's world: the regiment, the service, the Empire. She has already seen through all such systems.

Her experience of Brinsley Street School means she has gone down into some underworld, some pit. When therefore she visits the younger Tom and Winifred, they present one kind of representative marriage: of those who see through their world but stay in it. As modern manager, Tom foreshadows Gerald Crich in *Women in Love*, except that Gerald is passionately engaged, puts his heart and soul, unfortunately, into his role, and is both better and worse for that. Tom sees that the system he runs is horrible, and is callously detached. But the colliery is the next stage from the school: you spend your childhood being drilled in one, and your working life being used up in the other. If you are lucky, you do the drilling, but are still part of the system.

If Anton, as gentleman, has declined to enter that particular world, where you get your hands dirty but may make money, it remains the case that the Army is the archetype of all such organisations, and provides their behaviour, their discipline. The main aspect of Empire is that you take your civilisation and impose it on other people. That is not all there was to say about the old British Empire, but that much is true, and Skrebensky would have had to be a doctor or (curiously enough) a teacher to exemplify the positive things. It is equivocally positive that he is an engineer and can build the roads, bridges, and indeed railways, canals and aqueducts that will lead to a modernised society.

It is also crucial that before Ursula embarks on the second phase of the relationship with Skrebensky she has had two kinds of enlightenment at the university. First, she has lost her naive delight at entering the world of learning. She discovers that the teachers are in the same way compromised as managers and school-teachers: they are handing out tickets of admission to the higher parts of the system. But she does have one profound learning experience, a revelation. She has heard the fatal voice of Dr Frankstone saying: '"No really, [....] I don't see why we should attribute some special mystery to life – do you?"' But Ursula's microscope shows her a microcellular organism in a field of light, and this is a visionary moment, where she gains her sense of the 'special mystery'. From one point of view the organism is simple and primitive, from another it is absolutely pure, as from the hand of God. The message she derives from it is 'It intended to be itself.' It is a thought, or rather an impulse, which she has had before, about herself, but now it is conveyed as her Annunciation, the latest in the series which started with Tom's.

Beings that mean to be themselves should not submit to false disciplines, in schools, in collieries, in factories, universities, armies, empires, or they fail to become themselves. From this point, it is possible to look back to her early insight into Anton's failure ('"It seems to me [....] as if you weren't anybody"'). She had got to that thought already, and now, at the moment when she is receiving this illumination, she has received a letter from him saying that he is coming back and wants to see her: indeed he is on his way and they meet again, and renew the relationship.

The next chapter in which this happens is important, and little understood, so I give it a separate examination below. One can feel already that the relationship must be doomed. Young as she is, Ursula has seen what the men's world is like, comprehensively; she has to reject it and with it its representative Anton Skrebensky. The rejection shatters him, and her revulsion nearly shatters her. The book ends with what looks like a needed convalescence, and an opening out into a future which may permit some hope, but the rejection has been so radical and the things rejected so sweeping in scope (pretty well the whole social scheme) that one asks what is left to have hope in. The twentieth century's answer has been: political action. But the novel relates that to Skrebensky's, the younger Tom Brangwen's and Dr Frankstone's beliefs and lives, and shows it is no answer, but a failure of perception.

Lawrence's answer is implicit in the vision of the cell: the capacity of the living organism to become its self, which implies growth and change from within. The need of the individual is to be always, like life itself, in process. This is expressed, throughout the book, as being a traveller. As usual with metaphors, there is a negative implication. If travellers are always passing on, they can't also be building. A countervailing image, which also occurs crucially in the closing pages, is the resurrection-image of the nut which has to fall from the parent tree, seems to die, but breaks open and allows the new life to emerge from the ground where it has lodged. Trees are always rooted, always in process. The roots go down into the earth, the branches up into the air, where they respond to the weather. The tree became a kind of ancestral image for Lawrence, counterbalancing the sense of self as, like Tom, endlessly travelling.

5
The Rainbow: Language and Imagery

If all too much has been written about the first pages of *The Rainbow*, one still has to start there. It is pointed out that the sentences beginning 'But heaven and earth was teeming around them [....]' and especially 'the wave which cannot halt, but every year throws forward the seed to begetting, and falling back, leaves the young-born on the earth [....]' – and which go on, 'They knew the intercourse between heaven and earth [...]' – all this seems to sexualise nature. It would be truer to say that the reverse takes place: it naturalises what we single out as 'sex', and returns it to its place in the fabric of life.

It has also been said that these pages about the archetypal Brangwen men and women are a nostalgic idealisation of a life which was 'really' very hard, and not to be presented as better than what we have now. That too is to miss the point. Though I have made the case that the drive of the book has a real consonance with history, this prologue is not history, but foundational myth. In some sense myth does idealise: that is its function; but it is not dismissed by making the modern substitution myth = fabrication, mere untruth. The Book of Genesis is also mythopoeic: while it is dismissed by many as not true, it will go on being explored by others as poetry, and endlessly significant.

Then again, it would be difficult for the merely hard-headed to say that there were no relatively prosperous small farmers in the northern Midlands in the eighteenth and nineteenth centuries, or that the life described by Lawrence is not recognisable, and in some sense 'real'. It bears the same relationship to reality – and to myth – as that of Emily Brontë's Earnshaws at Wuthering Heights. She too was looking back to an ancestral age.

Furthermore, so far as a historical process is being indicated – and in the whole book, it is – it has nothing to do with the modern categories by which the 'myth' would be attacked: living standards, infant mortality, life expectancy, health provision, working conditions, social security. Rather it is about what the historian calls 'mentality'. I have avoided the word only because one could imagine Lawrence's opposition to the mentalisation involved even in coining it. It is about the movement from an unconscious identification with the life all round, a submersion in it, towards what we recognise as a modern consciousness, and in due course self-consciousness.

This too can be called myth-making: I have touched on the way in which Lawrence's perception of a pre-modern quasi-tribal mentality is close to the theories of anthropological writers of his time, and we have moved beyond that – see it too as a kind of myth. Here Lawrence and sympathetic readers should stand their ground. The processes of industrialisation and modernisation did take place, did change culture and consciousness in ways that the book conveys; it is to literature rather than to history and social science that we look for a sense of how it once felt to be alive. The writer does have to try to imagine that different sense of being in the world, to trace the ways in which modern consciousness has evolved; and reaching some sense of profit and loss is not a statistical enterprise.

If finally it is said, quite shrewdly, that none the less Lawrence is projecting backward on to that earlier world an understanding of its otherness which is peculiarly his, the answer must be 'What else can anyone do? And is not Lawrence's projection one of the most interesting insights we have?' There is no absolute provided by 'real' history, as real historians know.

The obvious mistake is to project backwards the modern consciousness which notes that if we are not like that now it is because we have moved on and it is all gain. The objection to Lawrence's enterprise raises an important issue because this issue of projection, or myth-making, is crucial to our understanding of the book, which is in so many places *about* projection, and in many places works *by* projection. We cannot dismiss anything as 'mere' projection, because that is an imaginative entering into things, and an unavoidable form of understanding, despite the dangers. This attempt to catch an earlier kind of embodiment forces us to think critically about the evolutionary process in society, and ourselves as product.

The subtlety and indirection of the approach is incorporated in elements of the language which look like bare notation, but silently

The Rainbow: *Language and Imagery* 71

prepare us for later metaphors. For instance, the second and subsequent sentences of the book seem neutrally descriptive:

> Two miles away, a church-tower stood on a hill, the houses of the little country town climbing assiduously up to it. Whenever one of the Brangwens in the fields lifted his head from his work, he saw the church-tower at Ilkeston in the empty sky. So that as he turned again to the horizontal land, he was aware of something standing above him and beyond him in the distance. (9: 6–12)

(If you come back to this after reading the last page of the book, Ursula's vision, you see that the same place is being looked at, a century later, and the houses on the hill, and the spire, are seen again, in a desperate attempt to feel hopeful.) The phrase here about the country town is made figurative by the word 'assiduously', implying an aspiration, as of a parish, a whole congregation, so the phrase 'country town' might imply something about the old Church of England. If the word 'empty' makes one pause a moment (has God gone away?) none the less the Brangwen looking at the tower feels an assurance in the words 'above him and beyond him'. Then one looks back at the other prepositional phrases: on a hill, up to it, lifted his head, up in the sky. These are silently mimetic of the movements of someone looking about, as if composing a picture, establishing relationships between the observer and the things seen. Also, the sense of what is 'above' or 'beyond' is capable of being part of a spiritualisation, a particular kind of metaphor.

The man, having looked up, 'turned again to the horizontal earth'. 'Horizontal' seems an odd word, not just because the earth could not be called 'level' since there are hills. In geometry, 'horizontal' has 'vertical' as its antithesis: the notion of two axes is being planted here. The vertical accent is the church-tower, and the conclusion 'above him and beyond him' puts both dimensions in plain language. More important, the sense of what is within a horizon, all that one can see from a fixed point, at once implies its opposite – the sense of the beyond. This leads into the next sentences:

> There was a look in the eyes of the Brangwens as if they were expecting something unknown, about which they were eager. They had that air of readiness for what would come to them, a kind of surety, an expectancy, the look of an inheritor. (9: 13–16)

This is said generally of all the Brangwens. But on the next page it is specified that it is the women who were different, who 'looked out from the heated, blind intercourse of farm-life, to the spoken world beyond'. That indicates a limitation in the sexuality of the 'male' notations. The 'womanly' notations now cumulate, and incorporate the sense of the beyond: her house 'faced out'; she 'looked out'; she 'stood to see'; she 'faced outwards to where men moved dominant and creative, having turned their back on the pulsing heat of creation, and with this behind them, were set out to discover what was beyond' – as distinct from the Brangwen men, who 'faced inwards to the teeming life of creation' and so were 'unable to turn round'. And again, 'the Brangwen wife at the Marsh aspired beyond herself [....] as a traveller in his self-contained manner reveals far-off countries present in himself' (12: 39–13: 2). The notion of the traveller comes in quite naturally, as the complementary opposite of the man working in the field, his vision bounded by what he can see from his fixed point on the earth.

The narrative voice comments here that 'The male part of the poem was filled in by such men as the vicar and Lord William [....] men who had command of the further fields.' To call all this 'the poem' is to give a hint that this is not mere social history. Another reason for not taking things literally is given a few pages later, when it is Tom Brangwen who meets and is impressed by a traveller, the foreign man he talks to in Matlock. So though it is said that 'the Brangwen woman' has this outward-facing impulse, it is he who exercises it to such effect that he marries a foreigner. Perhaps this is something he inherits on his mother's side: a female component of the Brangwen heredity, where the male aspect cleaves to the earth and the female aspect aspires beyond; and this has been pre-posited in mythical or figurative terms, as archetypal, a sort of Adam and Eve? Yet we are also being prepared for the ultimate development in the third generation, where it is the woman, Ursula, who takes on the role of being the adventurer into a widening circle, a finer consciousness.

Indeed, coming back to the opening pages after reading the whole book, one finds saddening reflections. It is Ursula who most 'strains to listen' to the 'lips of the mind of the world speaking and giving utterance' and what she hears in her time is disheartening. As for 'It was this, this education, this higher form of being, that the mother wished to give her children, so that they too could live the supreme life on earth' (12: 14–16) – one only has to think of Ursula in Brinsley Street School and at college. Her disillusionment casts back a bitter reflection on this early idealism – except that her vision of the living

The Rainbow: *Language and Imagery* 73

cell and the final rainbow keep the hope alive.

Something like a Fall takes place 'about 1840' when the canal embankment paradoxically confines the Brangwens inside their Eden while something diabolical takes place outside:

> But, looking from the garden gate down the road to the right, there, through the dark archway of the canal's square aqueduct, was a colliery spinning away in the near distance, and further, red, crude houses plastered on the valley in masses, and beyond all, the dim smoking hill of the town. (14: 1–5)

This may look like mere description, but 'spinning away' is what the Fates do; and the scene makes a crucial contrast with the spire and the hill of the opening. With the 'dark archway', a real component of a real structure, we have come upon the first notation of the overt leading figure of the book and one might ponder the effect of the most frequently met adjective, 'dark'. Both occur quite naturally here. In later uses the archway often links with or metamorphoses into other figures which seem to me to occur to Lawrence instinctively. It can also become, too easily perhaps, the rainbow of the title, or the Norman or Gothic arches of the churches visited, or the doorway which, ideally one spouse represents to the other.

The spire on the hill is just noticed, as on the first page. The vertical axis is set in the horizontal plane which is the circle of vision, a circumscription that one may aspire (as in 'the finer, more vivid circle of life') or fear to leave – it may be seen as the lighted circle in the dark which 'bristles' with the menace of unknown animals.

Moreover, the church on the hill, or the town on the hill (a quietly repeated reference throughout the book) are a subliminal Biblical allusion,[1] most notably to the Sermon on the Mount. The key text is: 'Ye are the light of the world. A city that is set on a hill cannot be hid'. The next verse is:

> Neither do men light a candle and put it under a bushel, but on a candlestick, and it giveth light unto all that are in the house. (Matthew 5: 14, 15)

[1] Made finally specific in *Women in Love* where Birkin 'saw the town on the slope of the hill, not straggling, but as if walled-in with the straight, final streets of miners-dwellings, making a great square, and it looked like Jerusalem to his fancy' (WL 255: 1–3).

This text was important for Lawrence, being associated with the candle-image which he used throughout his writing from *Sons and Lovers* onward. The seeming disjunction between the two Biblical images is bridged if one visualises, in the first, white houses on a hill in strong sunlight. That covert light image generates the other by a metaphoric shift, familiar as the cinematic fade. The two fuse in the next verse, which is a moralisation:

> Let your light so shine before men that they may see your good works and glorify your Father.

The 'dim smoking hill' is already a sad declension from the opening, a new reality. We need to keep in mind this constant ground-bass of Biblical reference. If we go back to the opening paragraphs, the phrase 'how should this cease' following 'Heaven and earth was teeming about them' triggers a reminiscence of Genesis 8: 22: 'While the earth remaineth, seedtime and harvest, and cold and heat, and summer and winter, and day and night shall not cease.' This is, actually, God's promise not to send another flood, his covenant symbolised by the rainbow. The Biblical Flood recurs in the book as an actual flood which drowns Tom. The Bible-myths prefigure eternal actual occurrences, and the sense which Brangwens and their descendants may derive from them.

Already the narrative is seeing again the landscape of the opening (as Anton and Ursula do in the final generation) and seeing it as changed:

> As they worked in the fields, from beyond the now familiar embankment came the rhythmic run of the winding engines, startling at first, but afterwards a narcotic to the brain. Then the shrill whistle of the trains re-echoed through the heart, with fearsome pleasure, announcing the far-off come near and imminent.
>
> As they drove home from town, the farmers of the land met the blackened colliers trooping from the pit-mouth. As they gathered the harvest, the west wind brought a faint sulphurous smell of pit-refuse burning. As they pulled the turnips in November, the sharp clink-clink-clink-clink-clink of empty trucks shunting on the line, vibrated in their hearts with the fact of other activity going on beyond them. (14: 21–31)

It's not obvious, yet hard to miss: we remember how the 'clink-clink-

clink-clink-clink' is of things chained together, and how the blackened colliers and the faint sulphurous smell 'tell'; and on a second reading words like 'vibrated' do vibrate. This 'other activity going on beyond them' is a sharp inflection into a minor key of the hitherto open-minded, even hopeful, questioning about the 'beyond'. This is what it is beginning to be like, now, in this part of England.

With the paragraph beginning 'The Alfred Brangwen of this period had married a woman from Heanor, daughter of the "Black Horse"' the narrative begins: here is a named individual, the first Alfred. The reader familiar with the whole book can look back at the first five pages and marvel at the economy with which the metaphorical seeds have been planted. The overt elements against which some readers strain, thinking them over-written, are not, ultimately, as important as the things which may not even be noticed: the spire on the hill, which creates the notion of what is above, and which carries automatically the other sense of what is around; the 'empty sky'; the circle of vision, which carries the other notion of what is beyond the horizon. The mere prepositions: up, above, beyond, out, outwards, behind, inwards – in their unnoticed way they generate the notions of outward-looking and outward-moving – of 'the traveller', of 'further fields' – and also the less overt sense of looking upward.

The first Alfred disappears in a paragraph, giving way to the first Tom, the patriarch who is the originating centre of consciousness. He meets the foreigner in the inn at Matlock; and it is no accident that his keen interest in this man coincides with a sexual encounter with the foreigner's girl. The generalised themes of the first pages have been given a personal focus.

As if incidentally, Tom's previous sexual experience, with a prostitute, is presented as 'something of a shock to him' because, for him as for the archetypal Brangwen men, the woman was the conscience-keeper, 'the angel at the doorway'. Another foundation has been laid; this 'doorway' links, not obviously at this point, with the archway in the aqueduct; is the continuation of the image-chain. The quotation is a complex allusion, to Coventry Patmore's 'The Angel in the House', but more generally to a recurrent Biblical phrase, especially as in Psalm 121: 'The Lord shall preserve thy going out and thy coming in, from this time forth and even for evermore.' The notion of guardianship can expand into that of opening up the world ('the finer and more vivid circle of life'); and the going out and coming in carries the note of married sexuality.

There follow the wonderful scenes of Tom's meeting his future wife, and his courtship, which all readers are touched by. She too comes from 'foreign parts'. The moment of meeting, the shock of recognition, the first gesture towards the other, the first actual touch are a great *topos* in Lawrence's work: but here too the maximum effect is created by the slightest notations. It is the merest chance passing-by of two unknown people, but '"That's her," he said involuntarily'.

> The feeling that they had exchanged recognition possessed him like a madness, like a torment. How could he be sure, what confirmation had he? The doubt was like a sense of infinite space, a nothingness, annihilating. He kept within his breast the will to surety. They had exchanged recognition. (29: 38–30: 2)

Another essential notation has been planted. The 'sense of infinite space, a nothingness, annihilating' is not so much a perception, more a dread. It is something Lawrence held in his consciousness and explored compulsively. In the subconscious spatial universe of the book, this dread is what you face if you move out of the horizontal circle, out of your old self, your known world, out of your field – in all its senses. Travellers are free of this infinite unknown; that is their attraction. But they take you out of your own circle into theirs, or they bring theirs into your life, or exclude you from it when you want to enter: these are the dangers they present. This is something fundamental about relationship with others, with the other. If you imagine your safe circle as that illuminated by a candle or lamp, then the other is the darkness always hovering outside, which threatens to break in.

To go back to the first age, the sentence about the Brangwen man aware of something standing above him and beyond him initially referred to the church tower, seemed spiritual in a conventional religious sense. But the next sentence 'There was a look in the eyes of the Brangwens as if they were expecting something unknown, about which they were eager' contains the important word 'unknown'. A conventionally understood religion is not unknown. One might skip twenty-five pages or so to the scene in church where Tom is looking at Lydia and her child Anna. He has gone 'for once' to church:

> The old clergyman droned on, Cossethay sat unmoved as usual. And there was the foreign woman with a foreign land vivid about her, inviolate, and the strange child, also foreign, jealously guarding something. (33: 9–12)

In the great scene where Tom goes to the vicarage to propose to Lydia, halts outside and watches her through the window, we, like him, are presented with a vision which intensifies this sense of the unknown. It is not only Mother and Child, archetypal pictorial motif. It is presented in terms of light and warmth, seen by the man outside in the roaring wind and 'the darkest of twilight'. The wind is itself a motif, and so is the time of year, March, the season of the equinox and its gales:

> There was a light streaming on to the bushes at the back from the kitchen window. He began to hesitate. How could he do this? Looking through the window, he saw her seated in the rocking chair with the child, already in its nightdress, sitting on her knee. The fair head with its wild, fierce hair was drooping towards the fire-warmth, which reflected on the bright cheeks and clear skin of the child, who seemed to be musing, almost like a grown-up person. The mother's face was dark and still, and he saw, with a pang, that she was away back in the life that had been. The child's hair gleamed like spun glass, her face was illuminated till it seemed like wax lit up from the inside. The wind boomed strongly. Mother and child sat motionless, silent, the child staring with vacant dark eyes into the fire, the mother looking into space. (42: 7–19)

It is a visionary moment, a suspension. The gaze turns from mother to child and back, and the child's translucency is like the candle which shines as if from within itself. (I think of La Tour's symbol, the candle-light which shines through the flesh of the child's hand which shelters it, and hints at Incarnation and the opening words of John's Gospel.) The iconic force of the picture is equalled by the psychological penetration; Tom feels excluded from her world; he is outside it as well as outside the room. The words 'light', 'dark', are working silently to reinforce what is simply seen, and the 'space' into which the woman looks is not just her separate past (people are often jealous of an unshared past) it is everything outside Tom's world.

Tom is unconsciously guided by a kind of piety. He has that way of looking up out of the situation he is in. We shared the moment when 'during the long February nights with the ewes in labour', 'he knew he did not belong to himself. He must admit that he was only fragmentary [....] There were the stars in the dark heaven travelling [....] Unless she would come to him, he must remain as a nothingness' (40: 3–9).

Here is the counterweight to Anton Skrebensky's feeling that 'his own things belonged to him'. But Tom's feeling, which is in one sense religious, a self-transcendence, is in another submissive, indeed dependent, since it acknowledges a need. The theme of 'travelling' has been made universal, and the polarity 'dark/light'. Like the other themes, they are planted and germinate in this part of the book, to take strange and sometimes horrifying form later.

For that matter, germination is an essential concept: turn back a page, and it is said of Tom, 'the facts and material of his daily life fell away, leaving the kernel of his purpose clean. And then it came upon him that he would marry her and she would be his life' (39: 35–7). That sense of the nut falling to earth, the husk breaking, and the kernel issuing clean is another *topos* in Lawrence's writing as a whole: it is given orchestral expansion at the end of the book in Ursula's transfiguring (or desperate) vision. Tom's simple conviction: 'she would be his life' implies an emotional investment which carries the threat of annihilation if the other person is removed or moves away, or just changes. Insofar as the other person is a 'foreigner', is unknown, the risk is not measurable. So, now, he focuses on the wedding ring on her finger: 'It excluded him. It was a closed circle. It bound her life' (39: 6–7). It is an example of the way that the visible is taken into the pattern-making, the symbol-making, of the consciousness, and is a form of projection.

The horizontal circle – what one sees, what one knows, what one owns, what one lives in and is familiar with – can in this way be linked with jealousy and dependence: what threatens to enter your circle or what excludes you from its circle. The vertical axis is a looking-up out of the circle to a realm from which help comes – or (strange consolation) where none of this human trouble is going on. At the end of the chapter, when Tom and Lydia are committed to each other, he looks up to the sky again for this kind of intimation as he goes out. It is then that we remember that he had done this before going in to have his meeting with her: he had 'looked up at the clouds which packed in great alarming haste across the dark sky'. He derives some sense of community with the ongoingness; as if establishing the vertical axis before he moves out of the darkness into the circle of light:

> She looked down at him as he stood in the light from the window, holding the daffodils, the darkness behind. In his black clothes she again did not know him, she was almost afraid.
>
> But he was already stepping on to the threshold, and closing the

door behind him. She turned into the kitchen, startled out of herself by this invasion from the night. He took off his hat, and came towards her. Then he stood in the light, in his black clothes and his black stock, hat in one hand and yellow flowers in the other. (43: 22–30)

It is 'an invasion from the night'. In this scene, words like dark, darkness, night; and the contrast between black clothes and yellow flowers, the light inside the room and the gathering dark outside – all this is operating its silent spell. If you press it into meaning you could say that what is happening is the arrival of the unknown, the beyond that the Brangwens had been looking for. When it arrives it is not one of the familiar things that the light has fallen on hitherto. It comes from outside the circle, will enter and may be a threat to old securities. It operates on both sides: he emerges out of the dark to her: she and the child, though in the light, have this dark element of the foreign into which they seem to look back.

They embrace and enter into a kind of trance, a sleep:

From which he came to gradually, always holding her warm and close upon him, and she as utterly silent as he, involved in the same oblivion, the fecund darkness. (45: 5–7)

That last phrase has a particular force, because we meet it again in the strange late scene of Anton's and Ursula's love-making. There it seems like jargon. Here it has its source and its original meaning. The 'darkness' in which Tom sits with Lydia in his arms is a lapsing out of consciousness, and is 'fecund' because it creates their being together as a couple. It comes upon them like sleep. In the later scene Anton and Ursula move into it as a matter of will and maintain it to spite the world. There the repetitions of 'darkness' are like an invocation which has to be obsessively repeated in order to work, and is a self-intoxication.

The end of the chapter re-establishes the vertical axis:

He went out into the wind. Big holes were blown into the sky, the moonlight blew about. Sometimes a high moon, liquid-brilliant, scudded across a hollow space and took cover under electric, brown-iridescent cloud-edges. Then there was a blot of cloud, and shadow. Then somewhere in the night a radiance again, like a vapour. And all the sky was teeming and tearing along, a vast disorder of flying shapes and darknesses and ragged fumes of light and a great brown circling halo, then the terror of a moon running liquid-brilliant into the open for a moment, hurting the eyes before she plunged under cover of cloud again. (48: 11–20)

This is not merely wonderful writing; by now one knows to give these signs their weight. Lawrence from the beginning in *The White Peacock* seems to be offering something dangerously like the notorious pathetic fallacy. The wind which blows in these crucial scenes is, perhaps, like the breath of God, but that is not said. The moon may be a power, but that is not said either. It is true that there are later very strange moon-scenes where the reader asks, what is going on here, and how am I to take this? – and this moment is a fore-runner. Like the moment before Tom entered the house, it breaks off from the human internal intensity, looks up and establishes the onward, mysterious, indifferent rush of all the world which dwarfs the personal goings-on yet makes them equally questionable: are they random and evanescent, or are they driven by hidden law? Either way, this is the world one belongs to.

One might explicate it to this extent: the onward movements in the sky make cosmic the notion of travelling. But there is no 'where to?': Ursula's later vision of the single cell shows it too moving in its circle of light, but its oneness with the infinite means that it has no destination beyond fulfilling its life-course. Tom looking up out of his circle assents to being a part of the whole in which he finds himself.

Tom's wedding ushers in 'The time of his trial and his admittance, his Gethsemane and his Triumphal Entry in one' (56: 17–19). This Christ-hood of all, believers or not, is conditional on their consenting to be reborn: is reserved for an elect. Tom's sense of this is put in terms which are now in danger of becoming over-familiar, but the point is a serious one:

> Behind her, there was so much unknown to him. When he approached her, he came to such a terrible painful unknown. How could he embrace it and fathom it? How could he close his arms round all this darkness and hold it to his breast and give himself to it? What might not happen to him? If he stretched and strained for ever he would never be able to grasp it all. And to yield himself naked out of his own hands into an unknown power! How could a man be strong enough to take her, put his arms round her and have her, and be sure he could conquer this awful unknown next his

heart? What was it then that she was, to which he must also deliver himself up, and which at the same time he must embrace, contain? (56: 20–31)

It is both a triumph and a crucifixion: the whole previous sense of widening the circle of vision has turned into a dread. This is psychologically acute; also a skilled dramatisation. Lawrence does not say he, Tom, at this moment suddenly had a drastic momentary sense of the momentousness of his commitment ... and so on in the conventional vocabulary of narration. These are the words one might use to try to represent the feeling. But in this kind of experience feelings are not verbalised. They arrive as this absolute physical sense of a world of dread, with no mind standing outside it, conceptualising. Lawrence's figures render what is wordless, physiological, a kind of panic. At the same time the repetition of 'unknown' is a tonal element which refers us to all that has been built up in the preceding pages as equally unverbalised or unconscious feelings – what one might call the Brangwen mentality. Now, by a familiar psychic process, the confident outward aspiration has become its complementary opposite or dark underside, a fear of self-giving or a fear of invasion.

Of course, this can at moments become conscious and can then be represented to the self:

> He realised with a sharp pang that she belonged to him, and he to her. He realised that he lived by her. Did he own her? Was she here for ever? Or might she go away? She was not really his, it was not a real marriage, this marriage between them. She might go away. He did not feel like a master, husband, father of her children. She belonged elsewhere. Any moment she might be gone. (58: 14–20)

Even this consciousness is dramatically realised: the short panicky sentences convey a breathless unease.

Tom's great vision occurs at the moment when he is handing over to the next generation, in church at the wedding of Will and Anna. Looking at the gothic window, with its dark stone tracery like a web holding the burning blue of the stained glass,

> He felt himself tiny, a little, upright figure on a plain circled round with the immense, roaring sky: he and his wife, two little, upright figures walking across this plain, whilst the heavens shimmered and

roared about them. When did one come to an end? In which direction was it finished? There was no end, no finish, only this roaring vast space. Did one never get old, never die? That was the clue. He exulted strangely, with torture. He would go on with his wife, he and she like two children camping in the plains. What was sure but the endless sky? But that was so sure, so boundless. (126: 4–12)

The two children may remind us of the children playing in the circle of light cast by the solitary lamp-post in *Sons and Lovers*; and in that book the word 'shimmering' became a code-word for the sign of life on the sunlit surface of things. I have suggested that this circle is the central ramifying figure not just in *The Rainbow*, but in Lawrence's whole work. We are being prepared for Ursula's visionary moments in the last two chapters: the circle of light with the eyes of wild beasts shining in the darkness around it, the cell in its own circle of light under the microscope, and the roaring circle under the tree where Anton and she make love. Here, Tom and Lydia are travellers, in transit under the boundless sky, one with their own infinite. Here the roaring of the sky is a triumph.

One might relate this intimation of Tom's to the opening paragraphs, where the elements of the figure are introduced: the land, the sky, the hill, the spire, the circle of vision, the sense of the beyond. These were for the first Brangwens just there, unconsciously taken in, waiting to have a meaning. But now they have been internalised and intensified: Tom holds them in a kind of consciousness, realises them as a significance: they can stand for the meaning of his life: it is his apotheosis. He has combined the notion of belonging in the circle with that of being a traveller, and it is the companionship of his wife which makes the union of the contraries possible. It is an important moment for the progress of the whole book, since it represents an onset of self-consciousness, something which people will have to wrestle with from now on.

And so, later, we come upon Anna, married, sitting in church, fixing *her* gaze on a little window she previously liked. This seems to repeat Tom's abstraction, but now, suddenly, the image seems to her ridiculous and pretentious. This is because a silent internal movement in her contrasts what it means to Will, and her resistance to it, which is her resistance to him. This is part of their married struggle, which Lawrence has just been entering into, with miraculous power. It is embodied, again, in their extraordinary unspoken conflict over the significance of Lincoln cathedral. Will's religiosity, his dependence on

Anna, his attempts to assert his independence, his respectability as social being – they are all him, and so is his reaching for significances he cannot quite focus. Equally, her perception of him is inseparable from her temperamental opposition to the things he values and stands for, and tries to make meanings from. She has to negate them.

So Anna, alienated from him by the conflict over values, perceptions and temperaments, has been unable to tell Will that she is pregnant, because the feeling between them is not right. The mood suddenly changes because, at tea with her back at the Marsh, Lydia tells Anna something about her natural father, and the group feels a kind of awe at their separateness as beings. As so often, the narrative doesn't say this flatly, but the mood-swing produces an internal change of attitude in her, so that, going home, 'as a sharp little moon was setting in the dusk of spring' and as 'the little church pricked up shadowily at the top of the hill',

> She put her hand lightly on his arm, out of her far distance. And out of the distance, he felt her touch him. They walked on, hand in hand, along opposite horizons, touching across the dusk. There was a sound of thrushes calling in the dark-blue twilight.
> 'I think we are going to have an infant, Bill,' she said, from far off.
> He trembled, and his fingers tightened on hers.
> 'Why?' he asked, his heart beating. 'You don't know?'
> 'I do,' she said.
> They continued, without saying any more, walking along opposite horizons, hand in hand across the intervening space, two separate people. And he trembled as if a wind blew on to him in strong gusts, out of the unseen. He was afraid. He was afraid to know he was alone. For she seemed fulfilled and separate and sufficient in her half of the world. He could not bear to know he was cut off. Why could he not always be one with her? It was he who had given her the child. Why could she not be with him, one with him? Why must he be set in this separateness, why could she not be with him, close, close, as one with him? She must be one with him. (165: 36–166: 13)

Tom's vision has been strangely metamorphosed. It is not only that he was looking back on a successful marriage, and recognising that that has been his life, while Will and Anna are still at the beginning, and struggling against each other. There is this distance between them partly because Will is a more 'modern' man than Tom (the word is given meaning by the whole drive of the book) and she is more modern than Lydia and has a more powerful will than the paradoxically named Will, so that though they are – just – within the same circle they are already on opposite horizons and in danger of going over the edge, out of sight of each other. Still, the wind that 'blew on to him in strong gusts, out of the unseen' is the wind that 'roared' to Tom in his triumph.

To turn to the next generation, to that moment when Skrebensky is about to take Ursula, it is now clear how much the scene has been prepared in these earlier moments of vision:

> It was very dark, and again a windy, heavy night. [...] They would soon come out of the darkness into the lights. It was like turning back. It was unfulfilment. Two quivering, unwilling creatures, they lingered on the edge of the darkness, peering out at the lights and the machine glimmer beyond. They could not turn back to the world – they could not. (417: 29–418: 4)

Here is the counterpart to the vision of the Brangwens 'about 1840', with the same sights and sounds. But the 'two quivering, unwilling creatures' are like an Adam and Eve peering out at the lights from the darkness they have invoked. Everything has been inverted; the Eden is itself tainted; the 'machine glimmer' is a strange anti-rhyme with what had 'shimmered' for Tom. While Milton's Adam and Eve had 'all the world before them, where to choose', these two 'could not turn back to the world'.

When they make love 'in the roaring circle under the tree that was almost invisible yet whose powerful presence received them' it is the tree which replaces the spire of the opening pages as vertical axis in the centre of the horizontal plane. It reappears, frighteningly multiplied, in Ursula's nightmare struggle in the final chapter, as trees 'thrust like stanchions upright between the roaring overhead and the sweeping of the circle underfoot'.

Looking back, one can see how the whole image- and narrative-structure has grown from the unobtrusive notations in the first pages. The spire on the hill seen by the man in the field generates all the subsequent 'horizontal plane' imagery, and notably the circle of light surrounded by the dark unknown: the vision of Tom, Will and Ursula. The arch of the viaduct, and what one sees through it, generate the 'vertical axis' imagery: the arches in church, the doorway, and the apotheosis of the rainbow.

I have made a distinction between the two which may seem arbitrary. The vertical component, the archway, is evidently mentalised, used rather deliberately as a structural motif, and its metamorphoses are signalled to the reader in chapter-titles and comments by the narrative voice. It is specific to this book, *The Rainbow* – is developed for it as structural device. The other complex, the light-dark circle, is found in the whole sequence of Lawrence's writings, from *Sons and Lovers* onwards, with ramifications in later short stories. One senses that it really did come unbidden to the pen, that Lawrence could not withstand it, and may not have been entirely conscious of the way it recurred, as part of his image memory-store. It engages him deeply at a personal level, and some of his profoundest experience is released into the texts through it.

But it is too simple to say that one image is conscious and intellectual, the other instinctive or unconscious. I do feel that the circle of light is personal, supplied initially by childhood memory, and deeply linked with the child's first sense of its place in a strange world of light and dark, safety and danger, self and other. But it is taken over by the creative imagination: used, pondered and developed as the converse image is used and developed.

And indeed, the two images are intellectually related, indeed convertible. The horizontal circle can be, in geometrical terms, rotated into the vertical plane, and it then stands on the earth as the arch or rainbow. We know that such a transformation was in Lawrence's mind because a similar rotation takes place in the *Study of Thomas Hardy*. There, one image, of an axle (horizontal) entering the hub of a wheel (vertical) transforms into the complementary image of a stem (vertical) bearing aloft a circle of petals (horizontal) with the centre of the flower, the pistil and stamens, taking the place of the hub. Moreover, in the *Study*, these images are pondered as conveying a complementary male-and-female genderedness. In one of Lawrence's surprising but natural transformations, the pairs – revolving axle and wheel, pistil and stamen – metamorphose into the movement of a dance in which male and female part and come together again, rotate together in a kind of gravitational attraction, and the thought-sequence then moves outwards to the movement of planets in their orbits. Looking across to *The Rainbow*, one thinks of the dance in the moonlit night-scene, or the movement together and apart of the two lovers in the other harvesting-scene. We are on the way to Birkin's image of a committed couple as a pair of planets in complementary orbit.

None the less, some distinction between the two types of image needs to be made. If we look at the final paragraphs of the book, this distinction between what is instinctive and what is intellectually constructed is given force. Of course, the final paragraphs of a profoundly meant book do have to rise to the occasion: there has to be a peroration, a tying-up or a signing-off or some such term, and this can hardly write itself. I have suggested that Lawrence has been ingenious here, in that to present the final vision as, conceivably, Ursula's convalescent euphoria avoids the charge that it is he who is slipping into the major key in order simply to escape the despair that might otherwise be the rational response to his total account. The conclusion embodies a saving hope, a faith in life as eternal rebirth, and this is conveyed in images familiar from the body of the book. The final rainbow is the last metamorphosis of the 'archway' motif, and this is either very neat and satisfying or rather too comfortably apt.

While she is still ill, Ursula has a precursive sense of recovery, not just her own:

> And again, to her feverish brain, came the vivid reality of acorns in February lying on the floor of a wood with their shells burst and discarded and the kernel issued naked, to put itself forth. She was the naked, clear kernel thrusting forth the clear, powerful shoot, and the world was a bygone winter [....] (456: 20–4)

This itself seems to me willed; we have met the figure before, and it is developed in the next paragraphs. There is a hint of sermonising, of a design on the reader, who has to be moved on to a new stance, as in

> In everything she saw she grasped and groped to find the creation of the living God, instead of the old, hard, barren form of bygone living. (458: 7–9)

But then, to do him justice, Lawrence feels the full awfulness of what he is trying to transcend, and his sermon becomes apocalypse. We are back at the opening scene of the whole book, horribly transformed:

> She saw the stiffened bodies of the colliers, which seemed already enclosed in a coffin, she saw their unchanging eyes, the eyes of those who are buried alive: she saw the hard, cutting edges of the new houses, which seemed to spread over the hillside in their insentient triumph, the triumph of horrible, amorphous angles and straight lines, the expression of corruption triumphant and unopposed,

corruption so pure that it is hard and brittle: she saw the dun atmosphere over the blackened hill opposite, the dark blotches of houses, slate roofed and amorphous, the old church-tower standing up in hideous obsoleteness above raw new houses on the crest of the hill, the amorphous, brittle, hard-edged new houses advancing from Beldover to meet the corrupt new houses from Lethley [....] a dry brittle, terrible corruption spreading over the face of the land, and she was sick with a nausea so deep that she perished as she sat.

The force of that is only deepened, for English readers, by the continuing process in the intervening years. But this is what Lawrence has somehow to transform. It is appropriate that he reaches for the rainbow, yet the quotation 'pat he comes, like the catastrophe of the old comedy' comes to mind:

And then, in the blowing clouds, she saw a band of faint iridescence colouring in faint colours a portion of the hill. And forgetting, startled, she looked for the hovering colour and saw a rainbow forming itself. In one place it gleamed fiercely, and, her heart anguished with hope, she sought the shadow of iris where the bow should be. Steadily the colour gathered, mysteriously, from nowhere, it took presence upon itself, there was a faint, vast rainbow. The arc bended and strengthened itself till it arched indomitable, making great architecture of light and colour and the space of heaven, its pedestals luminous in the corruption of new houses on the low hill, its arch the top of heaven. (458: 27–38)

At the least, this is apt and skilful: the heavenly architecture of light contrasts with the sordid 'development', as our planners now call it, and psychologically or spiritually, the reader welcomes the hopefulness. The point about rainbows is that, while they are certainly there, are not quite an illusion, they are none the less a trick of the light, and dependent on viewpoint. As we approach, they recede. Lawrence's serious intellectual point is actually conveyed by this: by the sheer desperateness, the insubstantiality of Ursula's hope, the element of faith. So I might press my charge about the metaphor being hopefully plucked out of the air, and he could reply that that was the point he was making, and his figure was chosen to project it, in all senses of the word. We have come down to matters of faith, in a world where people have to find their faith where they can, and must expect to be told it is an illusion.

The underlying metaphysical preoccupations of *The Rainbow* are carried by these non-conceptual vehicles, the language and the images, as much as by the process of the narrative and the elaboration of the world it takes place in. They take it right out of the social world of Lawrence's famous older contemporaries, Bennett, Wells, Galsworthy; even Forster's more troubled questioning is left behind. There is a link backwards, with Hardy, who in his odd way is always trumping his own metaphysical insights, but does actually have them. The way in which Lawrence keeps these issues open is one of his main achievements. The other analogy is with Eliot's pilgrimage, from *The Waste Land* to *Four Quartets*, but the difference is that Eliot, having found his home, closes the door behind him.

6
The Rainbow: 'The Bitterness of Ecstasy'

I take next the long, penultimate Chapter XV, 'The Bitterness of Ecstasy', analysing parts and skipping over others. It may seem invidious to single out one chapter. I do so because it is dense with the features which readers find hard to understand, because discussion of its content follows on from what was said above; and because it gives a balancing vision, where Ursula's developing and characteristically modern perceptions are set against the earlier accounts of Tom (his courtship, and his vision in church of the meaning of his life) and Will (his courtship, and his sense in the cathedral of some great outward impulse or aspiration). Those moments of illumination – and both deploy the central image of the circular field of light, with the travelling figure at the centre – are at heart religious: they convey the sense of life in a setting, a universe, felt as a meaningful, even a supportive, beyond.

For Ursula that sense is precarious. The chapter ends, for her and for Anton Skrebensky, in a despair, an emptiness characteristic of the new era – though at the end of the book she clings on to her rainbow-vision. But the preceding pages are a nightmare, and the parallel which suggests itself is Eliot's *Waste Land*, both in terms of the dead city, London, as city of the plain, and the sterile sexuality.

The momentousness of the investment in Ursula, as growing-point, as modern representative of the Brangwens and of twentieth-century Englishness, means that these late chapters in which she is the central figure carry both the onward narrative drive and the sense that patterns established in the first part are crucially modified, even subverted, in the second. This is felt most immediately in the imagery.

After Tom has been drowned in 'The Marsh and the Flood', the next chapter 'The Widening Circle' carries a clear implication. The circle is the horizon, literal and spiritual. It is that of consciousness, including consciousness of the world. The second half of the book repeats the narrative pattern in Lawrence's English-set novels – the pattern of his own early life. Education takes you out of the home-circle, first to the village school, and then to the town. So Ursula goes to college in Nottingham, where Anna had gone to school. The centre of gravity of English national life during the past century has been a sifting downwards of the mobile and talented towards London and the populous urban South East, and crucial later scenes in Chapter XV are set in London and on the south coast. The class-setting changes too: education brings clever young people into contact with other social groups, including the rich, the influential, the gifted cadres of society. We are on the way to *Women in Love* and its comprehensive social horizon.

Ursula and Skrebensky have this representative status: as they mature they define themselves more sharply than their parents in relation to their class, their generation, the nation. They are the movement of the times. In their love-affair, although in its first phase, in the earlier chapter 'First Love', they take the same walks in their courting as Ursula's parents – Lawrence is careful to note this – they are not as the affair enters its later phase replicating the conflict between selves that Tom had with Lydia and Will with Anna. They are refocusing certain issues. It becomes clear that Skrebensky's catastrophic dependence has moved beyond Will's, into another realm.

It is true that Anna's feeling for Will, especially his religious impulse, had a kind of contempt in it. She has a vein of rationalism which sees his yearning as ineffectual, aimed (it seems to her) at inessentials, and expressive of his mediocrity. Ursula's gradual comprehension of Anton Skrebensky repeats that process: she too is the more powerful person, and she comes to see through him and all round him. But the situation has been reversed in one important respect: it is Anton who carries forward Anna's rationalism into its twentieth-century social-political forms, while Ursula has inherited her father's religious impulse – again in a modern form. It now seems a saving wisdom that Will's urge is vague and undoctrinal. He is a seeker, does not impose formulae on the unknown, and does not synthesise what is best not put into words. To Anna's irritation, when she wants definitions, he refuses. He receives 'the Bible' and 'the Cathedral' as the whole unanalysable force of themselves, and wonders at their inexhaustibility. He takes them as metaphor-systems.

The scene in which Anna scoffed at the lamb and the flag in the church window as an ineffectual cliché-symbol is neatly organised: she is right to be unsatisfied by allegory and over-familiar imagery, so conventional that people no longer feel their meaning. But *he* is right to feel the something beyond, which the image can only gesture towards. (Jessie Chambers once pointed out Lawrence's fondness for the lines by George Herbert:

> A man that looks on glass
> On it may stay his eye,
> Or if he wishes through it pass
> And there the heavens espy.)

The huge set-piece in Lincoln Cathedral which followed took a truly adequate metaphor – the great cathedral – and in Will's and Anna's projection onto it of their feelings captured both their intellectual stance – his aspiration and her withdrawal – and through it their personalities coming into focus. There is a sexual connotation in his embodied sense of the onward-leaping arcade culminating at the altar; but like the opening paragraphs of the whole book is an expression of the wholeness of his personality and of life.

The first pages of 'The Bitterness of Ecstasy' are easy, swift narrative. The Brangwens have moved from the cottage by the church to the new house in Willey Green: a characteristic then-modern social move into town (a century later, the English reverse it). They are becoming suburban professional people in a 'grimy red-brick villa'. Ursula has survived her ordeal at Brinsley Street school, so is beyond that apprenticeship. She has just had a momentary inclination towards Anthony Schofield, whose attraction may have been that he was a throwback, like a natural Brangwen man of the earlier time. But she resists this, as if she knows it is a backward move, and hopeless for that reason. Now she settles into the new house and prepares for college in the autumn.

She is at first impressed by the college, projecting on to the 'pretty plaything Gothic form' something of her aspiration, much as her father had loved Lincoln, though now in a minor mode ('Her soul flew straight back to the medieval times [....]').

She finds botany satisfying: it is peaceful in the laboratory; she can work on her own; she draws well. In the vacation she visits the younger Tom and Winifred and finds that 'Something ugly, blatant in his nature had come out now [....] A materialistic unbeliever, he carried it all off by becoming full of human feeling, a warm attentive host, a generous husband, a model citizen.' Private good feelings contrast with his cynicism about his role. He is a modern social norm, and she knows she is against it.

She also finds on returning to college that she is seeing through it too. It is a continuation of the learning experience at the school: this place of education is an instrument of the society it serves. The teachers are 'middle-men handling wares they had become so accustomed to [....] What was Latin? – so much dry goods of knowledge [....] The whole thing seemed sham, spurious [....] It was a secondhand dealer's shop [....] a little side-show to the factories of the town [....] a little, slovenly laboratory for the factory [....] with a single motive of material gain, and no productivity [...] the religious virtue of knowledge was become a flunkey to the god of material success' (403). If this is her projection, it is an exceptional character feeling this mood, and the insight cannot be dismissed, since there is more truth in it now than there was then.

Ursula is about to be inducted into a descent into an underworld. The person conducting her is not now Winifred Inger, but Anton Skrebensky. It is important that immediately before she meets him again, she has her illumination, the self-defining vision of the living cell under the microscope. Before she sees it, she has a preliminary contrastive vision, meditative and low-toned. In classic terms, it is the dark night of the soul which mystics undergo before they receive their vision. It begins with the great basic structural metaphors of the novel:

> The last year of her college career was wheeling slowly round [....] She had the ash of disillusion gritting under her teeth. [....] Always the shining doorway ahead: and then, upon approach, always the shining doorway was a gate into another ugly yard, dirty and active and dead. Always the crest of the hill gleaming ahead under heaven: and then, from the top of the hill, only another sordid valley full of amorphous squalid activity. (404: 32–9)

Here is a case where the doorway-motif, though appropriate, might seem rather easy, a conscious deployment. But as so often, the structural device is inflected by something which gives it another life. The note introduced by 'ash' we recognise as a religious reference, the symbol of spiritual dereliction, the burnt-out self. Ash Wednesday places it in the Christian year – and here as elsewhere one is conscious of the parallel with Eliot. The crest of the hill is where one expects to see the shining city or the promised land, which have been replaced by the soot-stained mining town. The shining doorway is a late metamorphosis of the arch of the viaduct through which the early Brangwens saw the first industrial assault on the landscape: now it has become Ursula's more comprehensive, more analytical vision.

There is a moment of hopefulness ('No matter! Every hill-top was a little different, every valley was somehow new' 404: 40–405: 1.) Every valley shall be exalted, one remembers, from the Bible, and more especially Handel's *Messiah*. But dejection returns; and there follows the central image in Lawrence's whole work. That circle of light, in which Tom had seen himself and Lydia travelling through life, in his vision at Anna's wedding; or the circle in which Will and Anna had seemed to be travelling together when she announced the forthcoming birth of Ursula, this is now a circle in which Ursula is the only consciousness, and feels horror. The immediate link is with the 'ash' of the previous page, but the 'seed' is a link forward to the end of the whole book:

> That which she was, positively, was dark and unrevealed, it could not come forth. It was like a seed buried in dry ash. This world in which she lived was like a circle lighted by a lamp. This lighted area, lit up by man's completest consciousness, she thought was all the world: that here all was disclosed for ever. Yet all the time, within the darkness she had been aware of points of light, like the eyes of wild beasts, gleaming, penetrating, vanishing. And her soul had acknowledged in a great heave of terror, only the outer darkness. This inner circle of light in which she lived and moved, wherein the trains rushed and the factories ground out their machine-produce and the plants and the animals worked by the light of science and knowledge, suddenly it seemed like the area under an arc-lamp, wherein the moths and children played in the security of blinding light, not even knowing there was any darkness, because they stayed in the light. (405: 19–33)

Readers of *Sons and Lovers* will recognise the night-consciousness of Paul Morel, the child playing in the circle lighted by the solitary street-lamp. But now it has become the day-consciousness of Ursula and everybody else. To schematise, one can say it is Anna's and, we shall see, Dr Frankstone's and Anton's modern rationalising unconsciousness: for them it is all the world. But Ursula now finds herself looking out of the circle, and facing what may there be found or imagined, as threat. A kind of upheaval has replaced light with darkness – which she now has to face, or even to enter, though it is a dread.

94 *Lawrence's England*

She sees her own circle, her life, as occupied by the trains and factories of the mining country; 'the light of science and knowledge' is a self-deception: the business of the college. Her vision moves to the edge of the circle and beyond, and one can sense a universalisation: this is an indirect comment on the mentality of the commencing century, with its limitations and its hubris:

> But she could see the glimmer of dark movement just out of range, she saw the eyes of the wild beast gleaming from the darkness, watching the vanity of the camp fire and the sleepers; she felt the strange, foolish vanity of the camp, which said 'Beyond our light and our order there is nothing,' turning their faces always inward towards the sinking fire of illuminating consciousness, which comprised sun and stars, and the Creator, and the System of Righteousness, ignoring always the vast darkness that wheeled round about, with half-revealed shapes lurking on the edge.
>
> Yea, and no man dared even throw a firebrand into the darkness. For if he did, he was jeered to death by the others, who cried 'Fool, anti-social knave, why would you disturb us with bogeys? There *is* no darkness. We move and have our being within the light, and unto us is given the eternal light of knowledge, we comprise and comprehend the innermost core of knowledge. Fool and knave, how dare you belittle us with the darkness?' (405: 34–406: 9)

Dr Frankstone is as if waiting to come in – and so she does, three pages later. The passage continues:

> Nevertheless the darkness wheeled round about, with grey shadow-shapes of wild beasts, and also with dark shadow-shapes of the angels, whom the light fenced out, as it fenced out the more familiar beasts of darkness. And some, having for the moment seen the darkness, saw it bristling with the tufts of the hyena and wolf; and some, having given up their vanity of the light, having died in their own conceit, saw the gleam in the eyes of the wolf and the hyena, that it was the flash of the sword of angels, flashing at the door to come in, that the angels in the darkness were lordly and terrible and not to be denied, like the flash of fangs. (406: 10–19)

In the last paragraph, the word 'bristling' is one of Lawrence's code-words, first met in *Sons and Lovers*, in the passage about Paul's sense of night-time threat, as 'a kind of bristling in the darkness' and recurring in later works as a characteristic notation.[1] We met it earlier in *The Rainbow*, on p. 99, when Anna was talking to her father, trying in an analytical way to discuss people and reach meanings. 'But her father became uneasy. He did not want to have things dragged into consciousness. Only out of consideration for her he listened. And there was a kind of bristling rousedness in the room. The cat got up and stretched itself, went uneasily to the door.' The cat is going out of the circle of light, back to the darkness where it feels comfortable, unlike these rationalising humans. It is as if it knows better than Tom what is going on, and doesn't like it; Tom, equally wise but also not able to verbalise, is uneasy.

What was absent in *Sons and Lovers* (in the child's perception of threat) was the sense that the darkness contains not only the bristling wild beasts but the angels also (thus confirming the Genesis-and-Milton reference in the 'flaming brand'). Keeping out the one means keeping out the other. One has to be prepared to admit both, even if the angels are terrible. The angels might represent the victory which Tom won; he saw his married life as creating, from a male and a female constituent, one angel. One remembers that Rilke read *The Rainbow* – can imagine him assenting to both passages: these angels answered him when he cried to them. One might also point out how Biblical the language is here, following Lawrence's characteristic 'Yea' – even the language of the unbelievers. And those trains, that firebrand, prepare us for the moment when Anton and Ursula make love after the train has swept past with its trail of sparks, like the angel posted outside Eden.

The narrative voice pulls itself up here, and just goes on to say 'It was a little before Easter' – not that that is without significance – 'in her last year of college, [....] that she heard again from Skrebensky.' His re-entry has been most extraordinarily preluded. For a moment the memory of him makes him seem to her 'like the gleaming dawn, yellow, radiant, of a long, grey, ashy day'. The momentary question, why the contrast between dawn and 'ashy' day? can be given the rationalising answer – the dawn had been some years before, and the ashy day is now. All the same, it is a deliberately equivocal note, repeated when he actually appears.

But before he comes on-stage she has that other epiphanic vision – Lawrence's premonitory contrast – of the creature in a circular field of

[1] I have traced uses of this word in my article 'A kind of bristling in the darkness: memory and metaphor in Lawrence', *The Critical Review* (Canberra) 32, 1992, pp. 29–43.

light, the microscopic living cell, and these few seconds give a crucial, hopeful insight.

That too is given its important prelude, the scientific opinion of Dr Frankstone, a specific modern heresy:

> 'No really,' Dr. Frankstone had said, 'I don't see why we should attribute some special mystery to life – do you? We don't understand it as we understand electricity, even, but that doesn't warrant our saying it is something special, something different in kind and distinct from everything else in the universe – do you think it does? May it not be that life consists in a complexity of physical and chemical activities, of the same order as the activities we already know in science? I don't see, really, why we should imagine there is a special order for life, and life alone — —' (408: 15–23)

Dr Frankstone is well named: frank in the sense of overt but a bit simple, stone in the sense of heavy and impervious, and Frankstone as in Frankenstein, the hopeful inventor of monsters. She is the unknowing ancestor of the social engineers and tyrants of the following century. We hear her still, and she will always be about. But the narrative continues, in crucial contrast:

> [Ursula] looked still at the unicellular shadow that lay within the field of light, under her microscope. It was alive. She saw it move – she saw the bright mist of its ciliary activity, she saw the gleam of its nucleus, as it slid across the plane of light. What then was its will? If it was a conjunction of forces, physical and chemical, what held these forces unified, and for what purpose were they unified?
> [...] What was its intention? To be itself? Was its purpose just mechanical and limited to itself?
> It intended to be itself. But what self? Suddenly in her mind the world gleamed strangely, with an intense light, like the nucleus of the creature under the microscope. Suddenly she had passed away into an intensely-gleaming light of knowledge. She could not understand what it all was. She only knew that it was not limited mechanical energy, nor mere purpose of self-preservation and self-assertion. It was a consummation, a being infinite. Self was a oneness with the infinite. To be oneself was a supreme, gleaming triumph of infinity. (408: 27–409: 6)

In terms of light and shadow and mysterious annunciation it is related to the 'central' images I have been identifying. And in terms of significance, that relationship – of the circle of consciousness, the circle of life itself, the relationship between what is within the field of light and what is outside – is fundamental to the whole book. The implication is that Ursula, like the cell, must want to become herself, and that, however one understands the phrase, this must involve a oneness with the infinite. This is the heart of the novel, one of the focal points in Lawrence's work. It is a problem for us that 'oneness with the infinite' sounds like so many cheap mysticisms. One has to work to make it mean something. The word 'self' is equally problematic, and 'soul'; but they are needed, though one has to give them new applications. That is happening here, and Lawrence's advantage at this point is that he has the whole book behind him.

Self has been thoroughly explored, notably in the conflicts between Will and Anna. There is a self which is mere self – which asserts itself, opposes others, makes demands, or is dependent. That self is what we all share: it works alike in all of us: it is anonymous: the self as identified by Blake. There is another self (Blake's identity) which is trying to come into being, to become 'perfectly itself' – Birkin's later formulation in *Women in Love*. The struggle of Will and Anna has subsided or succumbed, and it is Ursula who must carry it into another era.

The vision of the single cell strips down to its basic constituent the whole sense of the living being as self or identity, so one is required to ask questions like, what is it? Since it is alive, it is a process, a becoming. Becoming what? Since it is already itself, it can only become more fully itself. Since it is – to reformulate the Frankstone doctrine – within the infinite living universe, obeying its laws, then it is also part of that infinite, and one infers that the infinite is, like the single cell, also entering into its being: an unending movement. There is no 'Where to?' therefore no teleology – that is the point about infinity. But every living thing is required to become itself if it can, within its own roaring circle, the circle of light, which is also the circle of consciousness, of self, of our world, of the universe. It is a mystery Dr Frankstone will not admit, because it is alive from within, and she wants to reduce life to mechanical components and outside determining forces.

One might glance aside here, to Eliot once more. Like Lawrence, he wrestled with this sense of the self, and there is a parallel, but a crucial difference, in the central image that each proposed. This, for Lawrence, is the circle of light, with, possibly, powers like angels and devils haunting round, offering or even threatening to come in – this permeability is as much a promise as a threat. The circle can be crossed: the angels can even be invited in. When his characteristic metaphor-shift occurs, and the circle round the nucleus becomes the shell of a nut or seed, then the life within is *required* to utter itself, to come out. It is not only its fate, but its nature. But for Eliot, the circle is a prison; the self is locked in, like Bradley's monad in its lonely world alongside all the other lonely worlds. It is a universal curse, requiring or permitting only the vault of faith. That leap seems to be out of this world, which is to that extent scorned. Eliot would reply that the Incarnation has resacralised a world otherwise corrupt; but the doctrine separates him from non-Christians.

The Ursula who is here pondering life 'nodalised in this shadowy moving speck', and who concludes that it intends to be itself, is receiving a Wordsworthian admonition, a sign. It can equally be said that her intuition is a projection, a mood – even a self-assertion, since she has already said that she too intends to be herself. Her positiveness might be undermined by its hopeful vagueness – would one know what it meant or how it felt, to be one with the infinite? And are the circumstances propitious, for her then, or for anyone now?

There is a dramatic psychological reality in her next mood:

> A great craving to depart came upon her. She wanted also to be gone. She was in dread of the material world, and in dread of her own transfiguration. She wanted to run to meet Skrebensky – the new life, the reality.
>
> Very rapidly she wiped her slides and put them back, cleared her place at the bench, active, active, active. She wanted to run to meet Skrebensky – hasten – hasten. She did not know what she was to meet. But it would be a new beginning. She must hurry. (409: 19–26)

The word 'transfiguration' refers back to her vision. The 'great craving to depart' initiates a theme taken up later, recurring as the more direct and urgent 'She wanted to go. She must be gone. She must be gone at once' when they are in London (422: 22–3), and her final mysterious utterance '"I want to go"' in the strange scene by the moonlit sea (444: 21). Her urgency is not something she could account for; it does not just mean that she wants to leave college now that she has seen through it. Here if anywhere is the unconscious bursting out and demanding action, even disastrous action. 'The new life' may also strike the reader as a tiny prefiguring of Eliot's 'Marina', where, for once in his work, a similar transfiguration is invoked.

There is a calculated ambiguity caught with brilliant aptness in the few bare notations when she sees Anton:

> He stood with the curious self-effacing diffidence which so frightened her in well-bred young men whom she knew. He stood as if he wished to be unseen. He was very well-dressed. She would not admit to herself the chill like a sunshine of frost that came over her. This was he, the key, the nucleus to the new world. (409: 31–6)

'The nucleus' *is* her projection. It links him unconsciously with the vision she has just had, and the course of the chapter shows how much she here misapprehends him, misconstrues intellectually, and at the same time how sharp her unconscious perception is. For in that 'sunshine of frost' – that unadmitted chill – she is perceiving unconsciously the way he is going to fail her. Readers might reach for the word 'subliminal' to account for it, but the technical term conceptualises. Lawrence gives a physical sensation in two modes, visual and sensory: not a thought, but this chilling light. The brief paragraph catches the swift rush of impressions, some of them conflicting.

> She laughed, with a blind, dazzled face, as she gave him her hand. He too could not perceive her. (410: 1–2)

This captures both the moment and the ultimate misapprehension of both of them: but one can understand that readers in 1915 and since were puzzled by the paradox.

The account of their courtship which follows conveys his attraction and her scarcely conscious reservations about him, which come at intervals to the surface, as in 'they were enemies come together in a truce. Every movement and word of his was alien to her being' (410: 10–11), or 'He seemed made up of a set of habitual actions and decisions.' That may seem obvious. More mysteriously, we have:

> In his dark, subterranean, male soul, he was kneeling before her, darkly exposing himself. She quivered, the dark flame ran over her [....] If she rejected him, something would die in him. For him it was life or death. And yet, all must be kept so dark, the consciousness must admit nothing. (410: 32–6)

This is so far from obvious as to pose another difficulty altogether. This is the mode of Lawrence's writing which many readers find intolerable or ridiculous. The crux is in the last words. If the consciousness is to admit nothing, Lawrence has to find terms in which to say what he is aiming at; must always be figurative, and may lapse into jargon. Here the word 'dark' has been used three times, 'darkly' once, in close proximity. We are approaching, on pp. 412–16, four of the most extraordinary pages in literature, most easily characterised by saying that the words 'dark', 'darkness' occur some forty times, and 'fecund' or 'fecundity' is associated with the darkness eight times. This is not the automatic writing it has been taken to be. Whether it is well judged is what we have to consider.

'Dark' is the most frequently used adjective in the book, and in the absence of a definition lends support to this charge that Lawrence has a set of unexplained technical terms, or that he is simply gesturing, caught up in a vision he cannot communicate and unaware of the repetitions. But you cannot use a word forty times in four pages, and not mean to or notice. 'Dark' is incipiently or actually metaphorical. It is part of the structure of oppositions which crystallise in those dark/light concentric circles. These are the terms in which Lawrence focuses his perceptions of life and consciousness and what is beyond that circle: is the condition of it, or perhaps the opposition to it – the unknown. The dark is something all-embracing to which we need to be attentive and open, even as we fear it. It is also within us.

There are also important traditional, indeed Biblical resonances, especially reference to the two key texts which start 'In the beginning ...' One is the contrast between original darkness and created light in the beginning of Genesis; the other is the development of that metaphor in John's Gospel, and especially the two verses

> In him was light, and the light was the life of men.
> And the light shineth in darkness, and the darkness comprehended it not.

At the back of the mind here is the concept that creation is the supervenience of light on a darkness which nonetheless remains there and active; these two remain elemental, universal: components of humanity as well as everything else. Paradoxically, this 'dark' element in Skrebensky, appealing to the corresponding 'dark' in Ursula, is what, for a time, transcends his ordinariness and gives him this power she responds to. For a time they relate at this primal level, but it is in the nature of modern life that sooner or later they have to come to the surface again, into the light.

And, as I have already suggested, the 'horizontal' configuration of the 'dark/light' circles can be rotated geometrically into an 'up/down' transformation, a world of light up here, and of darkness underneath; and the word 'subterranean' in the passage above sounds this underworld note. For Ursula, Skrebensky is a messenger or conductor, Hermes or Charon, taking her down. But at times he is also seen – projected – as a tiger:

> A glow came into his face, into his fine smooth skin, his eyes, gold grey, glowed intimately to her. He burned up, he caught fire and became splendid, royal, something like a tiger. She caught his brilliant, burnished glamour. (411: 31–4)

This is Blake's tiger, 'burning bright / In the forests of the night', who provokes the question, does he come from God's hand? This tiger may be one of the creatures glimpsed in the darkness outside the circle of light: is among those others, the wolf and the hyena, which make the darkness fearful. Ursula's finding him, for this moment, to be a tiger is important; for Lawrence the tiger was an aristocrat among animals. And Ursula is surely projecting onto him what emerges in herself, the 'brilliant burnished glamour'. The two young people are drawing out in each other these strange potentialities.

The narrative continues: 'Her heart and her soul were shut away fast down below, hidden. She was free of them.' This is deeply ambiguous: 'fast down below' may mean 'within her', but one may gather that she is also being taken underground into the world of darkness, and held fast, like Persephone. In this state she enters upon the night-scene, which begins, simply, with a one-sentence paragraph:

> It was a dark, windy night in March. (412: 10)

So it was when Tom courted Lydia. March is the time of the equinox and its gales. The point about the equinox is implicit in its name: for a brief season, light and dark have equal power. At crucial moments in the novel, there is an accompanying cosmic event – a full moon, perhaps – and in the 'circle of light' imagery, there is typically a 'roaring' wind. In the Bible, in Acts, the spirit of God descends on the Apostles at Pentecost like a 'rushing mighty wind'. Lawrence is not offering a pathetic fallacy, suggesting that the phenomenon replicates the human experience, or expounds it, or is expounded by it, as meaning. Rather the opposite: the question is raised but not answered. Simply, the two events happen at the same time in the same universe, and it is for us to catch a meaning if we can. With the moon-events, which I deal with later, this is hard. Lawrence does however, I think, in the wind-images imply that in an important moment like the coming-together of two people there is a spiritual implication, and if we hear the wind as the spirit of God – whatever that now means – so be it.

Asked where they shall walk, Ursula suggests the river, and they go to the 'dark, far-reaching water-meadows, beside the full river' – where one may hear a distant reference to the Styx. Anton draws her close to him, and they walk together as Will and Anna had done, and Will and the girl he met and 'spooned' with, also in Nottingham:

> They crossed the bridge, descended, and went away from the lights. In an instant, in the darkness, he took her hand and they went in silence, with subtle feet treading the darkness. The town fumed away on their left, there were strange lights and sounds, the wind rushed against the trees and under the bridge. They walked close together, powerful in unison. He drew her very close, held her with a subtle, stealthy, powerful passion, as if they had a secret agreement which held good in the profound darkness. The profound darkness was their universe. (412: 19–27)

From the outside, this would look like normal courting. But the words give it a quite other dimension. The simple sentence

> The darkness travelled massively along.

elides the river and the night into each other as the 'darkness' which is also their domain while this experience lasts, and the hidden part of them which it is liberating. We are now in the extraordinary pages where 'darkness' is the insistent motif.

Anton articulates it when he confides to her his perception of Africa, where he has been stationed: 'the strange darkness, the strange, blood fear'.

> 'I am not afraid of the darkness in England,' he said. 'It is soft, and natural to me, it is my medium, especially when you are here. But in Africa it seems massive and fluid with terror – not fear of anything – just fear. One breathes it, like a smell of blood. The blacks know it. They worship it, really, the darkness. One almost likes it – the fear – something sensual.'

She thrilled again to him. He was to her a voice out of the darkness. [...] Gradually he transferred to her the hot fecund darkness that possessed his own blood. (413: 11–22)

Had he (or, rather, Lawrence) been reading *Heart of Darkness*? As in that much discussed case, what we have here is the Westerner's projection. This is not about Africa or 'the blacks': it is about Anton Skrebensky's secret self, the darkness in him which he distances by identifying it with a far exotic region. But against this, the whole setting, so carefully, even remorselessly orchestrated by Lawrence, instates the whole notion of darkness in this actual moonless windy night in England, and much more in the condition which it releases in them.

There is a first sort of consummation, expressed as

He seemed like the living darkness upon her, she was in the embrace of the strong darkness. He held her enclosed, soft, unutterably soft, and with the unrelaxing softness of fate, the relentless softness of fecundity. She quivered, and quivered, like a tense thing that is struck. But he held her all the time, soft, unending, like darkness closed upon her, and she quivered as if she was being destroyed, shattered. The lighted vessel vibrated, and broke in her soul, the light fell, struggled, and went dark. She was all dark, willless, having only the receptive will. (413: 38–414: 7)

There follow three paragraphs in which the words darkness and fecundity recur, ending:

It was bliss, it was the nucleolating of the fecund darkness. Once the vessel had vibrated until it was shattered, the light of consciousness gone, then the darkness reigned, and the unutterable satisfaction. (414: 20–2)

It is hard not to feel this is overdone: the repetition of the words turns them into jargon. But Lawrence, as so often, is attempting to express something which others do not perceive, still less have words for. I think the intention here is to capture an ecstasy which he sees as an inversion, an opposite, of the positive things which Tom and Lydia, and even Will and Anna achieved, the balance they struck. Here there is no balance: it is all on one side, all darkness, and this is willed, unconsciously but powerfully by both lovers.

The shattered lighted vessel is probably a Shelleyan allusion – to Number 239 in Palgrave's *The Golden Treasury*, 'The Flight of Love':[2]

> When the lamp is shattered
> The light in the dust lies dead –
> When the cloud is scattered
> The rainbow's glory is shed.

Equally probably it is a reminiscence of the oil-lamp on the kitchen table which is such a power for the child in *Sons and Lovers*. It stands for what should shine in the surrounding darkness: consciousness certainly, but also a sustaining love. So that the 'nucleolating darkness' is the inversion of the living cell in its field of light (the word 'nucleus' on pp. 408 and 409 made links in this chain). The drive of these pages – 'darkness cleaving to darkness' – is not only of putting daylight consciousness to sleep, it is of deliberately going beyond, going definitively outside the safe circle, or down below. It is a Fall, not so much of Adam and Eve, as of Lucifer, or of Pluto and Persephone.

This gives Ursula a feeling that she now has a wisdom, a superiority. The disappointment, the cut-offness she felt in college as disillusionment, is transformed into a visionary power:

> 'The stupid, artificial exaggerated town [....] does not exist really. It rests upon the unlimited darkness, like a gleam of coloured oil on dark water [...]'
> In the tram, in the train, she felt the same. The lights, the civic uniform was a trick played, the people as they moved or sat were only dummies exposed. She could see, beneath their pale, wooden pretence of composure and civic purposefulness, the dark stream that contained them all. They were like little paper ships in their motion. But in reality each one was a dark blind eager wave urging blindly forward [...] they were dressed-up creatures. (414: 40–415: 12)

> 'What are you, you pale citizens?' her face seemed to say, gleaming. 'You subdued beast in sheep's clothing, you primeval darkness falsified to a social mechanism.' (415: 19–21)

---

[2]'This became a kind of Bible to us. Lawrence carried the little red volume in his pocket and read to me on every opportunity [...] all this was spread over a number of years, and meant more to our development than one knows how to put into words.' Jessie Chambers, *D.H. Lawrence: a Personal Record* (reprinted, Cambridge 1980) pp. 99–101.

It is a short step to the human carousel. Given this insight, Lawrence's shock of recognition when he saw Gertler's *Merry-go-round* in October 1916 is understandable. Gertler's image transforms representative people – the men mostly in uniform – into wooden puppet-figures circling and plunging on identical wooden horses. It is a powerful hostile metaphor. What Lawrence supplies is a mythopoeic convergence of cosmic powers. The negative insights already granted to Ursula are that school and college are mechanisms serving the larger mechanism of society. She has for a moment managed to divinise, by making effectively Luciferian, an individual twentieth-century man, Anton Skrebensky, representative of the crowd. The progression of their affair can be understood figuratively as this descent with him into the darkness, where she is Persephone to his Pluto, and then in the final chapter her necessary ascent back to life, a new spring. She has to leave him behind, to annihilate him. She finally has to recognise that he too is 'primeval darkness falsified to a social mechanism'. He is left in the Waste Land. Although this process, in her, is not conscious, at a deep level it is willed. An observer would say she does him terrible damage: the novel shows she has to.

For a time Skrebensky, sharing this 'primeval darkness' with her, shares her superiority:

> He too was free. He knew no-one in this town, he had no civic self to maintain. He was free. Their trams and markets and theatres and public meetings were a shaken kaleidoscope to him, he watched as a lion or a tiger may lie with narrowed eyes watching the people pass before its cage [...] So many performing puppets, all wood and rag for the performance! (416: 8–19)

> He was curiously happy, being alone, now. The glimmering grin was on his face. He had no longer any necessity to take part in the performing tricks of the rest. He had discovered the clue to himself, he had escaped from the show, like a wild beast escaped straight back into its jungle. (416: 25–9)

This casts a retrospective light on his 'Africa'. It is a continent of the mind, his mind. For a moment he feels comfortable in it. This is his apogee, and in this inverted state of grace the consummation of the two young colonisers of this darkness takes place. Before it happens, Lawrence again sounds a premonitory undertone:

> She waited, every moment of the day, for his next kiss. [...] He waited, but, until the time came, more unconsciously. When the time came that he should kiss her again, a prevention was an annihilation to him. He felt his flesh go grey, he was heavy with a corpse-like inanition, he did not exist, if the time passed unfulfilled. (417: 23–8)

The difference between them is conveyed: she is passionate and demanding, he is needy and complicated, and on the way to the disintegration which the end of the chapter conveys with awful power. In him the internal negative drive of the naked self which Tom and, much more, Will had displayed is now like a mortal disease, and one might ask how much this has in the intervening century spread like an infection. But that is to anticipate. First we have the climax:

> He came to her finally in a superb consummation. It was very dark, and again a windy, heavy night. [...] They were at the end of their kisses, and there was the silence between them. They stood as at the edge of a cliff, with a great darkness beneath.
> Coming out of the lane along the darkness, with the dark space spreading down to the wind, and the twinkling lights of the station below, the far-off windy chuff of a shunting train, the tiny clink-clink-clink of the wagons blown between the wind, the lights of Beldover-edge twinkling upon the blackness of the hill opposite, the glow of the furnaces along the railway to the right, their steps began to falter. They would soon come out of the darkness into the lights. (417: 34–40)

It is a deliberate effect, to stand again in imagination on this spot and see this view, and to think not just that two generations have passed, but that the world is changed, and that the 'darkness' is not just a time of day.

It is not now Eden that they are looking back on; but it was once. The suggestion that 'the world was all before them' is also negated. Where, now, are they to turn?

> So lingering along, they came to a great oak-tree by the path. In all its budding mass it roared to the wind, and its trunk vibrated in every fibre, powerful, indomitable.
> 'We will sit down,' he said.
> And in the roaring circle under the tree, that was almost invisible

yet whose powerful presence received them, they lay a moment looking at the twinkling lights on the darkness opposite, saw the sweeping brand of a train past the edge of their darkened field.

Then he turned and kissed her, and she waited for him. The pain to her was the pain she wanted, the agony was the agony she wanted. She was caught up, entangled in the powerful vibration of the night. The man, what was he? – a dark powerful vibration that encompassed her. She passed away as on a dark wind, far, far away, into the pristine darkness of paradise, into the original immortality. She entered the dark fields of immortality. (418: 5–19)

One wants to say, of that paradise, those 'dark fields', 'But surely they are light? That is what we have been told.' The negative inversion reminds us that Ursula and Anton remain in their dark underworld. As for the 'roaring circle' the mind goes back to Tom's vision of himself and Lydia, Will's and Anna's moment of travelling together. And the tree itself has powerful associations: with the Tree of Life, of the Knowledge of Good and Evil, and Northern mythical trees, such as Yggdrasil.

This tree's trunk 'vibrated in every fibre': tree and humans are equally in the wind, which may be the breath of God, and they vibrate to each other as the only way of being in harmony. A tree which 'roared to the wind' is accompanying or responding to the cosmic motion. The vibration which encompasses Ursula is the act of union with Anton, but more importantly her response to the 'dark wind' which transcends him.

Lawrence is dangerously close to excess here. Readers might mock this as self-parody. But it is self-consistent, and it is not obvious what he is doing – he would be more vulnerable if it was. One might look back at the similar risk taken in the first pages of the book, where the sexual and the cosmic are identified. Now we are on the dark side of that universe.

As for Ursula,

> Her soul was sure and indifferent of the opinion of the world of artificial light [....] she felt herself belonging to another world, she walked past [the train-passengers] immune, a whole darkness dividing her from them. When she went into the lighted dining-room at home, she was impervious to the lights and the eyes of her parents. Her everyday self was just the same. She merely had another, stronger self that knew the darkness. (418: 26–33)

The state of being in love is commonly thought of as being in another world, and thought of as good. The drive of the book suggests that the lovers need to be in another world because the real one is in decline; yet the world they are in is this negative, this darkness.

Their transcendence is subject to terrible reminders:

> 'I suppose we ought to get married,' he said rather wistfully. It *was* so magnificently free and in a deeper world, as it was. To make public their connection would be to put it in range with all the things which nullified him, and from which he was at the moment entirely dissociated. If he married he would have to assume his social self. And the thought of assuming his social self made him at once diffident and abstract. If she were his social wife, if she were part of that complication of dead reality, then what had his under-life to do with her? [....] Whereas now [....] she gave the complete lie to all conventional life, he and she stood together, dark, fluid, infinitely potent, giving the living lie to the dead whole which contained them. (419: 22–34)

Lawrence here uses words another novelist might use. It is a helpful intervention, since one gets a clearer sense of what has been going on. One may doubt whether his Anton could actually 'think' this, because it implies a consciousness he does not show elsewhere, and which would be self-annihilating. He does crumble later, for reasons indicated here, but he is not conscious of them. The paragraph moves back into Lawrence's 'unconscious' terms ('dark, fluid, infinitely potent') which have been given this momentary definition-by-inversion. And note the Biblical reference – to Christ's question to his mother, 'Woman, what have I to do with thee?'

Ursula's reply, 'I don't think I want to marry you', is a hint of a devastating honesty, which for the moment neither wants to pursue, because it would expose his inferiority and shatter the dream. So they have a premarital honeymoon in London. They enjoy what they have together, postponing the moment of truth-telling. The account is poignant, for what they are trying not to face slowly imposes itself on them, and on the world they are trying to maintain in face of the real one. This is notated briefly but aptly:

> They had revoked altogether the ordinary mortal world. Their confidence was like a possesssion upon them. They were possessed. [...]
> They were perfect, therefore nothing else existed. (420: 15–19)

That word 'possessed' is well chosen. It inflects what follows:

> All the time, they themselves were reality, all outside was tribute to them. (420: 36–7)

> They alone inhabited the world of reality [....] she began to think she was really queen of the whole universe, of the old world as well as of the new. She forgot she was outside the pale of the old world. She thought she had brought it under the spell of her own, real world. And so she had.
> [....] All the time, they were an unknown world to each other. (422: 5–16)

It is like a definition of love as supreme projection. There comes the moment when 'suddenly looking at a sunset, she wanted to go' (422: 22). It is like the beginning of, and the resistance to, a realisation – a putting-off.

They go to France, to Rouen – the cathedral where Emma Bovary had her first rendez-vous with Léon. Two brief paragraphs move us decisively on:

> For the first time, in Rouen, he had a cold feeling of death: not afraid of any other man, but of her. She seemed to leave him. [...] This was now the reality: this great stone cathedral slumbering there in its mass, which knew no transience nor heard any denial. It was majestic in its stability, its splendid absoluteness. (422: 31–9)

> They returned to London. But still they had two days. He began to tremble, he grew feverish with the fear of her departure. She had in her some fatal prescience, that made her calm. (423: 5–7)

In their first love, they had met and kissed in the village church ('"What a perfect place for a *rendez-vous*,"' he said in a hushed voice, glancing round.' 282: 1). It was in the same church that Skrebensky, listening to the sermon, believed 'his own things were quite at his own disposal'. The reader may also have captured the sense of a remarkable brief scene in a church in Derby, visited for a day, where Anton and Ursula had sat for a moment while men were repairing it, and they found 'the immemorial gloom full of bits of falling plaster, smelling of old lime, having scaffolding and rubbish heaped about, dust cloths over the altar'. For her, at that moment, 'Everything seemed wonderful, if dreadful, to her, the world tumbling into ruins, and she and he clambering unhurt, lawless over the face of it all' (275). Now the adolescent bravado has been lost. When one thinks even further back, to the scenes between Will and Anna where the church is the arena of their conflict – especially in Lincoln Cathedral – it is clear that we are now in a twentieth century where the significance of the church has shrunk: at best a silent monument, it can be used as a place of rendez-vous, is at worst a ruin.

Skrebensky's sense that he is on the verge of rejection, his fear, his dependence, transform into a horror associated with the Waste Land of London.

> He remained fairly easy, however, still in his state of heightened glamour, till she had gone, and he had turned away from St Pancras, and sat on the tram-car going up Pimlico to the Angel, to Moorgate Street on Sunday evening.
>
> Then the cold horror gradually soaked into him. He saw the horror of the City Road, he realised the ghastly cold sordidness of the tram-car in which he sat. Cold, stark, ashen sterility had him surrounded. Where then was the luminous, wonderful world he belonged to by rights? How did he come to be thrown on this refuse-heap where he was?
>
> He was as if mad. The horror of the brick buildings, of the tram-car, of the ashen-grey people in the street made him reeling and blind as if drunk. He went mad. He had lived with her in a close, living, pulsing world, where everything pulsed with rich being. Now he found himself struggling amid an ashen-dry, cold world of rigidity, dead walls and mechanical traffic, and creeping, spectre-like people. The life was extinct, only ash moved and stirred or stood rigid, there was a horrible clattering activity, a rattle like the falling of dry slag, cold and sterile. It was as if the sunshine that fell were unnatural light exposing the ash of the town, as if the lights at night were the sinister gleam of decomposition. (423: 9–29)

I had not thought death had undone so many, one remembers. And Eliot's *Waste Land*, his 'unreal city', is less fully and dreadfully notated than this. But the parallel occurs naturally. It is a reminder that Skrebensky has his representative status – that he is realised as a feeling individual as well as a sadly ordinary man. The breakdown which he now undergoes begins as a further half-admission of his ordinariness:

> He felt as if his life were dead. His soul was extinct. The whole being of him had become sterile, he was a spectre, divorced from life. He had no fulness, he was just a flat shape. Day by day the madness accumulated in him. The horror of not-being possessed him. (424: 10–13)

> He only became happy when he drank, and he drank a good deal. (424: 27)

Tom, we remember, had a phase of drinking-as-anaesthesia, but what a distance we have come! Similarly, Will's horrified sense of dependence has been extrapolated into something else.

Anton and Ursula have that last argument about politics in which their difference of views reveals the difference in their natures. She hates his democracy, she mocks his idea of Empire: in the end she says, '"I'm against you, and all your old dead things."' The words are simple, sound childish, but they go to the heart. 'She seemed [....] to strike down the flag that he kept flying' – we remember the lamb and its flag that Anna had mocked. Where Will was puzzled and wounded, Skrebensky is annihilated.

'Whitsuntide came', the festival of the coming of the Holy Ghost, with its wind-as-voice, and they go to stay in Sussex. Here Ursula has her Forster-like vision of England, remarkably like the panorama of the coast of England at the end of Chapter 19 in *Howards End*. Forster's tone fails him, as so often. We know that Lawrence read it. His own scene begins:

> The white track wound up to the rounded summit. And she must go.
>   Up there, she could see the Channel a few miles way, the sea raised up and faintly glittering in the sky, the Isle of Wight a shadow lifted up on the far distance, the river winding bright through the patterned plain to seaward, Arundel Castle a shadowy bulk, and then the rolling of the high smooth downs, making a high, smooth land under heaven, acknowledging only the heavens in their great, sun-glowing strength, and suffering only a few bushes to trespass on the intercourse between their great, unabateable body and the changeful body of the sky.
>   Below she saw the villages and the woods of the weald, and the train running bravely, a gallant little thing, running with all the importance of the world over the water-meadows and into the gap

of the downs, waving its white steam, yet all the while so little. So little, yet its courage carried it from end to end of the earth, till there was no place where it did not go. Yet the downs, in magnificent indifference, baring limbs and body to the sun, drinking sunshine and sea-wind and sea-wet cloud into its golden skin, with superb stillness and calm of being, was not the downs still more wonderful? The blind, pathetic, energetic courage of the train as it steamed tinily away through the patterned levels to the sea's dimness, so fast and so energetic, made her weep. Where was it going? It was going nowhere, it was just going. So blind, so without goal or aim, yet so hasty! She sat on an old prehistoric earth-work and cried, and the tears ran down her face. The train had tunnelled all the earth, blindly, and uglily. (429: 17–430: 3)

Ursula does Skrebensky and the men's world a kind of justice by feeling desolated by and for them, and admitting the energy, the courage alongside the blindness. Her question 'Where was it going?' looks forward to the puzzlement of the later Ursula and Gudrun in *Women in Love*, pondering the 'go' of Gerald Crich; it also looks back to her recurrent blind desire just to 'go' (there is an instance at the beginning of the quotation). There is an implicit contrast with the cell under the microscope, which does not mean to 'go', but to be itself. And within the image-world of the novel, a retrospective light is cast on Will's mole-like blind tunnelling-impulse: an implication has been drawn out.

They have their strange, Hardyesque experience, like a scene from *Tess*, of being alone up on the downs at night, with the stars; she bathes in the dewpond – the scene feels like one of Lawrence's ritual lavings and carries an echo of the bathe with Winifred Inger. They watch the dawn, one of Lawrence's favourite transformations. She weeps again, for the beauty of it, and he has been sensitised by his London-dereliction, and feels with her:

He too realised what England would be in a few hours' time – a blind, sordid, strenuous activity, all for nothing, fuming with dirty smoke and running trains and groping in the bowels of the earth, all for nothing. A ghastliness came over him.

He looked at Ursula. Her face was wet with tears, very bright, like a transfiguration in the refulgent light. Nor was his the hand to wipe away the burning, bright tears. He stood apart, overcome by a cruel ineffectuality. (431: 36–432: 3)

They have to go back to London – the next crucial moment has to take place there. He asks 'When shall we be married?' and she finally rejects the idea:

> 'I mean never,' she said, out of some far self which spoke for once beyond her.
>   His drawn, strangled face watched her blankly for a few moments, then a strange sound took place in his throat. She started, came to herself, and, horrified, saw him. His head made a queer motion, the chin jerked back against the throat, the curious crowing, hiccuping sound came again, his face twisted like insanity, and he was crying, crying, blind and twisted as if something were broken which kept him in control. (432: 37–433: 5)

It is vivid and horrible like the thrashing of Williams, her other infliction. Shaken and sorry for him, she makes it up with him for a time; they go off to a hotel together. These breakings off and compulsive returns, contrary impulses, doubts after certainties, are psychologically acute: are a tribute to the life-importance of the relationship, its weight: one can't just break off. But an end is approaching, and another crucial stage follows:

> When breakfast was over she lay still again on the pillows, whilst he went through his toilet. [...] His body was beautiful, his movements intent and quick, she admired him and she appreciated him without reserve. He seemed completed now. He roused no fruitful fecundity in her. He seemed added up, finished. She knew him all round, not on any side did he lead into the unknown. (438: 35–439: 1)

This sounds conscious, conceptual, compared with earlier experiences seized at the under-level of sensation and metaphor. But that is the point, now: the sequence has finally reached the level of thought, judgement, conscious decision. The word 'fecundity' glosses previous uses, going back to the experience of Tom and Lydia. It is a spiritual quality, and it inflects Ursula's conversation with the shrewd friend Dorothy:

> 'But do you love him?' asked Dorothy.
>   'It isn't a question of loving him,' said Ursula. 'I love him well enough – certainly more than I love anybody else in the world. And I shall never love anybody else the same again. We have had the

flower of each other. But I don't *care* about love. I don't value it. I don't care whether I love or whether I don't, whether I have love or whether I haven't. What is it to me?' (440: 5–11)

We are in the mental world of the opening of *Women in Love,* where Ursula and Gudrun have their conversation, intelligent and disabused, about marriage. Something more, something different, something unknown has to be created. It is not that 'love' is an illusion: we have had compelling illustrations of its nature and force in the preceding novel. But, as Ursula says: '"I could love a hundred men, one after the other. Why should I end with a Skrebensky? Why should I not go on, and love all the types I fancy, one after another, if love is an end in itself?"'

It's a brief exchange, and, like her disagreements with Skrebensky, unforced and natural. But the insight is wide in its implications. Lawrence has been taken since the 1930s as a prophet of sexual and emotional liberation: but the behaviour he has been thought to sanction is not liberated so much as compulsive, and here he is on the other side of merely sequential intensities, in 1915. The insight can be set against Skrebensky's feeling that his own things were quite at his own disposal: one implication might be that one's own things require 'self-fulfilment'. If it is said that Lawrence preached 'self-fulfilment', and that is what is sought in love, his reply would be that 'being oneself' is not the same thing, is a matter of becoming oneself in a world of others, who are there but not instrumental: the book is about that. In this last generation, Ursula is required to think harder and look further: and she is not fulfilled.

Once again, she is pulled back fom the brink of final rupture: she has failed her examination, so the world is putting pressure on her to marry, in default of a career. She seems to assent: 'Out of fear of herself, Ursula was to marry Skrebensky.' In this condition they go together to the 'tennis, golf, motor-car, motor-boat party' given by the 'lady of social pretensions'. Here, on the coast, the final terrible lovemaking takes place under the moon, and this wordless exchange ends the affair. It is the last of the strange moon-scenes in the book.

In that final love-making on the sand 'full under the moonshine' Ursula destroys Skrebensky, in a way more final than any verbal rejection could be. Next day they have an inarticulate farewell and leave. Skrebensky reverts into his breakdown, euphoric in the day, catastrophically robbed of independence at night:

> But at night, he dared not be alone [....] the hours of darkness were an agony to him. He watched the window in suffering and terror. When would this horrible darkness be lifted off him?
>
> [....] he was shocked almost to madness if he opened his eyes on the darkness. (446: 35–447: 6)

This was something Lawrence knew about (we meet this night-panic again in *Mr Noon*, where the central figure is a Lawrence-persona re-enacting these feelings). It is an ultimate development of similar states in Tom and Will. In the new generation it has become a form of life. Anton simply has to marry someone, turns back to an earlier girl, is accepted and 'sailed with his new wife to India'. The last chapter follows, in which Ursula too has to go down into her own underworld of sickness and despair, and then rise again, with her vision of the rainbow.

7
The Rainbow: Recurrences, Religion, Dependency

The Rainbow is a sequence, a network, of recurrences. Some are inevitable, given that three generations grow up in the same district, so that in courting they take the same walks. Doing so, they contemplate what is permanent, the land, but see it differently: the generations see the same spire on the hilltop, with the houses moving up to it. The successive glimpses of that view, with the silent reference back to 'the city that is set on a hill', show how the scene, and its absorption into the soiled mining town, was never neutrally observed and becomes increasingly charged. The suppressed allusion is part of a quiet religious ground-bass that is never the leading voice, and may not even reach consciousness.

Of course, there is religion, and Religion. What I have been recording is, for the most part, what Wordsworth, who also used the rainbow as a focus of insights, called 'natural piety' – the universal religious instinct. Religion as such, defined faith or theological doctrine, over time also becomes a recurring topic.

If you had asked the Brangwen men and women of the generations preceding Tom whether they 'believed', 'were religious' or 'were Christian', it would have seemed strange to them to be asked. This was so for most Western people before a certain date. The question arose only for educated people, readers and thinkers, mostly in towns. Lawrence conveys in those much discussed first paragraphs the degree to which the Brangwens' sense of life around them was naturally pious, in Wordsworth's sense. This may seem strange, since the poetic description of the cycle of seasons in the farmer's year sees all activity as sexual. But from the other aspect – that sowing seed in either way is the order of nature – a term like 'religious' is needed. Just as these people would stare at you if asked whether they were 'religious', they wouldn't know what you meant if you asked them about 'sex', and when it was explained would think you even more strange. We have singled out for inspection two strands which for them were part of the whole texture, which Lawrence restores.

Writing in 1914, Lawrence cannot wish away his consciousness of what he is doing, but the writing must be taken as his attempt to recover an integrity. The implication of his first paragraphs is that this world extends back in time to the point where it becomes quasi-mythical. To make the obvious parallel, we are in Lawrence's Book of Genesis, and these are the sons and daughters of God. The man in the fields sees the spire as a pointer to a power he accepts without analysis as 'standing above him and beyond him'. Tom Brangwen knows that he ought to go to church on Sunday like everyone else, but doesn't often do so. His religious sense does not express itself in Christian terms, but as the tendency to look up, at crucial moments, to a sky where the mysterious business of the universe is the visible activity of clouds, sun, moon. These are travellers like him.

He is in a way a seer: it is given him to know that whatever-it-is has put his wife in his path and 'without her he was nothing'. The actions which he performs preparatory to going on his 'bit of courting, like' are like a priest's ritual self-cleansing: the donning of a clean shirt and 'all clean clothes' is ceremonial, and an offering is required – a bunch of daffodils seems seasonal. Standing with 'the darkness behind', he sees his future wife and her child within the house as in a vision, and it is given to them both to say the right words and make the right movements.

His great moment comes when he is in his forties, when his stepdaughter is married and he presides at the wedding. He has his summating vision, that the meaning of his life has been his marriage, and in his slight tipsiness he goes on to make his speech about the nature of a married life, and how a man and a woman truly married go to heaven as one angel. Again, we remember that Rilke read *The Rainbow* and was struck by it. Did his own image of the angel, who tells man that what he has created (for instance the cathedral at Chartres) is great – did he find elements of that in Lawrence, or at any rate a confirmation? It is significant that for Tom the two people become one angel: it is like the Platonic recovery of one's other half. Rupert Birkin in a later generation and the subsequent book contests this idea of the two-in-one. Ideas of merging for him belong to the past. He wants two people in love to maintain their identities. This goes with increased consciousness of self, which cannot be abdicated.

Tom's speech is for these reasons a cultural moment of some

importance. The scene is also a triumph; Lawrence enjoys making it both touching and funny. While Tom is making the speech, his brother Alfred is offering a saturnine antiphon. Alfred is a modern man. He lives in town and works in the lace-making industry; he has that mistress, the strong-minded educated woman whom Tom visits and is impressed by. He hears that Alfred reads Herbert Spencer and Darwin with her. Alfred does not go to church, but has to come to his son's wedding, where he makes his presence and his dissent felt. The exchange between the exalted Tom, having his great day, and the dry Alfred, answering for all down-to-earth rationalists and cynics, is wonderfully caught; again it is an historic moment caught in a natural and unassuming way; the humour should not blind us to the deep seriousness. It is like an operatic ensemble: Tom floating his great aria about the divinity of love on earth is Sachs or Sarastro or Boccanegra, while Alfred interjects, in the pauses, his cutting Iago-like asides, the wives make gentle shocked noises and the husbands offer snatches of a drinking-song. At the end of the scene the eleven Brangwen men decide to sing carols to the newly-weds, as if to wish them a miraculous birth. As they go along Tom and Fred have a culminating philosophical conversation: it emerges that Alfred is proud to 'go alone' in life; but Tom has never wanted that. Going alone is what modern man may choose to do: or if he goes with others it is in Skrebensky's way a generation later, as social and political unit.

With Anna and Will religion becomes an intellectual issue, rather than a silent background element in all life. Anna as a child is (like Ursula in the next generation) conscious of the cycle of the Christian year – since she is not male, it comes to her as Christian rather than the succession of seasons which controls the farmer's life. It may be that Lawrence is tendentious in removing the Christian consciousness from his opening pages, making the Brangwen ancestors pious pagans rather than sound Church of England parishioners. With Anna he takes up the theme late in historical time. But the point is that this is an evolution from the original natural piety.

When Anna meets Will, the first thing they do is to go to church together, since visits and church-going both occur on Sundays. She becomes aware of Will as a distinct and odd identity by the way he sings the hymns in church.

She has already shown a Brangwen characteristic. At one point, she

> became an assiduous church-goer. But the *language* meant nothing to her: it seemed false. She hated to hear things expressed, put into

words. Whilst the religious feelings were inside her, they were passionately moving. In the mouth of the clergyman, they were false, indecent. She tried to read. But again the tedium and the sense of the falsity of the spoken word put her off. (99: 21–7)

This is like a specialisation of Tom's experience of school, of trying but failing to read the poetry which had stirred him when read aloud. He could not make anything of print. It is also like Ursula's experience later.

When Will's voice fills the church, Anna goes into a paroxysm of giggling: the congregation become aware of her and are shocked. The little incident is not just a piece of childish-adolescent hysteria. It expresses her sense of his exciting strangeness. His whole-hearted unselfconscious singing, as against her rebellious or self-willed cut-offness from the right-thinking and well-behaved congregation, identifies him as adherent, like Tom, and her as dissident, like Fred. But he is Fred's son, and she is Tom's daughter, so already the gender-roles are reversed. Her siblings are embarrassed by her, and disapprove. She is not conscious of what she is doing, and why. Yet she is becoming a distinct consciousness, and here is a symptom.

Will, it turns out, sings in his local choir – hence his willingness to fill the church with sound as the proper thing to do: also a hint that he is a social being, too much so, perhaps. His architectural interests, his reading, mark *him* out too, but this consciousness leads him into the path of righteousness. He has a passion for the church, for the religious world: one might say that religion is his religion. Indeed, he is absolutely undoctrinal, in an age when High and Low Anglicans were conscious of their theological and ritual differences, and both felt it important to distinguish themselves from Catholicism and Dissent. Will's religion is like the dream that Ruskin and Morris had of the Middle Ages – an evolved natural piety, of symbol and gesture, of religious art and metaphor, uniting people who might if they dropped into concepts interpret things in different senses and then fall into schism.

The huge set-piece prose-poem which conveys their visit together to Lincoln cathedral, his intoxicated sense of it and her mordant dissent, replicates the exchange between Tom and Alfred at the wedding, but turns that modest ensemble into a Brucknerian symphony. Again, a hostile critic would say that Lawrence is sexualising the experience: again the reply is that he is seeing 'sex' reincorporated into the whole life-experience. What we separate out as 'religion' is equally an impulse towards the whole of otherness, in the way that 'sex' is an impulse toward the other as made specific in the sexual partner.

None the less, inevitably both impulses become separated and identified: it is part of the development of consciousness that the book is about. From the opening pages we remember that the Brangwen women 'were different'; the difference was that they were aware of 'the lips and the mind of the world speaking and giving utterance'. These aspirations include the religious instinct; we read that 'she stood to see [....] where secrets were made known and desires fulfilled' and remember the General Confession and more than one other prayer, especially that of St Chrysostom: 'Fulfil now, O Lord, the desires and petitions of thy servants.'

This impulse towards knowledge and expression is made personal in the succeeding generations, which intensify it. In the chapters called 'Girlhood of Anna Brangwen' and the first 'The Widening Circle', Anna, and after her Ursula, are seen as young minds facing religion as a set of beliefs, of concepts. This is an evolution. Of Lydia, it is said, in the first of these chapters,

> She had some beliefs somewhere, never defined. She had been brought up a Roman Catholic. She had gone to the Church of England for protection. The outward form was a matter of indifference to her. Yet she had some fundamental religion. It was as if she worshipped God as a Mystery, never seeking in the least to define what He was.
>
> And inside her, the subtle sense of the Great Absolute wherein she had her being was very strong. The English dogma never reached her: the language was too foreign. Through it all she felt the Great Separator who held life in His hands, gleaming, imminent, terrible, the Great Mystery, immediate beyond all telling.
>
> She shone and gleamed to the mystery, Whom she knew through all her senses, she glanced with strange, mystic superstitions that never found expression in the English language, never mounted to thought in English. But so she lived, within a potent, sensuous belief that included her family and contained her destiny. (97: 14–29)

Here is an affinity with the silent assent of the Brangwen men. Lydia belongs to their generation. But she is also a bud or growth-point.

On the same page, by a very neat progression, Anna inherits her Polish father's rosary. At school, she learns the Latin words which are told to the beads. But she has the problem that Tom had with poetry. The rosary itself, 'the string of moonlight and silver', is let down by the words. 'What these words meant when translated was not the same as the pale rosary meant.' She is faced by the gap between the formulae of socialised religion and her own metaphorisations. The link with Tom's instinctive rejection of verbalisation is established, and it is here that Lawrence's first use in this book of the code-word 'bristling' occurs:

> Sometimes Anna talked to her father. She tried to discuss people, she wanted to know what was meant. But her father became uneasy. He did not want to have things dragged into consciousness. Only out of consideration for her he listened. And there was a kind of bristling rousedness in the room. The cat got up [....] (99: 6–10)

The narrative goes on to say that she became an assiduous church-goer, but the language meant nothing to her; and at this point she meets Will, and finds he is what used to be called 'churchy'. She is for a time impressed by his fervour. He is 'a hole in the wall beyond which the sunshine blazed on an outside world'. This projection fulfils her Brangwen-womanly role. But she goes on to find that his 'escape' is into a closed world. Will's churchiness is a sanctified drug to him, supplies emotion and colour, an outgoing. Anna however has a saving or dangerous intelligence: she listens to what is said in church and finds it inadequate, especially pious moralising ('She was not very much interested in being good [...] she wanted [...] something that was not her ready-made duty'). For that matter Will pays no attention to the banalities of Sunday sermonising either: 'He ignored the sermon [...] his real being lay in his dark emotional experience of the Infinite, of the Absolute.'

Lawrence's analytical intelligence takes hold of an affinity between the two – their unwillingness to be limited by ordinary social religion – and shows how it is the focus of conflict between them, since she is, in intellectual-historical terms, urging forward and he is holding on to what is age-old. So at one moment she forces him into the sort of definition he would rather not make ('You see, it means the Sacraments, the Bread,' he said slowly [....] 'You've to take it for what it means.') She responds with rationalising scorn, he is forced into unconvincing explication, and becomes angry. In that mood, he goes off to Nottingham, and comes back with a book on Bamberg Cathedral. He has made a gesture. What he likes about the book is that it presents images, pictures of carvings, which have to be taken as art; and 'He liked all the better the unintelligible text of the German. He preferred things he could not understand with the mind'. And this had been the point of the rosary for Anna.

So religion becomes one area where the conflict between their natures takes place. Will is trying to prolong into the future an attitude now challenged by strong individual persons who trust their own intelligence, so Anna has inverted the *values* of the Brangwen women while emphasising their *role* as consciousness-promoters. He is preserving the old openness to the unknown, but is beleaguered in that he has to do this in words, and can't manage it. They have their argument about the miracle at Cana: was the water really turned into wine? She is on strong ground, seems to win:

> Very well, it was not true, the water had not turned into wine. The water had not turned into wine. But for all that he would live in his soul as if the water *had* turned into wine. For truth of fact, it had not. But for his soul, it had.
> 'Whether it turned into wine or whether it didn't,' he said, 'it doesn't bother me. I take it for what it is.'
> 'And *what* is it?' she asked quickly, hopefully.
> 'It's the Bible,' he said. (160: 20–7)

She is disappointed, enraged. But it is a good answer, certainly the best he can manage.

It is a profoundly significant gesture when he destroys the little Adam and Eve figure he has been carving, when Anna makes the feminist objection to the Creation-myth that every man is born of woman. It is as if he can neither defend his religious consciousness nor realise that it would be in his carving that he could find an expression not confined to mere ideas.

There is the moment of truce when she tells him of her pregnancy; for that moment they are together in the circle of light, if on opposite sides. But the conflict goes on, and its strange outcome is that Anna celebrates her sense of victorious opposition with an unconscious Biblical allusion. Her dance, pregnant and naked, inverts the gender-roles of David and Michal, as she would have liked to invert the account of Eve's birth from the body of Adam. So Will is not David, the Lord's anointed, the giant-killer, the shepherd and leader of the people, the author of the Psalms, king and poet in one person. It is she who takes on his role as leader, and dances to her unseen Lord.

Surprising her in mid-dance, it is he who takes the jealous rationalising part. ('"What are you doing?" he said, gratingly. "You'll catch a cold."') At this point in their relationship the child Ursula is born, and Anna declares herself 'Anna Victrix'. That is qualified by another Biblical allusion: she is Moses on Pisgah, seeing the land she will never enter. And here she has the curious thought that she can toss 'the child forward into the furnace, the child might walk there [...]'.

Lawrence is interposing here. It is *his* thought that the mother who takes her fulfilment in her children is both failing to realise herself and imposing a sacrificial burden on the child. At this point too, he is making rather easy play with his structural images:

> And from her Pisgah mount, which she had attained, what could she see? A faint, gleaming horizon, a long way off, and a rainbow like an archway, a shadow-door with faintly coloured coping above it. Must she be moving thither? (181: 13–16)

But then the image becomes strange:

> She did not turn to her husband, for him to lead her. He was apart from her, with her, according to her different conceptions of him. The child she might hold up, she might toss the child forward into the furnace, the child might walk there, amid the burning coals and the incandescent roar of heat, as the three witnesses walked with the angel in the fire. (181: 35–40)[1]

> Sun and moon travelled on, and left her, passed her by [....] But she could not go, when they called, because she must stay at home now. With satisfaction she relinquished the adventure to the unknown [....] [but] still her doors opened under the arch of the rainbow, her threshold reflected the passing of the sun and moon, the great travellers [....]
>
> She was a door and a threshold, she herself. Through her another soul was coming, to stand upon her as upon the threshold, looking out, shading its eyes for the direction to take. (182: 10–23)

---

[1] Cf. *Sons and Lovers,* where Mrs Morel holds her baby up to the sun, as if to return him to where he came from – or sacrifice him. The furnace recurs in the final moonlit scene where Ursula annihilates Skrebensky. *Sons and Lovers* shows that mothers who abandon the task of becoming themselves and lay on their children the burden of fulfilling them are sacrificing them. Another Biblical parallel is Hannah vowing her son Samuel to the Lord (1 Samuel 1).

Over-apt or not, this makes a substantial point for parents, especially mothers, which Lawrence does not often allow. In general he thinks Anna's attitude is an abdication of the duty to go on travelling, which means becoming one's endlessly developing self. It might be retorted that this 'travelling' is ambiguous, given that sun, moon and earth do not leave their orbits and the later image of the cell, which also 'travels', remains one with the infinite, whose own 'travelling' is so metaphysically hard to conceive. One might say of Lawrence's image of the circle of light, which the cell also occupies, that it is like seeing oneself as the centre of the universe, which is usually meant as a criticism. If you reverse the 'travelling' image into staying at home, as Anna does, she is entitled to say that that *is* her orbit and her way to become perfectly herself: parenthood is one way people learn, not easily and not all of them, to stop being the centre of their universe, and become a doorway that others can pass through. Lawrence rarely allowed this, though it is really one 'moral' of his account of Tom's life – and a reason why one thinks so well of Tom. It may be suggested that finding that role naturally is a thing of the past. Lawrence does think that Anna at this moment is giving up, and I suppose my critical point about the relative easiness of the big metaphors here is that that easiness undermines the important point which he is momentarily conceding, also rather easily.

In the first chapter called 'The Widening Circle' we see that it is in the girl-child Ursula that the evolution of religious consciousness progresses, at the same time as she becomes the focus of the narrative. The progress goes alongside, but is not entirely equated with, straightforward intellection. It is an important moment for Ursula when 'she knew that $x^2 - y^2 = (x + y)(x - y)$', just as it is important to her to learn French. Algebra, in which terms are substituted and can be manipulated without changing their value or essence, was for Lawrence an important antithesis to metaphor. The foreign language, in which things have an equivalence to the native tongue but are strange and have their own logic of association, is interesting for that other reason. Ursula has also to contemplate, like her parents and grandmother, the language of institutionalised religion, which conflicts with her own image-making. In her own imagination

> The white-robed spirit of Christ passed between olive trees. It was a vision, not a reality. And she herself partook of the visionary being. There was voice in the night calling 'Samuel, Samuel!' And still the

voice called in the night. But not this night, nor last night, but in the unfathomed night of Sunday, of the Sabbath silence. (255: 1–6)

But this is pulled down by common perceptions:

How bitterly Ursula resented her first acquaintance with evangelical teachings. She got a peculiar thrill from the application of salvation to her own personal case. 'Jesus died for *me,* He suffered for me.' There was a pride and a thrill in it, followed almost immediately by a sense of dreariness. Jesus with holes in His hands and feet: it was distasteful to her. The shadowy Jesus with the Stigmata: that was her own vision. But Jesus the actual man, talking with teeth and lips, telling one to put one's finger into His wounds, like a villager gloating in his sores, repelled her. She was enemy of those who insisted on the humanity of Christ. (255: 26–35)

At this point, Will's refusal to verbalise, to intellectualise, is given its due. His own instinct is to seek adequate representation in art: 'he had collected many books of reproductions, and he would sit and look at these, curiously intent [....] He loved the early Italian painters [....] and always, each time, he received the same gradual fulfilment of delight [....] The whole conception gave him the deepest satisfaction, and he wanted nothing more' (258: 38–259: 15).

In both of them there is the instinct to find meaning, the distaste for conventionalisations, other than in art. Ursula finds significance, as her forebears had, in the harmony between the Christian and the solar year, with Christmas as miraculous rebirth of everything every year. Even here, consciousness provides a reservation: 'But it was becoming a mechanical action now, this drama: birth at Christmas for death at Good Friday' (261: 21–2). Like Lawrence, Ursula finds the emphasis on the crucifixion rather than the resurrection 'a mere confirmation of death'.

Like the conversations with Skrebensky later, Ursula's reflections are rendered as the instinctive reactions of a young mind, not intellectualised, with a natural element of adolescent hypersensitivity and the normal disgust with adult crassness. Yet it renders the movement of its time in important respects: this is how it must have felt to be turning away from traditional religious belief, as distinct from the way it might be conceptualised in the history of ideas. It doesn't happen as the result of reading Darwin and Spencer, though that reading might confirm the movement of the feelings.

And yet the ultimate religious experiences are given to Ursula, who is in her own way, like Tom and Will before her, a visionary. As Brangwen-woman she is carrying forward that openness to the beyond posited at the beginning of the book; and she is the culmination of those impulses in Lydia and Anna where a codified or socialised religion is rejected, not out of intellectually formalised scepticism or atheism, but because it is inadequate, cannot fulfil the need, is felt to be outworn.

Ursula's visions have been commented on above: they start with, and all have a visual and spiritual affinity with, that first sense of the lighted circle with the darkness haunting round – inhabited darkness, perhaps. There follows the single cell in its own circle of light, meaning to be one with the infinite; the roaring circle under the tree when Anton takes her; the vision of the train which is the mechanised counterpart of the cell; sunrise on the downs; the moon as furnace-door on the sand-dunes; the nightmare in the wood and then outside with the horses; her final vision of the rainbow redeeming the stricken landscape of her people, and the city on the hill. These are varieties of religious experience: the important sort, that you don't have in church.

There are recurrences of another kind in the novel, equally subtle in the way they are conveyed, and their relationship with, for instance, religious feeling. These are internal events, moods, which have to do with aspects of love, but could be seen also as aspects of religious feeling so far as religion is a stance towards the whole of life. One can name the phenomena: they are dependency, jealousy, infidelity. They are related in that persons possessed by a great love may realise, and fear, their dependence on it as the main meaning of their lives. Its removal might annihilate them. Jealousy is the fear that another may encroach on the relationship, or oust you altogether. Infidelity is the converse of the second thing, but may be a refusal to be dependent: may be the same psychic phenomenon inverted.

Recurrences of these things link the generations in the book. They offer a chance both to demonstrate permanent emotional realities and to show as time goes by how the phenomenon evolves, or is individually instantiated.

Dependency was something Lawrence was peculiarly inward with, profound about. One cannot doubt that he was conscious of it in his own relationships, spent much thought on it and much spirited effort combating it. On this topic he is one of the great authorities, and *The Rainbow* is a masterly analysis.

We meet it first in Tom. Married to Lydia, awaiting the birth of their first child, he finds she is withdrawn and depressed. 'She was not there for him' (61: 15) is Lawrence's simple way of putting it, and it sounds 'modern' to us. The phrase, explored, would open up all those issues about what is 'there' and how we see it. Her 'not being there' is a reverse aspect of her first appeal to him: that she was foreign and therefore exciting and strange. The wonder has mutated into anxiety. When she tells of her earlier life, in which he had no part, he feels excluded, himself not there:

> And there she sat, telling the tales to the open space, not to him, arrogating a curious superiority to him, a distance between them, something strange and foreign and outside his life [....] confounding his mind and making the whole world a chaos [....] (59: 34–40)

Her pregnancy has cut her off further, and in his deprivation he turns hostile, finding her 'cold, [....] selfish, only caring about herself, a foreigner with a bad nature'. The distance between them is expressed in one of the great thematic images:

> He sat with every nerve, every vein, every fibre of muscle in his body stretched on a tension. He felt like a broken arch thrust sickeningly out from support. For her response was gone, he thrust at nothing. And he remained himself, he saved himself from crashing down into nothingness, from being squandered into fragments, by sheer tension, sheer backward resistance. (63: 1–7)

The 'infidelity' which follows is not what we ordinarily understand by the word: rather that at one moment he is impressed that his brother has a mistress, visits her, finds her an interesting strong person, and has his certainties shaken. Since he is – it is his virtue and his strength – a simple man, he doesn't know what to make of this. It is Lydia who grasps the situation: '"You want to find something else",' she says (87: 34). She is far from simple, and her insight is unusual: she does the mental sum and comes out with the answer: '"You should not want so much attention [....] You are not a baby".' But then, this way of showing dependence (I need something) can turn into independence (I can get it elsewhere). She says '"You think you have not enough in me. But how do you know me? What do you do to make me love you?"' That turns the tables on him, and he reverts into opposition. 'She was again the active unknown facing him. Must he admit her?' It is a beautifully understood sequence. She demonstrates her superiority. Not only does she understand what is going on, she has the grace, denied most people, to make the essential gesture – though one might say this represents the mother in her as much as the wife. It is one of Lawrence's archetypal crossings-over.

> 'Come here,' she said, unsure.
> For some moments he did not move. Then he rose slowly and went across the hearth. It required an almost deathly effort of volition, or of acquiescence. He stood before her and looked down at her. Her face was shining again [....]
> 'My love!' she said. (89: 23–30)

The reconciliation is not just touching, it has its metaphysical aspect contained within the physical. He feels desire: it is expressed as 'She was there if he could reach her' and 'If he could come really within the blazing kernel of darkness [....]' (90: 24–5). At this point in the book, the last image seems jargon-like; one has to come back to it from later experiences to see that it conflates three images: the circle of light, the fallen nut, the pervasive sense of darkness. One accepts more easily (because it comes from a different store and is not opaque):

> They had passed through the doorway into the further space [....] She was the doorway to him, he to her. At last they had thrown open the doors, each to the other, and had stood in the doorways facing each other [...]
> And always the light of the transfiguration burned on in their hearts. (90: 37–91: 4)

I find it a bit heavy, like its recurrences.

Tom's jealousy is related to his dependency in the same way as this momentary impulse to infidelity. He has a profound emotional investment in his step-daughter Anna. One might say that she is related to his sense of his own youth. She comes into his life before his own children, is like a very late sibling. When Will comes to visit them, Tom is at first interested in him as strange and new. But then the feeling changes. 'There was no getting hold of the fellow, Brangwen irritably thought.' The note is repeated: 'Sometimes Tom Brangwen was irritated. His nephew irritated him.' This is Lawrence's way of recording a feeling that Tom is not conscious of; he is becoming jealous. The animal-images carry the feeling: Will is like a 'grinning tom-cat'. Lydia is more conscious:

> Brangwen was irritated. Nevertheless he liked and respected his nephew. Mrs Brangwen was irritated by Anna, who was suddenly changed, under the influence of the youth. The mother liked the boy: he was not quite an outsider. But she did not like her daughter to be so much under the spell. (107: 34–8)

There follows the crucial scene where Tom is forced to admit that he *is* jealous. It starts when Anna uses a transparent device to get out of the room with Will:

> 'Come with me, Will,' she said to her cousin. 'I want to see if I put that brick over where that rat comes in.'
> 'You've no need to do that,' retorted her father.
> She took no notice. The youth was between the two wills. The colour mounted into the father's face, his blue eyes stared. (110: 24–8)

He follows them out and sees them kissing in the barn,

> And a black gloom of anger, and a tenderness of self-effacement, fought in his heart. She did not understand what she was doing [....] She was a child, a mere child [....] And he was blackly and furiously miserable. Was he then an old man, that he should be giving her away in marriage? (111: 31–6)

The conflict of feelings, between his anger and his knowledge that it is now his role to get out of the way, forces him to become conscious of what is going on in him. He faces again the classic sense of dependency, fear of loss:

> She was going away, to deny him, to leave an unendurable emptiness in him, a void that he could not bear. Almost he hated her. How dare she say he was old. (112: 3–5)

He is, in her terms, old, as a father is old. He embraces that role, becomes really a father, and gives her away with a beautifully good grace.

In the next generation Will goes through experiences which are similar yet personal to him. The first days of his marriage are wonderfully rendered: first the delight in being cut off, alone in the cottage, out of the world, lost in each other, discovering their marriage: then falling out of that world. He is horrified to find that Anna, brisk, sensible and self-confident, 'would admit that outside world again, she would throw away the living fruit for the ostensible rind. He began to hate this in her. Driven by fear of her departure into a state of helplessness, almost of imbecility, he wandered about the house'. She knows there is an ordinary life to live, and doesn't mind. '"Can't you do anything?"' she said, as if to a child, impatiently.' He sinks into a black mood, is hostile to her, reduces her to tears. They have their first quarrel, and it is really over his dependency.

As with Tom, 'finding something else' becomes a question. Oddly and characteristically, the first time he goes off to Nottingham in a kind of fugue, it is that book that he comes back with, on Bamberg cathedral, with pictures of 'lovely statues of women'. This little infidelity is linked with his religious feeling, which is his way of transcending the life he feels trapped in – hence one reason for Anna's hostility to it. The second time, he goes to the music hall; sits next to a young girl, and fancies her. She represents 'the other'. Moreover, in his fantasy, 'She would be small, he would be able almost to hold her in his two hands. She would be small, almost like a child, and pretty. Her childishness whetted him keenly. She would be helpless between his hands' (211: 14–16).

That is his wordless image, put into words by Lawrence: it is, we should say now, a fantasy. We also see that she is both like and unlike his carving of the creation of Eve, which he had held in his two hands, creating her as he is now in his fancy creating this child-temptress. So the carving had also represented his search for 'the other' and in the conflict with Anna he destroys it. In this lapse, this irresponsibility, this other fugue, or escape from the reality of married life, Will has an hour in the park with the girl, 'spooning' as Gilbert Noon in a later book 'spoons' with his Emmie. The girl can take care of herself, knows exactly how far to let him go, and he does not force her. The incident spices his interest in Anna and hers in him: their sexual life is intensified. But the silent link between sexuality in this adventure, what it means for his sense of the other, and his religious aspiration towards another other, is established in the image of both as a childish female figure between his two hands.

Similarly, Anna's mockery of his cherished symbols, such as the lamb with the flag in the church window, or the whole great cathedral itself, is a form of jealousy. These are the ways in which he escapes her and the world, and she cuts him down. Once again, in the words, in the images, used to project his sense of the cathedral and what it means to him, there is, modern readers are too aware, a mimetic sexual imagery and rhythm. Once again, this is Lawrence relating things to each other as part of a whole life. Will's sexuality, like everyone else's, is not an absolute. It expresses him, and especially his aspirations outward, to the other. His religious aspiration is bound to be analogous. Both express his dissatisfaction with day-to-dayness, his being embedded in a social life – his work, for instance – which does not satisfy him, so that he is forced to look beyond.

Anna, about to turn aside into the final satisfaction of motherhood, as a kind of finale to their life alone together and a prelude to their becoming parents, dances that dance which consecrates her as Anna Victrix. One element of this is that she dances 'before her Creator in exemption from the man [....] She would dance his nullification.' Power has passed to the female line. It is the child Ursula that she is carrying. The next chapter is called 'The Child', and in the next, 'The Flood', Tom Brangwen is swept away. The age of the patriarchs is over. On the other hand, the 'Creator' to whom Anna dances is not Will's (however vaguely) Christian God, but much more like Adam's or Job's. Something of the Old Testament survives.

It is Will's next recourse, as husband not satisfactorily related to his wife, to turn aside in another kind of infidelity, and make demands on the female child. Again, one looks back to the previous generation. Tom was landed with Anna, had to make the best of something unsought and made a wonderfully good job of it. Will, less satisfied in his own life, turns to the child for more than she should be made to give. This topic too Lawrence knew all too much about. The author of *Sons and Lovers* drew a line under it by writing the later 'Foreword', which is a quasi-biblical text concluding that where the husband fails, the wife turns to the son. The complementary situation is that the husband may turn to the daughter. This may be a pattern which can be universalised. If all men fail, because in some sense the old patriarchy has become too strong for them too, forcing them into its mould, then it is of no interest to follow the careers of defeated sons dominated by their mothers. If women can escape the social curse, it may be that they have the future in them. Their fathers may try to dominate them, but are in any case weak, and offer no model that the daughters should want to follow. And this is the burden of Ursula's story.

The final recurrences of this kind in the book happen when Anton Skrebensky calls on the family and meets Ursula, as Will had called and met Anna years before. As Anton and Ursula become more interested in each other, lo and behold, Will and Anna become jealous ('Her father was gradually gathering in anger against him, her mother was hardening in anger against her', 281: 32–3). It helps, of course, that he is Polish in origin, as Lydia was; this makes him both strange and akin. Ursula too finds herself inventing a reason to get him outside, where they can kiss, as Anna had done with Will. The reason is itself a recurrence:

> 'I meant to show you my little wood-carving,' she said.
> 'I'm sure it's not worth showing, that,' said her father.
> 'Would you like to see it?' she asked, leaning towards the door.
> And his body had risen from the chair, though his face seemed to want to agree with her parents.
> 'It's in the shed,' she said. (280: 23–8)

It's neat, or too apt, whichever way you look at it. And there is a slightly obvious, slightly heavy moment in those places where Lawrence underlines the pattern:

> Hesitating, they continued to walk on, quivering like shadows under the ash-trees of the hill, where her grandfather had walked with his daffodils to make his proposal, and where her mother had gone with her young husband, walking close upon him as Ursula was now walking upon Skrebensky. (278: 24–8)

This is in the chapter 'First Love'. In 'The Bitterness of Ecstasy' the book opens out into Ursula's story in a way which transcends these easy parallels yet reinforces the drive of the whole. We observe, transfixed, the way in which Skrebensky's love for her becomes with terrible force his dependence on her, so that one finds a new meaning for phrases like 'she was all the world to him'; and how her eventual need to be utterly free of him rules out any kind of jealousy-provoking or testing his love or restoring some balance – which is what had gone on in the previous generations. There has to be an annihilation, a wiping-out, another Flood, followed by the rainbow which announces that life goes on in another creation.

8
The Rainbow: Scenes by Moonlight

All readers feel the power of certain scenes in *The Rainbow* where Lawrence's unique gifts reveal themselves. They divide into two categories: those we have warm memories of – mainly concerning old Tom the patriarch – and those we are disturbed by and find hard to understand. In the first group Tom is secure in the world which reveals itself to him as mysterious but reassuring: he is a co-traveller in the onward movement of everything, and is able to do the things which reveal themselves as right. In the second group first Will and Anna and then Ursula find themselves overtaken or suddenly illuminated; but the force, the power, that they feel or project is so other, so non-human, that it leaves them unsure what has happened, dismayed. These are night-scenes, and it is the moon which sheds the light, in the literal sense. The illumination (in the other sense) is the question. It is conveyed, or obfuscated for some readers, by the figures which baffled Jacques Berthoud (quoted in Chapter 3: I comment on the particular figures below).

This is not a new element in Lawrence. In *The White Peacock* there is a haunting scene in which the young protagonists watch the moon rise. One of them, Emily, says: 'I always think it wants to know something, and I always think I have something to answer, only I don't know what it is.' It is the two young women who have these intimations: the other, Lettie, says: 'Do you know, [...] I feel as if I wanted to laugh, or dance. Something rather outrageous' (WP 54–5). One may not notice it, but a link between moonlight and dancing has been silently established, as related to 'something rather outrageous'.

In *The Trespasser* the two lovers are not so much star-crossed as sun-and-moon-crossed in their stolen interlude on the Isle of Wight – an adulterous fugue which leads to the man's suicide. They swim in the day, and lie in the sun, getting burned. At nightfall they watch one apocalyptic moonrise. The man, Siegmund, recognises that the moon, once risen, has spilled its light on the sea, a libation. He sees too that he has spilled his life, and accepts the sacrifice. The disturbing thing is that 'Turning to Helena, he found her face white and shining as the empty moon' (T 133). His attempt at meaning is turned back on him: has he poured himself out for nothing, into something always avid and never fulfilled? Some identification between woman and the moon is a common trope; but Lawrence has made it mysterious and disturbing: not so much hostile as alien.

That second novel introduced other figures which recur in *The Rainbow* and elsewhere – a strange complex of motivic associations: between the sea, its saltness, corrosiveness, phosphorescence, especially under the cold white light of the moon: all spring from the sea-setting in *The Trespasser*. They carry over into later fictions, and reinforce the femaleness of the moon by summoning up related divinities – Aphrodite, born of the sea's foam, and Diana the huntress.[1] By another of Lawrence's recurring associations, a related figure is Lot's wife, who looked back and became a pillar of salt. These stage-properties seem arbitrary and inert until they are received as an active network of images which move into each other, touch other networks, orchestrate the drama and work their effect.

Publication of *Paul Morel*, the surviving draft of *Sons and Lovers* has made available another strange moonlit-scene. Paul, the Lawrence-figure, and Miriam, the Jessie-figure, are together when the moon rises. He is profoundly disturbed by it, almost overcome, and attempts incoherently to explain to her that the moon is a hostile force. The scene needs to be read in conjunction with two extraordinary pages (127–8) in Jessie Chambers's *Personal Record* of Lawrence's early life, where she describes three remembered moonlit scenes, all on successive holidays by the sea, where a hostile observer would think Lawrence's behaviour was that of a ... lunatic is the only word. Jessie could not remember what he said, except that it was wild, and she could get no purchase on it. In the draft novel, Paul Morel tries to put it into words. Again, the moon is hostile, damaging, and the force exerted has something to do with his relationship with the girl.

In *The Trespasser* the more extraordinary scenes are a mixture of

---

[1]Palgrave's *The Golden Treasury*: Poem 102 is Ben Jonson's 'Hymn to Diana': 'Queen and huntress, chaste and fair / Now the sun is laid to sleep, / Seated in thy silver chair / State in wonted manner keep.'

youthful lushness and visionary strength. The scenes which strike with comparable force in *Sons and Lovers* have a confident maturity (the *Paul Morel* scene was not carried over into the final version, perhaps it struck Lawrence as too personal to himself). The one which impresses most is that where Mrs Morel is thrust out into the garden by her drunken husband, and finds herself in 'an immense gulf of white light, the moon streaming high in face of her, the moonlight standing up from the hills in front, and filling the valley [...] almost blindingly.' In a trance she sees 'The tall white lilies were reeling in the moonlight, and the air was charged with their perfume, as with a presence'. She touches them, and when she comes back inside finds that she has pollen on her face, and brushes it off (SL 33–6). She is pregnant, carrying Paul, and the lilies may emblematise an annunciation: her brushing off the symbol may reveal her stern literal-mindedness, but neither she nor Lawrence offers a significance in the way that Siegmund does – or the earlier Paul Morel, in his incoherent way. The episode remains in the mind as out-of-this-world, what Eliot later called

> the unattended
> Moment, the moment in and out of time,
> The distraction-fit

It is for readers to make what they can of these scenes, and a practical course is to take them as a group and try to relate them. They suggest the possibility of some transcendence, if only of custom, banality, everydayness: still more, an incursion, a sudden awareness of the Other as a power which may even be harmful – a momentary god: specifically, a moon-goddess.

The comparable moments in *The Rainbow* carry us further. I see them not only as moments 'in and out of time', not just as the clock standing still. I go back to some remarks in Chapter 3. These transcendent moments can be seen as projections. Also, they do, without crudity, express something about the person projecting them, and that person's relations with the loved one. But it is also as if the world – and especially the moon – is telling them to attend, to realise something, to be aware of a crisis. It would be reductive to say that is all, but it gives us a hold on the experience.

Tom Brangwen's insights – his annunciations – convey his rootedness, also his openness. He perceives the Mother and Child from outside: they in the light, he in the dark. He sees them as foreign, strange, sublime, not his. But he approaches, takes them into his life, or opens his life to them. I quoted the passage where, after leaving Lydia, looking up at the windy sky, he perceives it as onward motion, endless travelling, with the brilliant moon alternately revealed and hidden. He takes the motion as that of the whole universe, and in his way he is travelling with it, is himself alternately obscured and enlightened. So the moon itself does not need to admonish him (Wordsworth's word). It is the later generations which find themselves addressed, and the moon checks, or liberates, or questions something in them.

Emily put it well, in *The White Peacock*: '"I always think"' (so this is her attempt at a meaning) '"it wants to know something"' (so it is some kind of subtle question or challenge) '"and I always think I have something to answer"' (so something in the respondent needs to be got out, and is personal to them) '"only I don't know what it is"' (the answer may not ever come. I might need to understand myself, or the world, more than I do or can). Her response tells us about her nature, just as Lettie's response ('"to laugh or dance. Something rather outrageous"') tells us she is dangerous – as the novel shows.

Will and Anna are suddenly admonished one harvest time. They are courting, and the moment has arrived where Will has to propose marriage.

> One evening they walked out through the farm-buildings at nightfall. A large gold moon hung heavily to the grey horizon, trees hovered tall, standing back in the dusk, waiting. (113: 17–19)

It is a harvest moon: 'gold' and 'hung heavily' promise fruitfulness. Entering a partly-reaped field, with the sheaves lying on the ground,

> They did not want to turn back, yet whither were they to go, towards the moon? For they were separate, single.
> 'We will put up some sheaves,' said Anna.
> So they could remain there in the broad, open place. (113: 27–30)

Every word tells, but especially 'separate, single'. I resist the temptation to dwell on every touch in this extraordinary scene. I sum it up by saying that the rhythm they establish, grasping and carrying the sheaves and setting them together in stooks, is like a dance, a rite. It emerges that Anna is the leader: she initiates the game or contest; she sets down her sheaves first; the rhythm in their coming and going sees that she is always first and he follows. He perceives this and tries to catch up; it becomes a contest, yet 'there was always a space between them'. The moon presides over this; for Anna it 'seemed glowingly to uncover her bosom every time she faced it', while he goes 'to the vague emptiness of the field opposite, dutifully' or is half-perceived in 'the dimness where he was'. In this equal rhythm 'there was the flaring moon laying bare her bosom again, making her drift and ebb like a wave' (a faint pre-echo of the wave-imagery in the episode in Lincoln cathedral, still more of the scene between Ursula and Skrebensky discussed below, where the rite is a real dance, and the wave-imagery becomes a dominant theme).

> Gradually a low, deep-sounding will in him vibrated to her, tried to set her in accord, tried to bring her gradually to him, to a meeting, till they should be together, till they should meet as the sheaves that they set together. (114: 39–115: 2)

A transformation takes place: he comes into the light. 'She saw the moonlight flash question on his face', and 'he was silvery with moonlight, with a moonlit, shadowy face that frightened her. She waited for him.' He is momentarily empowered; she is, by contrast, momentarily 'in shadow, a dark column' (115: 9).[2] The conflict declares itself: they meet at last, she wants him to put his sheaves down first, he says '"No, it's your turn".' The game turns serious. He takes her in his arms:

> He had overtaken her, and it was his privilege, to kiss her. She was sweet and fresh with the night air, and sweet with the scent of grain. And the whole rhythm of him beat into his kisses [...] He wondered at the moonlight on her nose! All the moonlight upon her, all the darkness within her! All the night in his arms, darkness and shine, he possessed of it all! All the night for him now, to unfold, to venture within, all the mystery to be entered, all the discovery to be made. (115: 37–116: 5)[3]

---

[2]Turning back to this point after reading the later scene with Ursula and Skrebensky at the wedding-dance, we recognise that the 'dark column' just outside the light is a metaphor-allusion waiting to become conscious – Lot's wife. She crystallises in the later scene: see below.
[3]Compare Jack's discovery in the night-scene in the 'Burns' fragment.

It is a key to so much in the book: this sense of a universe which is equally composed of light and dark – prime elements in the first creation. We remember that Lydia thought of God as the 'great Separator' (97: 23). The Christian god has indeed separated into three Persons; but she might have derived the figure from the first verses of Genesis: God initiated creation by separating light from dark. We now think of that as disposing of the dark; but for Lawrence the two elements go on coexisting as universal complementarities.

But also, the moment tells us something about Will, and it is good: he feels wonder and gratitude at coming on this unknown 'all'. He can accept 'all the night', both 'darkness and shine', and this is a moment of grace. The element of possessiveness, of working a will which represents a fear, is much less than in Skrebensky's case later.

The moon, which reflects the sun's light onto the world in darkness is a reminder, annunciator. Undoubtedly female, she here picks out Anna as leader in the dance; and in her harvesting Anna is always ahead of Will, by nature. However, he is, we remember again, Will by name, and makes himself catch up, catch her. He finds now that he desires her. What he desires is everything in her, especially what is other, hidden in the dark or night side of her, whatever is not like him and may be hostile.

How much of their relationship is caught in that game or rite or dance – she always ahead of him until she waits for him. And much is conveyed at the deeper level of the whole book: it prefigures the Apocalypse, the end-of-the-world contest between light and dark in the relationship between Ursula and Skrebensky, where the woman is not merely ahead of the man in the dance, or resisting him, but destroys him. It warns us not to take 'light and dark' as simple equivalents of right and wrong.

One might note that in another powerful night-scene, the one where Ursula and Winifred Inger descend naked into the river in what I take to be one of Lawrence's ritual laving-scenes – an initiation, indeed a baptism – there is no moon. They had been sitting indoors watching one of those thematic trains 'rushing across the distance'. 'The darkness sank, they were eclipsed' the narrative says, economically. At the river-bank Winifred's voice comes out of the 'cloud-black darkness.'

> 'I can't see the path,' said Ursula.
> 'It is here,' said the voice. (315: 34–5)

One feels bound to receive this as annunciatory; and the voice saying 'I shall carry you into the water' and 'I shall put you in' is that of a cult-leader, a baptist. The darkness is that of the uninitiated, who have not found the path.

Then the rain falls, chilling their 'flushed hot limbs'. At first it is pleasurable, but then, for Ursula,

> It made her cold, and a deep, bottomless silence welled up in her, as if bottomless darkness were returning upon her.

The narrative goes on to say 'she was chilled, as if from a waking-up'. Afterwards, exactly as in the later night-scene with Skrebensky after their consummation, she feels she needs to join ordinary uninitiated people on another train, yet feels her separation: 'she was alone, immune':

> All this stir and seethe of lights and people was but the rim, the shores of a great inner darkness and void. She wanted very much to be on the seething, partially illuminated shore, for within her was the void reality of dark space.
>
> For a time, Miss Inger, her mistress, was gone; she was only a dark void, and Ursula was free as a shade walking in an underworld of extinction, of oblivion. (316: 21–8)

Although the relationship continues for a time, ostensibly loving, with the older woman offering intellectual leadership as well as affectionate companionship, the sense is powerfully established of a destructive or barren initiation, a dipping into a Styx and a descent into the world of shades, from which one has to return to the upper air, the light. If not, one becomes like the unchanging stone at the bottom of the cold stream. The image mutates at the end of the book, linking the experiences.

But I have jumped forward: actually, Ursula's relationship with Winifred follows her first young love-affair with Skrebensky; and in that earlier chapter 'First Love', there was another moonlit night-scene, of dancing outdoors at the wedding of Fred Brangwen. The younger Tom Brangwen, later to marry Winifred, is there exerting his enchanter's recruiting power: he

> seemed to fan the flame that was rising. The bride was strongly attracted by him, and he was exerting his influence on another

> beautiful, fair girl, chill and burning as the sea, who said witty things which he appreciated, making her glint with more, like phosphorescence. And her greenish eyes seemed to rock a secret, and her hands like mother-of-pearl seemed luminous, transparent, as if the secret were burning visible in them. (294: 18–24)

It is an extraordinary set of notations, baffling unless you are familiar with them in previous uses, especially in *The Trespasser*. Aphrodite is heralded by these harmonies, as she inhabits first this woman, then that. No less remarkably, she transforms into a harpy if she is active and succubus-like; or Lot's wife if she turns aside. As for the secret, burning visible, 'It's the salt, you know, the phosphorescence ...' – or so one might murmur, as if that explained it. More helpfully, one might say that these are motifs which recur, which mutate into each other and into yet others, and serve the purpose of motifs in music-drama. One must follow them patiently and let them work. Here, they are going to explain themselves, if you follow their transformations and grasp the association-process.

The underlying logic is that the motif now introduced – bright moving sea-surface-images with a kind of Ancient Mariner electricity – this mutates into the waves of the dance, then goes under the surface, to become a flood, an underworld in which the dancers move. Consider the force of 'seemed to rock a secret': the one word 'rock' gives us the movement of the waves and the dance, a sense of being lulled magically to sleep, and of coming up against the rock. The note in 'fan the flame' and 'burning' goes on to generate images of something being smelted, having the heavy 'dross' removed. In this 'flux' the dancers melt together, two into one – that is the process which Ursula half-enjoys, half-resists. The magnetism exerted by the partner in the dance then turns her compass-point into a blade which she retorts upon the attempt to orient her. It is as if she has been forged in a cold furnace.

At any rate large powers are awakening, being revealed. The scene is set economically:

> Bright stars were shining, the moon was not yet up. And under the stars burned two great, red, flameless fires, and round these lights and lanterns hung (294: 30–3)

Ursula finds herself profoundly stirred, as if released:

To Ursula, it was wonderful. She felt she was a new being. The darkness seemed to breathe like the sides of some great beast, the hay-stacks loomed half-revealed, a crowd of them, a dark, fecund lair just behind (294: 40–295: 3)

At this point, the collocation 'dark, fecund' is familiar, but is here made animal by the great beast and its lair, and made active by the breathing motion, rhythmical like waves and music. This generates a set of complementary images: the breath-wave is internalised and then runs riot:

Waves of delirious darkness ran through her soul. She wanted to let go. She wanted to reach and be amongst the flashing stars, she wanted to race with her feet and be beyond the confines of this earth. She was mad to be gone. It was as if a hound were straining on the leash, ready to hurl itself after a nameless quarry, into the dark. And she was the quarry, and she was also the hound. The darkness was passionate and breathing with immense, unperceived heaving. It was waiting to receive her in her flight [...] She must leap from the known into the unknown. Her hands and feet beat like a madness, her breast strained as if in bonds.

The music began, and the bonds began to slip. Tom Brangwen was dancing with the bride, quick and fluid and as if in another element, inaccessible as the creatures that move in the water [...] The music came in waves. One couple after another was washed and absorbed into the deep underwater of the dance. (294: 40–295: 19)

'Waves' of music are a commonplace: but it has been taken here and worked into the structure of the imagery, made active and transformative. The darkness is 'breathing'; and this in-out movement is both that of the sides of the great beast, and of the waves of the sea in which the creatures swimming are also people gravely dancing. As for the wild impulse, it starts as a Diana-image (the quarry and the hound[4]) and so silently presages the moon. But for the moment, simply, 'She wanted to let go. She wanted to reach [...] she wanted to race [...] She was mad to be gone' – we recognise this as the urge 'to do something rather outrageous' as Lettie put it in the first novel, and it prepares us for the repeated impulse just 'to go' in the final scenes.

The sea-imagery has been generated by the notations about

---

[4]'Give unto the flying hart / Space to breathe, how short soever' (Jonson).

Tom and the beautiful fair girl 'chill and burning as the sea'. But it has been transmuted into wave-motion by the music and the breathing beast of the darkness. The 'mother-of-pearl' of her hands you might find on the shore at low tide, but now in the dance and the darkness we are deep under water. That sense of recurrently going deep down into an underworld is central to the second half of the book. It makes the darkness constitute a realm, not merely an absence of light.

These motives are deployed symphonically as Ursula and Skrebensky dance. Like her mother, she takes the initiative:

> 'Come,' said Ursula to Skrebensky, laying her hand on his arm.
> At the touch [...] his consciousness melted away from him. He took her into his arms, as if into the sure, subtle power of his will, and they became one movement [...] locked in a trance of motion, two wills locked in one motion, yet never fusing, never yielding one to the other. It was a glaucous, intertwining, delicious flux and contest in flux. (295: 20–9)

The words 'fusing' and 'flux' introduce the motif of metal being transformed: 'flux' neatly combines the wave-sense with the name of the fluid that men of that bygone age doing tinkering jobs (like Walter Morel) used in soldering things together;[5] and it is repeated:

> They were both absorbed into a profound silence, into a deep, fluid, underwater energy [....] All the dancers were waving intertwined in the flux of music [....] the dancing feet danced silently by into the darkness, it was a vision of the depths of the underworld, under the great flood. (295: 29–34)

Perhaps it is getting too explicit here, or too persistent, as when it goes on:

> There was a wonderful rocking of the darkness, slowly, a great, slow, swinging of the whole night, with the music playing lightly on the surface, making the strange, ecstatic rippling on the surface of the dance, but underneath only one great flood heaving slowly backwards to the verge of oblivion, slowly forward to the other verge.

---

[5] Also the notion of fluid change – 'flux' as in pre-Socratic thought. The word is used in the philosophical works (BEPW index, 'flux').

There is a sudden development. Ursula is at first 'aware of some influence looking in on her'. It becomes 'a great white watching':

> 'The moon has risen,' said Anton, as the music ceased and they found themselves suddenly stranded, like bits of jetsam on a shore. She turned, and saw a great white moon looking at her over the hill. And her breast opened to it, she was cleaved like a transparent jewel to its light. She stood filled with the full moon, offering herself. Her two breasts opened to make way for it, her body opened wide like a quivering anemone, a soft, dilated invitation touched by the moon. She wanted the moon to fill in to her, she wanted more, more communion with the moon, consummation. (296: 10–18)

It is extraordinary, as if the moonrise has caused the tide to go out all at once. 'Stranded' does it, and 'jetsam' – what you find at low tide; so, more spectacularly, does the sea-anemone. They too are exposed at low tide, and have the blatant sexual connotation. And if you look back to the earlier harvesting-scene and its implied dance, the light on Anna's clothed bosom has now become Ursula's spotlit theatrical nudity.

As if to mask and appropriate this dilated nakedness, offered not to him but to the moon, Skrebensky now eclipses her; he 'put his arm round her and led her away. He put a big, dark cloak round her, and sat holding her hand, whilst the moonlight streamed above the glowing fires. She was not there.' The narrative voice goes on to imagine 'her naked self' 'away there beating upon the moonlight.' But this impulse is suppressed by the sense that the people 'stood round her like stones, like magnetic stones,' and this mutates into the feeling that Skrebensky 'like a loadstone weighed on her'. ('Load' generates 'weighed'.) She wants 'the cold liberty to be herself, to do entirely as she liked. She wanted to get right away. She felt like bright metal weighed down by dark, impure magnetism. He was the dross, people were the dross' (296: 22–36).[6]

He tries to woo her, sensing her opposition ('Don't you like me tonight?')

---

[6]The compass-figure recurs in the final scene on the beach. It also harks back, with extraordinary aptness, to Ursula's relationship, as a child, with her over-demanding father, Will: 'Still she set towards him like a quivering needle. All her life was directed by her awareness of him [....]' 'by his clasping her to his body for love and for fulfilment, asking as a magnet must ask' (205: 21–3). She is now resisting this domination/dependency.

And she knew that, if she turned, she would die. A strange rage filled her, a rage to tear things asunder. Her hands felt destructive, like metal blades of destruction.

'Let me alone,' she said. (297: 2–5)

The metal blades have been generated by the previous 'bright metal', itself generated by the earlier image of smelting or transmutation, to produce this pure aggression, free of his 'dross'. Also by the sense of people like magnetic stones. He and the people round her want her to be in their circle. This mysterious henge, the circle of points like a compass-card, which the surrounding guests have become, with Skrebensky as the dominant or orienting force, are trying to make her point towards him. But if she has to be a compass-point, she turns herself into the double blade that compass-blades resemble. The sense that hands are the point where an internal force may cut at others has been waiting in the air since the beautiful fair girl's 'hands like mother-of-pearl seemed luminous, transparent, as if the secret were burning visible in them'.

That secret was linked with phosphorescence, with the sea, and thence with the underworld of the dance. But now another kind of electricity, the 'dark impure magnetism', is being exerted by Skrebensky. The force he exerts on her orients her towards hostility. He 'appropriates' her in the dance again, and part of her enjoys it:

> Always present, like a soft weight upon her, bearing her down [....] the weight of him sinking, settling upon her, overcoming her life and energy, [....] she felt his hands pressing behind her, upon her. [...] She liked the dance: it eased her, put her into a sort of trance [....] She received all the force of his power. She even wished he might overcome her. She was cold and unmoved as a pillar of salt. (297: 9–23)

There she is: Lot's wife, the turned-aside, the resistant woman, the glittering white pillar. She has been waiting, behind the images of phosphorescence. Salt is corrosive, coldly burning. That parallel too was first made in *The Trespasser*.

There is now an unconscious battle of wills between them, as there had been in the harvesting scene with Anna and Will, but more dangerous. Skrebensky's greater weakness makes him more oppressively demanding:

If he could only compel her. He seemed to be annihilated. She was cold and hard and compact of brilliance as the moon itself, and beyond him as the moonlight was beyond him, never to be grasped or known. [....]

So they danced four or five dances [....] always his will becoming more tense [....] And still he had not got her, she was hard and bright as ever, intact. But he must weave himself round her, enclose her, enclose her in a net of shadow, of darkness, so she would be a bright creature gleaming in a net of shadows, caught. Then he would have her, he would enjoy her. (297: 25–35)

We are back underwater. He is now a predator, she a prey, a fish in his net, in the overt image and his sense of the contest. But under the surface 'hard and bright as ever, intact' carries on the theme in 'cold and hard and compact of brilliance as the moon itself' and links the moon and the virgin Diana – so he may become Actaeon. As they walk together after the dance,

> She was bright as a piece of moonlight, as bright as a steel blade, he seemed to be clasping a blade that hurt him. (297: 39–298:1)

Then the full power of the moonlight bursts on him:

> he saw, with something like terror, the great new stacks of corn glistening and gleaming transfigured, silvery and present under the night-blue sky, throwing dark, substantial shadows [....] She, like glimmering gossamer, seemed to burn among them, as they rose like cold fires to the silvery-bluish air. All was intangible, a burning of cold, glimmering, whitish-steely fires. He was afraid of the great moon-conflagration [....] His heart grew smaller, it began to fuse like a bead. He knew he would die. (298: 3–12)

The sea-phosphorescence has become this dry night-fire, but the image of fusing[7] is carried over, and it is he who is melting down in the furnace to a single bead. The moon intensifies her mood:

> She seemed a beam of gleaming power. She was afraid of what she was. Looking at him, at his shadowy, unreal, wavering presence a sudden lust seized her, to lay hold of him and tear him and make him into nothing. (298: 14–17)

[7]BEF, index: fuse, fused, fusing; BEPW, index: phosphorescence.

She is Diana with her hounds; he has seen her naked sea-anemone self, and now 'Her hands and wrists felt immeasurably hard and strong, like blades' – the compass point transformed. But her way of destroying him is to seem to submit: 'She tempted him. [. . . .] Let him try what he could do.'

> And temerously, his hands went over her, over the salt, compact brilliance of her body. If he could but have her, how he would enjoy her! If he could but net her brilliant, cold, salt-burning body in the soft iron of his own hands, net her, capture her, hold her down, how madly he would enjoy her. [. . .] And always she was burning and brilliant and hard as salt, and deadly. Yet obstinately, all his flesh burning and corroding, as if he were invaded by some consuming and scathing poison, still he persisted. (298: 27–35)

The reader, lost in the swirl of imagery, may be reassured by some literal interpretations: the girl in her pale dress, in the bright moonlight, may well seem to burn in a frosty fire, and her ultimate coldness towards the man, her elusiveness even under his hands may make her seem slippery, like a fish. But the insistence on the corrosiveness of salt, so that even his 'soft iron' hands are at risk comes from Lawrence's myth-making. (Shakespeare's too: this is the 'sea change', now such a cliché, given its original power. What for Shakespeare may be 'rich and strange' is for Lawrence corrupted and deformed.)

The presences here: Lot's wife, Diana-Aphrodite, the sense that the phosphorescent foam of faery seas condenses into salt that corrodes soft iron, are not powers Skrebensky is conscious of, even if his internal processes are moved on by them. For us as for him they lurk in the imagery which Lawrence gives us. Indeed, how conscious Lawrence was himself in the writing is a question; I am sure he did not work these things out as quasi-logical sequences, but he could hardly be unaware that he was repeating, developing and combining images he had used elsewhere. But it was his method to accept what came unbidden, and this is, repeatedly, what comes. Certainly, he must have been contemplating, indeed intending, Skrebensky's dependent weakness, which here takes the complicated form of would-be possessiveness and sexual outgoing. He must also have been contrasting it with Will's more moderate weakness in the previous generation, and old Tom's strength. So he creates an imagery for what Skrebensky both invokes and fears, and it is thematic in *The Rainbow* – indeed in Lawrence's work as a whole.

What happens in that early scene foreshadows the ultimate destruction of Skrebensky by the same powers, incorporated in Ursula but given lethal force, at the end of their second affair. I quoted passages in a previous chapter: if one looks again at that sequence after re-reading this one, it becomes clear that at the climax Ursula, lying on her back on the sea-shore with Skrebensky on top of her, looks above him to the moon and is admitting the moon rather than him into her body – and he is half-aware of this rejection. A typology is involved, and in this first enactment was given its type:

> She took him in the kiss, hard her kiss seized upon him, hard and fierce and burning corrosive as the moonlight. She seemed to be destroying him. [...]
> But hard and fierce she had fastened upon him, cold as the moon and burning as a fierce salt. Till gradually his warm, soft iron yielded, yielded, and she was there fierce, corrosive, seething with his destruction, seething like some cruel corrosive salt around the last substance of his being, destroying him, destroying him in the kiss. And her soul crystallised with triumph, and his soul was dissolved with agony and humiliation. (299: 1–11)

The difference between the two occasions (apart from the fact that, this first time, there is no actual union) is that here she comes to herself, dissociates herself from her other 'burning corrosive self', is indeed shocked at herself, and becomes kind. 'She would bring him back from the dead [....] And she restored the whole shell of him. [...] But the core was gone.' It is a desperate attempt, by being 'nice', to cancel out what she is half-ashamed to find has happened, has burst out of her; and it doesn't really work. A shell is something empty found on the beach when the tide is out; also the discarded covering of a nut, as the core is the seed-part of a fruit.

There is a grim postlude:

> They went home through the night that was all pale and glowing around, with shadows and glimmerings and presences. Distinctly, she saw the flowers in the hedge-bottoms, she saw the thin, raked sheaves flung white upon the thorny hedge.
> How beautiful, how beautiful it was! She thought with anguish how wildly happy she was tonight, since he had kissed her. But as he walked with his arm round her waist, she turned with a great offering of herself to the night that glistened tremendous, a magnificent godly

moon white and candid as a bridegroom, flowers silvery and transformed filling up the shadows. (300: 22–31)

To 'turn' like that to the divinity is to reveal her true affinity, nothing to do with the man. It points forward to that final ecstasy on the sand, under the moon again, where she repeats and brings to conclusion the destructive process while seeming to give herself utterly to the man. The invitation or command on that second occasion comes when

> Suddenly, cresting the heavy, sandy pass, Ursula lifted her head and shrank back, momentarily frightened. There was a great whiteness confronting her, the moon was incandescent as a round furnace door, out of which came the high blast of moonlight, over the seaward half of the world, a dazzling terrifying glare of white light. They shrank back for a moment into shadow, uttering a cry. He felt his chest laid bare, where the secret was heavily hidden. He felt himself fusing down to nothingness, like a bead that rapidly disappears in an incandescent flame. (443: 30–8)

The furnace is not only the Biblical one with the three unscathed heroes. It is now inflected by the 'flux', the 'fusing' in the dance-scene, where once before Skrebensky felt fused down to a bead: for it is his nature which contains the dross, and is reduced to no more than this. Ursula's response, however, is to cry 'How wonderful! How wonderful!'

> The sands were as ground silver, the sea moved in solid brightness, coming towards them, and she went to meet the advance of the flashing buoyant water. He stood behind her, encompassed,[8] a shadow ever dissolving.
>
> 'I want to go,' she cried, in a strong dominant voice. 'I want to go.'
>   He saw the moonlight on her face, so she was like metal, he heard her ringing metallic voice, like the voice of a harpy to him.
>
> 'I want to go,' she cried again, in the high, hard voice, like the scream of gulls.
>   'Where?' he asked.
>   'I don't know.' (444: 3–24)

---

[8] The word conveys his being contained, subverted, and looks back to the compass-point in the dance-scene.

She is, in the other sense, possessed. The final 'I want to go' – is it aspiration, despair, bafflement? all three. As for the voice of the harpy, we are approaching a strange area of misogynistic dread in Lawrence's writing, which has its origin at this period, and in later works is morbid. In their final love-making on the sand 'full under the moonshine' Ursula destroys Skrebensky, in a way more ruthless than any verbal rejection could be. The terms in which this destruction is carried out flow from the word 'harpy':

> Then there, in the great flare of light, she clinched hold of him, hard, as if suddenly she had the strength of destruction, she fastened her arms round him and tightened him in her grip, whilst her mouth sought his in a hard, rending, ever-increasing kiss, till his body was powerless in her grip, his heart melted in fear from the fierce, beaked, harpy's kiss [....] She seemed unaware, she seemed to be pressing in her beaked mouth till she had the heart of him. Then, at last, she drew away and looked at him – looked at him. He knew what she wanted. (444: 27–36)

She insists on being taken 'full under the moonshine. She lay motionless, with wide-open eyes looking at the moon.' Afterwards,

> He seemed to swoon. It was a long time before he came to himself. He was aware of an unusual motion of her breast. He looked up. Her face lay like an image in the moonlight, the eyes wide open, rigid. But out of the eyes, slowly, there rolled a tear, that glittered in the moonlight as it ran down her cheek.
>   He felt as if the knife were being pushed into his already dead body [....] he watched [....] the unaltering, rigid face like metal in the moonlight, the fixed unseeing eyes, in which slowly the water gathered, shook with glittering moonlight, then, surcharged, brimmed over and ran trickling, a tear with its burden of moonlight, into the darkness, to fall in the sand. (445: 9–20)

He plunges away, from this 'motionless, eternal face' and that phrase crystallises what has happened. She has, for him, perhaps for herself, *become* the moon to which she has offered herself. It is an intensification of the experience of Siegmund in *The Trespasser*, who also turned to his lover and found her face white and empty as the moon. That was a passing impression, however deep and disconcerting; but what has happened now seems like a total annihilation of the man by a woman dedicated to a female otherness. As Skrebensky plunges away from her in horror, the word that is repeated six times in the narrative is not now 'dark' or 'darkness' but 'moonlight'.[9] It is as if Ursula has metamorphosed, become this alien power projecting its equivocal or hostile light. This is the projection of Skrebensky's desperation: his breakdown now is the counterpart of hers in the final chapter.

There was from the beginning a vein of misogyny in Lawrence: more exactly a fear of the power of women and a sense of the relative weakness of modern men. The whole drive of *The Rainbow* is that Ursula becomes the transmitter into the future of strengths which her father and lover do not have, although in the past the Brangwen men had been one pillar of the family arch. These fearful night-scenes make one ask whether that female power is also seen as destructive – the power of Aphrodite, or Diana, the corrosive salt born of the phosphorescent sea.

One answer is that in these moonlight scenes the perception of the moon is first Anna's and then Ursula's, and that of Anna and Ursula is Will's and then Skrebensky's. These are all projections, covering the defeat and retreat of weak men who cannot match a strong woman. That is true, but not the whole truth. If the scenes are taken together, the last is seen to fulfil the promise, or threat, of the first, and it is Lawrence who in the last is projecting both Skrebensky's projection and Ursula's as a fulfilment of his own similar indications in the first. It looks like his intention; there are moments in which the balance tips, and one would support this by pointing to later developments of the imagery, especially the beaked harpy's mouth, which I, like others, find morbid.

These images come from a personal store, and if they are not analysed or controlled they carry with them more of the user-source, tell more, than that person is conscious of. However, the source, the poet who is visited by these powers can, as they pass by, interrogate them. Lawrence did, at least at times. One effect of the division of the original *Sisters* and *Wedding Ring* into *The Rainbow* and *Women in Love* is that the final moonlit scene now occurs in the second novel, in the chapter pointedly called 'Moony'. There the Lawrence-figure Birkin, not present in *The Rainbow*, is a modern male self-consciousness trying

---

[9]It may now seem that the scene of their consummation, that 'dark windy night in March', is a success because there is no moon, so they can both give themselves to the darkness – for that moment their shared realm. Cf. the bathing-scene with Winifred Inger.

to find a good relationship with the chosen mate – Ursula in her later manifestation. She comes upon him one night obsessively throwing stones at the reflected image of the moon in a pond, and finding it constantly re-forming after his managing to dissipate it.

The action expresses something he is bringing towards consciousness. Equally clearly it conveys that the obsession is a projection – literally as well as psychologically, for it is the reflection rather than the moon itself that he is trying to disperse by projecting stones at it, and he cannot succeed, and knows it. He is telling us and himself something about himself. He calls the moon the 'accursed Syria Dea' – and that is Cybele or Astarte (ancestors of Aphrodite and Diana). In coming out with the formula he is saying, 'This is what I choose to identify the moon with, this is the power I fear, and why I am performing this action, which cannot succeed, except in so far as it conveys and relieves my feelings.'

This is a movement towards self-consciousness, and the scene suggests that this movement is required by Lawrence himself as an outcome, a product of the two-novel sequence. Ursula, aware that she is the implied target, gently persuades Birkin to stop. This is something they have to work out in their life together, if they decide to marry.

That lies in the future at the end of the book: as at the end of *The Rainbow*, it is left open, and the second novel may seem more hopeful because of this consciousness. Yet one reflects that for Lawrence consciousness was the problem as much as the solution. It would be no help if those for whom the moon seems to want to know something have been succeeded by those who think they know both the question and the answer.

Lawrence's parable tells its own tale: the image on the pond surface will always re-form. No good throwing stones: or even knowing why one is doing that: one must turn away, or change, which in Lawrence's terms means to become the next phase of oneself. The different Ursula of *Women in Love* at the beginning of this scene feels uneasy in the moonlight, as something she does not wish to be associated with; she does not feel an affinity or allegiance; and after Birkin's onslaught on the image she feels 'she had fallen to the ground, and was spilled out, like water on the earth' (WL 248: 7–8). Siegmund in *The Trespasser* used the same image. However, Birkin turns to Ursula and tells her that what he wants her to give him is 'that golden light which is you – which you don't know' (249: 30). That could only be the sun. It seems a lot to ask for, but at least it is not the moon.

9
England My England

England my England, published in the United States in 1922 and in England in 1924, collects the short stories written between July 1913 and July 1919. It exemplifies the points made in the opening chapter in interesting ways: some of the texts as we have them today, especially the title-story, derive from an extensive revision in January 1922, the very end of the period. On the other hand, 'The Mortal Coil', added to the Cambridge edition, was written in October 1913 and for some reason not collected. Dealing with the peace-time life of German army officers in garrison towns, it feels as if it had strayed from its companions in *The Prussian Officer*. It provides a link between the two collections and so between the pre-War and post-War worlds. Reading it alongside the title-story, 'England my England', reveals an unexpected affinity.

During the War period in which these stories were written, Lawrence was also drafting and re-drafting the 'Sisters' project, which became *The Rainbow*, with its distinct pre-War, and *Women in Love*, with its generalised post-War feeling, finally published in England in 1921. The point in treating this collection between the two novels is that it links the two worlds.

'England my England' is a wry allusion to the famous poem by Henley, usually read as celebratory, even jingoistic. As Lawrence uses it, the tone comes across as complex – part-sad, part-mocking, part-angry. In the story which leads into the volume, supplies its title and controls its tone, it is like an obituary. A lot is implied about a whole way of life pre-War. In most stories in the volume there is some echo of the War, and also this strange complexity of tone.

It is an interesting thought that the most important first-hand accounts of the conflict in 1914–18, the best renderings in fiction, took ten years to appear: it is as if the fighting men needed that time to come out of shock and collect their thoughts. What Lawrence reports in 1922 is a different kind of evidence, from the Home Front, as it was called. But it is in various ways significant, and prepares us for *Women in Love*. For instance, some stories deal with men who have returned from, or escaped, the fighting. Three deal with men wounded in action. Several deal with the effect of the separation of war on marriages, on the changed role of women – and the inability of men to handle the change. Only the title-story touches on the actual fighting.

'England my England'

This master-story also shows how crucial revision could be. If it had remained in the form of its first writing in June and rapid publication in the *English Review* in October 1915, one might pass over it briefly as an embarrassment. On re-reading it, this becomes a superficial reaction: looking at it again after reading the revised version of 1921–22, one sees how some things were developed later; also how the weakness (the unreality of the action at the front) is drastically curtailed.

The first form is given in an appendix in the Cambridge edition: a mere dozen pages, like an old-fashioned adventure-story for male readers of a magazine like *Blackwood's* or *The Wide World*. It culminates in a scene which might have led to an official citation or headline: 'Heroic wounded officer kills three enemy officers before being brutally finished off.' Yet this action, even on a first reading, is conveyed in a depressive mode leaving the reader cast down. When one looks for the reason, it seems to be that the story has as its centre a sad lucidity. One notices it first as the state of the wounded man returning to consciousness, becoming aware of his wounds and his situation, seeing the Germans come on the scene and deftly picking them off.

If you turn back a page or two, you see that he has the same lucidity in France before the final action, and this suggests a depressive condition. This is shown to have its origin in the first pages, back in peace-time England. So the lonely soldier was a casualty before he reached the front, and the trance in which he lies wounded, thinks at first of his wife and children as on the side of life, and then turns, still lucid, to the side of death – this is the culmination of his life. In joining the army he has become, in Shakespeare's phrase, absolute for death. For Lawrence he represents all the decent but unsatisfied men who acquiesced in – half-wanted – the slaughter which took them out of a life in which they could not manage to be happy.

The first draft has two numbered parts: the initial description of the old house and garden in England, in which Evelyn (as he is there called) looks as if he is happily working because it is a refuge 'filled forever with peace and sunshine and loveliness'. This is a backward-looking dream-picture; it becomes clear that the dream is clung to against the reality of a marriage in which there is tension between man and wife. This seems to be about his ineffectuality, his unwillingness to enter the world of work and provide more money for the family, and his dependence on his prosperous father-in-law.

The accident which cripples the favourite daughter (she 'fell on a sharp old iron in the garden') has the effect that the 'the distance was finally unsheathed between the parents' – the word unsheathed making the link between the accident, its cause in his ineffectuality (cannot even pick things up which might cause accidents) and the life it injures. In the second part, the War breaks out and seems to offer a solution. Evelyn volunteers, his wife Winifred is impressed, even sexually stirred, by this movement into 'life' – except that it is into death. The transition is summed up:

> He was really a soldier. His soul had accepted the significance. He was a potential destructive force, ready to be destroyed [....] What had he to do with love and the creative side of life? He had a right to his own satisfaction. He was a destructive spirit entering into destruction. (EME 225: 35–9)

A substantial point is made here, which is not weakened, as the end is, by remoteness from the actual experience (Lawrence had to imagine everything, didn't even know what a machine-gun was, and used the term inappropriately). Pre-War civilian life in twentieth-century England, and how it might be blighted at the core, was his preoccupation, and the sense that the War provided a way out for many was a tragic perception.

Even so, the final draft showed that that insight had come too easily. The six or seven opening pages of the first draft were strikingly expanded, so that the eventual death in France is reduced to some three pages out of a total of twenty-eight, and the culminating false heroics are eliminated: Egbert, as he is re-named, to imply an Old-Englishness which chimes with that of the cottage, kills nobody. On the other hand, the home life in 'the old Hampshire cottage that crouched near the earth amid flowers' is given an extended contemplation in which the simplicities of the first draft become complexities. It is a remarkable piece of writing: retrospective, analytical, summating, almost essayistic, yet making the ensuing narrative profound.

Though it was striking, the basic diagnosis in the first version had been too univocal. And the Lawrence doing the later revision may have recognised that the course of his own life from 1915 to 1919 had taken him too close to his protagonist's position for simple rejection. He could say of himself what he says of the re-named Egbert, reacting against war-hysteria and finding it hard to join the nation. He foreshadows Birkin in *Women in Love*:

> He had, however, the one deepest pure-bred instinct. He recoiled inevitably from having his feelings dictated to him by the mass feeling. His feelings were his own, his understanding was his own, and he would never go back on either, willingly. (27: 38–28:1)

> The deterrent was, the giving himself over into the power of other men, and into the power of the mob-spirit of a democratic army. (28: 25–7)

So when he has joined up:

> In the ugly intimacy of the camp his thoroughbred sensibilities were just degraded. But he had chosen, so he accepted. An ugly little look came on to his face, of a man who has accepted his own degradation. (29: 23–26)

Egbert is now less a case, more a person. That unique aspect is developed in the long opening section, which presents the pre-War history of the family.

It has been a distraction that the story seemed to have been based on the life and death of Perceval Drewett Lucas, his wife Madeline Meynell and the Meynell family of Greatham, where Lawrence was living in 1915, and which provides the setting. The analogies with these 'real-life' circumstances, as in the case of Ottoline Morrell, the original of Hermione Roddice in *Women in Love*, though obvious and striking are also adventitious. Being merely real, they gave Lawrence something to re-imagine, but are not significant beyond providing that stimulus. But then again, humanly speaking, people don't like to be used that way.

I doubt if there was any deep parallel between Lucas and Egbert, especially by 1921. On the other hand, between the two drafts Lawrence had been working on *The Rainbow* and *Women in Love*; so the true parallels and contrasts are with his own Will Brangwen, especially in his newly-married trance with Anna in their cottage; with the unsatisfied soldier Anton Skrebensky; with Gerald Crich and his father the kindly industrialist; with Rupert Birkin, who like Egbert has a small private income and cannot give himself to meaningless work in a society he has no faith in. And finally there are the young upper-middle-class people whom Rupert and Gerald associate with in London and country houses. They are all embodiments of 'England, My England'. The old cottage itself should be seen as Lawrence's Howards End, and Winifred's family as the rethought equivalent of Forster's Wilcoxes. *The Rainbow* had massively come up to the problem of living in the English social scheme post-1900 – how to fit in – whether one should even try. Egbert is the representative who won't try, and is unhappy.

What in *Howards End* was the crude contrast between Wilcoxes and Schlegels, where the marriage between Henry Wilcox and Margaret Schlegel is supposed to 'connect' two irreconcilable opposites, here becomes the more subtle coming together of the family of Godfrey Marshall, the successful and sympathetic businessman, and Egbert, who represents the intellectual wing of the southern upper-middle class. The marriage to Winifred Marshall really does connect two elements. One is the Chaucerian Franklin, Godfrey:

> At home he kept the hard head out of sight, and played at poetry and romance with his literary wife and his sturdy, passionate girls. He was a man of courage, not given to complaining, bearing his burdens by himself [....] He himself, with his tough old barbarian fighting spirit, had an almost child-like delight in verse [....] and in the delightful game of a cultured home. His blood was strong even to coarseness. But that only made the home more vigorous, more robust and Christmassy. There was always a touch of Christmas about him, now he was well off. (7: 20–30)

The other element is older, southern, finer:

> Well then, into this family came Egbert. He was made of quite a different paste. The girls and their father were strong-limbed, thick-blooded people, true English, as holly-trees and hawthorn are

English. Their culture was grafted on to them, as one might perhaps graft a common pink rose on to a thorn-stem. It flowered oddly enough, but it did not alter their blood.
And Egbert was a born rose. (7: 33–9)

This hybridisation is taking place in Lawrence's Howards End:

> The flame of their two bodies burnt again into that old cottage, that was haunted already by so much by-gone, physical desire. You could not be in the dark room for an hour without the influences coming over you. The hot blood-desire of by-gone yeomen, there in this old den where they had lusted and bred for so many generations. The silent house, dark, with thick, timbered walls and the big black chimney-place, and the sense of secrecy. Dark, with low, little windows, sunk into the earth. Dark, like a lair where strong beasts had lurked [....] It seemed to cast a spell on the two young people. They became different [....] They too felt that they did not belong to the London world any more. Crockham had changed their blood (8: 13–27)

There are reminiscences here of *Twilight in Italy* (the 'lair' in the church of San Tommaso), but much more of *The Rainbow* (the word 'dark' begins to be overused). That note, somewhat overdone, contrasts with the analytical clarity about Egbert's life:

> He had about a hundred and fifty pounds a year of his own – and nothing else but his very considerable personal atttractions. He had no profession: he earned nothing. But he talked of literature and music, he had a passion for old folk-music, collecting folk-songs and folk-dances, studying the Morris-dance and the old customs. Of course in time he would make money in these ways. (7: 10–16)

Lawrence has caught in a few casual sentences a way of English life. Here, in miniature, are the genuine innovators like Vaughan Williams and Cecil Sharp; the genuine talents like Ivor Gurney; and the diminishing band of followers like Heseltine and Cecil Gray, whom Lawrence knew – plus all the dilettantes 'tampering with the arts' as he devastatingly says. It is a part of the whole he is recording, and goes with the Georgian poetry that lingered on into the 1930s.

An un-Forsterlike implication of Lawrence's account is that it is the father-in-law's family that is really of the old England: the acquired culture is grafted on to them. Egbert's 'fatal three pounds a week' keeps him from coming to grips with life. But things are more complex than that:

> He was of a subtle, sensitive, passionate nature. But he simply would not give himself to what Winifred called life, *Work*. No, he would not go into the world and work for money. (12: 18–20)

Winifred has a point, but life is not *Work*. Lawrence knows that; and begins to move away from Winifred's point of view:

> If he had been weak Winifred would have been kind to him. But he did not even give her that consolation. He was not weak, and he did not want her consolation or her kindness. No thank you. He was of a fine passionate temper, and of a rarer steel than she. He knew it, and she knew it. (13: 21–6)

The strain on the marriage is sharply increased by the accident to the child, where the actual drama of the story suddenly unfolds, replacing this analysis, and the stalemate is given its false resolution by the outbreak of war and Egbert's volunteering.

> At the end of the summer he went to Flanders, into action. He seemed to have already gone out of life, beyond the pale of life. (30: 24–5)

The end follows in a couple of pages. What in the first version was a striking but simple perception remains a tribute to the dead multitude, but is more tragic because an individualised case is more subtly conveyed.

'The Mortal Coil'

If one has taken the intention and force of 'England My England', a charge of significance is transferred to 'The Mortal Coil'. Just as the first story seems on a first reading, in the initial draft especially, to be a men's magazine story gone morbid, so the other at first seems no more than a curious incident, what French newspapers call a *fait divers*, lending itself to another headline summary: German officer thinks he may have to kill himself, finds that his mistress and friend have died in his apartment by accident: one of Life's Little Ironies, and once again a popular kind of story in magazines (several of the stories start off with this kind of commercial appeal).

Like the others, it has a serious point, which relates it to the story of Egbert, the English middle-class semi-intellectual dilettante, his relationship with the family he has married into, and the world which wants him to 'do something' when he doesn't want to, since he sees through mindless activity. What is involved is more than class-consciousness, but starts there. One should call it an ethos, that of a caste. It is as if Lawrence is an ethnographer, looking in this case at the German minor aristocracy and officer class (Frieda's people) and in the other at the tension between the effective English entrepreneur and the well-bred upper class which was more content to 'be' than to 'do', but found that in 1914–18 the question was 'to be or not to be'.

Evelyn/Egbert commits a form of suicide by joining the army, which solves his problem. The young Baron Fritz Friedeburg is an officer in peace-time (like Anton Skrebensky). The army is one profession his class finds acceptable socially, especially younger sons not occupied with running estates. The first pages of the story establish that he has a crisis. He has been gambling: his class does that. Unfortunately he cannot pay his gambling debts: his class is supposed either to be rich or not to lose. Since he cannot pay, the code of the class determines that he has acted dishonourably, so he must resign his commission. This would face him, like Egbert, with the need either to take a civilian job, which he feels is a humiliation, a negation of his caste, or to kill himself.

One might say, now, that this is an antiquated code, and unreal. But one of the points made by both stories is that what is bred into you, your caste-formation, is, for you, more real than what the rest of the world thinks real, or what twenty-first-century rationalism thinks reasonable. It may express you perfectly.

On the other hand, the point of view of 'life' is well put by the beautiful and vital young actress-mistress Marta, vividly portrayed in the opening paragraph in her red silk dress. Yet her challenge is well met:

'And so you're done for, for three thousand marks?' she exclaimed, jeering at him. 'You go pretty cheap.'

'Three thousand – and the rest,' he said, keeping up a manly *sang froid*.

'And the rest!' she repeated in contempt. 'And for three thousand – and the rest, your life is over!'

'My career,' he corrected her.

> 'Oh,' she mocked, 'only your career! I thought it was a matter of life and death. Only your career? Oh, only that!'
> His eyes grew furious under her mockery.
> 'My career *is* my life,' he said.
> 'Oh, is it! – You're not a *man* then, you are only a career?'
> 'I am a gentleman.'
> 'Oh, are you! How amusing! How very amusing, to be a gentleman and not a man! – I suppose that's what it means, to be a gentleman, to have no guts outside your career?'
> 'Outside my honour – none.'
> 'And might I ask what *is* your honour?' She spoke in extreme irony.
> 'Yes, you may ask,' he replied coolly. 'But if you don't know without being told, I'm afraid I could never explain it.' (174: 20–40)

The argument continues. He points out that he can shoot himself – or become a waiter or a clerk, but won't do that 'because it wouldn't become me'. She looks at him and has to agree, but thinks he can somehow land on his feet like a cat.

> But this was just what he was not. He was not like a cat. His self-mistrust was too deep. Ultimately he had no belief in himself, as a separate isolated being. He knew he was sufficiently clever, an aristocrat, good-looking, the sensitive superior of most men. The trouble was, that apart from the social fabric he belonged to, he felt himself nothing, a cipher. (175: 25–30)

Lawrence has made a crucial point. This was the Skrebensky case as well as the Egbert case: for Skrebensky as for this other Baron Fritz, there was before 1917 no political mass-collective into which they could pay their 'cipher' and be among the other zeros in the mass. Lawrence makes the further point:

> The free indomitable self-sufficient being which a man must be in his relationship to a woman who loves him – this he could pretend. But he knew he was not it. He knew that the world of man from which he took his values was his mistress beyond any woman. He wished, secretly, cravingly, almost cravenly, in his heart, it was not so. But so it was. (175: 37–176: 2)

Careless readers often reach for Nietzschean or 'Leadership principle' clichés about Lawrence, but it is to misread. This is the obverse or followership-principle, and Lawrence is against it, as these stories demonstrate. Egbert finds he is against the 'mob-spirit of a democratic army', which is his virtue, but he couldn't manage the previous life either, without his father-in-law's money. He is 'fine' to no effect. As officers Skrebensky and Fritz can manage; but are hopeless against the social pressures which they would feel outside the army. They too are 'fine' to no purpose. They do not have the essential 'free indomitable self-sufficient being' which can withstand the pressure of a system – or its absence.

Fritz Friedeburg has the stultified self-knowledge, the depressive lucidity, of Egbert. He knows what he is, and has a respect for it which prevents him doing or being what other people press him to do or be for practical reasons. This is what it means to belong to a caste. But it is not enough to belong and be defined by the caste, especially when you find that you cannot live either as the caste requires or as others suggest, and you don't have self-possession in the real sense postulated by the girl:

> '[. . . .] What am I without my pride?'
> 'You are *yourself*,' she said. 'If they take your uniform off you, and turn you naked into the street, you are still *yourself*.' (177: 27–30)

The title of the story comes from Hamlet's 'To be or not to be' – the soliloquy of the potential suicide. The 'mortal coil' is not just active noisy life, but the things which coil round you as constrictions: they have to be shuffled off as you shuffle off. Fritz's silent moment enacting Hamlet's speech also enacts one of Lawrence's central images:

> He sat staring in front of him, a dull numbness settled on his brain. He was watching the flame of the candle. And, in his detachment, he realized the flame was a swiftly travelling flood, flowing swiftly from the source of the wick through a white surge and on into the darkness above. It was like a fountain suddenly foaming out, then running on dark and smooth. Could one dam the flood? He took a piece of paper, and cut off the flame a second. (177: 13–19)

One can say, he has contemplated suicide for a moment ('Put out the light, and then put out the light . . .' comes to mind also). The flame cut off is life cut off. But that does no justice to the whole figure, the unconsciousness of the gesture, and the sense of life as flame. The interruption does not cause the flow to cease.

The next day Fritz carries out his duties with his platoon, marching into the country on manoeuvres. Lawrence conveys his commitment to the automatism of service life, and under it the determined despair. At the end of the day, returning to his private fate, he finds that Marta and her friend have been asphyxiated in his apartment – a sheer accident caused by fumes from the stove. The bodies are being taken away, a police officer has to interview him about the deaths. Lawrence brings the story to a close with a seemingly dismissive or cursory paragraph; it half-hides the real point of the story: faced with this actual accidental death, cutting off a person who was in her vividness an embodiment of life, his previous life seeming all the more to be unreal, his suicide would have the same unreality. So, as he answers the policeman's offficial questions,

> Friedeburg continued to answer. This was the end of him. The quick of him was pierced and killed. The living dead answered the living dead in obscene antiphony. Question and answer continued, the note-book worked as the hand of the old dead wrote in it the replies of the young who was dead. (189: 20–4)

If you are already dead, why kill yourself? But then again, why not?

'The Blind Man'

'The Blind Man' could also be said to be about death in life, but raises the possibility of a resurrection: both states are metaphorical, and both deepened by tacit Biblical allusions. It is a subtle story, conducted by descriptive and narrative touches which seem prosaic or naturalistic. It opens with Isabel Pervin awaiting one November evening the arrival of her 'oldest and dearest friend' Bertie Reid, who is visiting her and her husband for the first time. There had been no previous visit because the two men were deeply incompatible. But her husband Maurice, at home, having been blinded in France, has suggested a visit. Her tension now is deftly conveyed: she is listening for the sounds of the arrival of Bertie and her husband's movements – much as a blind person might listen. A page or two of retrospect describes the life together of the blind man and the wife – 'peaceful with the almost incomprehensible peace of immediate contact in darkness'. The last word carries three significances: this November evening and night is dark; the blind man lives in darkness, but is happy in it for reasons which are developed; and 'darkness' is, we know from *The Rainbow*, an active state complementary to the light of day. It is conveyed as Maurice's realm, and in the course of the story both Isabel and Bertie find themselves going out into the dark to the farm buildings behind the house, where Maurice is contentedly working in his treble darkness, somewhat like old Tom Brangwen. They have to approximate his state, or come up to the border of his realm. Is it disability, or something better than normality? Does he have a knowledge to give?

In the first paragraph, it is said that Maurice 'had a disfiguring mark on his brow' possibly a reference to Cain: has Maurice like all soldiers said 'Am I my brother's keeper?' and been told 'The voice of thy brother's blood crieth unto me from the ground, and the LORD set a mark on Cain, lest any finding him should kill him'. The distinction marks him out, or sets him aside, as special.

In the climactic scene outside in the dark the blind man and Bertie make contact, literally. Maurice has asked, since he can't see himself and doesn't like to ask Isabel, who will tell him something comforting, 'Is my face much disfigured?' Bertie replies that the disfigurement is more pitiable than shocking. Then this happens:

'Do you mind if I touch you?'
 The lawyer shrank away instinctively. And yet, out of very philanthropy, he said, in a small voice: 'Not at all.'
 But he suffered as the blind man stretched out a strong, naked hand to him. Maurice accidentally knocked off Bertie's hat.
 'I thought you were taller,' he said, starting. Then he laid his hand on Bertie Reid's head, closing the dome of the skull in a soft, firm grasp, gathering it, as it were; then, shifting his grasp and softly closing again, with a fine close pressure, till he had covered the skull and the face of the smaller man, tracing the brows, and touching the full, closed eyes [....] He seemed to take him in, in the soft, travelling grasp.
 'Your head seems tender [....]' Maurice repeated [....] 'Touch my eyes, will you? – touch my scar.'
 Now Bertie quivered with revulsion. Yet he was under the power of the blind man, as if hypnotised. He lifted his hand, and laid the fingers on the scar, on the scarred eyes. Maurice suddenly covered them with his own hand, pressed the fingers of the other man upon his disfigured eye-sockets, trembling in every fibre [....]
 Then suddenly Maurice removed the hand of the other man from his brow, and stood holding it in his own.

'Oh, my God,' he said, 'we shall know each other now, shan't we? We shall know each other now.' (61: 38–62: 27)

It is an extraordinary imagining, both as drama, as human understanding, and in the way it is worked out in detail. And one feels the New Testament typologies as very active. One of them is an inversion of the Scriptural originals – the Gospel scenes where Christ restores the blind to sight by touching their eyes. Now the miracle is that the power-figure is himself blind, but is trying to restore a spiritually incapacitated man to something deeper than sight. The incapacitated man is also a doubting Thomas, but is *made* to touch the saviour's wound, and is horrified because he cannot bear to touch or be touched. So the Cain figure, reserved for God's purposes, who has gone through his crucifixion in Flanders, has it in him to be a resurrected Messiah – but only to those who can... perhaps the phrase is 'really see'.

The story has its doctrinal Lawrentian point. He said explicitly in a number of places that sight is a dominating faculty, too close to the conceptualising tendencies of the consciousness, and the adjunct of all rationalising. The essence of sight is that what is seen is other, but instantly transformed by the mind into known categories: when we say 'Ah, yes, I see' we often mean we have reduced the other to our terms. But touch is immediate and non-mental, the way in which we admit we don't know this thing, and need to grasp it.

The paradox is that Lawrence had the most acute visual sense of any writer – though it is true that he usually sees everything as if for the first time – and he deploys it in this story. We do vividly see his characters as they find their way through the triple darkness: but it is also a matter for them in the darkness of balancing, of hearing, of smelling, of 'sensing'. It is supremely so for the blind man himself, as he shaves himself, sits down at the table, eats his food. What he had with his wife at the very beginning of the story was summed up as 'immediate contact in darkness'. If you look back at the scene of the 'touching' the notations are equally complex, and here above all the touching or sensing is connected with something one is tempted to call 'knowledge' – but redefined.

However, the ending of the story is a silent comment on the parabolic happening. It has done wonders for Maurice, precisely because he can't see. Isabel can, and this is what she sees:

There seemed a curious elation about Maurice. Bertie was haggard, with sunken eyes.

'What is it?' she asked.

'We've become friends,' said Maurice, standing with his feet apart, like a strange colossus.

'Friends!' re-echoed Isabel. And she looked again at Bertie. He met her eyes with a furtive haggard look; his eyes were as if glazed with misery. (63: 6–14)

These references to eyes, especially to their meeting, make the blunt point that it is not an advantage to be blind: you may escape some traps that the sighted fall into by not really seeing what is before them, but also you don't see what they can. Sometimes it tells you a lot:

But she was watching Bertie. She knew that he had one desire – to escape from this intimacy, this friendship, which had been thrust upon him. He could not bear it that he had been touched by the blind man, his insane reserve broken in. He was like a mollusc whose shell is broken. (63: 20–4)

But then again, the 'mollusc whose shell is broken' is neither a visual image nor something which can be touched. It signals briefly Lawrence's apocalyptic vision in the years after 1915, triggered largely by the visit to Cambridge, the contact with Bertrand Russell (who seems to be lurking in the figure of this other Bertie) and the horror of the rationalising false apostles in his train. The hard shell which protects a little soft ego, and may transform into a clock going tick-tock, tick-tock, prompts the desire to step on it. The man blinded by the war, who can operate only by the other senses, especially touch, is saved from being a mollusc. Within a shell he could not operate humanly at all. But the sighted man, the social man, the intellectual friend, the man dedicated to being alone, stands for a class not broken down by the War, remaining insulated within the hard shell of a rationalising social self. My summary puts crudely what Lawrence renders delicately as drama and as parable.

'Hadrian'

This is a masterly story. In its setting and atmosphere it sketches the solidity and reality of a whole novel, as in the first parts of *The Lost Girl* and *Aaron's Rod*, with its examination of the class setting in a Midlands town. The family background: the defunct pottery business with the works adjoining the home, the dying father, the two sisters threatened with becoming old maids – this is conveyed with economy. We recognise also one of Lawrence's social themes: the young woman like Elsa Culverwell born into the prosperous shopkeeper class, and faced with the problem that if she marries, it must be 'beneath' her, since she has no social equals. We also recognise the 'two sisters' theme memorably treated in 'Daughters of the Vicar' or later in *Women in Love*. In this story Matilda and Emmie Rockley are facing the future, when their father is dead and they inherit his money: this wealth will make them untouchable (the word seems to come naturally).

One recognises, with more surprise, that to this theme Lawrence has added a reworking of the *Wuthering Heights* legend. Lawrence's Heathcliff is the charity boy Hadrian. Emily Brontë's old Mr Earnshaw, on business in Liverpool, decides to bring home and adopt the outcast child Heathcliff, and has to face the outraged reactions of his biological children – except that his daughter Catherine discovers an affinity with Heathcliff, which grows into a profound love. Something similar happens with Ted Rockley and Hadrian, 'an ordinary boy from a Charity Home, with ordinary brownish hair and ordinary bluish eyes and of ordinary rather cockney speech'.

The story is a working out of this situation and the outraged feeling it first caused. The War is a factor, in that the adult Hadrian had emigrated to Canada, but has joined up and come back to England, and so revisits the house. The essential part of the story recounts this visit, and Lawrence conveys the awkwardness of his arriving before he is expected, the at first contemptuous attitude of the sisters, which covers an intense excitement at seeing this new aspect of him, but is disguised as a rather dry way of putting him down.

The crucial scene occurs at night, 'near midnight' as Lawrence mildly specifies (the witching hour). Matilda, forgetting – the psychologically over-acute will smile – that Hadrian is sleeping there, goes to her father's room. She has been brooding over the situation and her feeling of anxiety about her future. 'Her mind seemed entranced', Lawrence says. 'At last she felt she must go to him.'

> It was near midnight. She went along the passage and to his room. There was a faint light from the moon outside. She listened at his door. Then she softly opened and entered. The room was faintly dark. She heard a movement on the bed.
> 'Are you asleep?' she said softly, advancing to the side of the bed.
> 'Are you asleep?' she repeated gently, as she stood at the side of the bed. And she reached her hand in the darkness to touch his

forehead. Delicately, her fingers met the nose and the eyebrows, she laid her fine, delicate hand on his brow. It seemed fresh and smooth – very fresh and smooth. A sort of surprise stirred her, in her entranced state. But it could not waken her. Gently, she leaned over the bed and stirred her fingers over the low-growing hair on his brow.

'Can't you sleep to-night?' she said.

There was a quick stirring in the bed. 'Yes, I can,' a voice answered. It was Hadrian's voice. She started away. Instantly, she was wakened from her late-at-night trance. She remembered that her father was downstairs, that Hadrian had his room. She stood in the darkness as if stung.

'Is that you, Hadrian?' she said. 'I thought it was my father.' She was so startled, so shocked, that she could not move. The young man gave an uncomfortable laugh, and turned in his bed.

At last she got out of the room. (99: 18–40)

The reader notices that there were two sleepers here. The phrases 'But it could not waken her ...' and 'Instantly she was wakened ...' suggest that she has been sleep-walking (perhaps for years?) The touch of the hand on the face, the surprise it creates in her, remind us of Jack Haseldine touching Mary Renshaw's face with his lips, and discovering the world, so to speak. It also re-works the situation in 'The Blind Man'. It is all delicately under-expressed, to suggest something which can be taken simply as an odd little experience, a strange chance. But strange chances wake people in more than one sense, as Hadrian's reaction shows:

Hadrian too slept badly. He had been awakened by the opening of the door, and had not realised what the question meant. But the soft, straying tenderness of her hand on his face startled something out of his soul. He was a charity boy, aloof and more or less at bay. The fragile exquisiteness of her caress startled him most, revealed unknown things to him. (100: 11–16)

As for Matilda, her pride makes her withdraw. 'Her hand had offended her, she wanted to cut it off.' However, the father resolves the situation – at first sight dictatorially and manipulatively – by threatening to alter his will in Hadrian's favour if Matilda does not marry him. This seems outrageous, except that the dying man actually facilitates the coming together which the chance touch foretold, but which embarrassment and social pride would normally prevent. There is a crucial conversation near the end:

> 'You don't want me then?' he said in his subtle, insinuating voice.
> 'I don't want to speak to you,' she said, averting her face.
> 'You put your hand on me, though,' he said. 'You shouldn't have done that, and then I should never have thought of it. You shouldn't have touched me.'
> 'If you were anything decent, you'd know that was a mistake, and forget it,' she said.
> 'I know it was a mistake – but I shan't forget it. If you wake a man up, he can't go to sleep again because he's told to.'
> 'If you had any decent feeling in you, you'd have gone away,' she replied.
> 'I didn't want to,' he replied. (106: 13–25)

It is an inversion of the sleeping beauty motif. Waking him, without meaning to, she has really wakened him, also without meaning to – and for that matter wakened herself. But since he is now really awake, he cannot dissemble.

> '[. . . .] Let us marry and go out to Canada – you might as well – you've touched me.'
> She was white and trembling. Suddenly she flushed with anger.
> 'It's so *indecent*,' she said.
> 'How?' he retorted. 'You touched me.' (106: 29–34)

'That same evening' she tells her father she will marry Hadrian, without explanation. It sounds irrational or forced by the inheritance, but is, properly considered, a true resolution. 'Properly considered' means, here as elsewhere in Lawrence, taken as profoundly figurative, indeed as parable. The dying father is able to say to Hadrian, 'Ay, my lad, I'm glad you're mine.' So the original adoption has become a real fatherhood.

The story has been known as 'You Touched Me', which was evidently appropriate. But it gets to the heart of the story too quickly and crudely, gives the point too easily, and Lawrence wanted to call it 'Hadrian', the name now adopted. As for the theme of touch, it is one of the great themes in Lawrence, and produces some of his greatest moments (we met it in 'The Blind Man'). This is one of the main ways in which people who cannot talk their way to each other – or prefer not to – nevertheless meet. No meeting can be more direct, and the implications go beyond what we could ever manage to say. The story shows this. There is also a complex cultural hinterland, especially the hint of a fairy-tale or miraculous transformation, as in the Gospels, where Christ touches or is touched. We remember that at the beginning Matilda and Emmie are compared to Mary and Martha, who in their contrasting ways waited on the Saviour. In her anguished reflection on the touch, Matilda uses the Biblical phrase about cutting off the offending hand. This is the hand which steals things or may not be allowed to be unclean, but the Song of Songs also points out that it is the hand used in making love. All this is delicately combined with the sleeping beauty tale, where the prince's kiss has become the princess's touch. It is also linked to those fairy-tales where the neglected step-child, poor apprentice or adopted orphan is transformed by a kiss, or performs the right action at the right moment, and marries the master's or the king's daughter.

This seemingly plain tale about graceless people of the kind Lawrence knew in his home town is a very delicate transformation of the ordinary and banal. It retains their vigour and plainness, which is a strength, but sheds a miraculous light on it. Given that in his fictions Lawrence persistently comes up to the frontier between the everyday and its transformation by a modern, though not a literalist, religious understanding, one might even say that he throws light on the New Testament. Bringing the dead to life is plainly a miracle if conceived literally. Bringing the living to life seems easier, but is rarely managed. It might be seen as a miracle: the figure of Lazarus can be taken for most people in their everyday death-in-life. This leads us straight to 'The Horse Dealer's Daughter'.

'The Horse Dealer's Daughter'

'An odd little story', is again a possible first reaction: another of those curious ironies or strange spiritual processes which produce an unexpected outcome, so that lives are determined. After a few re-readings it turns into one of the most extraordinary and profound things Lawrence ever wrote, while retaining that initial oddness, where one starts to say 'truth is stranger than fiction' and then realises that it is fiction which is giving us a truth stranger than other fiction. It gives examples of Lawrence's great recurring themes raised to mythological or religious status; yet this deliberateness is so delicately handled that neither the device nor the meaning may be noticed.

As with 'Hadrian', we are in the opening scene in one of those declining midland trading families. The three brothers and their sister, in the kitchen of the big house where their horse-dealer father was once rich and dominant, are now faced, on his death, with ruin. The house has to be sold, they have to leave. The men have somewhere to go, but Mabel refuses to say what she is going to do. This scene presents them as declaring their intention and brutally pressing her for an answer which she refuses to give.

One notices on the way a fairly easy symbolism. Of Joe, the eldest, it is said that 'his bearing was stupid'. As the brothers turn to watch the last horses being led away, we see that there are four horses, to match the four humans, and 'Every movement showed a massive, slumbrous strength, and a stupidity which held them in subjection'. Joe watches 'with glazed hopeless eyes. The horses were almost like his own body to him. [....] He would marry and go into harness. His life was over, he would be a subject animal now.'

That makes too easy a point – but Lawrence then refines it. Fred Henry, the second brother, 'watched the passing of the horses with more *sang froid*. If he was an animal, like Joe, he was an animal which controls, not one which is controlled. He was master of any horse [....] But he was not master of the situations of life.' It is he who begins to press Mabel about her future, and persists, while she persists in her refusal to answer. She 'sat on like one condemned, at the head of the table'. On a re-reading one sees the point of that: she has formed an intention, but it is one she cannot disclose, and the word 'condemned' is a hint.

There now enters the other main character, the young doctor Jack Fergusson, who is introduced as a friend, or drinking-companion, of the brothers. He addresses Mabel courteously, to put the same question:

> 'What are *you* going to do then, Miss Pervin?' asked Fergusson. 'Going to your sister's, are you?'
> Mabel looked at him with her steady dangerous eyes, that always made him uncomfortable, unsettling his superficial ease.
> 'No,' she said. (141: 25–9)

It is on re-reading that one picks up the references to eyes, to looking, to meeting a gaze, to being 'unsettled' or changed by it. These are normal elements of social exchange, but can be the strangest, and looking without saying anything, is, like touching, a way of disclosing oneself or making contact without seeming to or even meaning to.

At the end of this scene there are a few paragraphs of retrospect and summary. The men have gone off, so the attention turns to Mabel:

> For months Mabel had been servantless in the big house, keeping the home together in penury for her ineffectual brothers. She had kept house for ten years. But previously it was with unstinted means. Then, however brutal and coarse everything was, the sense of money had kept her proud, confident [....]
>
> No company came to the house, save dealers and coarse men. Mabel had no associates of her own sex, after her sister went away. But she did not mind. She went regularly to church, she attended to her father. And she lived in the memory of her mother, who had died when she was fourteen, and whom she had loved. She had loved her father too, in a different way, depending upon him, and feeling secure in him, until at the age of fifty-four he married again. And then she had set hard against him. Now he had died and left them all hopelessly in debt. (142: 25–41)

Then there is a paragraph in which subtler notes are quietly sounded:

> She had suffered badly during the period of poverty. Nothing, however, could shake the curious sullen, animal pride that dominated each member of the family. Now, for Mabel, the end had come. Still she would not cast about her. She would follow her way just the same. She would always hold the keys of her own situation. Mindless and persistent, she endured from day to day [....] It was enough that this was the end, and there was no way out. She need not pass any more darkly along the main street of the small town, avoiding every eye [....] This was at an end. She thought of nobody, not even of herself. Mindless and persistent, she seemed in a sort of ecstasy to be coming nearer to her fulfilment, her own glorification, approaching her dead mother, who was glorified. (143: 1–14)

The harmonies attending the repeated words 'end' and 'darkly' are transformed by 'fulfilment' and the repeated 'glorification'. It may be only on re-reading that one grasps that she means to join her mother by killing herself. It is possible to think that she means 'to approach her dead mother' simply by attending to her grave. The next paragraph shows her taking her little bag, but then its contents, 'shears and sponge', have mythical or Miltonic and Biblical overtones.[1] She goes 'quickly, darkly' along; and it is in the nature of this case that one hardly knows whether the two words carry all their significances overtly or are given them by the context.

She attends to the grave 'in a state bordering on pure happiness'. Fergusson passes from his house to the surgery, and 'glancing across the graveyard with his quick eye he saw the girl at her task at the grave'. Something strange then happens, another silent contact across a distance:

> She lifted her eyes, feeling him looking. Their eyes met. And each looked away at once, each feeling in some way found out by the other. He lifted his cap and passed on down the road. There remained distinct in his consciousness, like a vision, the memory of her face, lifted from the tombstone in the churchyard, and looking at him with slow, large, portentous eyes. It *was* portentous, her face. It seemed to mesmerise him. There was a heavy power in her eyes which laid hold of his whole being, as if he had drunk some powerful drug. He had been feeling weak and done before. Now the life came back into him, he felt delivered from his own fretted, daily self. (144: 3–12)

The notations are now beginning to multiply and complicate each other. One would not need to be re-reading to be struck by 'Now the life came back into him, he felt delivered [....]', but it is only later that one recognises that she has here in one way done for him what he has in another way to do for her, including the administering of the potent drink.

Shortly after, coming out of the surgery to do his rounds, he sees her again across the field.

> Why was she going down there? He pulled up on the path on the slope above, and stood staring. He could just make sure of the small black figure moving in the hollow of the failing day. He seemed to see her in the midst of such obscurity, that he was like a clairvoyant, seeing rather with the mind's eye than with ordinary sight [....] He felt, if he looked away from her, in the thick, ugly, falling dusk, he would lose her altogether. (145: 6–13)

---

[1] The Miltonic reference is to 'Lycidas': 'Comes the blind fury with th'abhorred shears / And slits the thin-spun life.' 'Lycidas' (89 in *The Golden Treasury*) is structured on the parallel between drowning and baptism.

He nearly does. Suddenly realising that she is walking into the pond, he has to run down and try to rescue her. Lawrence describes the process:

> He slowly ventured into the pond. The bottom was deep, soft clay; he sank in, and the water clasped dead cold round his legs. As he stirred he could smell the cold, rotten clay that fouled up into the water. It was objectionable in his lungs. Still, repelled and yet not heeding, he moved deeper into the pond. The cold water rose over his thighs, over his loins, upon his abdomen. The lower part of his body was all sunk in the hideous cold element. And the bottom was so deeply soft and uncertain, he was afraid of pitching with his mouth underneath. He could not swim, and was afraid. (145: 32–40)

This is powerfully repulsive. The repeated 'clay', with its Shakespearean and proverbial associations, suggests that the physical horror threatens to become mortal. At one point 'he touched her clothing' – a reversed Biblical reference may stir for some readers. And as the rescue proceeds, there are stronger notes:

> And so doing he lost his balance and went under, horribly, suffocating in the foul, earthy water, struggling madly for a few moments. At last, after what seemed an eternity, he got his footing, rose again into the air and looked around. He gasped, and knew he was in the world. Then he looked at the water. She had risen near him. He grasped her clothing, and, drawing her nearer, turned to make his way to land again. (146: 7–13)

It remains entirely possible to read 'rose again', 'in the world', and 'she had risen' as being merely what happened.

Fergusson is able to revive her on the bank ('He could feel her live beneath his hands, she was coming back') so now he has done literally for her what she had spiritually done for him at the earlier moment – but 'literally' begs a question. There follows the extraordinary final scene when he has got her back to the house, removed her wet clothes and wrapped her in blankets (in pictorial terms this has elements of the succession: Deposition, Pietà, and Entombment, to be followed by Resurrection).

Given some whisky, she comes to. 'She looked full into his face, as if she had been seeing him for some time.' He is cold and wet and 'mortally afraid for his own health [....] He had begun to shudder like one sick.' However,

> Her eyes remained full on him; he seemed to be going dark in his mind, looking back at her helplessly. The shuddering became quieter in him, his life came back in him, dark and unknowing, but strong again. (147: 11–14)

Once again, the spiritual effect (shall we say?) operates on him: she has done again for him the equivalent of what he did for her. He finds he has to remind her of what happened. 'Was I out of my mind?' she asks; and 'Am I out of my mind now?' These are obvious questions, and his obvious or simple answer is maybe, to the first question. But to the second he answers 'No'. He respects her deeper insight: 'He felt dazed, and felt dimly that her power was stronger than his on this issue.' He wants to go upstairs and find dry clothes, 'But there was another desire in him, and she seemed to hold him. His will seemed to have gone to sleep [....] But he felt warm inside himself. He did not shudder at all.'

Suddenly she becomes conscious that she has no clothes on – 'For a moment it seemed as if her reason were going.' To her question 'Who undressed me?' he has to reply that he did.

> For some moments she sat and gazed at him awfully, her lips parted.
> 'Do you love me, then?' she asked.
> He only stood and stared at her fascinated. His soul seemed to melt.
> She shuffled forward on her knees, and put her arms round him, round his legs, as he stood there, pressing her breasts against his knees and thighs, clutching him with strange, convulsive certainty, pressing his thighs against her, drawing him to her face, her throat, as she looked up at him with flaring humble eyes of transfiguration, triumphant in first possession.
> 'You love me,' she murmured, in strange transport, yearning and triumphant and confident. 'You love me. I know you love me, I know.' (148: 11–24)

The reader may remember that in the pond the water 'clasped dead cold round his legs'. One may also know that a crouching figure clasping the knees of a standing or sitting person is the classic posture of the supplicant in myth and art. But that is a detail. The extraordinary scene continues, in which his reserve, even his horror, his fear (is she really mad?) falls away as his merely social or personal shell is broken, he gives way to her, drops on his knees beside her, and holds her. To her question he can now reply 'Yes'.

> The word cost him a painful effort. Not because it wasn't true. But because it was too newly true, the *saying* seemed to tear open again his newly-torn heart. And he hardly wanted it to be true, even now.
> She lifted her face to him, and he bent forward and kissed her on the mouth, gently, with the one kiss that is an eternal pledge. [...] He never intended to love her. But now it was over. He had crossed over the gulf to her. (150: 9–17)

They have done a miraculous thing. One's first-reading impulse to say, 'Oh yes, how strange, but I suppose something like that could really happen' – this turns into an acknowledgement that Lawrence has gently and carefully shown exactly what has gone on, in terms of emotional process, and has kept it also at a level of spiritual and human significance which lifts it right out of the realm of mere reporting, however imaginative.

It is one of the great stories. It is linked to 'Hadrian' and others by this theme of closing the gap or crossing the gulf, and doing so by means – especially touch or gaze – which are not ordinary social negotiation through speech. But what in 'Hadrian' is taken at the fairy-tale level here becomes religious. What has been performed is a baptism, which has always symbolised death to one life and resurrection in the next.

I justify the term by pointing to one of the great *topoi* in Lawrence's writing. Going down into water and coming back out of it is always for him a type of baptism, and of all ritual lavings and immersions. This was true even in the earliest writings, where the notions of washing and rebirth are syncretically linked with classical notions of visiting the underworld – perhaps with a guide – and returning to a new life. Orpheus and Persephone are mythical precursors.

One could see it already in *The White Peacock*. The scene in which the narrator and central consciousness Cyril bathes in a pond with his much-loved friend George, who is seen, naked, to have a beautiful body, and who holds Cyril close and dries him – this has for modern readers the vibration of covert homosexuality. But this is not the main intention. 'The Horse Dealer's Daughter' also looks back to the scene in *The Rainbow* where Ursula bathes with Winifred Inger. The same vibration is felt there, and this time intended: the relationship has an undoubted sexual component, the chapter is actually called 'Shame' and, superficially received, was one of the main reasons for the banning of the book.

But this later epiphany teaches us to go back and read those earlier occasions with more insight. As for bathing and drying the body of the loved one, it is what parents do for babies. It is also what the miner's wife and mother do for their dead son and husband in 'Odour of Chrysanthemums' where the scene is evidently a Pietà and Entombment. When a man does it for an adult male friend, the action may seem equivocal, but if you look forward to the scene in *Aaron's Rod* where the Lawrence-figure Lilley anoints and massages the body of the sick Aaron Sisson, the scene has, I think, no intended sexual import: it is a ministration somewhere between medicine and religion. Indeed it prefigures the scene in the late story 'The Escaped Cock' where the priestess of Isis anoints and rubs the body of the crucified saviour: this is the prelude to an intercourse; but that is presented as a sacred ritual or ultimate communion. One cannot say it always is, but that is its potential meaning.

To come back to 'The Horse Dealer's Daughter', one might say that Dr Fergusson is, in newspaper-headline terms, Mabel Pervin's saviour: he has returned her to life. The story shows that in a deeper sense she, by her gaze and later by her actions and words, has equally saved him, released a deeper life in him. The art of the story is such that one is left looking at those words and asking, has one made a simple positive statement or has one been led to a religious truth? The deeper question is: how would one know the difference?

'Tickets Please' – 'Monkey Nuts' – 'Wintry Peacock' – 'The Last Straw'

'Tickets Please' returns us to the civilian world of wartime, where men have to live and work with women in a changed role, and find it hard to do so. The young women who now act as conductors on the trams are 'fearless young hussies' with 'skirts up to their knees', and they are 'perfectly at their ease' in their new role. John Thomas, the inspector (his name is mockingly relevant), thinks this is a situation he can exploit, goes out with all the pretty ones but refuses to commit himself. He is in Lawrence's words 'a nocturnal presence' – a theme initiated in *Sons and Lovers*, where people 'from the night' have no daytime or worktime substantiality. He has 'no idea of becoming an all-round individual', which among other things would mean making a choice and settling down. Shrewdly, the girls grasp this tactic, and refuse to be exploited one by one. They form into a group, a pack, corner him and physically assault him, demanding that he make a choice. In this collective attack their hair is 'wild', Lawrence notes, and for very attentive readers since *The White Peacock*, that is the sign of the maenad. '"You ought to be killed",' one of them tells him. But he will not give in, '"not if they tore him to bits"' (44: 3). So he is like Pentheus and they are the Bacchantes in a modern re-staging of *The Bacchae*. The classical parallel, when it is pointed out, is a surprise at first: it gives the story a depth, a perspective back into mythical time, without being obvious.

'Monkey Nuts' is another story of the emergence of women in wartime. Two soldiers, the young Joe and the more seasoned and self-possessed Albert, working in a railway yard ('After Flanders it was Heaven itself') are loading corn harvested locally, and are faced with the phenomenon of the Land Girl. Again the unfeminine costume is part of what disturbs them as they face 'a buxom girl, young, in linen overalls and gaiters. Her face was ruddy.' This was one of Lawrence's favourite adjectives, always implying vitality. At first, characteristically, the interaction is only the look exchanged. The younger man, Joe, is smitten, but cannot respond, so the girl has to use other means – even goes so far as to send him a telegram summoning him to a meeting. They do meet, but it is as if he can never recover the initiative or accommodate himself to the reversal of roles. The older, more confident Albert tries opportunistically to take over the affair, but is rejected by the girl; she wants the younger one, who cannot face her, and retreats into himself. There is no analysis: the events can be seen from the outside only and remain baffling. This is a precise rendering of the situation: what Joe cannot himself grasp is not put into words by Lawrence. On the other hand, Albert has a cocky self-confident turn of speech, which is repulsive to the girl.

It is an obscure failure on Joe's part; he turns it into a bitter rejection of her, so she is defeated for her presumption. The men revert into their own relationship, which is that of mates, with Albert subtly dominant. So being 'mates' can be a male consolation for a failure to relate to women, especially the new women. The War has brought women out, and also knocked men back.

A similar, equally curious failure is notated in 'Wintry Peacock', one of Lawrence's rare first-person narrations. As always with this mode, one has to ask if the author's voice is to be identified with the narrator's: especially since on a first reading there seems to be an alliance – as self-serving men – between the narrator and the returned soldier Alfred Goyte: an alliance against his wife. She is deceived by Alfred in more than one way; and verbally by the narrator: so there builds up between them this complicity against her. At the beginning Alfred has not yet reached home from France, but is on the way. The wife asks the narrator to translate as he reads to her a letter from a Belgian girl who has given birth to what sounds like Alfred's child and now seeks to rejoin him in England. The narrator is astute: in this delicate situation, he tactfully mistranslates as he reads, saying that the child is a little brother and has been called Alfred out of affectionate memory of the soldier by the family he befriended. The wife, listening, is by no means convinced; her ready jealousy makes her assume the child is Alfred's.

She has an odd insinuating manner with the narrator (or is this his instinctive lack of sympathy?). She makes up to him with a boldness which, like that of the girl in 'Monkey Nuts', disconcerts the man. What she is using on him might be called charm, but is more than that; he expresses it by more than once calling her 'witch-like' as she gets her way over the letter.

As for the peacock of the title, the bird, if the woman is a witch, is her familiar. Her relationship with it is what a psychiatrist might call a displacement or transference: she gives it the love that her absent husband cannot have, or does not deserve, or will not return. The bird determines the action by getting lost in the snowy landscape, nearly dying. The narrator finds it, rescues it, and so has occasion to return it to the farm up on the hill, where the rescue assembles other members of the family, including Alfred, now returned. His father, a sympathetic character, explains that the peacock, Joey, has been one issue between the couple: there was 'a bit of a to-do between 'em' and the bird flew away: the main issue was 'this letter job'. He makes what is either a very cynical or a very sensible remark about the letter and the feeling it has brought to the surface:

> 'What's good o' makkin' a peck o' trouble ower what's far enough off, an' ned niver come no nigher ... 'Er [the wife] should ta'e no notice on't. – Ay, what can y' expect.' (87: 18–21)

The last phrase unpacks as: if men are sent off for years on war service, risking their lives and leaving their wives at home, it is inevitable that some will seek comfort, or love, or sexual relief in affairs with foreign women. Children will be born. One has to shrug.

The narrator leaves, is intercepted by Alfred, who wants to know about the letter, which his wife has burned. The narrator tells him how he too has deceived the wife, and gives the gist of the deception. They enter into their male complicity. Alfred says that the child may be his, may not. That is to imply that the Belgian girl is 'loose' and so entitled to no respect. In any case, '"I've never got that letter, anyhow".' So he is in the clear with both women. As a last twist he asks: '"Why didn't you wring that bloody peacock's neck – that bloody Joey?"' The narrator is startled, asks why, and hears '"I hate the brute [....] I had a shot at him."' So he too was jealous, and that is why the bird escaped. Alfred has one moment of thinking '"Poor little Elise"' – which is another give-away: she is not 'loose' – but then bursts out laughing, for he is in the clear. '"But I'll do that blasted Joey in [...]"' The narrator ends 'I ran down the hill shouting also with laughter.'

Two men have allied themselves in opposition to a woman, much as the soldiers in 'Monkey Nuts' unite in opposition to the bold, outgoing Land Girl. It is a union of resentment, or weakness or misunderstanding. The pattern is repeated in other stories, though the alliance may also be of women against men.

The father's not unsympathetic peace-making comments seem to put the whole matter in a long human perspective; but the lasting and puzzling resonance is provided by the peacock. We remember that in *The White Peacock* the bird had been the emblem of a misogynist's fear or resentment: 'the very soul of a lady', 'all vanity and screech and defilement'. Odd when you think of it – the book should have been called *The White Peahen*. The bird here is male, but still the vehicle of a hostile misogyny. The wife when first seen is wearing a 'preposterously short skirt' – emblem of the wartime emergence. She addresses the narrator boldly, tries to make him join in complicity with her in her determination to read a letter addressed to the husband, makes her own predetermined sense of what the narrator actually mistranslates, burns the letter, but still gives the husband a row – deserved, of course. In her bold insinuating manner she is repeatedly likened to a witch – which may be the narrator's malice, but is also how we are led to take her. The peacock which flies to where the narrator finds him is like an emissary; but is also the object of the husband's jealousy, getting a love which he thinks due to him. The rights and wrongs are all confused, but are cut through by Alfred and the narrator agreeing to stand together as men. How Lawrence himself may have felt, he is excused from telling us by his method, and that is its point; but we can turn to other stories to construct an attitude. It is not a simple for or against.

He is once more a kind of anthropologist: an observer of the ways of tribal people.

'The Last Straw', first published as 'Fanny and Annie', deals with another paternity case. Fanny has come back to her north Midlands steel-making native town, having bettered herself as a lady's maid in the south. Indeed she is now lady-like. She has been jilted by a socially desirable man down there, and is now resignedly coming back to marry Harry Goodall, her childhood boyfriend, who has stayed at home and remained resolutely working-class. He meets her at the station and the scene-setting delicately and wittily suggests that the lurid light in the sky from the furnaces 'lighting the desultory, industrial crowd' illuminates her descent into an inferno. Or is she a Eurydice? Actually, the force of the whole story is contrary: it is a homecoming to her own people, but that means accepting their ways, their values.

Harry turns out to be a better match, a better man, than Alfred Goyte. For one thing, he can sing and do it well, and we have seen that this is a virtue, even a grace. One might think of Harry as another Burns figure (and Burns got into trouble because of his charms) or even an Orpheus. But the possible solemnity of that is neatly undermined. If there is a defect in his singing it is only that 'he handled his aitches so hopelessly':

> 'And I saw 'eaven hopened
> And be'old a wite 'orse —'

'He had a good voice, and he sang with a certain lacerating fire, but his pronunciation made it all funny. And *nothing* could alter him' (159: 3–10). And that indicates his problem, or rather her problem, if she allows it to be so. It is also his virtue, to use a word Lawrence appropriated.

The central incident in the story comes when scandal erupts at a wonderfully wittily described Harvest Festival service, which Fanny attends as visibly Harry's intended. The hymns are the obvious ones, but the story gives

> Come ye thankful people come,
> Raise the song of harvest home ...

and the anthem 'They that sow in tears shall reap in joy' an unexpected overtone. Harry sings solo parts, looks and sounds well. Listening, and contemplating him, Fanny's complicated feelings begin to settle towards him 'as if his flesh were new and lovely to touch. The thorn of desire rankled bitterly in her heart.'

But as his voice sinks, a middle-aged woman stands up in the congregation and shouts a denunciation of him 'in God's holy house.' He is a 'scamp as won't take the consequences of what he's done.' The congregation are thunderstruck, but Harry 'stood there, looking down with a dumb sort of indifference on Mrs Nixon, his face naive and faintly mocking'.

Mr Enderby, the Vicar, brings the service to a close with a tactful improvised prayer, and when everybody leaves apologises to Fanny. Harry merely remarks '"We've had a bit of an extra"' – a performer's term for an addition to the programme. Mr Enderby asks what it was all about, and Harry replies, '"The daughter's going to have a childt, an' 'er lays it on me."' Pressed, he goes on '"It's no more mine than it is some other chap's."' The girl, Annie, is '"always in an' out o' th' pubs wi' th' fellows."' Mr Enderby, thus informed, thinks that none the less Harry should sing at the evening service as arranged – though we are to understand that this will be anticipated as an event and will draw an audience. Harry accepts, which is brave.

Fanny has all along been faced by the prospect of a new life which may be a descent – if not into an inferno, at least into a class she thought she had left for 'higher' things. She is now faced with the realities of that life: it is implied that Harry's family, his mother in particular, fear that after this revelation she may feel she is too good for them. On the other hand, she has no better alternative in view. Harry's father acts the part of old Mr Goyte in 'Wintry Peacock'. He and Harry's sister Jinny question Harry:

'What's 'er say, then?' asked the father secretly, of Harry, jerking his head in the direction of the stairs whence Fanny had disappeared.

'Nowt yet,' said Harry.

'Serve you right if she chucks you now,' said Jinny. 'I'll bet it's right about Annie Nixon an' you.'

His father looked at him enquiringly.

'It's no more mine than it is Bill Bowers' or Ted Slaney's, or six or seven on 'em,' said Harry to his father.

And the father nodded silently.

'That'll not get you out of it, in court,' said Jinny. (165: 8–21)

It is like the point Alfred Goyte and his father made. In this society, if young women are 'loose', they have no rights. Everyone accepts that. Here, only her mother will take Annie's part – very bravely and openly, in church, to the horror of all who hear, but it has no ultimate force. This is partly because, as we learn, the mother herself is not respectable. Fanny makes her decision. She says she won't go to church that evening, to see Harry face the public again. 'There was a sudden halt in the family.' She resolves their fear by going on '"I'll stop with *you* to-night, Mother."' By calling Mrs Goodall 'Mother', and staying at her side in this emergency, she has taken sides. She has made a wise judgement by not going to the spectacle in which Harry may be humiliated further, but has thrown in her lot with the family.

So the 'last straw' has broken the back of false social pride, or been clutched by a drowning person, or been drawn to decide a fate. This was a tough and quite 'unfair' society where the men were 'no better than they should be': that is to be expected. But it is the women who are left with the consequences, have to understand that and conduct themselves accordingly. To hold your head up in that society, you have to be not so much righteous as able to face facts and act prudently. Fanny shows she can do that.

That is to make heavy weather of an exquisitely light, witty story, whose every touch counts. I have explained some of the jokes, heavily enough, to make the necessary points, but there are more. Those who think Lawrence had no sense of humour may need to have the rest explained to them.

A recurrent feature in several of the stories is the apparent alliance between two men in relationship to a woman, or two women in relationship to a man. It *seems* like that – an alliance – perhaps against a force which may be hostile, or at any rate other and strange. But where the men ally themselves, especially in 'Monkey Nuts', it is as if they were afraid, or baffled. The present-day reader, alert to gender-politics, may find the stories at first obscure, even upsetting. In 'Wintry Peacock' and 'The Last Straw' the off-stage girls landed with a baby and no husband seem betrayed, and the comments of the older male relatives of the presumed father seem cynical. The portrayal of the witch-wife Mrs Goyte and the outraged mother of Annie seem comedic, even hostile. Is this evidence of Lawrence's misogyny? I think not. The decision made by Fanny, the other woman, depends on the crystallising moment when she sees the whole situation, the whole culture, and decides to accept it. She is, we feel, a strong person, knows herself to be stronger than Harry, whose attitude to her has throughout been one of silent submission (when he's not singing, that is). She is going to be able to handle marriage to him. It will not be what she had once hoped for; but good enough.

As for Albert and Joe, they seem to have repulsed the forward Land Girl: but actually Joe cannot manage her, because she is too strong for him, and she has nothing but scorn for Albert's 'forwardness'. If she seems defeated, they are more so. In 'Samson and Delilah' the returning husband finds himself tied up and dumped outside the pub by order of his outraged wife, whom he had deserted years before. He accepts this symbolic punishment: having once 'loosed the bonds of love' he finds his treatment appropriate and the bonds from now on acceptable. He says he respects her for her action: '"A bit of a fight for a how-de-do pleases me, that it do".' We presume they settle down again, if not as equals – for she has demonstrated her power. In 'The Primrose Path' the uncle-figure Daniel Sutton is given a day's silent examination by his nephew as he goes about his affairs. He seems a strong, indeed rough, man's man; but the progress of the day's exposure is to reveal him as 'a chaos of a man' unable to handle his feelings, unable to relate to his women, and destined to leave or be left by them. He can only be nice to dogs. Men don't come out well, in these stories, and their alliances are out of weakness.

These are ordinary lives, though it is worth observing how wide the range of Lawrence's direct observation is, how many kinds of people he knew and could represent without condescension or idealisation. In the major stories a transcendence takes place, is equated with a resurrection from that ordinariness. In 'England My England' itself, Evelyn/Egbert is not ordinary, though he is in important ways representative. His failure to find transcendence tells us something about his England as well as about himself, and he ushers us into the world of *Women in Love*.

10
Women in Love: Introduction

The endings of Lawrence's novels can be profoundly ambiguous. Often, he seems to have a tragedy on his hands, yet is unwilling to end on a negative note: there has to be some hope. It is as if he passes the question over to the reader.

So *The Rainbow* ended with that glimpse of an Apocalypse – though the radiance may be an illusion, another projection. The undertone of a Biblical structural analogy has played throughout it, unfolding from Genesis to Revelation. An Apocalypse is part-terrible, part-hopeful: the end of one world, but also a Second Coming. A new age begins – or so the believer may hope.

Women in Love ends without that hope, yet a strange half-consolation is offered. Rupert Birkin contemplates the body of his friend Gerald Crich, whom he loved, and who also represented a class, a generation, England itself:

> He turned away. Either the heart would break, or cease to care. Best cease to care. Whatever the mystery which has brought forth man and the universe, it is a non-human mystery, it has its own great ends, man is not the criterion. Best leave it all to the vast, creative non-human mystery. [...]
>
> God can do without man. God could do without the ichthyosauri and the mastodon. These monsters failed creatively to develop, so God, the creative mystery, dispensed with them [....]
>
> It was very consoling to Birkin, to think this. If humanity ran into a cul de sac, and expended itself, the timeless creative mystery would bring forth some other being, finer, more wonderful, some new, more lovely race, to carry on the embodiment of creation. [...] To be man was as nothing compared to the possibilities of the

creative mystery. (WL 478: 28–479: 14)

It's a bleak consolation. The proper Biblical parallel would be the Book of Job, that profound pre-Christian opening-up to the same mystery: the ways of creation. Lawrence offers a twentieth-century equivalent, which is able to metaphorise ideas about evolution.

One thing that happened between the separation of the two books was that Lawrence, in the years after 1915, reviewed his own belief-system. He came to feel that in his recourse to metaphor he had been too ready to 'come out of the Christian camp' in his use of the old symbols. His reading of the pre-Socratics moved him back behind Christianity, even the Old Testament, to a different set of metaphors which, for a time at least, better represented his fundamental intuitions. The results are clear in parts of *Women in Love* – too clear, sometimes, resulting in patches of dogmatic jargon where the ideas have not receded into the texture.

But it was not just a matter of reading Burnet on early Greek philosophy and thinking that Heraclitus represented better than the Bible some of his own instinctive mental movements and attitudes. More important, there was the War: blind nation against nation in tribal madness. This was the end of the world he had been born into. It was not an Apocalypse: no god had called time and was coming in judgement. It was the working out of a process which could be called evolutionary but demanded an end to nineteenth-century notions that evolution was inevitably onward and upward. A cosmic disaster, the modern equivalent of an Ice Age or the impact of a meteorite, had put a cataclysmic end to a phase of time and a form of society. As in past disasters, there were going to be some survivors, who had to make a new life, somewhere.

Two other differences from *The Rainbow* come to mind. The characters in that novel do talk to each other, characteristically and entertainingly at the beginning, and have moments of serious intellectual discussion – especially Will and Anna, Ursula and Anton Skrebensky. But *Women in Love* immediately strikes the reader as in one aspect a series of intense debates about their society and their world by a larger group of intelligent educated people, trying to make explicit a sense of their individual and social lives.

The other difference is that there is little violence in *The Rainbow*: Ursula's thrashing the boy Williams sticks in the mind as heralding something new and worse, even though Anton's willingness to fight for his country still seems like play-acting, unreal. In *Women in Love* violence is a main connecting thread: it crops up as if inevitably in the discussions; it becomes actual in crucial episodes, and precipitates the final scenes, which are like a crystallisation of the whole book. Most importantly, we are by dramatic means led to see how personal lacks and needs lead to that violence. It expresses the world of the novel, which is why specific reference to the War would have been – however massively – only an instantiation of what he was showing. Its massiveness could even be taken as abnormal and meaningless, while Lawrence brings the phenomenon down the inescapable personal level.

The two leading male characters, Rupert Birkin and Gerald Crich, are protagonists in this disaster. Birkin proposes to live on into the new era, if not in England: it is his role as prophet and witness. Gerald, for all his class-superiority, represents most people, and is swept away to his death, as surely as if he had been killed in the War – nor is it possible, as with the myriads of nameless war casualties, to say that his death is meaningless. It is certainly ominous that in his childhood he had killed his brother, and the other characters ponder the significance of that death. It may even be significant that in the death-process he initiates the last act by striking a German man. But since the War overtook Lawrence during the prolonged writing process, it has no actual part in it. One might imagine a Gerald Crich who had served in France as an officer and been marked by the experience, and a Birkin who had refused to serve, or like Lawrence, escaped through ill-health. But Lawrence didn't need the War to make his point: the book is all the more remarkable for having made its diagnosis from before, outside and beyond the War, which was 'only' (one might say) an eruption of the condition he explores. It was the whole of English society, Western industrial society, that was his concern, and not just its symptomatic wars. And the possibility that Western society has gone further down the spiral since he wrote means that the book remains sharp-sighted and comprehensive despite its date: the most serious, ambitious and comprehensive English novel of the twentieth century.

Readers since 1945 have noted with a start of surprised recognition the little prophecies which are thrown out as gloomy para-jokes: for instance Gudrun and Loerke playing into each other's negative mindset:

> As for the future, that they never mentioned except one laughed

out some mocking dream of the destruction of the world by a ridiculous catastrophe of man's invention: a man invented such a perfect explosive that it blew the world in two, and the two halves set off in different directions through space, to the dismay of the inhabitants: or else the people of the world divided into two halves, and each half decided *it* was perfect and right, the other half was wrong and must be destroyed; so another end of the world. (453: 9–16)

Loerke and Gudrun are plainly set against any positive one might find in the book. However, such positives are not easy to find. Here, for instance, is Birkin:

'What people want is hate – hate and nothing but hate. And in the name of righteousness and love, they get it. They distil themselves into nitro-glycerine, all the lot of them, out of very love. – It's the lie that kills. If we want hate, let us have it [....] but not in the name of love. – But I abhor humanity, I wish it was swept away. It could go, and there would be no *absolute* loss [....] don't you find it a beautiful clean thought, a world empty of people, just uninterrupted grass, and a hare sitting up?' (127: 10–27)

One might say, blessed are the hares, for they shall inherit the earth – but then one thinks, but what about Bismarck, the well-named violent buck-rabbit? Maybe he is infected by the interfering humans who want to depict him, to control him.

Birkin's words are not just a momentary flight of negative fancy, a mood. Very near the beginning of the book, at the wedding-party at Shortlands, the home of the Criches, he and Mrs Crich consider whether people 'don't really matter':

'Not many people are anything at all,' he answered, forced to go deeper than he wanted to. 'They jingle and giggle. It would be much better if they were just wiped out. Essentially they don't exist, they aren't there.' (25: 1–4)

She makes the sensible reply: there they are, whether they exist or not. The discussion is then taken up in a general conversation with the other guests, changes tack and bumps up against race, nationality, commerce, competition and war. It is all half-joking, and yet is meant. Here is Gerald:

'A race may have its commercial aspect,' he said. 'In fact it must. It is like a family [....] to make provision you have got to strive against other families, other nations. I don't see why you shouldn't.'

'You can't do away with the spirit of emulation [....] it is one of the necessary incentives to production and improvement.' (28: 29–38)

As the argument quite mildly proceeds, Gerald produces a half-comic example:

'If I go and take a man's hat from off his head, that hat becomes a symbol of that man's liberty. When he fights me for his hat, he is fighting me for his liberty.'

Birkin states his own counter-position:

'[...] it is open to me to decide, which is a greater loss to me, my hat or my liberty as a free and indifferent man. If I am compelled to fight, I lose the latter.' (29: 16–30)

Hermione Roddice is asked if she would let anyone snatch her hat off her head:

'No,' she replied, in a low inhuman tone, that seemed to contain a chuckle. 'No, I shouldn't let anybody take my hat off my head.'
'How would you prevent it?' asked Gerald.
'I don't know,' replied Hermione slowly. 'Probably I should kill him.' (29: 38–30: 2)

The exchange plays at the level of half-joking discussion, but the whole novel shows it to be deadly serious at heart, as Gerald's death and Hermione's assault on Birkin prove. The notional hat represents one's sense of self, one's place in society, one's love, and the way the one involves the others.

If we look back to the beginning of that conversation, we see that Mrs Crich wanted Gerald to have a friend – he has never had one. She says it pointedly to Birkin, who deflects the appeal by saying to himself 'Am I my brother's keeper?' is then shocked to remember that the child Gerald did kill his brother, and broods over the question: can there be a true accident? So the archetypes Cain and Abel preside over the following discussion and turn Hermione's threat into something more than personal to her.

As the conversation continues, the topic switches to the earlier scene outside the church where the bride raced the groom to the door, and won. Gerald says – he would – it 'defies normal standards of behaviour', but Birkin retorts, 'Anybody who is anything can just be himself and do as he likes.' The bride did a rare thing: she acted spontaneously on impulse and 'It's the only really gentlemanly thing to do – provided you're fit to do it.' There follows the exchange everyone remembers:

> 'You think people should just do as they like?'
> 'I think they always do. But I should like them to like the purely individual thing in themselves, which makes them act in singleness. And they only like to do the collective thing.'
> 'And I,' said Gerald grimly, 'shouldn't like to be in a world of people who acted individually and spontaneously, as you call it. – We should have everybody cutting everybody else's throat in five minutes.'
> 'That means *you* would like to be cutting everybody's throat, ' said Birkin.
> 'How does that follow?' asked Gerald crossly.
> 'No man,' said Birkin, 'Cuts another man's throat unless he wants to cut it, and unless the other wants it cutting. This is a complete truth. It takes two people to make a murder: a murderer and a murderee. And a murderee is a man who is murderable. And a man who is murderable is a man who in a profound if hidden lust desires to be murdered.' (33: 5–20)

Birkin's remarks have a steely logic: Gerald's easy generalisation does imply his own tendency to violence, but he cannot see it. In this couple of pages Hermione and Gerald have given unconscious notice of their own potential —yet it is Birkin who in the debate seems the odd man out. The paradox is that his 'singleness' – made by the others to seem eccentric or antisocial – is distinguished by them from what 'everyone' does – which is the unconscious drive to violence of the collective. We remember Skrebensky, Gerald's precursor in *The Rainbow*. Something deeper is now being uncovered in his attitudes, in the years when 'everybody' accepted the War – except those few who singled themselves out and suffered for it. The effort to find 'singleness' affects not only life in the large social setting; it starts with the individual's life with the chosen woman as sexual partner, and the chosen man as loved friend. The action shows the search for new kinds of relationship taking place, in a world which does not conceive the need, is even hostile to the idea, so far as it can be said to be at all conscious – for all the superficial discursiveness of its representatives, including supposed intellectuals.

11
Women in Love: The Chapter as Focus: 'Breadalby'

The novel unfolds in an easy natural-seeming sequence. Each chapter has its setting. The narrative opens with the sisters at home in Beldover, and returns there from time to time. There are episodes in the old country-houses Shortlands and Breadalby, drives by car into the countryside, boat-trips on the ponds and lakes, excursions to London – and finally, once the two couples have formed, they leave England for that strange excursion into the Alps, which was meant to be a pleasure and turns out to be the end of a world.

The events represent the movements of people with homes and places of work (Beldover, Ursula's school, Gerald's colliery) where the upper class might also go to a country-house party at weekends, or to London on business or pleasure. In this sequence, the four main characters meet, become involved, hesitate about their commitment, at last become two couples. There follows that crucial exit from England, in terms which suggest a transition into another world or epoch. Since it becomes a disaster, one might have expected that the new setting would be presented as one of Lawrence's underworlds. On the contrary the underworld is established at the outset as Beldover and its miners: the exit is up into the eerie unheavenly, life-denying upperworld of ice and snow which Lawrence had pondered in *Twilight in Italy*. Birkin and Ursula, we assume, have now left England for good; Gerald dies and goes home to be buried; Gudrun is left up in the air.

Within each chapter there is a succession of incidents, some of them strange, but not more so than much of life. They determine or confirm the relationships in normal ways. So, at the surface level, we have a naturalistic novel, almost like one of the great nineteenth century novels – *Middlemarch*, for instance, with its two sisters who were women in love in an earlier English Midlands setting.

But through this natural-seeming narrative Lawrence is setting up and constantly extending a network of significances which cannot afford to be obvious, and may escape notice, but which give the book its breadth of application, its psychological and spiritual profundity, and its mythopoeic element. The problem, as with *The Rainbow*, is that to expound it point by point is tedious, but if you don't see these points you have only skimmed the surface. I take one chapter, 'Breadalby', sketch the necessary analysis, show some of the links backwards and forwards which tie it in to the network, and point to some significances.

Breadalby is the country home of Hermione Roddice, and in her half-curious, half-condescending way she has invited Ursula and Gudrun to stay as two of her party of guests. A social-historical point made here is that the old social structure is being eroded (Birkin and Gerald note this in conversation, and Gerald half-resists it). Once, the children of Will Brangwen, a lower-middle-class person, would not have been invited (Will himself is conscious of being out of place at Shortlands, the Crich home, in 'Water-Party'). But Hermione recognises Gudrun as an artist, and therefore classless, and the sisters also count as intellectuals, or at any rate emergent. They display this in their emphatically coloured dresses, hats and stockings, which mark them out both from the uniform black of the mining-folk and the formally dressed upper-class people who also represent their class in their clothes. (We have forgotten that men once wore black to work, and women's daytime colours were sober. Gerald wears black.) So the sisters are gazed at as equivocal beings by those above and below them – much to their irritation. In this way they show themselves to be 'single' – Birkin's term.

At the start of the chapter they have been fetched from the station by the Roddice car. Entering the park, they see the beautiful old house in its man-made grounds 'like an English drawing of the old school'. '"Isn't it complete!"' Gudrun says, and this is equivocal: what is complete has ceased to grow on. Gudrun adds that she doesn't love it, but appreciates it as 'final'.

That note, about the English and the European past, sounds throughout the book. Later in the chapter, Birkin, also a guest, sits in bed, extends Gudrun's thought and follows his own. His mild musing turns into a rejection of the place, and of the present world as sequel to the past:

> how lovely, how sure, how formed, how final all the things of the

past were – the lovely accomplished past – this house, so still and golden, the park slumbering its centuries of peace. And then, what a snare and a delusion, this beauty of static things – what a horrible, dead prison Breadalby really was, what an intolerable confinement, the peace! Yet it was better than the sordid scrambling conflict of the present. If only one might create the future after one's own heart [....] (97: 7–14)

This foreshadows the development of the theme in the later chapter 'A Chair', where Birkin and Ursula, now committed to each other, consider for a moment acquiring possessions, see a beautiful old chair in Beldover market, buy it and at once repent. Birkin makes the standard 'Arts and Crafts' point that nothing so beautiful is now made by machine. England had something to express when it made that chair; but now one has to '"fish among the rubbish heaps for the remnants. [....] There is no production in us now, only sordid and foul mechanicalness"' (355: 30–2). Ursula (neat psychological point) is irritated by his preaching, and says she is '"sick of the beloved past"'. '"Not so sick as I am of the cursed present,"' he retorts. They have one of their characteristic little tiffs. She says she doesn't want old things, and he completes the argument – his way, of course – by saying they don't want things at all. They don't want a home.

This is progression to a crucial point: she finds it hard to accept (rightly, one thinks, as ordinary person). They give the chair to a young couple getting married because the woman is pregnant: the man accepts that he is trapped, while the woman finds it natural to be setting up a home, however humble.

This first theme, of past and present, has its ultimate development in the final phase in the Alps, where Gudrun and Loerke

> played with the past, and with the great figures of the past, a sort of little game of chess, or marionettes, all to please themselves. They had all the great men for their marionettes, and they two were the god of the show, working it all. As for the future, that they never mentioned, except one laughed out some mocking dream of the destruction of the world [....] (453: 6–11)

And Birkin's imagined new world of no homes is taken up and extended by Gudrun, imagining a life with Loerke, or free spirits like him:

'And Loerke *is* an artist, he is a free individual. One will escape from so much [....] I shall get away from people who have their own homes and their own children and their own acquaintances and their own this and their own that. I shall be among people who *don't* own things and who *haven't* got a home and a domestic servant in the back-ground [....] Oh God, the wheels within wheels of people – it makes one's head tick like a clock, with a very madness of dead mechanical monotony and meaninglessness. How I *hate* life, how I hate it. How I hate the Geralds, that they can offer one nothing else.' (464: 6–19)

Here is an example of how a set of ideas ceases to be the possession of one exponent, speaking for the author, and is extended or denatured by others. Gudrun's expression is not Birkin's: in her emphases one hears her distinctive voice, and her rejection of what Birkin also rejects sounds like a hysterical horror. This hints at what underlies her overt self-possession, and the real basis of her final rejection of Gerald. It is his tragedy that he is identified with the old life; she is right about that. It is her tragedy that she cannot actually link with anyone because she fears that nothing can have meaning. It is not an illogical fear, for she lacks Birkin's residual faith in life itself. The 'mad clock' image, the meaningless tick-tock, is something Lawrence was a prey to himself, and we met it in *Twilight in Italy* and *The Rainbow* as a condition of modern life and its absence of any substitute for faith.

Back to 'Breadalby', where for the moment Ursula has found 'a magic circle drawn about the place, enclosing the delightful precious past'. But the spell is broken by all the talk, 'like a rattle of small artillery', mental and very wearying. Lawrence deftly sketches the group of guests, sitting in the grounds 'spattering with half-intellectual, deliberate talk'. The leaders are Hermione and the Bertrand Russell figure Sir Joshua Malleson. Hermione 'lifting her face like a rhapsodist' goes off into an aria about education: 'the joy and beauty of knowledge in itself'. Here is another theme, for 'knowing' in the sense of incorporating, possessing intellectually, is the mainspring of Hermione's internal life. There had been that discussion of it in 'Class Room' where Hermione rhapsodised to Birkin in front of Ursula and the children. What is known is held stationary: if something or someone escapes that possession it threatens Hermione's equilibrium. We see this happening, and it leads to her form of violence.

Here, at the end of the rambling exchange, Birkin has snubbed her by refusing to join the group which she dominates, making them all go for a walk with her 'like prisoners marshalled for exercise'. She is undermined by his refusal, but compensates, saying 'with a curious stray calm: '"Then we'll leave a little boy behind, if he's sulky."' And she looked really gay while she insulted him.' None the less she has lost her equilibrium, feels compelled later to seek him out. She finds him copying the Chinese drawing of geese because, he says, one gets more of China this way 'than reading all the books'.

> 'And what do you get?'
> She was at once roused, she laid as it were violent hands on him, to extract his secrets from him. She *must* know. It was a dreadful tyranny, an obsession in her, to know all he knew. For some time he was silent, hating to answer her. Then, compelled, he began:
> 'I know what centres they live from – what they perceive and feel – the hot stinging centrality of a goose in the flux of cold water and mud – the curious bitter stinging heat of a goose's blood, entering their own blood like an inoculation of corruptive fire – fire of the cold-burning mud – the lotus mystery.' (89: 12–21)

Her urge to 'know' has been trumped: she is left speechless at his claim to 'know' something she cannot possibly grasp. Nor, actually, can we: Birkin has here launched into one of Lawrence's esotericisms, also expounded in the philosophical works, and one can be blunt and say this tells one nothing about China. However, there is point in Birkin's bringing it out here, precisely to flummox Hermione. Also, it is 'in character': Birkin does, like Lawrence, throw out these excursus-like bursts of private theory, as for instance on the African statuette in Halliday's flat. But the sceptical reader, or those who know about China and African art, may dismiss them as flights of fancy.

But then again, the business about the flux and the cold-burning mud can, for a moment, seem entirely appropriate, as when in the next chapter but one Gudrun is actually sitting 'staring fixedly at the plants that rose succulent from the mud of the low shores'. Here is something caught in the imagined setting, and vividly extended in Lawrence's direction. Moreover, when it continues 'Ursula was watching the butterflies' something about the perceptions of the sisters is turned into something about their natures.

However, it was a mistake to imagine that any character but Birkin could entertain these ideas discursively, as if they were common property, so that there is a difference between giving Gudrun the nightmare clock-image, which we can share, and giving anybody but

Birkin the doctrinal material. The notorious occasion is the one in 'Excurse' where Ursula, kneeling before Birkin, puts her hand 'full on his thighs, behind' and we get a formal exposition of Lawrence's then-current notions about this part of the body as the source of a mysterious life-flow. This is conveyed as her rhapsodic vision, but ordinary readers feel, tartly, that one could only be feeling like this if one had recently been reading the philosophical works of D.H. Lawrence and was trying hard to make them work. This is something that hasn't caught on, and won't. It links with the excessive preoccupation with men's 'loins', which can be read as homoerotic – a note which Lawrence wanted not to sound.

At this moment in 'Breadalby' Hermione is not merely checked by Birkin's evidently hostile attitude, but broken by it:

> 'Yes,' she said, as if she did not know what she were saying. 'Yes.' and she swallowed, and tried to regain her mind. But she could not, she was witless, decentralised. Use all her will as she might, she could not recover. She suffered the ghastliness of dissolution, broken and gone in a horrible corruption. And he stood and looked at her unmoved. (89: 30–5)

She re-establishes herself by putting on a characteristically eerie dress and presiding over the dinner table and the talk: 'this ruthless mental pressure, this powerful, consuming, destructive mentality that emanated from Joshua and Hermione and Birkin and dominated the rest.' After the meal she more or less commands the guests to dance, so leading naturally into one of Lawrence's *topoi*. Watching Gudrun dance, Gerald 'was unconsciously drawn to her. She was his future.' One thinks ahead to 'Water-Party' where her dancing before the Highland cattle suggests her self-confident aggressiveness; and also the later dance in the Alpine Gasthaus. At Breadalby, in the general dance which follows, Birkin's ability to forget himself 'so that he danced rapidly and with a real gaiety' makes Hermione hate him again for escaping her. Watching him, the Contessa makes an important recognition: '"Mr Birkin, he is a changer".' Hermione registers this with a deathly despair.

Birkin's dance foreshadows his strange little dance for Ursula in 'Water-Party'. What the Contessa saw in him as a 'changer' is there felt by Ursula as his oddity – his singleness, one might say: 'somewhere inside her she was fascinated [...] Yet automatically she stiffened herself away, and disapproved.' She is still making the orthodox social judgement, at this stage.

The following day at Breadalby, Birkin finds himself having that meditation about the things of the past, and how they are a confinement. Later, at breakfast, looking round at the other guests, he thinks 'how utterly he knew' them; 'how known it all was, like a game with the figures set out, the same figures, the Queen of chess, the knights, the pawns, the same now as they were hundreds of years ago [....] But the game is known, its going on is like a madness.' Near the end of the book, when Gudrun and Loerke 'played with the past [....] a sort of little game of chess' one may have forgotten that Birkin had had this vision before them. An important point is being made: Gudrun, Loerke and Birkin share crucial insights about their worlds: the difference is that he is constructing a saving faith while they retreat into a cynical self-sufficiency.

Here, Birkin's gloom about what is so utterly known is a silent comment on Hermione's compulsion to know. Suddenly he gets up and goes, and Hermione registers his departure – another moment of panic. She counters it by an exercise of will; she proposes that they all bathe: the third of her quasi-commands to the group. There is now some dissent. Her brother Alexander says he must go to church and read the lessons, and in the little discussion which follows it becomes clear that he feels he has to do this because it is expected of him as local landowner; he is not a Christian, but he believes in 'keeping up the old institutions' (revealing terms).

It is a neat touch, realistic and significant. In *The Rainbow* everyone went to church. It was not just a convention: the main characters had some element of faith remaining, or it was a real issue. In *Women in Love*, except for the wedding and funeral – social occasions – nobody goes to church except Alexander, for whom it is a caste matter, like his politics and his landowning. It goes with the eighteenth-century house. The weather is fine and warm, so, though he must of course wear a hat, he can carry his gloves, which he waves to the guests as he leaves.

The bathing scene follows. Within this chapter, it is a brief episode, neat but pointed. Within the first part of the book, that set in England, the 'water scenes' are cumulatively significant. It is another of the *topoi*: going down into water carries deep meanings for Lawrence. The realist base is the fact that Felley Mill Pond and Moorgreen Reservoir are remembered places, dear to him. They figured in *The White Peacock* and *Sons and Lovers*. They are now given significance in a sequence of episodes where the perceptions of the characters add weight. Some things seem slight but are building up the theme: as when, in 'An Island',

Ursula later finds Birkin mending an old punt, and he says, naturally enough, '"I hope it won't let me to the bottom, that's all. Though even so, it isn't a great matter, I should come up again"' (123: 33–5). This is given retrospective weight in 'Water-Party'. There Gerald, who in 'Diver' had been seen breaking the surface but confidently swimming in the 'uncreated' element, finds that he now has to dive dangerously deep in a life-and-death search, and comes up horrified:

> 'If you once die,' he said, 'then when it's over, it's finished. Why come to life again? There's room under that water there for thousands.'
>
> '[. . . .] it's curious how much room there seems, a whole universe under there; and as cold as hell, you're as helpless as if your head was cut off.'
>
> 'And do you know, when you are down there, it is so cold actually, and so endless, so different really from what it is on top, so endless – you wonder how it is so many are alive, why we're all up here.' (184: 3–20)

It was John the Baptist who had his head cut off. Diving deep, total immersion, as death to an old life and initiation into a new one gets its significance from the Christian doctrine of baptism, familiar both from the Book of Common Prayer and *Lycidas*. There the drowned friend is imagined as visiting 'the bottom of the monstrous world' and then 'mounted high / Through the dear might of Him that walked the waves': the parallel with baptism there turns drowning and mourning into triumph.

But Gerald, the unbeliever, is unable to come back up in that sense. His incoherent words here are a premonition of his eventual mounting high, into the mountain realm which is also cold, endless and has room for thousands. So when he goes down into water he is not baptised, and when he goes up into the air he is not redeemed. Both realms are for him negations, anti-life.

'Water-Party' is massive: and no reader can escape the sense of multiple significances being deployed, as for instance, the little touch when Birkin lights the lanterns of Ursula's canoe:

> 'You've got the heavens above, and the waters under the earth,' said Birkin to her.

'Anything but the earth itself,' she laughed [....] (175: 14–16)

These spatial levels are an important theme, and generate the idea of being on a dangerous surface, likely to fall through it and be lost beneath, or to rise into a life-denying space. The extraordinary little four-page chapter 'Sketch Book' has Ursula and Gudrun on that muddy bank, being approached by Gerald and Hermione in a boat. In a characteristic contest of 'unthwarted and unflinching wills' these two wrangle over Gudrun's proffered sketch-book which falls into the water and has to be pulled out by the now apologetic Gerald (who in this process has his 'loins' exposed to inspection). I suggested that the scene gives a momentary reality to Lawrence's esotericism about water-plants. They are vividly seen, so that the preoccupation emerges from the setting.

But then again, in 'Gudrun in the Pompadour' Halliday reads out Birkin's over-earnest letter: and there Lawrence seems to enjoy parodying himself, and we hear about 'all this process of active corruption, with all its flowers of mud. [...] Pussum, you are a flower of mud [....] We're all flowers of mud [....] It's perfectly wonderful, Birkin harrowing hell' (383: 37–384: 3).

One is left pondering the contrasts: Lawrence can first propose his pre-Socratic system of the twin streams of corruption, which strikes us in the abstract as willed and unconvincing; and then in 'Sketch Book' show it for a moment brilliantly instantiated; and finally guy it through Halliday. It seems for a moment as if he has recognised that his esotericism looks ridiculous, and has brilliantly sent himself up. For a moment this is a relief – but then one has to turn yet another somersault – for, of course, it helps to place Halliday and the others as the real flowers of mud that they are.

To return to Breadalby, the bathing-scene is a grotesque ballet – a procession of fantastically garbed figures crossing the grass, assembling as a mythological genre-picture of gods and nymphs, with Gerald as Dionysus, Malleson as river-god and Hermione about to become a vengeful Diana. But there are other overtones: the little Contessa swims 'like a rat', and so joins the other rat-figures, the young husband-to-be in 'A Chair' and Loerke. These are the cool outsiders who look on and can swim away, detached or exploratory. Looking at the group Gudrun notes another important parallel:

> 'Aren't they terrifying? [...] Don't they look saurian? They are just like great lizards. Did you ever see anything like Sir Joshua? But

really, Ursula, he belongs to the primeval world, when great lizards crawled about.' (101: 10–13)

There is a glancing reference back to this in 'Water-Party', when Gerald is glimpsed after his prolonged and desperate dive, and Gudrun sees him climb out of the water 'slowly, heavily, with the blind clambering motions of an amphibious beast, clumsy' (182: 38–9). More important, it is a foreshadowing of Birkin's ultimate vision of all these people passing away, as bypassed by the movement of 'the creative mystery'. 'These monsters failed to develop.' So the Contessa's vision of Birkin as 'changer', which horrifies Hermione, is a sign of grace: he can evolve.

The bathing-scene also reveals splits in the group which Hermione is desperately trying to hold together, as a herd. Alexander has to pursue his aristocratic role, Birkin is profoundly dissident, and Gudrun and Ursula refuse to swim, which is a sign of grace in them. When Gerald is 'once more the properly-dressed correct young Englishman' he asks Gudrun why she wouldn't swim. She answers '"Because I didn't like the crowd".' She is not a joiner. She and Ursula make the same point to Gerald in 'Water-Party' when they insist on leaving the crowd for their swim, their dance, their singing.

A minor issue here was nakedness. It would be unthinkable for these conventional social beings to bathe naked, and in their procession to the pond their curious costumes are noted. This reminds us of an earlier moment in Halliday's London apartment. There the young men moved about self-consciously naked, and Birkin, at first surprised, joined in. There was even a conversation about it, which pointed up their self-consciousness, but had a hint of idealism. Gerald has travelled in hot countries, and is surprised to be told by the Russian young man how '"perfectly wonderful"' it must be to '"feel the air move against me and feel the things I touched [....] I'm sure life is wrong because it has become much too visual."' The man is near, or longs for, a recovered state of innocence. His nostalgia for Eden looks forward to Birkin's later wistful longing for the somewhere still to be found, with a few other people, where one could wear few clothes or none. It also foretells his strange – or quite natural – actions after Hermione attacks him.

Gerald, however, looking at the naked Russian, feels repelled: 'Was that all a human being amounted to? So uninspired! thought Gerald.' The reaction tells one something about him. In the scene at Breadalby, on the other hand, although he makes a point about not being able to swim without a costume, once he is given a scarlet silk kerchief he is rather pleased to 'flaunt himself a little in the sun, lingering and laughing, strolling easily, looking white but natural'. One notices later in 'Water-Party' that the sisters, having escaped the crowd, quite naturally slip out of their clothes, bathe naked, and dance themselves dry. Later moments of nakedness seem a strong contrast, but are linked. In 'Gladiatorial' Birkin and Gerald strip in order to wrestle with each other (one may sense a reference to Jacob and the angel). And in 'Excurse', when Birkin and Ursula are finally committed to each other, they drive deep into the old remains of Sherwood Forest and

> They threw off their clothes, and he gathered her to him, and found her, found the pure lambent reality of her forever invisible flesh. (320: 19–21)

Hermione, now, in contrast is weirdly attired, and 'crossed the lawn like some strange memory'. She is the dominant character in the whole chapter: the sequence of events is frustrating her obsessive need to control them, and to shepherd her dependent guests; for the independent-minded Birkin, of course, and to some extent Gudrun and Ursula too, keep getting loose. Her dominance is the obverse side of a profound dependency, a total abjection, centred on Birkin. If she cannot keep him in her orbit, she disintegrates.

We remember that in the very first chapter, at the wedding ceremony, she 'was thinking only of Birkin. [...] She wanted to stand touching him. She could hardly be sure he was near her, if she did not touch him.' At the end of the ceremony 'Hermione crowded involuntarily up against Birkin, to touch him. And he endured it.' This may seem a shrewd psychological insight. It is also one of Lawrence's submerged Biblical allusions – to the woman 'with an issue of blood' who touched Jesus in the crowd:

> And Jesus said, who touched me? When all denied, Peter and they that were with him said, Master, the multitude throng thee and press thee, and sayest thou, who touched me? And Jesus said, somebody hath touched me: for I perceive that virtue[1] is gone out of me. (Luke 8: 44)

---

[1] Lawrence used 'virtue' in this sense in *The Trespasser*, 'Delilah and Mr Bircumshaw', 'St Mawr' and 'David'. The reader may also remember 'Hadrian', first called 'You Touched Me', and 'The Blind Man'.

The allusion is suppressed because it is not desirable to endorse what is satirically called Birkin's *Salvator Mundi* image, but the concept of the sick person seeking aid is operative. Hermione's desperate hold on Birkin and his fighting clear are a main current of the early narrative, the other being the development of the love between Birkin and Ursula. What Birkin wants to maintain is his 'singleness' in a relation with a woman, so that they constitute a couple without this possessiveness. Hermione has to be fought off. It is not just a reaction: the search is developed intellectually as the basis of marriage and social life.

This concern begins to emerge in the group discussion about social identity – one of the formal discussions in the book, where the personae express views in tune with their characters while Birkin develops his opposition. Malleson leads off by saying that 'the great social idea [...] is the *social* equality of man.' Gerald demurs: some people, he says, are fit only to do subordinate tasks: the unifying ideal is 'the work in hand' and it is the business of production which holds men together. This is his industrial version of Skrebensky's 'service' collective ideal. It is mechanical, but his society *is* a mechanism. Pressed about love between men and women, he says that such relations are 'my own affair'. The disjunction is pointed out, but he fails to see that it matters. Hermione makes a solemn remark to the effect that 'in the spirit we are all one [...] all brothers there' and Birkin turns on her with a credo which we recognise as endorsed by Lawrence:

> 'Just the contrary, Hermione. We are all different and unequal in spirit – it is only the *social* differences that are based on accidental material conditions. We are all abstractly or mathematically equal, if you like. Every man has hunger and thirst, two eyes, one nose and two legs. [...] But spiritually, there is pure difference and neither equality nor inequality counts. It is upon these two bits of knowledge that you must found a state. Your democracy is an absolute lie – your brotherhood of man is a pure falsity, if you apply it further than the mathematical abstraction. [...]
>
> '[...] what have I to do with equality – with any other man or woman? In the spirit, I am as separate as one star is from another [....] Establish a state on *that*. One man isn't any better than another, not because they are equal, but because they are intrinsically other [...]' (103: 24–40)

We note the first use of Birkin's 'stellar' image. The argument is important not just because it gives Birkin the occasion to formulate his view. The merely theoretical or political high-mindedness of Malleson and Hermione is given weight by the anguished attempt by Gerald's father Thomas Crich, 'The Industrial Magnate' of a later chapter, to live by the late nineteenth-century Christian version of this liberal social consciousness. He is the Victorian patriarch of the mining area. He finds that his Christian heritage of general benevolence and his acts of specific generosity have no real effect, since he is not, in the classic prescription, willing to sell all that he has and give it to the poor. But he is eaten up by the problem of wanting to live well and is ultimately broken by the conflict. It crystallises in his wife's fierce opposition to his self-deception, his being willing to be preyed on by parasites, but not to be whole-hearted either way. So the mild remark that Ursula now makes to Gerald at Breadalby ('"But won't it be rather difficult to arrange the two halves?"') is later dramatically instantiated, at length, by Gerald's father.

There is a link backward with the affair Gerald had had with the Pussum in London. He was uneasily aware that he had used her, made her instrumental in his characteristic way; and in half-guilty conversation with Birkin suggested that his conscience would be easier if he had given her, say, £10. So now, when Gerald says, lightly and impercipiently, '"Between me and a woman the social question does not enter. It is my own affair."' Birkin's quick '"A ten-pound note on it"' may pass unnoticed, as it does by the unconscious Gerald, but is a neat touch, and helps to make the point that, though men and women in love are also part of society, the economic argument accounts fully for nothing.

The upshot of the conversation for Hermione is that she is filled with 'violent waves of hatred and loathing [...] coming strong and black out of the unconsciousness.' Birkin's determined singleness means that he escapes possession; and her instability is triggered by his escape. The scene which follows, where she attacks him, prefigures the late scene in which Gerald attacks Gudrun and nearly kills her, when a similar struggle has been played out, with Gudrun in her own way insisting on her 'singleness'.

The remarks and incidents leading to Hermione's violence began in the 'Shortlands' chapter with her saying '"Probably I should kill him."' Within a couple of pages, Birkin, talking about 'singleness' again, had that brush with Gerald, who thought '"We should be cutting everyone else's throat",' to which Birkin made his classic response about the murderer and the murderee. In the next chapter, 'Class-room', Birkin fell out with Hermione in front of Ursula, and spoke violently, unforgiveably, out of his opposition to '"your fixed will".' He went on: '"But your passion is a lie [...] it is your will. It's your bullying will. [...] You want to have things in your power [....] your lust for power, to *know*."' Indeed he was carried away:

> 'You want it all in that loathsome little skull of yours, that ought to be cracked like a nut. For you'll be the same till it *is* cracked, like an insect in its skin. – If one cracked your skull perhaps one might get a spontaneous passionate woman out of you, with real sensuality.' (42: 31–5)

It was all the more unforgiveable for being true; and it presages Hermione's attempt now to crack *his* skull in revenge at Breadalby: she pays him back. Feeling compunction, he has sought her out in her room, finds her writing, and sits down to read. She brings the ball of lapis lazuli down on his head, twice, but his book deflects the second blow. He says: '"No you don't, Hermione [....] I don't let you"' – so declaring that he is not a murderee.

Barely conscious, he leaves the house, and has his extraordinary epiphany. He is just aware that 'he was moving in a sort of darkness'.

> Yet he wanted something. He was happy in the wet hill-side, that was overgrown and obscure with bushes and flowers. He wanted to touch them all, to saturate himself with the touch of them all. He took off his clothes, and sat down naked among the primroses, moving his feet softly among the primroses, his legs, his knees, his arms right up to the arm-pits, then lying down and letting them touch his belly, his breasts. It was such a fine, cool, subtle touch all over him, he seemed to saturate himself with their contact.
>
> But they were too soft. He went through the long grass to a clump of young fir-trees [....] The soft sharp boughs beat upon him, as he moved in keen pangs against them [....] To lie down and roll in the sticky, cool young hyacinths, to lie on one's belly and cover one's back with handfuls of fine wet grass, soft as a breath, soft and more delicate and more beautiful than the touch of any woman; and then to sting one's thigh against the living dark bristles of the fir-boughs; [...] and then to clasp the silvery birch-trunk against one's breast [...] this was good, this was all very good, very satisfying. Nothing else would do, nothing else would satisfy, except this coolness and subtlety of vegetation travelling into one's blood. (106: 36–107: 20)

At the level of realism one can say: well, of course he is suffering from shock and concussion, so he has a kind of fugue – people do. It is also a natural reaction away from people and their violent possessiveness to escape into the open, and to drop social and emotional complications with one's clothes, and go back to Eden. But there is more to it than that.

It is something Lawrence had attempted to catch in *The White Peacock*:

> Over the hill, the big flushed face of the moon poised just above the tree-tops, very majestic, and far off – yet imminent. I turned with swift sudden friendliness to the net of elm-boughs spread over my head, dotted with soft clusters winsomely. I jumped up and pulled the cool soft tufts against my face for company, and as I passed, still I reached upwards for the touch of this budded gentleness of the trees. The wood breathed fragrantly, with a subtle sympathy. The firs softened their touch to me, and the larches woke from the barren winter-sleep, and put out velvet fingers to caress me as I passed. (WP 152: 5–13)

It's early writing, and lush. The moon may represent something female, like Hermione, and the need to escape is comparable. The trees offer 'friendliness', which seems satisfying and uncomplicated because not human. But what Birkin has is like a paradisal pre-human equivalent of sexual intercourse where he is taken out of his humanity and united with these other forms of life. There is even a hint that he ejaculates: 'He knew now where he belonged. He knew where to plant himself, his seed' – and of course 'seed' links humans and plants.

Within the argument of the whole book the episode epitomises Birkin's dissatisfaction with social life, with people as they are, his feeling that they may become unable to evolve and so may be superseded, his willingness to contemplate a world where we humans have destroyed ourselves, leaving the hare sitting up in the grass, his feeling that other forms of life are sane and self-contained. The trance, or vision which is granted him as an intense physical experience, rendered in the terms of human sexual love, is a religious experience. The sexual analogy is the one that humans turn to, so raising the old question about the Song of Songs: which way does the analogy lead?

The English literary analogy is with Marvell's *The Garden* (No. 112 in *The Golden Treasury*), where the controlling wit, the intellectual parallel with Eden, cool the same kind of erotic notation:

> No white nor red was ever seen
> So amorous as this lovely green.
>
> When we have run our passions' heat
> Love hither makes his best retreat:
> The gods, who mortal beauty chase,
> Still in a tree did end their race.
>
> What wondrous life is this I lead!
> Ripe apples drop about my head:
> The luscious clusters of the vine
> Upon my mouth do crush their wine;
> The nectarine and curious peach
> Into my hands themselves do reach;
> Stumbling on melons as I pass,
> Ensnared with flowers I fall on grass.
>
> Meanwhile the mind from pleasure less
> Withdraws into its happiness [....]
>
> Annihilating all that's made
> To a green thought in a green shade.

Marvell inverts the Eden-reference as Lawrence does. Eve is a late-comer, an intruder:

> Such was that happy Garden-state
> While man there walk'd without a mate:
> After a place so pure and sweet
> What other help could yet be meet!
> But 'twas beyond a mortal's share
> To wander solitary there:
> Two paradises 'twere in one
> To dwell in Paradise alone.

Birkin's Eve joins him in paradise later, in 'Excurse'. His entries into the realm of non-human life in this world contrast with Gerald's epiphanies, which are equally characteristic, but negative. Gerald is seen throughout the book as a kind of projectile. In 'Diver' the sisters comment on his 'go' as they watch him hurl himself into the water. He merely breaks the surface, and is able to exult in the momentary dominance of the element. But in 'Water-Party' he has to dive deep and stay down as long as he can, is defeated and comes out horrified. In the Alps he is first of all a projectile again, on his toboggan and his skis; but that too is surface-skimming, and in the final episode he goes up into the region where there is no life. We also remember that long circuitous walk into the night after his father dies and he fears he is losing his grip on his life: his unconscious pilgrimage takes him to his father's grave – from which he has to go to Gudrun's bed to recover his sense of self. In him, the association of death with desperate dependence is as if consecrated. And at the end, just before he collapses in the snow, we may not notice, as he himself scarcely notices, the little crucifix in the snow – which gives him the strange sense that he is going to be murdered. What do we make of that? Jesus Christ as murderee?

These extreme contrasting experiences of Birkin and Gerald make narrative sense, and we can simply take them as what happens. They may be rationalised as symbolic elements in the human story. They are also like brief openings in the clouds, moments of vision in which the two main male characters, in extremity, are felt to be negotiating a universe which transcends the daily here and now. In a society in which nobody goes to church, it is in moments and settings like these that a meaning – for Birkin – or lack of meaning – for Gerald – may be glimpsed. We came to see, in *The Rainbow*, that such extraordinary moments are varieties of religious experience. They occur in *Women in Love*, but now are rare, and for Gerald, annihilating because they answer to the nothingness which he projects.

12
Women in Love: Birkin and Lawrence: Loerke

The leading voice in most of the discussions is Birkin's: he puts forward the ideas that others find strange, and he contests their received ideas – or indeed what they think are their advanced ideas. The reader soon grasps that he is a Lawrence-figure; but that is not a simple identity.

More than most authors, Lawrence in his novels used his own experiences to formulate or explore – and now and then to contest or even mock – his own thought. In this way he could develop or test what other authors might have presented as concluded. There was point in doing this through a persona who was like him; otherwise this viewpoint could only be presented or implied by the narrative voice, and the drive of the novel would be taken over by it. In *The White Peacock*, in *Sons and Lovers*, in *Women in Love* and later in *Mr Noon*, *Aaron's Rod* and *Kangaroo*, there is a Lawrence-figure. Cyril Birdsall in *The White Peacock* is also the narrator, and is heard to say Lawrentian things, so that he becomes the most immediate of these representatives. Paul Morel in *Sons and Lovers* is given a family and a childhood very like Lawrence's – the differences are minor. He is not the narrator, but there has been a perception that the narrative voice does not distance itself from him, so that the novel is 'unfair' to Miriam Leivers and to Paul's father. I have made the case elsewhere that the narrative structure of the book and its imagery – now that we have it in its original form, with Garnett's excisions restored – do distance the action and permit an independent judgement of Paul. Even so the point is a real one, and not confined to *Sons and Lovers*. It happens in a specific form in *The Rainbow*, as we saw. Readers find themselves thinking, Who is saying this? Is it Lawrence? So we come full circle: there is real point in his having a representative, so that the Lawrence voice can be played off against others.

The related difficulty was met in the discussion of 'Elsa Culverwell'. If Lawrence gives the narrative voice to a character, that person is bound to be heard saying things which only Lawrence could come up with – otherwise he can't get his novel to convey what he wants it to. The issue was usefully fudged in *The White Peacock*: Cyril can not only tell us things he can't have known, he can have thoughts only Lawrence could have, but we don't mind hearing Lawrence through this disguise. In the 'Burns' fragment Jack Haseldine feels extraordinary things, but then he is an artist and in any case doesn't put them into words. It is Lawrence's supreme gift to render the wordless – intuitions, aspirations, fears, projections – as metaphor. Elsa Culverwell on the other hand was always showing an expressive gift, a novelist's gift – indeed Lawrence's gift – when she is not, we suppose, a specially remarkable person.

There is an additional problem in the mature and programmatic novel *Women in Love*; for here Lawrence wishes to convey his own set of developing ideas about English society and the relationships possible within it. This cannot be formal exposition, it must be dramatic, but it needs to be expressed in a pointed, extensive and sequential way. It also needs to be contested. That could produce a familiar problem: the wordy set-piece debate found in the ordinary novel of ideas, using the novelist's *porte-parole*, as in Shaw, where one dreads the moment when the spokesman begins to put everyone right.

So a Birkin is called for. He needs to be an intellectual, and to have a verbal gift. Yet he cannot be allowed to be always conscious, always coherent, still less always right. He has to be human, and to be a character of the same substance as the others, with limitations. He needs to be a seeker; to feel that he has not yet got all the way there, to fail sometimes to get things out successfully and to have to reformulate them, to be subject to mood, to have defects and limitations. He needs also to be resisted, even by the people who love him, and to be effectively criticised for his failings. So others, especially Ursula, who loves him, make effective points against him. It is both her gift and her failing that she often fails to see what he is getting at, and in doing so more than half-implies that it is over-sophisticated intellectualising or grasping at phantoms, and that she, in her instinctive way, is closer to the truth. This is an important possibility, which at moments he contemplates. None the less, he *is* Lawrence's representative; if he does not himself represent or express all that the book does, it is because the narrative, independently of him, presents a massive drama, especially the conflict of Gerald and Gudrun, of which he is, like us, the horrified spectator. This is not presented through his consciousness, and he has no words for it.

The novel, therefore, has two elements represented by the couples who are the principal actors. The Birkin–Ursula drama is positive: an attempt, which looks like being successful, at an emotional partnership by a pair emerging from traditional English society: a marriage, a life together – of a sort. I say that because I think the ordinary reader comes out on the other side of being moved and convinced, and says of specific aspects, 'Well, no, actually.'

The other drama, of Gerald and Gudrun, is an imaginative triumph, and horrifying. There is an implication that if we cannot manage what Birkin and Ursula are trying for, we are likely to go the way that the other couple goes. It is a disaster, and more likely to happen because more representative – more like us. The further implication is that it is these two who represent the drive of modern Western society, and war is the national expression of what we see happening at the personal level. That is why Birkin, contemplating the frozen corpse of the man to whom he had offered love, feels that humanity faces catastrophe. The natural reaction of the reader who has been swept along by the final chapters is to be profoundly taken aback, and to feel that since 1921 not much has changed. And yet we are still here, so ...? Once again that is the way the book leaves us really thinking, not just briefly convinced, and that, actually, is its continuing force.

An important aspect of the Gerald–Birkin relationship is that Birkin proposes that bond which complements their love for a chosen woman, and has related importance and continuance – blood-brotherhood, he calls it. Love would be a better word. But that raises a problem – still – for the reader. Is this covert homosexuality, or acceptance that bisexuality is a norm? Or is Birkin proposing a new relationship which escapes our conventional categories? We do know with some certainty that between 1915 and 1917 Lawrence faced in himself a homosexual component, and I have shown how in the philosophical works of the period he made this into a kind of poetry.[1]

If we look back to *The White Peacock*, the very touching relationship between Cyril Beardsall and George Saxton, with its high point in that scene where they bathe naked together, presented a long, close, indeed loving relationship between two young men, one of whom – George – finds it hard to succceed in his love for women, while the other – Cyril

---

[1] Especially in 'The Crown' and 'The Reality of Peace'. See BEPW, index: homoeroticism.

– hardly tries. What they have together is better than what they can manage with women.

That first approach to the topic was either simplified or complicated by what I believe to be Lawrence's own imperfect consciousness – at that time – of himself and what he was writing. This was abetted by a general public unconsciousness or innocence: also by a literary tradition going back to the classics (the Nisus and Euryalus story); the Bible (David and Jonathan); *Lycidas*, that elegy for a loved young man which supplies a number of allusions in Lawrence's first novel; and the general public school, university and service ethos of male friendship. This old tradition had its ambiguities, perhaps useful ones. It did assume that manly men could perfectly well have a noble friendship, passing the love of women. It is something Lawrence now wishes to re-animate, on the other side of the horrified silent crystallisation of ambiguity which followed Wilde's trial and imprisonment.

The abandoned 'Prologue' to *Women in Love*, written in the Spring of 1916 and deleted early in 1917, makes two things clear – or rather its abandonment does. In this earlier opening to the novel the relationship between Birkin and Gerald has lasted already for four years. 'They knew they loved each other, that each would die for the other.' 'Birkin felt a passion of desire for Gerald Crich', while Gerald 'felt a great tenderness towards Birkin'. Crucially, Birkin

> recognised that, although he was always drawn to women, feeling more at home with a woman than with a man, yet it was for men that he felt the hot, flushing, roused attraction which a man is supposed to feel for the other sex. Although nearly all his living interchange went on with one woman or another, although he was always terribly intimate with at least one woman and practically never intimate with a man, yet the male physique had an attraction for him, and for the female physique he felt only a fondness, a sort of sacred love, as for a sister.
>
> In the street, it was the men who roused him by their flesh and their manly, vigorous movement, quite apart from all individual character (501: 35–502: 6)

The narrative goes on to tell how he had felt a keen attraction to 'the soldier who had sat pressed up close to him' on a train, and a 'young man in flannels on the sands at Margate, flaxen and ruddy like a Viking of twenty-three', and, revealingly, a strange Cornish type of man, with dark eyes like holes in his head, or like the eyes of a rat, and with dark, fine, rather stiff hair, and full, heavy, softly-strong limbs. Then again Birkin would feel the desire spring up in him, the desire to know this man, to have him, as it were to eat him, to take the very substance of him. (505: 1–5)

He sums it up:

This was the one and only secret he kept to himself, this secret of his passionate and sudden, spasmodic affinity for men he saw. He kept this secret even from himself. He knew what he felt, but he always kept the knowledge at bay. His a priori were: 'I *should not* feel like this,' and 'It is the ultimate mark of my own deficiency, that I feel like this.' Therefore, though he admitted everything, he never really faced the question. He never accepted the desire, and received it as part of himself. He always tried to keep it expelled from him. (505: 21–8)

This is a painful honesty, and one assumes it comes from Lawrence. The Cornish man is surely a reminiscence of William Henry Hocking, with whom he had had a relationship like the earlier one with Alan Chambers, the George Saxton of *The White Peacock*. However, all this can only get in the way of writing *Women in Love*, which cannot afford to seem to be about repressed or sublimated homosexuality, or accepted bisexuality, or just not knowing where one stands. It has to start from a basis which is self-assured and can be shared by most readers.

Nor can it be burdened with the other part of Lawrence's own psychic baggage, the part indicated in the remark about 'a sister', where one feels like adding 'and mother'. It is also made clear in the 'Prologue' that Birkin's affair with Hermione Roddice was, in this draft, a rewriting of the Paul Morel–Miriam Leivers relationship in *Sons and Lovers* – and indeed Lawrence's own relationship with Jessie Chambers. It only becomes a sexual relationship because he insists that they *must* now do this, and she consents to sacrifice herself, both of them then feeling that it is a failure, a betrayal. She is devoted and submissive, and he first exploits her and then rejects her because she is ... too much like his mother, we presume.

It was an act of intelligence and self-knowledge on Lawrence's part to reject all this and start again. Lawrence's Birkin has to have Lawrence's independence of mind and his alienation from society, but not his psychosexual problems. He must be able, from a more neutral base, to seek for an ideal sexual relationship with a woman, both of them being as free to do so as humanly conceivable. He also wants an ideal relationship with another man.

The Rupert Birkin we have in the published text has, for all we know, no parents: no problem there. He is not working-class. He is an Oxford graduate, former Fellow of Magdalen, and is now an Inspector of Schools – like Matthew Arnold. His being upper-middle-class and Oxford makes his affair with Hermione more probable – she does not have to inspect him curiously from above as she does the Brangwen girls. His work in schools gives him a natural contact with Ursula.

He is not homosexual or bisexual: the desire for a lifelong bond with another man is a strong emotional need, even an intellectual one, but not sexual. This is demonstrated when the two wrestle naked but are not erotically aroused, even though Birkin recognises that Gerald is beautiful. The only physical form their love takes is that at several crucial moments they instinctively clasp hands – always a profoundly significant gesture for Lawrence: one might call it a pure contact between whole people. At the end of the book, that contact survives in Birkin's mind: '[...] how once Gerald had clutched his hand, with a warm, momentaneous grip of final love.'

Conclusively, this non-sexual male bond is specifically set off against the powerful figure of Loerke, the German sculptor who enters the book in its final phase. On a first reading he is a baleful, villainous man. On second thought, he is interesting because he has some of the characteristics Lawrence was careful not to give to Birkin, and so becomes a counterweight, an anti-Birkin, but linked to Birkin in his own form of 'singleness'. He is first met in the company of his humble, dominated, young male lover, who is about to be cast off without compunction. The argument with the sisters about Loerke's statue – the naked girl on the horse – elicits the information that he did indeed sexually exploit the young model, because he likes only very young women. He is prepared to have a relationship with Gudrun, though she is older, because she is beautiful and – more important – he recognises in her his own clinical detachment from the world, his entire self-sufficiency. He and she are the people in the book who don't need anyone else, resent being needed, and finally reject the needy person. He tells Gudrun about the poverty of his childhood in the slums of central Europe: he has starved, stolen, and possibly prostituted himself:

'And how did you live then?' asked Ursula.
He looked at her – then, suddenly, at Gudrun.
'Do you understand?' he said.
'Enough,' she replied.
Their eyes met for a moment. Then he looked away. He would say no more. (425: 36–426: 2)

Hence, in part, his ruthless detachment. His reflection on his experience has influenced his art, inevitably. It has distanced him from life and suffering. He says startlingly modernist things about art: he is well on the way to the Bauhaus, and indeed to abstraction. There is an implication here both about the course of art in the twentieth century, and why it went that way: once again Lawrence is prophetic.

Loerke is clear that in the twentieth century people are subjected to, even created by, their labour. It is not just their social role, it is their nature. For that reason art, which once served religion, must now serve industry. The beautiful factory will take the place of the cathedral, and people will worship in it by working. His art will make the factory beautiful. This is the explicit opposite of what Birkin has been saying about work, and carries Gerald's willing but unconscious instrumentality to the point of perverse illumination.

So Loerke is Birkin's distorted image. They are both powerfully confident of their intelligence and insight, both physically slight, almost insignificant. They both have a sardonic turn of phrase. They both mean exactly what they are saying, in the company of people who are less intelligent and less conscious. The fact that Gudrun finally gravitates towards this strange power once she has seen through Gerald and his needy dependence is an indication that one major movement of the intellect in the century would be towards this standing-off, this dissociation.

Near the end of the book Gudrun contemplates the change of relationship:

At least, it was time for her now to pass over to the other, the creature, the final craftsman. She knew that Loerke, in his innermost soul, was detached from everything, for him there was neither heaven nor earth nor hell. He admitted no allegiance, he gave no adherence anywhere. He was single and, by abstraction from the rest, absolute in himself. (452: 21–6)

The word 'single' has been Birkin's theme. Applied to Loerke, it catches exactly their inverted relationship. It is a sign of the difficulty of Birkin's position that it may side-slip into this perversion.

Birkin, however, is not an artist or a writer. Perhaps it is a mistake that he is not, since his impulse just to leave, to have no home, no work, means that he is left with no obvious point in his life beyond the marriage to Ursula, which sounds as if it is going to be childless, and possibly stormy. What will they do? To be a rootless expatriate was either a pointless or a harrowing experience in the twentieth century. Writers and artists took their talents with them, but if one looks back now on most of the English and American writers in self-chosen exile in the 1920s and 1930s – some of whom the Lawrences knew – they seem mostly an exported variant of the London-based triflers Lawrence was so scornful about. Writers of genius, such as Lawrence, could turn their exile to advantage. Birkin cannot. Loerke, on the other hand, doesn't need to leave what he is so profoundly dissociated from.

In not making Birkin a writer, Lawrence may have thought he was making him more representative – but could later have come to feel that he had actually weakened his case. Birkin's leaving England seems to be motivated entirely by the condition of England itself. This is portrayed to grim effect – one can share the revulsion – yet as Birkin says to Ursula, other societies are as bad in their own way. But if as England's leading young writer Birkin had written a great and healthgiving book which had been suppressed as obscene, he would have a personal justification which also revealed the deathly social instinct in his country.

Lawrence may have come to see this. In the 'Nightmare' chapter in *Kangaroo*, the story of his life from 1915 to 1918 is told, to explain why the Lawrence-figure Somers, who is a writer, finds himself in Australia. It does recount a persecution, and does explain the urge to leave, but even here there is no *Rainbow* case. The horror recounted is that of English wartime public hysteria: the currents of persecuting massemotion overbearing the instincts of the decent individual. What England was against in those years was not so much Germany as 'singleness'. 'England My England' touched on that mass-emotion, and began to convey a defeated impulse to stand out against it. It was part of the current of feeling which banned *The Rainbow* and hunted the Lawrences out of Cornwall. 'Singleness' really was persecuted at that time. That history would have supported Birkin's instinct and helped to explain his self-exile.

A postscript. Birkin and Gerald have a conversation about Loerke: Gerald is puzzled at the attraction he exerts. Birkin offers a diagnosis: Loerke is '"a good many stages further than you or I can go".' He explains:

> 'Stages further in social hatred [....] He lives like a rat, in the river of corruption, just where it falls over into the bottomless pit. He's further on than we are. He hates the ideal more acutely [....] yet it still dominates him. I expect he is a Jew – or part Jewish.' (428: 17–21)

It sounds to us, now, like anti-Semitism. But Lawrence's 'rat' image is always more complex than that. Look back at the 'Cornish' man, who also had the eyes of a rat, at the sharp-sighted little Contessa in 'Breadalby', at the young working-man trapped into marriage in 'A Chair'. They share a detachment from the social group, a self-sufficiency and independent judgement which gives them their aura of separateness. That is why people may be against them, as they are against rats: the animals are disturbingly other.

One characteristic dilemma of Jews, on the other hand, especially intellectuals and professionals in the old Germany, was that those who most earnestly wished to be assimilated were still rejected as alien by popular sentiment and by nationalist theoreticians of the *Volk*. They couldn't win. But Loerke's total detachment makes him the leading 'rat' figure in the sense of a completely disabused outsider, who no longer wants to have any part in the society he sees through – and he expresses his detachment in his art, with its curious ability to express what industrial society is now about: its unconscious religion. This places him not alongside, but 'a good many stages' ahead of Birkin, who still has feelings of pain and resentment about his society, such that he has to get out; and who if he were a writer would convey this in books like *The Rainbow* and *Women in Love*.

The historical irony is that after 1933 Loerke's 'singleness' would be seen as a provocation. His art would be declared *entartet* – degenerate – as *The Rainbow* was in England in 1915. He would either join Birkin in exile, or be killed.

13
Women in Love: The Project

An attractive aspect of Birkin's nature is that he can switch off his intensity, indeed his mental activiity, and just let things be for a time. We see him doing it more than once, most notably in 'Excurse' when he and Ursula have had a very human row and she has walked off in a fury. He falls silent, and as it were deflates. She comes back with a flower for him, and in musical terms they can start a new positive movement.

None the less the intensity of his preoccupation, his search, is one driving force of the action. It is clear that he is trying to find a new way of being in love, and to find the person who will accept him, and it. That is the hard part. Ursula, he becomes convinced, is the person he wants to set out with on this journey; but she finds it easier to accept him, for all his complications, than this new way of his – for the usual reason that she has her own ideas, and they are at the outset conventional.[1] They seem to remain so, it has to be said.

It is not hard for her to abandon the project of the 'little grey home in the West' because from the start she rejects her own home; both the sordid industrial setting, Beldover, and the house that is shown sad and empty when her parents have left it, so that she wonders how it could ever have been her home. She agrees to present the lovely old chair to the young couple about to be married because the girl is

---

[1] At one point Ursula says to him '"You don't want to serve me"', and he retorts angrily '"What you want me to serve, is nothing [....] it is your mere female quality [....] it's a rag doll".' This foreshadows the later novella *The Captain's Doll*, in which the little cleverly made image of the Captain symbolises the attempt to capture him, or his nature, by the women who love him. It is an essential possessiveness, and includes the artist's possessiveness in trying to capture another's nature in a representation.

pregnant. The young man is being trapped into marriage because of his sexual adventure, and is resigning himself to it. It is suggested, however, that the girl is having her maternal urge fulfilled, and is going to run the marriage. Ursula has more complicated feelings about this than Birkin does. It's right for them, she says, which sounds immensely condescending but might actually be a touch envious. He is against all that.

The two families presented for inspection are Ursula's and Gerald's. Ursula's we may think we know from *The Rainbow*, but actually it has changed. Will has lost his openness, his searching, and become a stupid, conventional, lower-middle-class prototype. Yet he has his moment when Birkin absentmindedly calls to propose to Ursula, finds her not there, has to engage in conversation with Will, and comes out with his 'liberated' thoughts about marriage, which is 'over' if the participants regret it. This is actually inconsistent with his overall search, and with what he himself says more than once. He is thinking that Will, in his conventionality is a 'roomful of old echoes'; but Will scornfully retorting 'in and out like a frog in a galleypot' is for moment a source of folk-wisdom. But when Ursula in her absent mode says she is going to leave home, and adds that Will has always bullied her, he proves the truth of it by hitting her, so joining the violent majority doing what Birkin at the outset of the book called 'the collective thing' – and that is not 'right for them' at all; for him they are 'the common ruck'. For Ursula the blow is a decisive moment: she leaves and joins Birkin for good: they get married.

That external impetus crystallised the issue; but it is another matter entirely to grasp and accept the kind of relationship Birkin is seeking with her. There is an issue of 'character' here. Before that first failed proposal Ursula watched Birkin stoning the image of the moon, and grasped that *she* was in some sense the target, or women like her, or all women. Birkin, however, carrying out his compulsive, repetitive and above all delusory action is giving way to an unconscious drive. However, one hint contained in the imagery – that the moon-image, restoring itself, converts from polyp to rose – suggests that one aspect of the thing he is attacking is the thing he wants, and not separable. He identifies this with the not-otherwise-to-be-expressed characteristic of Ursula that she has a golden radiance in her, and he wants her to bestow it on him. This is not like the moon, and is what he loves in her: something she is not conscious of and does not control. It is his perceptiveness to see and prize it, but he can only have it with the rest of her.

So an odd, not obvious aspect of the art of that chapter 'Moony' is that after the highly symbolic episode at the pond we only *seem* to drop into the everyday. Birkin makes his call and has that conversation with Will. It actually starts with Birkin remarking in passing that it was a full moon two days earlier, and Will doubts whether the moon really affects the weather – small talk, but highly relevant. It may dawn on us later that Birkin has been throwing stones into the pond again, the pond now being the Brangwen home. What re-forms as image is first Will's total conventionality, and then Ursula's unwillingness, when she is told about the call, to take on Birkin's ideas:

> She knew what kind of love, what kind of surrender he wanted. And she was not at all sure that [...] it was this mutual unison in separateness that she wanted. She wanted unspeakable intimacies. She wanted to have him, utterly, finally to have him as her own, oh, so unspeakably, in intimacy [....] And subtly enough, she knew he would never abandon himself *finally* to her. He did not believe in final self-abandonment. He said it openly. It was his challenge. She was prepared to fight him for it. (264: 29–265: 2)

This is Ursula as moon, and the moonlight is the reflection of old ideas about love which actually minister to the ego. What Birkin wants, the sun aspect, is partly what he divines as her intrinsic nature, and partly what he works out intellectually as his ideal, his project. It is a piece of realism that the two things are so hard to separate.

The intrinsic nature, the true self, is identified in his mind with his concept of 'singleness', and this has been a topic since that early moment when the bride had the grace, as he saw it, to race the groom to the church. It produced the crucial interchange with Gerald which set the agenda for the whole action of the novel. And it is essential that 'the collective thing' not only produces concepts and habits of possessive love: it produces a violence, which is shown in the course of the book to be related, and reveals that some are murderers and most are murderees. It all coheres.

The whole ensuing action is the unfolding of this process. We have seen Birkin, attacked by Hermione, refusing to be a murderee. At the end Gudrun very nearly becomes one. In 'Water-Party' she hits Gerald for no reason except that it is in her nature. 'The first blow', she says, 'And I shall strike the last.' Towards the end:

> She knew her next step – she knew what she would move on to,

when she left Gerald. She was afraid of Gerald, that he might kill her. But she did not intend to be killed. A fine thread still united her to him. It should not be *her* death which broke it. – She had further to go [...] (452: 12–16)

And in the eventual enactment:

But Gudrun had moved forward. She raised her clenched hand high, and brought it down, with a great downward stroke, over the face and on to the breast of Gerald.

A great astonishment burst upon him, as if the air had broken. Wide, wide his soul opened, in wonder, feeling the pain. Then it laughed, turning, with strong hands outstretched, at last to take the apple of his desire. At last he could finish his desire.

He took the throat of Gudrun between his hands [...] (471: 26–33)

The apple of his desire is her Adam's apple: the old Adam, we might say. Gudrun's violence imitates Hermione's, but Gerald's reaction is not Birkin's: it is the collective thing.

If one asks where is this leading – surely away from ideas of love? the answer is no. Hermione and Gudrun are both women in love – Gerald's love is like theirs and turns to violence because it cannot face singleness. They are in complementary rather than opposite positions: rejection by Birkin in Hermione's case, rejection of Gerald in Gudrun's. What Gudrun rejects in Gerald is his absolute dependence on her which threatens her kind of singleness – which is absolute refusal of commitment to anyone.

She turns instead to Loerke because he has his own kind of singleness, which chimes with hers. They are both artists, and there is more than a hint here that twentieth-century artists, in their world of abstraction, no longer need people. As Loerke puts it, '"you *must not* confuse the relative world of action with the absolute world of art".' Ursula's angry denunciation of him is not just the conventional person's rejection of what sounds like art-nonsense, it is a perception which links art to the whole drive of the book. Gudrun confirms him:

'*I* and my art, they have *nothing* to do with each other. My art stands in another world, I am in this world.'

Women in Love: *The Project*   221

Loerke murmurs his agreement. But Ursula has the last word. To the aesthetes it sounds amateurish and philistine, but it is the truth:

> 'As for your world of art and your world of reality,' she replied, 'you have to separate the two, because you can't bear to know what you are. [...] The world of art is only the truth about the real world, that's all – but you are too far gone to see it.' (431: 1–29)

Birkin in his singleness is none the less committed to a relationship, but has to find one which is not dependent, exploitative or merely conventional, and which is maintained with an equally single, conscious, willing person. A problem here is that this endeavour requires in both partners extraordinary self-knowledge – unless they are phenomenally unselfconscious and at the same time independent – if it is not to sink into the ordinary sorts of infatuation and possessiveness. We know that in other contexts Lawrence deplored hyper-consciousness; but it seems we do not escape paradoxes, and this is the arch-paradox in his work, which does itself supremely raise consciousness.

Birkin expounds to the resistant Ursula his notion of the two people permanently linked in a sort of orbit like planets, separate but related. The formulation is crucial, but is so well known that I do not need to quote it. She retorts that she will not be a satellite, and they have a characteristic falling-out over his metaphor. Her own conception – that he should 'serve' her – sounds remarkably like being a satellite. She retains the old belief in love as a chivalrous affair in which the knight vows himself in service to the lady. Birkin will have none of that.

Their arguments, their quarrels, are deftly dramatised. It is born in on the reader that what can be done by intense discussion and disagreement is intelligently and persistently pursued, but that in the end even Birkin is let down by his verbalisation. Failing a truly adequate formula, he can only point, and if the other person is not looking in the same direction, she will not see what he is pointing at. He is not defining concepts so much as trying to discriminate experiences and life-stances, indeed pointing to an unknown.

Moreover Birkin grasps that the essential indefinable something in Ursula which he loves is impossible to seize completely in words. He does his best to find images: he calls it the golden light which she seems to shed; or it is like the rose which he glimpses when the 'moony' polyp is stubbornly re-forming. The whatever-it-is is in there among the things he would rather not have to deal with – part of this whole person with her own ideas about 'love'. And in the end he has to admit that love is the only word for what he feels, despite all the accretions from the past which have so conventionalised it, despite the particular demands on him which Ursula makes – and despite the appalling exemplifications of 'love' in Hermione, Gudrun and Gerald.

So the ordinary reader, smiling at their quarrel in 'Excurse', thinks they have had an up-and-a-down which is in its way profound; but talking like that, arguing like that, cannot settle things for good. There is no alternative to getting on with a life together – and that is what they agree to do. But here the ordinary reader is in for a profound shock. As soon as they have committed themselves, Birkin immediately proposes that they resign from their jobs. For him it is the first thing to do: for us it would be the last.

Of course, he can afford it – he has that £400 a year, a comfortable income in those days, and living in Europe would have been cheaper than living in England. One thinks back to Egbert in 'England My England', who had only £150, and whose part-dependence seemed unsatisfactory or anomalous compared with his father-in-law, who had earned his wealth.

The issue here is not just employment, how one might be occupied: it was first raised by Ursula, who in 'Moony' had said, '"I looked at England and thought I'd done with it".' At that moment Birkin had replied, '"It isn't a matter of nations [...] France is far worse"'; but she had insisted '"I felt I'd done with it all"' (249: 6–10). That makes one think they are going to go right out of Europe. Pressed, Birkin is vague in 'Excurse' and for a moment Ursula moves back, becomes more realistic: '"We've got to take the world that's given – because there isn't any other".' He then comes out with his notion that

> 'There's somewhere where we can be free – somewhere where one needn't wear much clothes – none even – where one meets a few people who have gone through enough, and can take things for granted – where you can be yourself, without bothering. There is somewhere – there are one or two people –'
> 'But where –?' she sighed.
> 'Somewhere – anywhere. Let's wander off. That's the only thing to do – let's wander off.' (316: 1–9)

It's the merest daydream, not made more real by his saying 'It isn't really a locality, though [....] It's a perfected relation between you and me, and others.'

But if one were to say that that is something he might attempt in England, he would have none of it. The urge to get out is primary, and the mild Utopianism is merely consequential. The whole novel as it progresses makes the case against this irredeemable England.

And here we have to face the other element, also a shock, in Birkin's search. A link is found in the discussion between Birkin and Gerald in 'Marriage or Not'. Birkin asserts: '"One should avoid this *home* instinct, it's a habit of cowardliness".' It doesn't have to be, one thinks: one might see it as courageous, an act of faith. Gerald mildly says there's no alternative, and Birkin seems to drive on: but actually he swerves. Seeming to do Will retrospective justice, he says:

> 'We've got to find one. – I do believe in a permanent union between a man and a woman. Chopping about is merely an exhaustive process. – But a permanent relation between a man and a woman isn't the last word – it certainly isn't.' (352: 14–17)

The logic of his argument is that this private exclusiveness of marriage produces tightness and meanness and insufficiency, therefore we need the '*additional* perfect relationship between man and man' and this is 'equally creative, equally sacred, if you like'.

Gerald makes what seems to him the obvious point that '"there can never be anything as strong between man and man as sex love is between man and woman".' Birkin insists: '"You've got to admit the unadmitted love of man for man. It makes for a greater freedom for everybody, a greater power of individuality".' Gerald crucially declines: '"I can't feel it, you see".'

That chapter ends with a reflection from the authorial voice, not from Birkin. It points out, plausibly, that Gerald as conventional person would accept a conventional marriage to Gudrun – but that would be 'to become like a convict condemned to the mines of the underworld'. It goes on:

> The other way was to accept Rupert's offer of love, to enter into the bond of pure trust and love with the other man, and then subsequently with the woman. If he pledged himself with the man he would later be able to pledge himself with the woman: not merely in legal marriage, but in absolute, mystic marriage.
>
> Yet he could not accept the offer. There was a numbness upon him, a numbness either of unborn, absolute volition, or of atrophy. Perhaps it was the absence of volition. For he was strangely elated

at Rupert's offer. Yet he was still more glad to reject it, not to be committed. (353: 16–25)

There is no real logic in this. It strikes one as mere theory, put across as something given. It might be Birkin's dream, but sounds also like Lawrence's. It seems unreal.

Once more, the ordinary person would accept that profound comradeship, which we might well call a kind of love, exists between people of the same gender who work together, perform some social role together, meet in the same places, are rooted in the same society, see each other through bad times. In the twentieth century, service life in wartime threw people together and forged bonds which were the major benefit of those disasters. The people concerned felt this deeply. But the merest possibility of all that is denied if the moment you decide to get married you also decide to leave your country for a wandering life. Birkin sees no inconsistency here, yet is denying himself what he needs, as Lawrence did.

He would reply, I think, that he was looking for something even deeper. It comes out at the very end when Birkin contemplates Gerald's frozen body:

Cold, mute, material! Birkin remembered how once Gerald had clutched his hand, with a warm momentaneous grip of final love. For one second – then let go again, let go for ever. If he had kept true to that clasp, death would not have mattered. (480: 13–17)

There follows a discussion with Ursula, who cannot grasp what Birkin wanted, or his despair. '"Aren't I enough for you?"' she asks. '"As far as woman is concerned,"' he says, '"But I wanted a man friend, as eternal as you and I are eternal [....] another kind of love".' It does seem more deep than what men usually have with friends, and the question arises which Lawrence probably wanted to block off: is this a kind of idealised homosexuality or bisexuality? Or has Lawrence really glimpsed something 'unadmitted' in the sense that we have not learned to identify it? It is one of the ways in which the book leaves one thinking on.

The other obvious issue is: children. On the third page of the first chapter Gudrun says flatly: '"I get no feeling whatever from the thought of bearing children".' Ursula is uncertain: '"Perhaps one doesn't really want them, in one's soul – only superficially".' Then she adds: '"When one thinks of other people's children ..."' and Gudrun says '"Exactly".' Extraordinary! It's a mere blanking-out. The Pussum finds herself pregnant by Halliday, and says '"Isn't it beastly!"' Halliday wants to give her £100 – to pay her off or buy an abortion. When she is next met, in The Pompadour, 'she was thinner'. The young pregnant woman in 'A Chair' is, as Ursula says, getting a home together, and it is now that she makes her ambiguous remark '"It's right for them – there's nothing else for them."' Pregnancy as social clincher, as forcing people into marriage, was an issue at the time and after; but here it clouds the issue of children actually desired by married people. We observe that Thomas Crich dotes on his youngest child Winifred, who loves him. There is Anna still, as matriarch, and there is a glimpse of family life with children when Birkin calls at the Brangwen home. But that is all, and the contrast with the generations of *The Rainbow* is bleak. The 'few other people' whom Birkin hopes to find and live with seem all too likely to be childless too. What sort of community is that?

14
Women in Love: Character

Lawrence's presentation of the participants in this drama seemed incomprehensible to his first readers. The feeling was summed up by Middleton Murry, an intelligent critic favourable to Lawrence: writing about *Women in Love* in *The Nation and Athenaeum* in 1931, he could 'discern no individuality whatever in the denizens of Lawrence's world'. 'Man and woman are indistinguishable as octopods,' and 'they writhe continually, like the damned, in a frenzy of sexual awareness of one another.' We remember that Edward Garnett, responding to early drafts of 'The Sisters' seems to have made a similar point, provoking the celebrated letter in which Lawrence said he was not trying to portray 'the old stable ego', and substituted his figure of carbon, the basic element which underlies the apparent opposites of coal and diamond. He was wanting to demonstrate that kind of universal beneath the surface of human behaviour. He would be understood as time went by.

What the traditional reader expected to see was sharply differentiated personalities seen from outside. What the important twentieth-century novelists have wanted to show was consciousness felt from within. The first tends to reveal peculiarities, even oddities; the other to show universals. In recent times two intellectual movements have shifted readers closer to Lawrence. There has been the long psychological endeavour which started in his time, one effect of which has been to posit in the psyche basic constituents or mechanisms of a universal kind. More recently there has been a sense of the self as both socially constructed and unstable, so that it is less like the hard little personal individuality posited in Garnett's time. From these points of view Lawrence's characterisation seems more comprehensible; but there remains a difficulty, a structural or methodical procedure which we have to grasp.

The strangeness, the originality of *The Rainbow* resides mainly in the kaleidoscope of rapidly transforming metaphor which we have to learn to take as representing the perceptions of the people. These are presented as pure images because the feelings are wordless states, and to put them in the form of verbalisations of the 'it seemed to her that ...' or 'he thought that ...' kind is a misrepresentation. There can be no words after 'that ...' because the feeling is not a thought but an immediate wordless impression, before conceptualisation. *Women in Love* is much less image-conducted, but has a related difficulty. This is, to grasp the emotional drive behind the actions (the speech is often an action). One character, Birkin, does introspect in a way which is reported, and relates his feelings to his actions. He is in that sense too the central character, and we grasp his relationship with the author, who is therefore an authority on what goes on within him. But the other characters have to be perceived from outside as we perceive characters in the drama and people in real life – by how they look, what they say, what they do, even what they wear. There is almost no authorial analysis of the kind which points out motive – we have to do that. The characters are other, and at moments extreme. They are of one kind, and it is a mistake to see this as not human, or even strange. In *Women in Love* the most characteristic images render internal states: moods and overpowering implosions. Again, they are, as in life, wordless. We do not say to ourselves 'I feel a sudden ...' What we have is a surge or a collapse, a warmth or a coldness, an impulse towards or away – or some other figure much better expressed by Lawrence. Once again, as in *The Rainbow*, we have to feel them and let them work.

Murry's contemporaries, both readers and the popular novelists they felt comfortable with, retained a conception of character which went back, through the nineteenth-century novel and Dickens's hyper-individuated minor characters to eighteenth-century conventions of theatre and journalism: the 'character-part' consisting of externally observed personal oddities. Minor characters could be this kind of caricature; but even main characters had to be in some way explained, summed up, understood: to function like a closed economy. This led to the theoretical requirement of 'truth to character' touched on in the discussion of 'Elsa Culverwell'. To call a book by a character's name was half a promise.

Oddly enough, there *is* one very striking character-part in *Women in Love*: Hermione Roddice. She has an utterly individual style: her clothes, her features, her voice, her manner are caught with Dickensian sharpness of eye and ear – even the way she moves, the way she puts questions without a rising inflection (no question mark at the end of the sentence) so that she seems to be both summing people up and putting them down while appearing to interrogate them. Early readers who knew her said, 'Ah, Ottoline Morrell to the life – or rather, cruelly caricatured.' The unfortunate result was that Lawrence was thought to be merely portraying the 'real-life' original.

But the Ottoline element is merely the surface of Hermione. Jessie Chambers saw herself in Hermione, and was not wrong. The psychic mechanisms, the compulsions, the needs which drive the fictional Hermione from within, the superficial self-command concealing inner turmoil, the aggressive neediness, are not only shared with actual people like Jessie: they are the universal which links Hermione to other characters in the book, notably Gerald Crich, who has the same affliction in a different key. This universal also links backwards with characters in *The Rainbow*: old Tom's momentary dependence on Lydia, Will's dependence on Anna, Skrebensky's total collapse when Ursula rejects him. What in Tom, even in Will, seemed normal or human – part of a whole life – was seen to grow in Skrebensky to obsession, to breakdown. Now in *Women in Love* the process is perceived as an essential characteristic of twentieth-century social and emotional failure.

Consider the progression of Gerald Crich from what he is at the beginning of the action: the diver full of 'go', the seemingly free individual with an impulse to dominate, to manage, to control, to possess – to use people. Compare that with what he is at the end: unable to accept that the affair with Gudrun is over, unable to move back into his singleness, and in that defeat feeling that his only course is to murder the person who will not let him possess her. That curve has its turning point on the night when he walks in a trance to his father's grave, and on to Gudrun's bed, where he pours himself into her.

The parallel with Hermione is clear. She also seems dominant. But she is completely dependent on Birkin, and when he moves away can only express her disintegration as violence. In his small way Will Brangwen repeats the pattern. When Ursula decides to marry Birkin she also rejects her father, woundingly, and he expresses his anger and above all his incoherence (he cannot express himself otherwise) by striking her. She is then hurt and upset because she is not herself a violent dependant and cannot understand what she has triggered in him.

Gudrun and, at the end of the book, Loerke are the diastole to this systole. They will not be dependent on another, and when Gudrun finds she has acquired this dangerous dependent Gerald she feels no obligation, rather disgust, and finally casts him out. She feels an affinity with Loerke because he too wants no hangers-on. He and Gudrun have their art, but the abstraction of their emotional life must have some bearing on what they produce and how it is valued.

This behaviour, sometimes strange, sometimes violent, is not acccounted for in terms by Lawrence, not explained. It just seems to happen, and can seem dismaying. But it is also extremely like what we read every day in the newspapers – also unexplained – or meet in our lives; and if we enter into the metaphors we get, not the 'explanation' but what it feels like within the characters. If we grasp that and then step outside we understand the phenomena.

So, oddly enough, the bafflement which Murry expressed in his alienated zoological comparison – that everyone in the book is strange and not to him recognisable as human – this might have been taken as getting near the truth. Except that the real question for baffled readers was: were they outside the aquarium looking in, or inside looking out? A related failure of vision is caught at moments in the book. Gudrun, for instance:

> Ursula seemed so peaceful and sufficient unto herself, sitting there unconsciously crooning her song, strong and unquestioned at the centre of her own universe. And Gudrun felt herself outside. Always this desolating agonised feeling, that she was outside of life, an onlooker, whilst Ursula was a partaker, caused Gudrun to suffer from a sense of her own negation, and made her, that she must always demand the other to be aware of her, to be in connection with her. (165: 26–34)

For once, Lawrence offers something like a diagnosis. More urgently, here is Gerald:

> And once or twice lately, when he was alone in the evening and had nothing to do, he had suddenly stood up in terror, not knowing what he was. And he went to the mirror and looked long and closely at his own face, at his own eyes, seeking for something. He was afraid, in mortal dry fear, but he knew not what of. He looked at his own face. There it was, shapely and healthy and the same as ever, yet somehow, it was not real, it was a mask. [...] His eyes were blue and keen as ever, [...] He could see the darkness in them, as if they were only bubbles of darkness. He was afraid that one day he

would break down and be a purely meaningless babble lapping round a darkness. (232: 7–20)

Without generalising, Lawrence is offering insights into the effect on social and individual nature of life in twentieth-century society. He is identifying a drive towards a stultifying uniformity, a psychological totalitarianism, which expresses itself as lack of individual meaning, lack of identity, lack of felt community other than all being in the same predicament: the whole turning to violence. To offer the old style of character portrayal, where everybody is hyper-individual, would have been to fail to see his own point.

This is why 'singleness' – Birkin's watchword – is such a paradox. It is one thing to be superficially unique in the way Hermione is – that is merely to have mannerisms. It is another thing to be truly single – to grow into one's own individuality. Here is the first use of the term:

[Birkin] affected to be quite ordinary, perfectly and marvellously commonplace. And he did it so well, taking the tone of his surroundings, adjusting himself quickly to his interlocutor and his circumstance, that he achieved a verisimilitude of ordinary commonplaceness that usually propitiated his onlookers for the moment, disarmed them from attacking his singleness. (20: 14–19)

There follows that first discussion with Gerald about how 'anybody who is anything can just be himself and do as he likes', with Gerald dissenting, and his own logic leading him to endorse violence ('everybody cutting everybody else's throat'). The book proves both of them right, in a way, except that Gerald is in the overwhelming majority. Birkin's point is silently made by the continuous exposition of 'character' which underlies the violence. That psychic drive establishes not singleness but the internal mechanism which enforces uniformity. It is an aspect of what can still be called human nature. It also exemplifies the two aspects of the biological axiom: all individuals belong to a genus, but each is also unique. The conscious human is free to follow Birkin's insight – at the cost, it seems, of eventual exile, internal or real.

One aspect of traditional character-portrayal was the use of the narrative voice to say things like 'as he said this, she thought that ...' – that is to say, to maintain an analytical narrative which keeps up a moral current bank balance as the action unfolds. This tended to emphasize conventional kinds of ulterior motive or self-interest, or allowed the virtuous to resist all that and stay in credit. Little of this sort goes on in *Women in Love* – though it has to be said that it is helpful when it occurs (as in the analysis of Gudrun quoted above). Rather the individuals are shown dramatically to be in certain states, moods or dispositions, ranging from withdrawal to passionate attachment and to violence. Out of less agitated states they speak, discuss, expostulate with each other. There are also moments of illumination which might be called heavenly or deathly, and these include, for Birkin and Gerald, sexual ecstasy.

If we were to categorise the *dramatis personae*, it would not be in conventional ways. There are the possessed, notably Hermione and Gerald. There are the self-possessed, notably Gudrun and Loerke. There are the seekers, Birkin and Ursula, who have to steer a course between the other pairs.

Birkin and Ursula have the advantage of being closely related to Lawrence and Frieda, which means that a substantial personal reality comes across – is established by description of how they look, what they do, what they say. There seems no need for analysis. Gudrun and Gerald are at first mostly observed from outside. Gerald is given a kind of glamour, conveyed by Lawrence's characteristic 'Northern' imagery of frost in sunlight – very apt, given his fate. He is also his succession of actions, which have a revealing consistency, and he acts his social role as captain of industry. Gudrun is her clothes, and especially her voice with its high sharp tones and emphases. She is her aggressive self-exposing actions in 'Water-Party', culminating in that 'first blow' that she gives Gerald. She is her art of little self-contained images. Above all, she is her fierce self-sufficiency, which gives her a surface social competence like Gerald's.

But the final chapters, when Birkin and Ursula have dropped out, move into a real interiorisation. We now enter into Gerald's states in particular. In personal terms it is now a chaos: obsessional dependence has replaced his earlier insentience about people, when they were instrumental. Gudrun refuses this: it is her defining state that she is not going to serve anybody else's needs, rejects them as a tiresome demand, even a threat. Gerald has ceased to be an exciting equal; and she consciously rejects at one moment the possibility that she might act as his emotional backer in a public career where she would be the real power. She has to cut him off – something which has never happened to him before, so his need turns murderous. All this is conveyed with great power; but I have turned into analytical terms what is presented as wordless feeling, desperate internal impulse, silent conflict, masked by seemingly self-possessed conversation.

Gudrun is resolutely 'single' by nature, and so presents an important qualification to Birkin's search. The late alliance with Loerke, who has no interior life that is shared with us, shows that through experience and conviction he is as 'single' as Gudrun – which is why they so appreciate each other. Loerke does not feel forced, as Birkin does, to enter into a formal exile from the country he despairs of and the neighbours who will not let him show up their lack of singleness: he, Loerke, is always in a silent internal exile and can remain cold and detached among the other people. Nor does he feel, as Birkin does, the need to find the right permanent relationship with one woman and the complementary love for one man. Like Gudrun, he can use people and drop them, in an instrumentality which is colder than Gerald's. He stands out in the whole book as the perfectly isolated being: his 'singleness' is not something he is trying to grow into as the full expression of his individual being; it is an arrested, a 'finished' thing, and in Lawrence's terms what is finished is dead. True singleness is the condition of being alive among others, and consenting to uniqueness. This can feel like being alone, which is why many people fear it in themselves and may hate it in others.

15
Women in Love: Lawrence's England

Given the title of the book, and the skilful way in which the relationships between the two pairs of central characters are followed, it may seem that the overall intention is to demonstrate the possibility of an ideal marriage – or, as the cliché used to put it, 'a normative human relationship'. But that is to abstract the people and their feelings from their setting. They themselves are very conscious of where they live and what it does to and for them. It is the matrix, the main condition of their lives, and Lawrence gives them this consciousness as a way of refracting his own. We watch the four young people moving from place to place in the natural course of their lives, and what they see and react to is a presentation of the England they inherit, may help to carry on if they stay, or which they reject if they leave.

In the first chapter, after their revealing conversation about marriage, the sisters ask themselves why they are still at home, break off and go out. On the way 'Ursula was aware of the house, of her home, round about her. And she loathed it, the sordid, too familiar place [....] this obsolete life.' They walk out into 'the amorphous ugliness of a small colliery town'. Lawrence moves into a searing description of the landscape, in which the word 'black' sounds like a knell. If one thinks back to *The Rainbow* the much-used word 'dark' had a cosmological ring, calling up its opposite 'light' as the other term of creation. Here 'black' initially means just that: the coal dust which covers the earth and everything else and testifies visibly to a century of industrialisation. The *Rainbow* sense survives in Ursula's feeling that she is in 'a dark uncreated hostile world'. As for the inhabitants, the colliers' wives, with their 'watchful underworld faces', are a tribe who have their abjection born into them. They see the sisters in their bright colours, and are instinctively mockingly hostile ('"What price the stockings!"'). Gudrun wishes them annihilated.

There is a later scene where two labourers see the sisters walking, again in their defiant life-colours. The older man says he would give his week's wages for five minutes with Gudrun – '"Her with the red stockings"' – which is a kind of tribute, even a longing. The younger says '"It's not worth that to me".' So: the older man is brutal but vital, from a previous generation. The younger one has had the life, the desire, bred out of him.

In touches like this Lawrence builds up the sense of his horror, now, at the landscape, the world he had pictured affectionately in *The White Peacock* and still comfortably in *Sons and Lovers*. What men have done to the land reflects back on them: they are now its product. The note recurs in this chapter ('Coal Dust') which leads into the scene with Gerald's Arab mare at the railway crossing, which tells us how he uses his colliers as well as his horse.

The later chapter 'The Industrial Magnate' tells the story of Gerald's father Thomas Crich, and how he as patriarch is succeeded by Gerald as modern manager. In brief, it is the history of the mining industry which Lawrence had seen unfolding in the lives of generations of his own family. His father had lived and worked under the old 'butty' system, where groups of workers under their leader, the butty, had been like subcontractors, had produced the coal in their own style or at their own speed, and been paid accordingly. That system had passed away with mechanisation and the increasing pressure for economical production: what we recognise today as 'productivity', where more must be produced with less. Gerald is the prophet – or in twentieth-century terms, the dictator – of this movement. His father watches with some horror, seeing that it has to happen, but seeing also what it does to the people he had wanted to care for.

Lawrence here writes with authority: he does it in personal terms, because it is on people that the process has its effect. Yet one cannot escape the sense of inevitability, nor the sense that since his time the whole process has reached its natural conclusion: there were a million British miners at the beginning of the twentieth century, a few thousand at its end. Gerald's blind efficiency accelerates final social and personal defeat. So it is not just psychologically acute that when his father, Gerald's own link with the previous world, a kind of conscience or better nature, dies at the end of his long despair, Gerald is overtaken by a sense of horror, of not-being, which he cannot understand. When he wanders off into the night, and tramps, in his evening dress, round the darkened countryside, his first stop is at his father's grave. He then plunges off to Gudrun's bed in order to pour himself, his horror, into her. And this, of course, this unconscious need, eventually horrifies her too and causes her to stand off from him. None of this is crudely stated: one has to ponder the sequences, the impulses, the actions and reactions. But it is in these ways that the book silently creates its full social force, in human terms.

I suggested that the two roadmenders represented two generations of a tribe losing its primitive vigour. As for its morality, that is conveyed in 'A Chair'. The young, rat-like man is consenting to a tribal mating-convention. If you get caught out breaking one rule, you have to obey the other: marry and rejoin the majority.

This was a theme Lawrence contemplated quite often. It occurs in *Sons and Lovers*, especially when Paul Morel is determined not to 'do the right thing' by Miriam, yet is painfully aware that he is exposing her to social exclusion. He talks about it to his mother and Clara Dawes (who can have an affair with him because she is married, and not so exposed); they hear his progressive rationalising, but know better because they are women and it is on them that the pressure most falls. There was that moment in *The Rainbow* when Ursula feared she was pregnant. Later, in *Mr Noon*, the topic creates the mordant comedy of the first half. In *The Lost Girl* Alvina escapes the expectations of one tribe by marrying into another older European one. In *Aaron's Rod* Aaron Sisson, nearing middle age, realises he has subsided into a sort of trap – ordinary married life with children – and on an impulse gets right out.

One literary antecedent was Hardy's *Jude the Obscure*, which took the case of the serious and in one sense innocent young man trapped into marriage by a scheming woman falsely claiming to be pregnant by him. The end result is a tragedy. In Lawrence's short stories 'Wintry Peacock' and 'The Last Straw' the tribal mentality is for those moments given its due – its element of realism and prudence, justice even, including the woman's point of view. But that is for the tribe – or as Ursula puts it, '"It's right for them – there's nothing else for them".' Birkin is absolutely determined to have none of that; and in *Women in Love* as in that group of three later novels, the rejection of the old tribal morality is an important element of what takes him (and Gilbert Noon, Alvina Houghton and Aaron Sisson) right out of England, in search of a place or community where social forces are not recognised. Is there such a place?

This whole world of Beldover, where the social, the personal and the setting are inseparable, is aptly summed up when the Brangwen sisters go back to the house that their parents have just moved from, and are horrified to see this, their home, in its abandoned abjectness. '"What *must* we be like,"' says Gudrun, '"if we are the contents of *this*!"' '"Vile!"' says Ursula, '"It really is."' One might think for a moment what a trajectory has been represented in the two novels: from the beginning of *The Rainbow* to this. Yet one also remembers the early glimpse through the dark archway of the colliery 'spinning'. This is what has been spun.

This chapter, 'Flitting', heralds the other more final move – out of England – recounted in 'Continental'. And this revulsion is related to Birkin's rejection of the mere idea, now, of having a home, and possessions in it, and being in that way rooted. One might think that a hard case is being made: not everywhere is as ugly, even today: there is today more consciousness, and the movement started in Lawrence's time; he has contributed.

But it is not a matter of appearances: what is at stake is the kind of life. Here the Crich family narrative complements the Brangwen family narrative. These are the other inhabitants who in their own way did most to make the landscape and the town: they did not dig the coal, but they employed the miners, and acquired their wealth by the spoiling of the landscape and the institution of this way of life.

Breadalby and Shortlands, the big houses, are part of the setting. Breadalby in particular has the glamour of the English past, the agrarian world of landowners and country-folk before the pits were sunk. It carries into the twentieth century the aura of the eighteenth – the old aristocratic family, the grounds, the servants. Hermione holds court and permits herself to take an interest in cosmopolitan intellectuals and artists who have their own equivocal social status. But the Brangwen sisters are cut off from their own background.

Shortlands is the home of the industrialists, the Criches, who have taken the place of the landowner, have real present power because they employ most of the local working population, and give patronage to the rest. The annual event recorded in 'Water-Party' is the modern equivalent of holding court and dispensing bounty – Thomas Crich is also an alms-giver.

The London which the two pairs visit is represented by Halliday's apartment and The Pompadour. As the train runs through the grim urban setting into the London terminus, Birkin asks Gerald '"Don't you feel like one of the damned?"' Gerald laughs: he can't see it; but Birkin persists: '"It is real death".' This is the London of Skrebensky's breakdown, the Waste Land. They meet again in the café, a 'dim world' of 'shadowy drinkers' in the tobacco smoke. It is another underworld – though for Gerald it is 'an illuminated new region among a host of licentious souls [...] dim, evanescent, strangely illuminated faces.' The people they meet were memorably dismissed in 'England, My England' – those who 'tamper with the arts'. The Pussum professes a horror of black beetles, but is not afraid of blood: she proves it by jabbing a knife across Libidnikoff's hand – which causes Halliday to go faint and vomit. It is part of the violence which pervades the book, but has a perverse, almost nonsensical bad-child quality peculiar to this group. Birkin watches, 'white and diminished'. In Halliday's apartment Gerald goes to bed with the Pussum, a sort of transaction made in front of the others, except that he doesn't pay her. At the end of the stay, we are told, Gerald and Halliday have a 'nasty and insane scene'. 'Gerald was on the point of knocking-in Halliday's face; when he was filled with sudden disgust and indifference' – an exact foreshadowing of the final violence on Gudrun in the Alps.

It is a world of empty sophistication and triviality, the froth of metropolitan life. It is not even, in Gerald's terms, dominated by the work-nexus. It is rapidly sketched, but no more is needed. In the later scene, Gudrun at The Pompadour hears members of the group laughing as Halliday reads aloud that ill-advised letter in which Birkin preaches his gospel, and the setting and the reception it gets make one revise one's opinion and think one sees what he means after all. Gudrun, disgusted, takes the letter and stalks off with it; the chapter ends with her crying '"I feel I could *never* see this foul town again – I couldn't *bear* to come back to it".' There is something metropolitan about her characteristic over-emphases, and it is an apt curtain-line. The next chapter is 'Continental' and they are all four out of England.

To return to Shortlands, which for a significant part of the story is the place where Gerald's father is slowly dying: Gudrun joins the staff as Winifred's art-teacher, and this permits the relationship with Gerald to develop. It is not far from the Brangwen home: both houses are in the blackened colliery area. There is an evening when Gerald walks her home, and they stop and kiss under the railway bridge: for a moment it excites her to think this is just like the miners in their courtship ritual. The other moment, when he walks from Shortlands to the grave and then into Beldover to her house suggests the interdependence of the two classes as well as his dereliction now that what could be called the moral base of his social role has disappeared.

It was a fragile base: paternalist charitableness could be seen as self-deception on Thomas Crich's part, and Gerald does not deceive himself. But without that element he is reduced to the credo he announces at Breadalby: that the industrial machine is that: a machine, though its servants, outside their work, are 'free to do as they like'. He discovers that he has no idea what that might be. He feels his identity is slipping away. Lawrence dramatises this crisis in terms which have a resonance we have learned to detect:

> As the evening of the third day came on, his heart rang with fear. He could not bear another night. Another night was coming on, for another night he was to be suspended in chains of physical life, over the bottomless pit of nothingness. And he could not bear it [....] He could not fall into this infinite void, and rise again. (337: 29–35)

His 'excurse' into the countryside around, in this catatonic state, echoes and contrasts with the other parallel movements: Birkin's shocked exit from Breadalby into a countryside which he feels welcomes him back to Eden; his later 'Excurse' in the car with Ursula; the departure from England; the moments towards the end of the book when the two couples venture out of the Alpine Gasthaus into the otherworld of the mountains; Gerald's last going off, alone, into that anti-life. The first exits are into aspects of England; the last ones are into something like space.

In 'Excurse' the alienated Birkin and Ursula drive around in his car (modern touch). At first there is no real destination; it is like Gerald's unconscious wandering walk, before he comes to himself and makes for Gudrun. Birkin and Ursula also come to themselves, and find they are in Southwell. They hear the Minster bells playing the evening hymn, have that conversation in which they recognise that the Minster is the English past. She sees it with pleasure, remembers that Will and her mother had visited it. Birkin finds a memorable figure: 'It looks like quartz crystals sticking up out of the dark hollow' – an extrusion from the immensely past. For Ursula 'It was like dim, bygone centuries sounding'; it is 'the dream-world of her childhood'. Standing in the inn-yard 'smelling of straw and stables and petrol' she finds 'the world had become unreal. She herself was a strange transcendent reality.' They have found their way to each other, but it seems to be a condition in which they have left the world of social England behind. On the other hand their true marriage, their sacramental love-making, takes place when he drives into the heart of the old Sherwood Forest, as if to go back beyond history, or at any rate modernity, into a natural state.

The drive of the whole book is that one might have moments in which there is access to an original England in places remote from people; but if you want to have a social life of a different kind you have to get right out. There is no real argument about this: Ursula is carried along by Birkin's determination. Hence the importance of the scene on the boat in 'Continental'. They leave at night, and so it is dark, but Lawrence now recurs to his *Rainbow* imagery and turns the absence of light into a symbolic darkness which surrounds the travellers in their movement from one kind of life to another, which may be more fruitful. Ursula stands

> watching the small, rather desolate little lights that twinkled on the shores of England, as on the shores of nowhere, watched them sinking smaller and smaller on the profound and living darkness [....]
>
> 'Let us go forward, shall we?' said Birkin. He wanted to be at the tip of their projection. So they left off looking at the faint sparks that glimmered out of nowhere, in the far distance called England, and turned their faces to the unfathomed night in front [....] the black unpierced space ahead. (387: 17–27)

On the next two pages the note is sounded repeatedly. The essence is that they are falling 'like one closed seed of life' through a space which will take them to where they may rest and germinate in a new life; and the 'darkness' metaphor mutates:

> Her heart was full of the most wonderful light, golden like honey of darkness, sweet like the warmth of day, a light which was not shed on the world, only on the unknown paradise towards which she was going, a sweetness of habitation, a delight of living quite unknown [....] (388: 16–20)

This is the light Birkin had always seen in her, identified with her. Now it is projected into their future. As for him:

> He was falling through a gulf of infinite darkness, like a meteorite plunging across the chasm between the worlds. The world was torn in two, and he is plunging like an unlit star through the ineffable rift. What was beyond was not yet for him. (388: 25–9)

There is an issue of 'character' here: she is instinctively hopeful; he feels a kind of dread. When they land ('This was the world again') they are in the 'superficial unreal world of fact. Yet not quite the old world. For the peace and the bliss in their hearts was enduring.' This carries them through the sense that they have crossed a Styx into the desolated underworld of the station. The railway journey starts in darkness. They pass a farm, and she is reminded of her childhood at Cossethay. As they go on she feels exhausted and depressed: 'No new earth has come to pass.' But as they approach the Alps, 'This was the other world now.'

The final chapters show how strange, how anti-life, this other life is – so that finally Ursula tells Birkin she cannot bear it, and they move on – to the South, in the first instance, and, one supposes thereafter to a wandering life together. The notes sounded in this chapter 'Continental' cumulatively tell us that this whole transition is not an easy movement from old to new, dark to light. None the less there is no turning back.

Leaving England is one of Lawrence's great *topoi*. We meet it again in *Aaron's Rod*, *The Lost Girl*, *Mr Noon*, *Kangaroo*. The memorable image of England like a coffin sinking into the waves as the boat crosses the Channel is found in *The Lost Girl*:

> England, beyond the water, rising with ash-grey, corpse-grey cliffs, and streaks of snow on the downs above. England, like a long, ash-grey coffin slowly submerging. [...] It seemed to repudiate the sunshine, to remain unilluminated, long and ash-grey and dead, with streaks of snow like cerements. That was England! (LG 294: 12–16)

Kangaroo remembers and re-uses that vision. In all these novels the same transition is narrated, and is clearly life-determining for the characters. They are moving from one world, one life, to another.

There are two elements here: the old and over-familiar, the now hated – and the new, which has to be discovered. Of all the characters concerned, especially Birkin, and Somers in *Kangaroo*, the reader, especially the ordinary English reader, who has read the books and stayed in England, is entitled to say that their impulse – just getting out in the hope of a new life, somewhere, with a few congenial fellow-expatriates – is unreal. It is particularly unreal if you also want to have that relationship with another man, because a wandering life prevents it, while staying at home may provide it. And indeed Gerald is lost on the way: he dies, having said in any case that he cannot see what Birkin's whole project is about. The end of the book seems to show us a Birkin who is either defeated or not in sight of success. One cannot believe in all that he is doing.

Presumably Lawrence accepts that as a possible reaction. Partly it is his story, and of course in 1921 it was not over. There was more for him to learn and to report. Here, at the end of *Women in Love*, he has something much wider in implication to say to the ordinary reader, and it is – do you grasp what you have been shown about England, your England, and its people? Is it still basically true? Does it apply, in some sense, to Western society? Are you so sure *you* have got it right? Can you be content with what you have? What are *you* going to do?

I have made the ordinary person's objection to Birkin's utopian project of a community 'somewhere' – which is all too likely to be an odd little group of people, some with personality problems. But the objection only applies to the specific, personal, even idiosyncratic, Birkin enterprise in the 'now' at the end of the book. One might speculate that the Birkin we have had presented to us is likely to move on intellectually as well as geographically. Our reservations should not too much affect our response to the case about English, about modern industrial and post-industrial society, that Lawrence has been so massively making throughout the two great novels taken, as he meant them to be taken, as related. What was it Ursula said in response to Gudrun and Loerke? 'The world of art is only the truth about the real world, that's all – but you are too far gone to see it.'

Index

Abstract Expressionism, 12
Abstraction, 214, 220
Acorn, 53, 86
Africa, 102, 105
Anemone, 143, 146
Angels, 75, 94, 95, 117
Annunciation, 59, 67, 139
Aphrodite, 134, 140, 146, 150
Arch, archway, 45, 52, 73, 85, 86, 127
Army, the, 59, 67, 159
Art, 220–1
Ash, 92, 93
Astarte, 151

Bacchantes, 177
Baptism, 138, 172, 175, 198
Bathing, 112, 197, 200, 210
Bauhaus, 214
Bennett, Arnold, 30, 35, 39, 40, 88
Berthoud, Jacques, 50–1
Bible, The, 45, 48, 54, 74, 90, 108, 122, 148, 162, 167, 169, 211
   Genesis, 45, 54, 69, 74, 100, 117, 138, 163, 184
   1 Samuel, 123
   Job, 185
   Zechariah, 47
   Song of Songs, 205
   Psalms, 75
   Matthew, 62, 73
   John (Gospel) 10–11, 77, 100
   Acts, 101
   1 Corinthians, 62
   Apocalypse, 54, 138, 184
   Christ's powers, miracles, 164, 169, 173, 201
Birkin as representative, 209
Blake, William, 10, 97, 101
Bristling, 94, 95, 121
Brontë, Emily: *Wuthering Heights*, 29, 31, 55, 69, 166
Burns, Robert, 17, 27, 28, 36, 180

Burrows, Louie, 63, 64

Cain, mark of, 163, 188
Candle, 73–4, 77, 161
Carbon, 226
Carousel, 105
Cathedral, 214
   Bamberg, 130
   Lincoln, 82, 90, 91, 110, 119, 131
   Rouen, 109
   Southwell Minster, 238
Cell, 67, 68, 80, 82, 92, 96, 126
Chambers, Alan, 212
Chambers, Jessie, 8, 18, 64, 104, 134, 212, 228
Character, 34, 230
Children, 224–5
Christianity, 118–22, 203
Church, 57, 58, 73, 76, 109, 118–19, 197
Circle of perception, 51, 52, 72, 73, 75, 76, 78, 81, 85; *see* Image
   of consciousness, 97 *and see* Image, Imagery
   of light, lamplight, 93, 122, 126
Conrad, Joseph, 6, 103
Corke, Helen, 64
Crucifix, 46
Cullen family, 16, 30
Cybele, 151

Dance, dancing, 85, 122, 131, 136, 138, 139–47, 196
Dark, darkness, 26, 73, 77, 78, 79, 80, 84, 93, 94, 99–100, 102–4, 106, 138–9, 204, 229
   blazing kernel of d. 128
   of blindness, 162, 164
   d. fields of immortality, 107
   nucleolating d., 104
David and Michal, 122
De la Mare, Walter, 6
Democracy, 202

Dependency, 62, 126–32, 146, 201, 206, 220, 228, 229, 231
Diana, 64, 134, 141, 145, 146, 150, 199
Dickens, Charles: his characters, 227
  Bleak House, 31, 33
Dross, 140, 143
Duckworth, 5, 16

Eden, 42, 43, 45, 47, 56, 73, 84, 106, 205–6, 238
Ego, old stable, 226
Eliot, George: *Middlemarch*, 36, 191
Eliot, T.S., 88, 89, 97–8, 110
Empire, 66, 67, 111
England, 192, 215, 222–3, 233, 238–41
English Review, 5, 153
Equality, 202
Eurydice, 180
Eve, 206
Eyes, gaze, 170, 175

Fecund, fecundity, 79, 100, 113
  fecund darkness, 103, 141
Feminism, 65
Flaubert, G., 2, 5, 6, 8, 11, 29, 45
Flux, 140, 142, 195
Forster, E.M.: *Howards End*, 33, 36, 40, 88, 111, 156–7
Frankstone, Dr, 67, 68, 93, 94, 96
Fuse, fusing, 142, 145, 148

Garnett, Edward, 5, 6, 7, 27, 31, 32, 226
Gertler, Mark, 105
Go, to; want to go, 98, 109, 148, 206
  just going, 112
  to be gone, 141

Haggs Farm, 17, 22, 27
Hands, 23, 140, 144, 146, 167–9, 213, 224
Hardy, Thomas, 21, 23, 88, 112, 235
Harpy, 148–50
Heinemann, 6, 7
Herbert, George, 91
Hill, city/town on, 73, 75
  crest of, 92

Hirai, Masako, 36
Hocking, William Henry, 212
Holly, 19, 156
Home, 193–4, 215, 217, 223, 236
Homosexuality, homoeroticism, 64, 175, 196, 210
Horizons, opposite, 84
Horizontal, vertical axes, 71, 78, 84, 101
Hueffer (Ford), F.M., 5, 6

Image, imagery, 41, 45, 85–6, 150
  animal-images, 50, 52, 61, 93, 94, 101, 105, 129, 141, 157
  circle (light, dark) 51–2, 67, 75, 76, 77, 78, 81, 82, 85, 89, 90, 93, 96
  clock, 165, 194
  compass-point, blade, 51, 140, 143, 148
  doorway, 92, 93, 123, 128
  furnace, 123, 145, 148
  mollusc, 165
  nut, 68, 78, 86, 98, 204
  peacock, 178–80
  rat-figures, 199, 212, 216, 235
  sea-images: salt, phosphorescence, corrosion, 134, 140, 142, 144, 146, 147, 148
  seed, 69, 93, 98, 205, 239
  shell, 53, 86, 147, 165
  spire, tower, 71
  stars, 61, 202
  stone/kernel, 53–4, 128, 139, 143
  sun, 151
  sunshine of frost, 99, 231
  tree, trees, 52, 68, 84, 106, 107, 126
  wave, 69, 137, 140, 141–2
  wind, 52, 77, 80, 83, 84, 106
  and see Arch, Circle of perception, Space
Industrialisation, 56, 64, 67, 70, 112, 193, 202, 203, 214, 233–4, 238
Inferno, 42, 180, 181
Infinite, oneness with, 96, 97
Instrumentality, 203, 214, 232

James, Henry, 5

244 Index

Jealousy, 128–32
Jerusalem, 73
Jew, Loerke as, 216
Joyce, James, 2, 7, 8

Kernel, 78, 86, 128
Kinkead-Weekes, Mark, 55

Lawrence, D.H.
  his aesthetic, 2, 7–15
  his esotericisms, 195–6, self-parodied, 199
  uses his own experience, 208, 231
  his misogyny, 150, 182
  as reviser, 3–8, 152, 153–5
  reviews his beliefs, 185
  but eliminates his psychosexual baggage, 213
Works
  Cambridge edition, 1–3, 7
  Aaron's Rod, 3, 12, 35, 176, 208, 235, 240
  'Burns Novel' fragment, 3, 16–30, 34, 49, 137, 209
  'Captain's Doll, The', 217
  Complete Poems, 'Foreword', 9–10
  'The Work of Creation', 13
  'Crown, The', 210
  'Daughters of the Vicar', 16, 36, 166
  'Elsa Culverwell', 3, 16, 27, 30–8, 166, 209, 227
  'Escaped Cock, The', 176
  England, my England, 37, 152ff
  'England, my England', 19, 153–8, 215, 222
  'Foreword' to *Sons and Lovers*, 11
  'Fox, The', 22, 37
  'Honour and Arms' ('The Prussian Officer'), 3
  'Insurrection of Miss Houghton', 16, 30
  'Introduction' to M. Magnus, 3
  Kangaroo, 3, 37, 208, 215, 240
  'Ladybird, The', 22
  Lady Chatterley's Lover, 4
  Look! We Have Come Through!, 37
  Lost Girl, The, 3, 17, 30, 31, 35, 235, 240
  Movements in European History, 35
  Mr Noon, 3, 14, 35, 115, 130, 208, 235, 240
  'Odour of Chrysanthemums', 176
  Paul Morel, 4, 7, 8, 16, 30, 37, 134–5
  Phoenix I, 13
  Phoenix II, 12
  Plumed Serpent, The, ('Quetzalcoatl'), 3
  'Prelude, A', 22
  Rainbow, The ('The Sisters', 'The Wedding Ring'), 4, 8, 9, 13, 16, 29, 31, 37, 175, 194, 215, 227, 235
    structure, 14; suppressed, 14
  'Reality of Peace, The', 11, 210
  'Scargill Street', 16
  'Second Best', 48–9
  Sons and Lovers, 4, 5, 8, 16, 18, 24, 28, 33. 59, 82, 93–5, 104, 123, 131, 135, 176, 208, 212, 234, 235
  Study of Thomas Hardy, 14, 85
  Trespasser, The, 29, 133–4, 140, 144, 149, 151
  Twilight in Italy, 35, 46, 56, 157, 191, 194
  White Peacock, The ('Laetitia', 'Nethermere'), 4, 7, 8, 13, 16, 18, 22, 27, 28, 29, 32, 34, 37, 133, 136, 175, 177, 205, 208, 209, 210, 234
  Women in Love, 4, 37, 63, 114, 150–1, 166, 208, 209
  'Prologue' to *Women in Love*, 211, 212
Lawrence, Frieda, 9, 63, 64, 159, 231
Leavis, F.R., 11, 39, 40
Loadstone, 143
London, 90, 110, 236
Lot's wife, 134, 137, 140, 144, 146
Lucas, Perceval, 155

Male friendship, 223–4
March, equinox, 77, 101
Marvell, Andrew, 205–6
Memory, m.-store, 41, 46
Metaphor, 41, 43–6, 51, 54, 70, 227, 229 *see* Image

Meynell family, 155
Milton, John: *Paradise Lost*, 47–8, *Lycidas*, 172, 198, 211
Mining industry, 234
'Momentary god', 46, 54
Moon, moonlight, 80, 114, 126, 133, 134, 143, 145, 148–50, 205, 218–19
  harvest-moon, 136
Morrell, Ottoline, 155, 228
Moses on Pisgah, 123
Murder, 189, 204, 228
Murry, J. Middleton, 226, 227, 229
Myth, mythology, 48, 54, 69, 70

Nakedness, 200–1, 204
Narrator, first-, third-person, 31–5
Nation and Athenaeum, 226
Night, 79
North, northern, 35, 56, 231

Orion, 23
Orpheus, 175, 180

Palgrave: *Golden Treasury*, 104, 134, 205
Past, the, 192–4, 197
Patmore, Coventry, 75
Persephone, 101, 104, 105, 175
Planets, 221
Poland, Polish, 55, 56, 132
Pre-Socratic philosophers, 185, 199
Projection, 35, 40, 48–51, 54, 70, 98, 103, 150, 151, 206

Rabbit, 23, 25, 26, 37, 187
Religion, 40–1, 47, 90, 116, 120–2, 124–6, 205–6
Resurrection, 54, 125, 162, 169, 173, 183
Rilke, R.M., 11, 95, 117
Roaring sky, circle, wind, 81–2, 84, 97, 101, 106–7, 126
Rouen, 109
Russell, Bertrand, 165, 194

Sand, George, 11
School, 57, 65–6, 72
Self, itself, oneself, 96, 97, 219, 226
  perfectly itself, 97
Shelley, P.B., 104
Shimmering, 82
Singing, song, 21–2, 33, 37
Singleness, 189, 192, 202, 203, 213, 214, 219, 220, 230, 232
Sleeping beauty, 33, 168
Social difference, 202
Space, 76, 127, 139
Spontaneity, 189
Stars, 77
Styx, 102, 139, 240
Surrealism, 12

Touch, 76, 163–4, 167–9, 170, 175, 201
Train, railway, 42, 43–4, 57, 74, 93, 95, 106, 111–12
Traveller, travelling, 61, 68, 72, 76, 78, 80, 117, 123–4

Underwater, 141, 145, 198, 206
Underworld, 43, 92, 139, 142, 175, 191, 233, 237
Unknown, 76, 77, 79, 80

Violence, 186, 188–9, 203–4, 218, 219–20, 230, 237
Virtue, 201

War, 59–60, 63, 210
  of 1914–1918, 152, 166, 176–8, 185–6, 215
Whitsuntide, 111
Wordsworth, William, 49, 98, 116

OHIO UNIVERSITY LIBRARY
Please return this book as soon as you have finished with it. In order to avoid a fine it must be returned by the latest date stamped below. All books are subject to recall after two weeks or immediately if needed for reserve.

JUN 1 7 2005
MAY 0 6 2005
TODAY

CF